Praise for

(barcode: D0000975)

"A zany caper… Fenske… niscent of a tame Carl Hiaasen on Cupid juice.

—*Booklist*

"This delightfully witty debut will have readers laughing out loud."

—*RT Book Reviews*, 4½ Stars

"Hilarious! A wild, sexy romp with a fresh, fun take on love."

—Lani Diane Rich, *New York Times*
and *USA Today* bestseller

"Fenske's wildly inventive plot and wonderfully quirky characters provide the perfect literary antidote to any romance reader's summer reading doldrums."

—*Chicago Tribune*

"An awesome debut novel… I really had fun reading this quirky romance."

—*Night Owl Reviews*, Reviewer Top Pick

"Utterly sensational and entirely unique."

—*Romance Fiction* on Suite101.com

"Fresh and sassy…a must read."

—*BookLoons*

"[An] uproarious romantic caper… Great fun from an inventive new writer; highly recommended."

—*Library Journal*

"An adorable, comical story with a unique, romantic plot that will tickle your funny bone!"

—*Dark Diva Reviews*

"A real gem… a funny, sexy, screwball romance that is reminiscent of early Jennifer Crusie."

—*The Romance Reader*

"Pure romantic and comic entertainment."

—*Romance Novel News*

"Entertaining and hilarious with quirky and very likable characters. A solid debut."

—*Under the Boardwalk*

"Pure wacky fun."

—*Cheeky Reads*

"A laugh-a-minute adventure that is perfect for a reading escape."

—*SOS Aloha*

"This book was the equivalent of eating whipped cream… sure it was light and airy, but it is also surprisingly rich."

—*Smart Bitches Trashy Books*

"This story hits the spot for laugh-out-loud, fun reading!"
— *Reviews by Martha's Bookshelf*

"Hilarious… The plot is completely over-the-top, which I adore when it's done right (and this is done right)."
— *The Book Swarm*

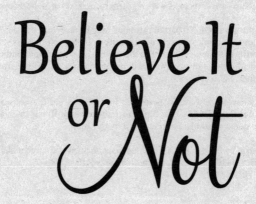

Believe It or Not

TAWNA FENSKE

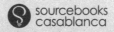

sourcebooks
casablanca

Copyright © 2012 by Tawna Fenske
Cover and internal design © 2012 by Sourcebooks, Inc.
Cover photos © Getty/I Love Images; Getty/Aki Horluchi

Sourcebooks and the colophon are registered trademarks of Sourcebooks, Inc.

All rights reserved. No part of this book may be reproduced in any form
or by any electronic or mechanical means including information storage
and retrieval systems—except in the case of brief quotations embodied
in critical articles or reviews—without permission in writing from its
publisher, Sourcebooks, Inc.

The characters and events portrayed in this book are fictitious or are
used fictitiously. Any similarity to real persons, living or dead, is
purely coincidental and not intended by the author.

Published by Sourcebooks Casablanca, an imprint of Sourcebooks, Inc.
P.O. Box 4410, Naperville, Illinois 60567-4410
(630) 961-3900
Fax: (630) 961-2168
www.sourcebooks.com

Printed and bound in Canada.
WC 10 9 8 7 6 5 4 3 2 1

*For the Bend Book Bitches: Sheri Abbott,
Larie Borden, Dianne Capozzola, Cherri Miller,
J. J. Shew, Stephanie Anderson Stroup, Karen Tippetts,
and Nancy Zurflu. Thank you for the love, laughter,
and unwavering support. Without our summers
of smut, none of this would have happened.*

Chapter 1

VIOLET MCGINN STORMED INTO HER MOTHER'S HOSPITAL room with her hair on fire.

Literally, as it almost happened.

"Would you please put out that candle!" she snapped, batting flames away from her long, dark hair as she dodged the dreadlocked stranger. He sighed and retreated to a far corner of the room, where a tie-dyed huddle was chanting something that sounded suspiciously like pig Latin.

"Violet!" Moonbeam cried. "Baby, you made it!"

"Mom, my God!" Violet rushed forward and shoved a pile of silk scarves off the chair beside her mother's bed. She dropped breathlessly into it and covered Moonbeam's hand with her own. "I got on the first flight out of Maine after Butterfly called. What happened? Was it the stairs in front of the house? That one board I've been telling you to get fixed? How badly are you hurt?"

Moonbeam patted Violet's cheek. "That's my girl, always seeking. You never could ask just one question at a time. It's so good to see you, sweetie. How was your flight?"

"Mom," Violet said, trying not to grit her teeth. "What the hell happened?"

"Well, I was just telling Salmonberry, it was exactly like what you predicted in your vision."

Violet frowned. "My vision?"

"Of course. The psychic vision you had when you visited for the Invocation of Isis."

Violet stared at her mother, wondering what drugs they'd given her. And whether there was a dispenser in the cafeteria.

"Mom, what are you talking about?"

"You remember, dear. It was the last time you visited. We were outside on the porch and you were getting ready to leave and you had a psychic vision—"

Realization dawned, and Violet shook her head. "Mom, we've been over this a hundred times. I'm an accountant. I'm not psychic. There's no such thing as—"

"Oh, Violet, don't start this again. What happened today is irrefutable proof of what I've been saying for thirty-three years."

"It's irrefutable proof that the board at the top of the stairs was loose," Violet argued. "I just happened to notice it, that's all."

She squeezed her mother's hand, trying to get a grip. It was like this every time she visited home. Well, not exactly like this. Her mother wasn't usually in the hospital, tethered to an IV pole, looking frail and bruised and a little stoned. Come to think of it, had Moonbeam ever been to a hospital? Even Violet's birth had taken place at home.

Violet cleared her throat. "I checked out the data online for this hospital, and I was glad to see that patient-satisfaction scores, infection rates, and reported patient falls are statistically—"

"Oh, Violet," Moonbeam interrupted. "Let's not start with the numbers right now, sweetie. Tell me, is there a man in your life?"

Violet resisted the urge to beat her forehead against her mother's bedside table. Instead, she looked around the room for anyone else who might deserve a beating. It wasn't difficult.

"Would you please stop touching my mother?" Violet snapped, whirling to face the bespectacled man hovering behind her with a stick of incense in his hand. "I'm pretty sure you're not supposed to have anything on fire in here."

He smiled. "Yes, but the elemental serpentine energy of the human body lies coiled at the base of the body, and when you're in touch with your Kundalani—"

"Please don't touch *anyone's* Kundalani, right now. Please? Just give me a minute with Moonbeam, okay?" She turned back to her mother. "What are the doctors saying, Mom? Did you break anything? How long do you have to be here? Do we need to call a specialist?"

"Oh, Violet, again with the questions!" Moonbeam smiled drunkenly as she pressed her fingers against the back of Violet's hand. "Always seeking, that's my girl."

Violet tried hard not to grit her teeth. "Mom—"

"I've broken my pelvis and a couple bones in my left leg. Oh, and two bones in my right arm, but that's all. No, wait. There was something with my toe, too. Do you think I could get a prescription for medical marijuana?"

"Marijuana is beside the point right now. What does the doctor say?"

"He wants to rush me into surgery, but I don't think that's necessary. I joined this group on attitudinal healing and I know a man who does biodynamic cranial therapy, so maybe if I just—"

"Dammit, Moonbeam! You've broken at least half a

dozen bones. A doctor told you that surgery is what you need. It doesn't sound *optional*. Don't you think maybe—"

"Violet dear, I want to do this naturally. I want—"

"It's a major injury, Mom, not childbirth."

A bald woman sitting cross-legged on the floor at the foot of the bed cleared her throat. "Crystal power really is the best thing for restoration of universal life energy. Maybe if your mother waited for her ultradian healing response and then—"

"Hey, Raven," Violet interrupted. "When did you get your medical degree?"

She brightened, looking like a happy chipmunk. "Actually, I was just recently certified as a divine spiritual healer online, and I think—"

"Unless there is now an *MD* after your name, this is not helping." She turned back to Moonbeam and squeezed her hand. "If an orthopedic specialist thinks surgery is the best thing, that's what we need to do."

"But surgery is so invasive," Moonbeam protested. "And I have readings booked out through December, so I need to make sure I'm there for my clients."

"Can't Butterfly take them?"

"Too busy."

"Sunshine?"

"Too unenlightened."

"Marzipan?"

"Too mentally unstable."

This, coming from a woman who believed Vipassana meditation could cure cancer. Violet sighed and put her head in her hands. Her mother was kind. Her mother was sweet. Her mother was the most sought-after psychic in Portland, Oregon.

And her mother was also a complete nut job. How was this going to work?

"I'm so proud of you for having this vision, Violet," her mother chattered. "I always said you had the gift. Raven, didn't I always say Violet had the gift?"

"You said Violet had the gift."

"See?"

As Moonbeam prattled on about crystal power and chakra alignment, Violet felt the familiar trap closing around her. She considered gnawing off her own leg to escape.

But she knew what she had to do instead.

She pulled her head out of her hands and looked up at her mother, blinking against the cloud of smoking sage coming from somewhere behind her.

"Okay, Moonbeam," she said. "I've got a deal for you."

There was never a point in Drew Watson's childhood where he stood before his third-grade class and announced, "When I grow up, I want to own a male strip club."

Yet here he was, thirty-five years old, making a damn good living doing just that.

Sort of.

"It's not a strip club," he explained for the hundredth time to the hulking man seated at the bar without a shirt on. "It's just a regular bar Sunday through Thursday. A nice place to listen to music and grab a drink."

"Right, but you do have strippers, right?"

"Male exotic dancers," Drew agreed, running a rag over the same spot on the bar he'd been wiping for the last ten minutes. "We started offering it on Friday and

Saturday nights after we had a bit of success bringing in some Chippendales dancers for a one-night show."

At the other end of the bar, his dopey ex-brother-in-law grinned. "*A lot* of success. Tons! We made gobs of money. And now I get to dance. I always wanted to be a dancer, and now I get to be one."

"That you do, Jamie," Drew agreed, saying a silent thank-you to his ex-wife's brother for devising the plan that had saved the whole damn bar after the divorce.

Not that Catherine had been pleased to have her younger brother stripping or her ex-husband running a bar where men threw their shirts at screaming women, but annoying his ex wasn't necessarily a negative in Drew's book. Plenty of *other* women were pleased. They flocked to the bar in droves, scheduling bachelorette parties and rowdy girls' nights out, and slipping their phone numbers to Drew on a disturbingly regular basis.

It was totally worth the ribbing from his buddies, the raised eyebrows at high school reunions, the eye rolls from his straitlaced ex-wife, the occasional pick-eter, and the constant disdain from the owner of Miss Moonbeam's Psychic Pservices next door.

"I sure would like a job," sighed the shirtless stranger seated at the bar. "I've got my stage name all picked out and everything."

"Try next door," Drew suggested. "They're hiring."

"The psychic place? I'm not psychic."

"Neither is the owner, but that doesn't seem to stop her," Drew said. "I meant the tattoo place, though."

"But I want to be a stripper. I'd work really hard. You have all these cool lights and stages and poles and stuff, and it seems like a fuckin' awesome place."

"It is," Drew agreed, "and I'll definitely keep your application on file in case something opens up. Hey, Jamie?" He turned to his ex-brother-in-law, feeling oddly on edge. "Have you seen Miss Moonbeam today?"

Jamie shook his head. "Nuh-uh. I keep seeing people standing outside, staring at their watches and looking mad."

Drew had noticed the same thing, and it had him worried. Though he'd butted heads with the old bat quite a lot over the years, he didn't want anything bad to happen to her. Not even if it meant he could nab her studio and expand the bar. Not even if it meant she'd stop harping on him about the exploitation of the human body. Not even after what she'd done four years ago, when—

"Does she still have those pet mice?" he asked Jamie.

"I think so. Why?"

"If something's happened to her, no one's feeding them. I'd better check."

Jamie beamed. "That's really nice of you, boss."

"That's me," Drew said, digging some food scraps out of a nearby bus tub. "A regular Mother Teresa."

The shirtless guy at the bar looked up. "Dude, you're gay? I mean, I figured, with you running a male strip club and all, and I don't have a problem with it or anything and I still really want to work here—"

"I'm not gay," Drew said as he moved toward the door that separated his shop from Miss Moonbeam's. "And it's also not a strip club. And I'm also not hiring. But thanks for coming by. I'll call if something opens up."

"Promise?"

"Sure."

Drew unlocked the door separating his bar from the psychic studio. As he stepped inside, he was greeted by a heavy wave of patchouli fragrance that nearly knocked him backward. Coughing a little, Drew stepped into the dimly lit shop. He detoured around the display of horoscope-themed key chains, lucky bamboo in colorful pots, and texts on telekinesis, moving toward the back where he'd seen the little white mice running in their wheel. He spotted them in the corner, their pink noses twitching in the dim red light that glowed from a lamp in the opposite corner.

"Hey, guys," Drew murmured, stepping closer to their cage. "Look, I brought you some peanuts and some leftover spaghetti and a piece of lettuce."

The mice stood on their hind legs, sniffing the air in anticipation. Drew pried the lid off and handed in the goods, arranging them in the green dish in the corner. The mice scurried over gratefully, selecting their first course with an obvious eagerness. Drew watched, smiling.

"What happened to Moonbeam, huh?" he asked, pressing the lid back in place. "She wouldn't just leave you guys here alone, and she always tells me when she's going on vacation."

The mice looked up from their meal, contemplating the question. One of them dropped his noodle and pressed his front paws against the side of the cage, his whiskers twitching in response. Drew touched a finger to the glass.

A door rattled behind him. Drew whirled around, alert to the sound of keys clattering against the front door. He squinted in the half darkness, watching as the door eased open, spilling light onto the dusty floor. A figure emerged through the doorway, sunlight streaming in behind her like a waterfall. A woman, Drew realized.

A very pretty woman, he amended, noticing the long, dark hair, the perfect curve of her hips in fitted jeans that tapered down into tall boots with pointy heels like the ones his ex-wife used to wear. Cashmere sweater in a nice champagne hue, an expensive-looking leather jacket. Drew couldn't tell what color her eyes were, but he could guess.

Amber. Her eyes would be amber.

He took two steps forward, ready to greet her. But the motion must have caught her by surprise. She screamed and grabbed a copper Buddha statue off the counter. He saw her eyes flash with aggression as she zeroed in on him in the dim light.

"Who are you and what the hell are you doing in my mother's shop?"

Drew put his hands up in surrender. "Hey, relax."

He saw her blink in the dim light as she gripped the statue in one hand. "Who's that? Are you looking for money? How did you get in here? What do you want?"

He cocked his head to one side. "Drew. No. Key. Mice."

"What?"

He offered a smile, trying to look nonthreatening but knowing he probably looked like an unshaven ax murderer with an unhealthy fondness for '80s concert T-shirts. "I was answering your questions. In the order you asked them."

"Are you mocking me?"

"No. Are you going to kill me with Buddha? Because I think there might be a karmic law against that."

He watched her hesitate, then sigh. She set the statue

on the counter and fumbled for the light switch beside the door. She flicked it on, but instead of a bright poof of illumination, the light trickled out in dim mauve hues.

"Mood lighting," she muttered, glancing up at the ceiling. "God bless Moonbeam."

Feeling more confident she wasn't about to beat him to death with a religious symbol, Drew took a tentative step forward, hands still raised in surrender. "I'm sorry, did you say Moonbeam is your mother? You must be Violet. She talks about you all the time. I'm Drew. I own the business next door."

"You're the tattoo artist?"

"Not that business. The other one."

Her eyebrow quirked. "You own the male strip club?"

He sighed. "It's not a strip club; it's a bar. We just happen to have male exotic dancers a few nights a week."

"I know all about it," Violet said, giving him an appraising look. "Moonbeam wasn't pleased when you started bringing in the strippers. She's *really* not pleased you want to take over her studio space to bring in *more* strippers."

"Are you going to lecture me about my exploitation of the alpha body? Because if you are, can I at least put my hands down first? My arms are getting tired."

She was studying him in earnest now, her eyes flitting over his features with something he might have mistaken for interest if she hadn't just been on the brink of beating him to death. He decided to study her as well, taking in the long, dark hair, the sternness of her features, the eyes that weren't amber at all, but the most remarkable, breathtaking shade of violet.

"Your eyes are amazing," he said without thinking, then wanted to kick himself.

She widened them in surprise and bit her lower lip. "Thank you. That's how I got my name." She cleared her throat, softening her voice a little. "You can put your hands down. Did you say Moonbeam gave you a key?"

"We have keys to each other's shops so we can use them in case of emergencies."

"How did you know about Moonbeam's accident?"

"Moonbeam had an accident?"

Violet frowned. "What emergency were you talking about?"

"The mice," he said, nodding at their cage. "No one was here to feed the mice."

"Oh." She blinked. "I didn't even think of that. Thank you. That was nice of you."

Drew took another step forward, genuinely worried about Moonbeam now. "Is your mom okay? What happened?"

"She fell down some stairs, but she'll be fine. She's in surgery right now."

He watched her bite her bottom lip again, more worried than she seemed to be letting on. Should he offer a hug? No, definitely not. He'd only just met her, and she'd assume he was just trying to cop a feel. Not an unappealing thought by any means, but probably not the best move, with Buddha sitting there poised for bludgeoning.

"She's not, um, having someone do this surgery at home, is she?" Drew asked.

Violet smiled a little at that. "Believe me, she'd be sprawled on the kitchen counter with a vision-seeker using shamanic cosmology to cure her broken pelvis if she had her way. I managed to convince her maybe an orthopedic surgeon was a better option."

"I can't believe she went for it."

"Yeah, well, I struck a deal with her."

There was an edge to her voice, something that made Drew wonder if she'd been forced to sell her soul to a pagan deity. Knowing Moonbeam, it was possible. "A deal?"

Violet sighed. "I'm going to fill in for Moonbeam until she's back on her feet again. I talked to my employer, and they're going to let me work from here for a month or two so I can help keep Mom's business running while she recovers."

"Your employer," he repeated, assessing her in earnest now. Her hair was straight and glossy, and he wondered what it would feel like to slide his fingers through it. "What do you do? Besides the psychic thing, I mean."

"I'm an accountant. In Portland. Portland, *Maine*," she clarified.

"You moved from Portland, Oregon, to Portland, Maine?" He laughed. "Didn't want to hassle with learning to spell a new city?"

She flushed a little, but her eyes were still friendly. Guarded, but friendly. "Portland, Oregon, is 3,198 miles from Portland, Maine—one of the longest distances between two cities in the continental United States. I wanted space. Something new. Something…" She paused, her eyes flitting past the tie-dyed scarves, the glass jars of incense, the crystal ball on the corner table. "Something *normal*," she finished.

"Normal," he repeated.

"Yes."

Drew nodded, wondering whether she always bit her lower lip this much. His thoughts veered a little there as he considered how that lip would feel between his teeth as he nibbled softly, then traced his tongue over—

"But you're here now," he said, interrupting himself before he got too carried away. "Filling in for your psychic mother. You don't look like a psychic."

She straightened sharply. He took a step back, wondering if she'd reach for Buddha again.

Instead, she folded her arms over her chest. "What does a psychic look like?"

"Sorry, I didn't mean that in a bad way," he said. "I'm sure you're a very good psychic."

She looked away. "Right. Well, I just came in to grab Mom's appointment book and assess the space. I'm thinking if I move a desk in over there, I can do my accounting work during the daytime over in that corner of the shop and keep the psychic thing contained over here with the sofas."

"Sure, sure," he said, feeling half the blood leave his brain as she moved past him, her hair brushing his bare arm as she strode toward the back of the shop. "Let me know if you need help moving furniture or anything."

He turned and watched her bend down to flip a latch on the teak cupboard at the back of the shop. Drew reminded himself a gentleman wouldn't stare at her ass.

Then he remembered he wasn't a gentleman. It was an amazing ass, round and full and—

"Are you staring at my ass?" Violet asked without turning.

"You psychics ruin all the fun," Drew answered, not feeling particularly embarrassed.

"There's a mirror in the cupboard. I can see you staring."

She grabbed the appointment book and stood up. Her gaze froze on the cupboard door and she got a funny, faraway smile. "I made this dent when I was eight," she said, running her thumb over the gouge in the wood. "I threw a serpent mandala because I didn't want to go to Iyengar class."

"You too?"

Violet dropped her hands to her side and looked at him again. Tucking the book under her arm, she offered her hand to shake. "It was a pleasure meeting you, Drew."

"Likewise, Violet," he said as he engulfed her hand with his. She met his eyes then, and something warm and electric sparked between them.

Violet pulled her hand back and studied him for a moment. Then she shook her head. "A male strip club, huh?"

He sighed. "A bar. A bar that routinely hosts shows for male exotic dancers."

"Right." She shook her head again and tucked her hand into the pocket of her leather jacket. "I'll let Moonbeam know you were taking care of Zen and Qi. She'll appreciate that."

"Her what?"

"The mice. Their names are Zen and Qi."

"Oh. Of course. Well I wouldn't be too sure about Moonbeam appreciating the help. She's not overly fond of me or my business."

Violet smiled. "What's not to love about scantily clad men writhing around on stage?"

"Exactly!" Drew said with more enthusiasm than he meant. Violet gave a knowing look, and Drew started to assure her he was perfectly straight. Then he decided against it. Nothing screams "closeted homosexual" like announcing to a strange woman that you aren't gay.

Drew cleared his throat. "Hey, if you're not doing anything tomorrow night, we've got a special performance at the club. The Men of Texas. They're supposed to be pretty good. There's an extra cover charge, but I could put your name on the guest list if you want to check it out."

Violet looked startled. "Not really my scene." She hesitated, then shrugged. "Maybe that's a reason to do it."

"You like butt rock?"

"Pardon me?"

"Not a proposition. Or a medical condition. Butt rock, you know? Hair metal, glam rock, eighties power ballads, MTV, fist-pumping power chords?"

She shook her head. "I have no idea what you're talking about."

Drew grinned and began to pound a drumbeat on the countertop. Feeling Violet watching him, he launched into the chorus of the Scorpions' "No One Like You."

He half expected her to roll her eyes or walk away, but she laughed. "Butt rock, huh?"

He stopped drumming and looked at her. *God, she's beautiful*.

"We can call it glam rock if *butt* isn't a common part of your vocabulary."

"What makes you think *butt* isn't a common part of my vocabulary?"

"You know, I'm not sure this is a topic for a first conversation."

She rolled her eyes. "*Butt* is totally a part of my vocabulary."

"I'm sure it is. Anyway, butt rock... er, *glam rock*... is the best kind of music for male entertainers. The beat's perfect, and the music tends to appeal to women in our target demographic."

"You don't say."

Drew grinned. "So you want to stop by tomorrow?"

"Maybe."

"How about if I put your name on the list, just in case?"

"Okay." She nodded. "Thank you. I'd better get back to the hospital for visiting hours."

She started to move toward the door, but her heel caught on the frayed edge of the Oriental rug. She toppled forward, and Drew grabbed her without thinking.

"Oh," she gasped, looking up at him. Their eyes locked, and Drew was suddenly very conscious of the thinness of her sweater, the heat of the room, the flash of light in her eyes. In that moment, he would have preferred removing the skin from his forearm with a carrot peeler to taking his hands off her.

He let go of her and took a step back. "There you go," he said, offering an awkward pat on the shoulder. "You take care."

She blinked, then nodded. "Thank you. You, too."

He watched her walk away, deliberately not staring at her ass.

Chapter 2

BY THE TIME VIOLET GOT BACK TO THE HOSPITAL, Moonbeam was beginning to come out of anesthesia. She already had a cluster of visitors waiting outside to see her as soon as the nurse allowed it.

"Did they say how she's doing?" Violet asked Butterfly, whose pale curls were exploding from beneath an orange turban. The rest of her was covered from head to toe in tie-dye, and her tattered Birkenstocks were a concession to the hospital's footwear requirement. A tarot-card reader herself, Butterfly had been Moonbeam's best friend since Violet was still in diapers—organic cloth ones, of course. Though Violet had never known her father, she'd grown up with the love of two distinct, albeit odd, parents in her life. Butterfly was like a second mother to her.

"They aren't really telling us much," Butterfly said, looking worried. "None of us are technically family, you know, and there are all these rules now about privacy."

"Let me go see if I can find someone, okay?" Violet said. She watched the frown lines grow shallower on Butterfly's forehead and felt better for being able to help.

Violet walked past the nurses' station, halfway expecting someone to stop her. No one did. She kept walking down a tiled corridor, not entirely sure what she was looking for, but fairly certain it would be clad in a white lab coat.

She didn't have to look long. As she rounded another corner, she ran smack-dab into exactly such a specimen. Her breath came whooshing out in an unladylike *oof* as she collided with a male body that was—of course—dressed in a perfectly starched lab coat.

He caught her by the shoulders, holding her upright to keep her from toppling over. Violet gasped, more stunned to be grabbed by strange men twice in an hour than she was by the shock of impact. She was still tingling from the feel of Drew's hands on her shoulders, a little baffled by her response to him, since his enthusiasm about male exotic dancers made her pretty sure he was gay.

She looked up at the doctor and smiled. He smiled back. *Not gay*, Violet decided.

The doctor peered down at her and released her shoulders. "I'm so sorry, are you okay?"

"I'm fine, I'm fine. It's my fault. I wasn't watching where I was going."

She looked up into a pair of warm, brown eyes the color of Cadbury milk-chocolate eggs.

"Can I help you find something?" he asked, his eyes filled with concern, rather than creamy fondant.

"I was just looking for someone who could tell me how my mother is doing."

"Who's your mother?"

"Moonbeam... er, Lily McGinn."

The doctor offered a weak smile and pulled off a surgical cap to reveal a thatch of thinning, caramel-colored hair with a slight bald patch. "Of course. You look just like her. She's a spirited one, isn't she?"

"That's one way to put it."

He laughed and extended a hand. Violet shook it, trying not to be creeped out by the purple gloves she sincerely hoped were clean. He seemed very nice, and surely doctors washed their hands regularly.

"I'm Dr. Chris Abbott, your mother's orthopedic surgeon," he said as he pumped her hand with a little too much enthusiasm. He released it then, and smiled again. "The surgery went great. Have you gone back to see her yet?"

"Well, no. The nurses said she's still coming out of the anesthesia."

"Come on," he said as he touched her shoulder and steered her down another corridor. "You might as well be there when Moonbeam wakes up."

"Oh. Thank you."

He led her back to a room where Moonbeam lay blinking on a hospital bed, wrapped up in bandages with an IV snaking into her arm. As Violet approached, Moonbeam opened her eyes and smiled weakly.

"Hi, honey," Moonbeam whispered, her throat scratchy from the anesthesia. "How are you doing?"

"I'm doing fine, but I'm not the one who just got carved up. No offense, Dr. Abbott," she amended quickly, glancing over her shoulder at him.

"Call me Chris, please," he said, winking at Violet. "Hey, Moonbeam, how are you feeling?"

She smiled. "Snowy."

Dr. Abbott gave Violet a conspiratorial smile. "Morphine. She seems to like it."

"I'm sure she does."

Moonbeam yawned, then shut her eyes again. "I'm just going to take another nap, okay?"

"Whatever you want, Mom. I picked up your appointment book. Looks like you've got Mrs. Rivers at six p.m. Anything special I should know?"

But Moonbeam was already fast asleep.

"It sometimes takes a while for people to really come out of the anesthesia," Dr. Abbott offered. "Really though, she's doing well. You're welcome to go tell her fan club out there that you got to see her. She should be back to herself in another thirty minutes or so, and I'll have the nurse come tell you which room she'll be in."

Violet looked up at him, noticing for the first time the pleasant crinkles around his eyes. He was cute in that wholesome, enriched-wheat-bread sort of way. Very stable. Very nice. Very *normal*.

Normal had been in short supply for most of Violet's early life, so she smiled.

"Thank you, Dr. Abbott. I really appreciate it."

"Chris."

"Chris," she agreed, broadening her smile. "My mother is lucky to have you."

That evening, Violet got to work setting up her temporary accounting practice in one corner of Moonbeam's shop. She'd dragged a small desk out of the storage area and arranged her laptop and desk calendar and her pencil case with all the number-two pencils perfectly sharpened and aligned.

She could hear the faint sound of music from the other side of the wall, and wondered if Drew was still working. Not that she was interested. Not that *he* was interested. If her hunch was right, he was batting for the other team.

Still, her ears strained to pick up the sound of his voice, or at the very least, the notes of the song. Def Leppard, she realized. Something off the *Pyromania* album, maybe. "Photograph"—that was it. She hummed along with it as she clambered up onto the desk with a hammer in one hand.

She was standing there studying the wall when she heard a voice behind her.

"I don't usually see Moonbeam up on the desk. Is that a special psychic technique they only practice on the East Coast?"

She spun around, startled less by Drew's voice than by the electric blue of his eyes. His hair was as rumpled as it had been earlier, standing up in dark spikes that looked like someone had rubbed his head on the carpet. She couldn't tell if it was a hairstyle or a lack of one. Either way, there was something oddly endearing about it.

Stop staring, Violet.

She realized he was still waiting for an answer, and considered making something up to suggest a correlation between increased elevation and enhanced psychic powers. Instead, she shrugged and held up the hammer.

"If I'm going to be running my accounting office out of this place for a little while, I want it to look professional," she said. "I took down one of the tapestries so I can mount a nice framed landscape photo."

"Anyone ever tell you standing on a desk in stilettos is a bad idea?"

"No."

He sauntered toward her. "Allow me, then. Standing

on a desk in stilettos is a bad idea. Get down before you end up in the hospital with Moonbeam and I end up playing the psychic for you both."

She started to protest—not just the fact that he was telling her what to do, but the notion she was "playing" at anything. But before she could say a word, the hammer slipped from her grip and landed on her toe.

"Ow!" she yelped and lifted her foot.

Bad idea, she thought as she began to topple in her ridiculously high boots.

She didn't even see Drew move. It was like he just lifted his arms and she fell right into them. Her breath caught in her throat as she felt his hands grip her rib cage, the back of her knees. She looked up and found her herself nose to nose with him, his arms snug around her body, his breath ruffling her hair. He smelled like warm cotton and cherry Coke and something else she couldn't name that made her heart clench.

His eyes held hers, and she watched his Adam's apple move as he swallowed. "Standing on a desk in stilettos on only one foot… even worse idea."

"Duly noted."

"Are you okay?"

"I think so."

"Does your foot hurt?"

"What?"

"Your foot," he said, his arms still tight around her. "You dropped the hammer on it. That tends to smart a little."

"Oh. Right." Violet bit her lip. "I think it's fine."

His eyes were still fixed on hers, and Violet shivered. "Okay then," he said. "I'm going to put you down now."

Violet felt a flutter of disappointment, then did a mental eye roll at how dumb that was. He lowered her safely to the ground and took a step back.

Then he bent to pick up the hammer.

"Where do you want it?" he asked.

"What?"

"The painting, not the hammer." He grinned. "That was almost the punch line to a really filthy joke."

She blinked, trying to come up with something witty to say, something to show she wasn't completely discombobulated by his nearness.

Way to play it cool, Violet.

"Never mind," he said. "Hang on, let me grab my drill. Also not a filthy joke, for the record."

He retreated to the storage area between their shared space and returned a few seconds later with a cordless drill, a packet of drywall anchors, a couple of silver hooks, and some screws. "Let's get this thing mounted. Here, you can keep the hammer."

She started to protest, but really, he seemed to know what he was doing. Besides, did she want to climb back up on the desk? She sighed and stepped aside while Drew set his keys and cell phone on the shop counter and stepped up onto the desk with maddening ease. He looked down and nodded at the frame leaned up against the wall. "That's a nice photo."

"Thanks. It's Mount Hood."

"I know."

"Studies have shown artwork in offices and waiting areas has a calming effect on people, with eighty-four percent of study participants preferring landscape or nature scenes."

He gave her an odd look, and Violet felt like a dork. "I like statistics," she said. "And data."

"I like mountains. Can you hand me the photo?"

She stooped down and picked up the frame and offered it to him. "Thank you for doing this. Really, I appreciate it."

"Not a problem."

He got to work fiddling with a device Violet couldn't quite identify. As if reading her thoughts, he smiled down at her. "If you'd like to make a crack about the guy who works with male strippers using a stud finder, now would be the time."

"Pardon me?"

He held up the gadget. "Stud finder. It's how I know where to screw. You can make a crack about that, too, if you like."

"I'll pass," Violet said as primly as possible, trying not to stare at his hands.

On the counter beside her, his cell phone buzzed.

"Can you see who that is?" he asked with a couple screws between his teeth. "What's it say on the screen?"

Violet peered down at the iPhone. "Sam?"

"My partner. I'll call back. Give me another screw?"

This time, she forced herself not to blush. He had a partner. Of course. Named Sam. Clearly Drew was not an option. Not that she'd ever considered him to be. Not in a million years.

No, she had more pressing issues to deal with. Nursing her mother back to health. Keeping her accounting practice and Moonbeam's business afloat. Figuring out how to be a fake psychic. Typical stuff.

"One more screw, please?"

Violet bit her lip and handed him one, determined not to notice the way her hand tingled when he touched her.

⚊⚊⚊

The next evening, Violet was ready to jump out of her skin.

Preparing to do a fake psychic reading would be hard enough without worrying about her mother's health. But from the moment Moonbeam had come out of anesthesia the night before, she'd been a handful not only for Violet, but for every member of the medical staff.

Could she have some medical marijuana?

No.

What about burning sage in the room?

No, definitely not. Her neighbor was on an oxygen tank.

Watsu would really help the healing process; did they have a swimming pool on-site?

No.

It went on like that all evening, and eventually, Violet began to notice the nurse eyeing the cords snaking out of the wall. Violet could see the wheels turning in the nurse's head: *one good tug, and it could all stop…*

You had to hand it to Moonbeam, though. She was spirited. Just like Dr. Abbott had said. Dr. Abbott, with his warm chocolate eyes and thinning caramel hair. And yes, his slightly vanilla personality. Nothing wrong with that. If Violet wasn't mistaken, he'd looked down the front of her blouse at least twice while adjusting Moonbeam's IV pole. He was interested in her, at least a little. She could do worse than a doctor, assuming he wasn't married with a wife and one-point-two kids at home.

So now here she sat in Moonbeam's shop, cozy in the chair that still held the shape of Moonbeam's rump. She had five minutes before her first psychic reading. What the hell was she going to do?

Next door, Violet could hear the faint hum of some obscure '80s hit. She tried to tune it out, but found herself lured by an odd wave of nostalgia as she recalled the crackly speakers and gym-sock smell of a middle school dance. One of the few Moonbeam had allowed her to attend.

Whitesnake, she thought. That was the band. The song was called "Trouble."

Focus, Violet. This isn't helping.

An astrological chart. She could do that. She could waste at least ten minutes of the appointment printing one off on the computer and talking to the woman about her birth sign. That was good, right?

But it wasn't enough. Violet was going to have to make something up. She sighed, feeling a sense of dread snake up her spine as the little bell tinkled on the door, signaling Mrs. Rivers's arrival.

"Hello, Mrs. Rivers," Violet said, standing up. "Did you get my telephone message?"

"Yes," replied the mousy-looking woman picking her way toward the back of the shop. She looked like a light breeze might topple her over, and she jumped like a scared cat when she bumped against a rack of key rings.

Cheating husband, thought Violet.

"I hope your mother is okay," Mrs. Rivers said. "I've used her services a few times, but I have to admit, I never knew she had a daughter."

"Yes, well, I live in Portland."

Mrs. Rivers looked at her quizzically.

"Portland, *Maine*," Violet amended, feeling foolish. "Shall we get started?"

"Oh. Oh, yes, of course. So is this common?"

"What?"

"For psychic abilities to run in families this way. You know, you and your mother—"

"Yeah, sure. Very common. Can I get you some tea?"

Mrs. Rivers gave her a goofy smile. "You're the psychic. What kind of tea do I like?"

Violet resisted the urge to roll her eyes. This was one of Moonbeam's favorite tricks.

"Chamomile," Violet replied, feeling guilty already.

Mrs. Rivers looked delighted. "Oh! You're as good as your mother!"

Absolutely, thought Violet, turning to switch on the Insta-Hot. *I can read the notes in the appointment book, just like Moonbeam.*

"So how long have you been in business?" Mrs. Rivers asked as they waited for the water to boil.

"Oh, almost ten years. Right after I got out of college."

"Really? You went to college to be a…?"

"Oh. Psychic. Right. Um, actually, my degree is in accounting. I'll be running an accounting practice over in that corner of the shop while I'm here. If you know anyone who needs my services…"

"A psychic accountant? Oh, you'll be in very high demand."

"Right. I actually don't combine the two. Unethical, you know?"

"Of course," Mrs. Rivers said, and Violet felt like a heel.

She turned in her chair and retrieved a mug from the cupboard, along with a tea bag and two sugars—just the way Mrs. Rivers liked it. "So you're a Gemini, right?" Violet began. "Let me just pull up your astrological chart here on the laptop and we can go over your—"

"Actually, I don't want to do the astrological chart this time."

"No?"

"No. I want to know something… um, personal."

"Personal?"

"Yes. You see, I have this friend."

Violet sighed. "Mrs. Rivers…"

"Okay, okay, you're too good," Mrs. Rivers said, looking guilty. "You're right, it's me."

"Go on."

"It's just… I want to know about Frank."

"Frank? Right, good old Frank. What do you want to know?"

"Well, he's just been acting a little suspicious lately, and there have been a couple times when I've wondered if maybe there's something going on and—"

"You want to know if he's cheating?" Violet guessed.

Mrs. Rivers's eyes grew wide. *Jesus*, Violet thought. *When a woman has to ask a total stranger if her husband is fooling around, she already knows the answer. Why is she asking me?*

"I'm just so—," Mrs. Rivers began.

"Yes. Yes, he is cheating. I'm sorry."

"But—"

"Statistically speaking, twenty-two percent of men cheat. Really, it's best to move on. Once the trust is gone, you really don't have much left, do you?"

Mrs. Rivers looked dumbstruck. "But how—?"

"The *how* isn't the point, Mrs. Rivers. The point is, you can't let things go on like this."

"I can't?"

"No, you can't. And I think you know what you need to do."

"I do?"

"Think about it."

Mrs. Rivers furrowed her brow, concentrating hard. "I guess you're right. So how long has this been going on?"

"About two weeks longer than you've suspected it."

"Really?"

"Yes."

"Okay. So I need to confront him, then. Maybe I could bring him here and you could talk to him? I mean, he can't deny it with you. You're a psychic. You see everything."

"Right. See, that's really not the best idea. Why don't you and Frank sit down and have a heart-to-heart talk. And even if he denies it, I think there's a more important lesson in here for you."

"There is?"

"Yes. You need to start standing up for yourself. You need to not let Frank—or any other man—control the way you feel about yourself. You need to be strong. How will he respect you otherwise?"

"Well, I guess…"

"Don't guess. Know! Be strong! Be assertive!"

"Okay!"

"Now go out there and kick some ass!" Violet shouted, pounding her fist into her palm with a smack.

Mrs. Rivers looked befuddled. "Wow. You're a lot different than your mother."

"Yeah, well, she taught me everything I know. I just put my own twist on it."

"Okay," Mrs. Rivers said brightly, glancing at her watch. "So it looks like our time is up."

"It is?"

"I only signed up for a half hour this time."

"Right," Violet said, feeling a weight lifting from her shoulders. "So I'll just run your platinum MasterCard now."

"Wow. That's really amazing how you just know things like that," she said, digging in her purse.

God help this woman, Violet thought as she reached for the credit card machine.

By the time she'd run the card, issued a final pep talk, and ushered Mrs. Rivers out the door, Violet was feeling exhausted. And thirsty. And yes, a little bit guilty.

Did Moonbeam still keep a bottle of tequila behind the—

"Nice work there," a voice said.

Violet stood up fast, smacking her head on top of a bookcase. "Ow! Dammit, Drew, how long have you been standing there? Were you eavesdropping? What do you want?"

"Ten minutes. Yes. Toilet paper."

"What?"

"Just answering your questions again. In the order you—"

"Right," she said, trying hard to hold on to her indignation instead of noticing the bright blue of his eyes. "So you *were* eavesdropping?"

"Not intentionally. The walls are pretty thin, and I

share a corridor with your mom's shop. I was just stock-
ing the restrooms for tonight and I noticed we were out
of toilet paper and—"

"Right. I know. The access door to the storage closet
is in Moonbeam's shop."

"Wow!" Drew said. "You must be psychic!"

Violet frowned. Was he being a sarcastic bastard or a
naive one? *Sarcastic*, she thought, eyeing the back of his
head as he opened the storage unit. Definitely *sarcastic*.

"Anyway," he said from inside the closet, "since
you're psychic, you probably already know that Frank
isn't Mrs. Rivers's cheating husband."

"What?"

"Frank is her squash partner. They both play pro-
fessionally. They were ranked in the top-ten doubles
teams on the world circuit a couple years ago, and I'm
pretty sure Frank wouldn't be happy to hear you think
he's cheating."

"But—"

"Of course I'm sure you already knew that," he called
over his shoulder. "Being psychic and all."

Violet closed her eyes and counted to ten. Maybe
this wasn't so bad. Maybe the squash partner really *was*
cheating. Maybe he wouldn't be so angry. Maybe—

"So Drew," she said, interrupting her own thoughts
in desperate hopes of canceling them out. "Do you often
eavesdrop on my mother's sessions?"

"Not intentionally," he called from inside the closet.

"Right. Not intentionally. I was just wondering if her
technique has changed much over the years."

"You mean does she still prey on gullible people and
tell them exactly what's written all over their faces?"

He turned around with his hands full of toilet paper and grinned at her. "Pretty much."

"I wouldn't use the word *prey*, exactly—" Violet began.

"No? What word would you use?"

"My mother is empathetic."

"Of course."

"She's kind," Violet added, not sure why her cheeks were heating up. "Moonbeam is keenly in tune with the emotions of others."

"Absolutely. Nothing wrong with that at all. Hell, I'm not even sure she knows she's full of it."

"Am I sensing a little skepticism here about psychic powers?" she asked, folding her arms over her chest.

"Would that be your sixth sense or your seventh sense at work there?"

Sarcastic. Definitely sarcastic.

Of course he had to be good looking. And of course he also had to be gay. Why could she never meet any straight, handsome, funny men who weren't complete smart-asses?

Dr. Abbott, she thought, and forced a little smile.

Drew began to juggle the toilet paper with maddening ease, and Violet watched, fascinated in spite of herself.

"Hey, are you coming tonight?" Drew asked, still juggling the toilet paper.

"Tonight?"

"The Men of Texas. I've got your name on the list."

"Oh, right. I mentioned it to my mother's best friend, and she thought it sounded exciting. I'm not so sure. It's not really my scene."

"Your mother's best friend watching the Men of Texas? This I've gotta see."

"Yes, well, I'll try to be there."

She watched him juggling the toilet paper for a few more minutes, disgusted with herself for being so strangely amused, so fixated on his hands.

Hands reserved for his partner, Sam, she reminded herself. *Knock it off, Violet.*

"Did you know Oregon is the most active juggling state in the U.S.?" she blurted.

He stopped juggling and stared. "What?"

"Yes. Approximately fifty-three percent of the state's population can juggle. Portland is also home to the only retail all-juggling store in North America."

"This data fetish you have is fascinating."

Violet blinked, not sure if he was teasing or genuinely fascinated. He was smiling, but that could mean anything.

"Well, I knew about all that because I've been contracted to do some accounting work for the guy who runs the juggling shop," she said. "But there really are a lot of interesting statistics related to Oregon. Have you heard that Oregon has the highest concentration of strip clubs in the nation?"

"I've heard that," Drew said slowly, studying her with something that was either amusement or the expression of a man trying to remember if he had mental-health services on speed dial.

"It's not true," Violet said. "Oregon actually has the *second* highest concentration of strip clubs in the nation. West Virginia beats us."

"I didn't realize we were competing."

"It has to do with the Oregon Supreme Court ruling

that adult bookstores, nude dancers—it's all considered free speech, so it's protected. It's part of why Portland thrives on the whole offbeat counterculture thing. Legalized medical marijuana, physician-assisted suicide, bacon-wrapped doughnuts—"

"I never thought I'd hear *doughnuts* and *suicide* in the same sentence," Drew said. "At least not in a way that made sense. You really are a wealth of wacky data, aren't you?"

Violet bit her lip. "I can't help it. Part of being an accountant, maybe."

Drew's eyes were locked on her mouth, and Violet stopped biting her lip and stared back. He shook his head and turned away from her. "Hope to see you tonight, Violet."

He walked away juggling his toilet paper.

Drew couldn't believe he'd invited Moonbeam's daughter to see the Men of Texas. What the hell had he been thinking? Sometimes he forgot he ran a bar with strippers and not an exotic sushi restaurant.

The nature of his business, and particularly the addition of the twice-weekly male-stripper shows, had annoyed the hell out of his ex-wife. It didn't matter that the stripper thing had been her brother's idea, or that Jamie saw it as the fulfillment of his lifelong dream. Catherine had expected Drew to talk her baby brother out of what she saw as a ridiculous plan, and the fact that he refused annoyed Catherine to no end.

As a high-powered divorce attorney, Catherine probably could have fought him for a share of the bar, but she hadn't been the least bit interested. In fact, she had only set foot in the bar twice during their entire two-year marriage.

"Professional women find that sort of thing gauche," Catherine had told him so many times he'd stopped counting.

And Violet was definitely a professional woman. That's why Drew choked on his cherry Coke when she came wandering through the door at ten p.m., looking saucy and stern in a pair of slim black pants and a purple wraparound top made of some sort of stretchy material. The stilettos she wore gave a sexy wiggle to her walk. Drew tried not to stare.

That became impossible as Violet's companion joined her. She looked like someone's grandmother, with fine, pale curls and a plump bosom. Of course, no grandmother he knew wore a red bustier under a tie-dyed cape, with purple Birkenstocks to round out the ensemble. Drew had to blink several times to take her all in. Had he seen her around Moonbeam's shop before? If he had, she sure as hell hadn't been wearing leopard-skin stretch pants.

He watched as the two of them ambled over to a corner table and smiled up at the waiter. To her credit, Violet maintained eye contact, despite the fact that the waiter was clad in nothing but a green loincloth designed to look like leaves. Grandma was slightly less subtle. Her jaw was hanging so far open, Drew could have lobbed a basketball in there.

As soon as they'd ordered their drinks, Drew walked over to their table. Violet looked up at him, those odd-colored eyes luminescent beneath the black lights.

"You made it," he said, smiling down at her. "I didn't think you would."

"Yeah, well, I've actually never been to a show like this before." She looked around in obvious wonderment. "I wasn't too sure about it, but we had kind of a rough day at the hospital with Mom, and Butterfly thought we could use a distraction. Oh, I'm sorry. Drew, this is Butterfly, my mom's best friend. Butterfly, this is Drew… er…"

"Watson. Drew Watson," he said, extending his hand for Butterfly to shake. Instead, she grabbed it, flipped it over, and began to study his palm. Drew stared at her for a minute, then looked to Violet for help.

She just shrugged. "Right. Drew owns the place, Butterfly."

"Really?" Butterfly asked, glancing away from his palm momentarily to look up at him with renewed interest. Her eyes were as globe-like as the butt cheeks of the dancer on stage behind them.

"So you must, um, really like the nude male figure?" Butterfly asked.

Drew laughed. "Not nearly as much as I like the nude female figure."

The two women exchanged a look, and Drew got ready to offer up the usual defense. He wasn't gay. He didn't have a thing for naked men. It was just that from a marketing standpoint, exotic male dancers were—

"Sir, Mr. Watson, sir." A bouncer came running up to the table, his brow furrowed in concern. "We've got a situation again."

"A fight?"

"No. It's Jamie. He's refusing to go on."

Drew sighed, trying hard not to grit his teeth. He

looked back at Violet and Butterfly, both of whom wore the identical female expression that said, *The second you leave, we'll be talking about you.*

"Will you ladies excuse me for a minute?" Drew said. "I've got a crisis to avert."

"No problem," said Violet, reaching up to take her drink from the waiter. A strong drink, from the look of things. "Thanks again for inviting us."

"No problem. Really. Make yourselves at home."

"Of course. Because my home is filled with half-naked men writhing on the floor."

Drew let that one pass and hurried off down the hall toward the dressing room. *Jamie.* God. What now?

Rounding the corner into the dressing room, Drew followed the sounds of muffled sniffling to a sofa in the back corner. There sat his ex-brother-in-law, looking forlorn and a bit drunk in his fireman costume—lined with Velcro for easy removal, of course.

"What seems to be the problem, Jamie?" Drew said, coming to sit beside him.

Jamie looked up at him, his eyes red-rimmed and goopy. *Jesus*, Drew thought. *And women throw their panties at this guy?*

"It's Sid," Jamie sniffled. "He called me a wuss."

"Right. Remember what we talked about with the sticks and stones…?"

"But it really hurt my feelings, boss," Jamie said, his expression so wounded that Drew couldn't help but feel sorry for him. Well, as sorry as he could feel for a man who'd been named Mr. Oregon Bodybuilder for three out of the last five years.

"You have to get through this, Jamie," Drew soothed.

"Those guys just tease you to get a rise out of you. If you don't let them get to you, they'll stop."

"But dancing is my art," he sniffed. "They don't understand how it wounds me when they make a mockery of something that's so emotionally valuable to me."

"Hey," Drew said. "Remember those pretty girls in the front row last week? They could have tucked that hundred in anyone's shorts, but whose did they choose?"

Jamie smiled a little at that. "Mine."

"Exactly. And who did we pick out of all the dancers to perform at that movie star's bachelorette party next month?"

Jamie's smile got wider. "Me."

"And who's going to fund his college education entirely off tips from his job here?"

By now, Jamie was glowing. "Won't that be great? Maybe I'll even keep going and get my master's in social anthropology."

"I'm sure that will serve you well," Drew agreed. "So are you almost ready to go on? The Men of Texas are relying on you to get the crowd warmed up for them."

"I've got it covered, boss," Jamie said, standing up and putting on his fireman's hat that said RED HOT. "You can count on me."

Then he trotted away, leaving Drew to stand there staring after him.

"I should have been a preschool teacher," he muttered.

By the time Drew got Jamie pumped up and settled a dispute between the Men of Texas over whose costume had the most sequins, a full hour had gone by. The bar was packed with two bachelorette parties and an assortment of tipsy women taking advantage of the late-night drink specials, so Drew hadn't had a chance to check on Violet. Was she enjoying herself, or had she gotten offended and left by now?

As he rounded the corner next to the main stage, Drew got the answer to that question.

"Hey, big boy! Take it off! Woooooohooooooo!"

Violet was standing on the table—which, thank God, he'd had the foresight to bolt into the floor—wobbling in her stilettos as she called out to one of the Men of Texas.

Somehow the tie on her wraparound top had come loose, displaying a flash of black bra Drew tried hard not to notice. Violet shrieked again, and the dancer on stage lobbed his T-shirt at her. She leaned out to catch it—a tough move even if her balance hadn't been compromised by the contents of the four empty cocktail glasses on her table.

Violet yelped. Drew ran.

He reached out and caught her just in time, feeling her tumble into his arms in a cloud of bourbon and warm flesh.

He looked down at her in his arms and felt his libido surge. "You really have to stop falling like this."

"But it's so fun to have you catch me!" She looked blearily into his eyes and smiled. "Why aren't you naked?"

"Why aren't you under the care of a good therapist?"

"I am!" she shrieked with delight. "Does that mean you'll take off your clothes?"

Drew tried not to smile as he glanced around the room. "Where did Butterfly go?"

"She went next door to clean the mouse cage. Apparently bourbon makes her want to tidy."

"And it makes you want to stand on tables and scream at naked men."

"Doesn't it do the same for you?"

Drew sighed. "No."

Violet nodded knowingly. "Tequila then. Hey, can you take me home?"

"What?"

"I was going to take a cab, but since you're standing here holding me, I thought maybe…"

"Right," Drew said, and set her on her feet. He looked up at the stage, where one of the Men of Texas seemed to be winding down. "Let me go find Sam."

Violet sighed looked strangely sad for a moment. "Sam. Right. Good old Sam. I might hate Sam."

"What?"

"I've never met Sam, so I guess that's not fair, is it?"

Drew took a step back, not really sure what to say. "Okay. I need someone to look after things while I run you home, so we need Sam. Are you staying at Moonbeam's house?"

"Yes. Definitely."

"Do you think you can tell me how to get there?"

"Pretty sure." She signaled a passing server with a drink tray, her mind already on something besides the Men of Texas or her evident distaste for his business partner.

"Okay. Well then, I'm glad you've enjoyed yourself here."

Drew went to get his keys, shaking his head a little as he rounded the bar. He was willing to bet his next mortgage payment this was not a woman who got drunk and screamed at scantily clad men in bars.

Come to think of it, he wasn't sure *drunk* or *screaming* were even part of her repertoire. He wasn't sure about the scantily clad men, but he preferred not to dwell on that.

"Hey, Sam," he called to the busty, middle-aged blonde woman behind the bar. "Can you cover things for a few minutes?"

"My sitter's with the kids for another three hours, so I'm good. What's up?"

"I need to run Moonbeam's daughter home."

Sam glanced up from the beer taps and squinted toward the table where Violet sat swaying to the music. "That the girl who's been trying to spank the dancers all night?"

"Probably."

"Good luck. You'll have your hands full with that one."

Drew felt his mind veer into dangerous territory with the thought of having his hands full of anything to do with Violet, so he turned and headed back toward her table.

He found her perched on the lap of one of his dancers, a drunken smile on her lips.

"So then I found out that my date had bet his best friend ten dollars that I had breast implants," she was hollering into the dancer's ear. "Can you believe the nerve?"

The dancer shook his head in wonderment, looking down her shirt in awe of the gift that had dropped into his lap.

"Come on, Violet," Drew said, hauling her up out of Joey's arms. Joey looked glum for a minute, but perked up at the sight of her pert little butt walking away from him. Drew scowled at Joey and ushered Violet in front of him, steering her toward the door.

As soon as Drew got her into the car and extracted some driving directions from her, Violet began to chatter at warp speed.

"It was so nice of you to invite me out like this," she gushed. "Moonbeam would have a stroke if she knew. Is that bad to say about my mom when she's in the hospital? It really is too bad you're gay. You're awfully cute. Sort of like John Cusack."

"I'm not—"

"I know you and Moonbeam haven't always gotten along and she told me you're exploiting the human body, but those guys seemed pretty happy and with all those tips they're being fairly compensated and the temperature was good so they have nice working conditions so I don't think you're so horrible."

"Well—"

"I was just telling Butterfly how nice you were to feed the mice like that. Do you come over to Moonbeam's shop a lot? Because I'll probably need a lot of help over there. Do you want to know a secret?"

"I—"

She leaned close—as close as she could with the seat belt yanking her backward—and whispered against his cheek.

"I'm not a psychic. I'm an accountant with Barton and Withrow in Portland, Maine."

"Yeah, you mentioned the accountant thing already," Drew said, not sure if it was the liquor on her breath or something else making him mildly dizzy. "It's nice you've got a few different career skills to fall back on. I mean, besides the psychic thing."

"No, no, you don't understand," she slurred. "Psychics don't exist."

"Oh. Okay. Well, then, you're a pleasant figment of my imagination."

She smiled at him… a little sadly, it seemed. Then she lost her train of thought as she became distracted by the buttons on the radio. Drew studied her. *What an odd woman.* They drove in silence for a few minutes until Drew pulled into the driveway of Moonbeam's house. He jerked the parking brake, but kept the car running, not ready yet to walk her to the front door.

"So who won the bet?" he asked.

"Huh?"

"Your date bet his friend you had breast implants. Just curious who won."

"Pig."

He grinned. "Yup."

She smiled at him. "It's okay, I guess, since you're gay."

Before he could react, she'd grabbed his hand and shoved it into the front of her shirt.

"See?"

"Uh—"

"Now you have your answer!"

"Um, Violet?"

"My date never did get to find that out."

"Right. Violet?"

"Pretty impressive, huh?"

"Absolutely, but Violet?"

"Yes?"

"I'm not gay."

"You're not?"

"No."

She stared at him. She looked down at his hand, not in any hurry to remove it. She looked back up at him, seemingly bewildered.

"You're sure you aren't gay?"

"Positive. I've even been married before."

"Married?"

"To a *woman*," he added. "A woman even more high-strung than you are."

"But I was so sure you liked men, and then there's your partner, Sam, and—"

"Sam is my *business* partner. And a woman."

"So you're not—"

"No."

"But—"

"Violet, I'm as gay as these are silicone and you're a psychic."

"Oh."

"So I think the gentlemanly thing to do would be to remove my hand from your very nice, very real, very unpsychic breast."

She smiled, looking startlingly sober all of a sudden. Then she put her hand on his, holding it there. "And what if I don't want you to?"

Chapter 3

THERE WAS A DISTANT VOICE IN THE BACK OF VIOLET'S head telling her to remove the stranger's hand from her breast and bid him a polite good-night.

Of course, the fact that she was hearing voices was not a good sign. It wasn't surprising, considering how much time she'd been spending with Moonbeam and how much bourbon she'd consumed, but still.

"Not gay?" Violet repeated, looking down at his hand. It was still on her breast, which was probably because she'd locked his wrist in a death grip and held it in place at the opening of her top.

"Not gay," he confirmed. "And as much as I'm enjoying this, I'm not looking forward to dealing with you when you sober up and accuse me of molesting you. So I'm going to pull my hand back nice and slow, and you're going to let go of my wrist on the count of one, two, three…"

Violet took a deep breath and released his wrist. She waited one heartbeat. Two.

"Okay, removing my hand now," Drew said, his voice a little strained.

Three heartbeats, four. Violet shifted in her seat. Just a tiny movement, but enough to feel her flesh press harder against his palm.

She made a small whimper in the back of her throat.

Drew closed his eyes and cursed under his breath.

"Okay," Drew said, and pulled his hand back. He took another breath, this one shakier than the last. "Right, so I'll be going now."

"Yes, of course," Violet said, trying hard to sound sober. "Thank you for the ride. Good night, Drew Watson."

"Good night, Violet."

Violet sat there, trying to regain her composure. She folded her hands in her lap and took a breath, her head still spinning a little from the bourbon and all the heat in the car.

She flipped the visor down and looked at her reflection, wondering how her lipstick had gotten smeared across her face. Had she really left the house with that much eyeliner? She had a vague memory of Butterfly urging her to get sexy before they set out for the evening, but she couldn't recall intentionally trying to look like a hooker.

She felt her brain start to spin, so she flipped the visor back up and folded her hands on her lap again.

Beside her, Drew cleared his throat. "So, this is where you'd get out of the car."

"What?"

"This is my car, not your bedroom. I can see how you might be confused."

"Oh. Right. No, I was just leaving." Violet fumbled the door open, her fingers shaking and a little sticky. "Good night, Drew."

"Here, let me help you inside," he said, unbuckling his seat belt.

"Oh, no," Violet said, thrusting her hand out to push against his chest. She'd only meant to force him back against his seat, but here she was, groping his pecs. *Very nice pecs*. Violet drew her hand back. "Stay here. I'll be fine, really."

He gave her a skeptical look. Violet turned away and swung her leg out of the car, wobbling a little as she found her footing on the rain-soaked pavement. "So, thanks again," she said brightly, swinging the other leg out of the car as she turned back to look at him.

Drew's eyes held hers for several beats, not even blinking. Violet resisted the urge to lunge back into the seat and grab him by his shirt collar and—

"No problem," Drew said, blinking at last. "You sure you don't want me to walk you to the door?"

Violet shook her head and stood up, gripping the side-view mirror for balance. She stood there for a moment, looking out over the street, then down at the droplets of rain smeared across the roof of his car. "I'm fine," she called down to him, straining to keep her voice nonchalant. "The door is ten yards away."

There was a long pause. Inside the car, Drew cleared his throat. "Violet?"

She bent back down and peered through the door of the car. "Yes?"

His eyes were dark, his expression unreadable. She could see his chest rising and falling.

"Fix your shirt," he said at last.

Violet's hand flew to her chest. Her fingers touched the lacy edge of her bra. "Oh. Right. Yes, of course."

Drew shook his head and closed his eyes, muttering something under his breath. Was he mad? Annoyed? Violet wasn't sure. Judging human emotion was Moonbeam's strong suit, not hers.

She fumbled with the tie on her wrap top, covering

her bra. Then she stepped back from the car. "Well, thanks again," she said.

Drew opened his eyes, looking more composed than he had a few seconds ago. "Good night, Violet."

Violet took another step back and pushed the car door shut. Drew put the car in gear and backed out of the driveway, then stopped, his brake lights flickering. Violet stood still for a moment, watching his windshield wipers swishing back and forth. Watching the beam of his headlights flickering in the rain. *Watching him*.

Finally, she realized he was waiting for her to get safely in the house. Waiting one hundred feet away at the end of the driveway, well out of her reach, which was probably smart.

Violet wobbled up the steps and waved to him from the porch before turning and letting herself in with her key. She shut the door behind her and flashed the porch light off and on, letting him know she was safely inside.

Then she turned around and peered through the window, watching him again. She noticed how he gunned the engine and tore off down the street, much faster than he'd arrived. She saw his taillights fade into the inky fog. She stared after the car, long after it had been swallowed up by the damp blackness.

"Not gay," she repeated to herself. Then she turned and staggered down the hall to her room, not bothering to take her stilettos off before she crashed onto the bed.

———

Violet moved gingerly the next morning. It took ten minutes to peel her parched tongue off the roof of her mouth, and another ten minutes to tiptoe through her

alcohol-saturated memory bank to recall what she'd
done the night before.

Had she really downed four Manhattans?

Had she really told Drew Watson she was a fake psychic?

Had she really forced him to grab her boob?

She contemplated all of it as she drove her rental car
across town to the Hollywood District of Portland. Her
boss back in Maine had referred her to a guy who ran a
juggling shop and needed a bit of accounting work, and
Violet had been happy for the distraction.

Accounting. That's what she did for a living. Not
this crazy psychic thing. Hell, she didn't even believe
in psychics.

But the fact that she'd said that to Drew last night had
been a grave tactical error.

She owed it to her mother to preserve the reputation
of her business. To shield it from a man who, accord-
ing to Moonbeam, had been coveting her studio space
for years.

So she just had to make sure Drew knew she had been
kidding. She could insist Moonbeam was a real psychic.
She could insist that *she* was a real psychic. That wasn't
so hard, was it? Lord knows she'd have to do it anyway,
if she wanted to keep Moonbeam's business running.

She breathed in the scent of rain-washed pavement
and damp grass as she pushed open the door to the
little shop called Serious Juggling. She froze in the
entryway, heart thudding in her ears as she spotted a
familiar figure.

"Drew?"

He spun to face her, looking as startled as she was.

He recovered faster, his bewilderment replaced by an

appraising look that lingered a few seconds extra on her breasts. "Hey, Violet. You're looking surprisingly vertical."

She straightened a little, knowing it was probably futile. Her dignity was hopelessly lost after last night. "Thank you for the ride last night. And for being a gentleman."

"Gentleman?" He quirked an eyebrow. "How drunk were you?"

She flushed and glanced past him to see if any other customers had heard. Everyone seemed to be engaged in conversations about knives and hoops and juggling clubs, so Violet looked back at Drew.

"I meant that *some men* might take advantage of a woman in an inebriated state. You didn't follow me into the house and throw me on the bed and have your way with me, so thank you for that."

Drew grinned. "If I'd thought that was an option, I might have gone for it. My instincts got a little fuzzy after you glued my hand to your breast."

She glanced toward the cash register again and lowered her voice. "Do you have to bring that up?"

"Absolutely. It was the highlight of my week. Maybe even my year. Do you always bite your lip like that?"

"What?"

"Your lip. That's got to hurt."

Violet pressed her lips together and ignored the question. "Why are you here?"

"Thought I'd broaden my horizons a little, move on from juggling toilet paper to juggling knives or flaming swords. Looked this place up online after you mentioned it yesterday. How about you? What do you want to juggle?"

"Paperwork. I'm here to pick it up so I can do some accounting work."

Drew shrugged. "Paper's not very easy to juggle. How about balls?"

"Balls?"

"Balls," he repeated, grabbing a set of three multi-colored ones off a display. "Get your mind out of the gutter, Violet. Show me your juggling skills."

He tossed the three balls to her. They watched as all three dropped to the floor.

"Impressive," Drew said.

"I have skills. Marketable ones. Juggling just doesn't happen to be one."

"Ever tried it?"

"No."

"Come on, I'll show you. It's fun."

Violet wasn't the least bit interested in juggling, but she could see the clerk still deep in conversation with another customer. When Drew reached out and caught her wrist, Violet suddenly forgot about the paperwork.

"Take a couple steps this way," he said. "Good. Okay, feet apart, elbows at a ninety-degree angle, bend your knees a little. Here you go."

He placed a red, beanbag-like ball in her right hand and Violet felt a funny, electric jolt as his fingertips brushed hers. He closed her hand around the ball and gave a tight squeeze. Then he released her.

"Toss the ball back and forth between your hands," he said. "That's it—a nice, gentle arc."

"Like this?"

"Pretty much. Toss a little higher, about eye level. When you're comfortable with that, try closing your eyes while you toss."

Violet obeyed, feeling only mildly silly standing in

the doorway of a downtown Portland shop with her eyes
closed throwing a beanbag ball back and forth with a
man she'd only just met. Even with her eyes closed, she
could sense Drew beside her. She felt the faint rustle
of his breath stirring her hair, the heat from his bare
forearms. He smelled wonderful—something clean and
soapy mixed with the faint smell of cherry cola. She
breathed him in and felt her head start to spin.

"Whoops," Drew said.

She opened her eyes to see him catch the ball just
before it hit the ground.

"Not a problem," he said, standing upright. "I think
you're ready to handle two balls now."

She flushed and stole another glance toward the
cash register.

Drew grinned. "Mind out of the gutter, Violet. Here's
your other ball."

"I wasn't—"

"Yes you were."

She was, so she shut up and took the second ball.
"Now what?"

"Toss the first one up. While it's in the air, toss the
second one underneath it."

She did as he said—at least, she thought she did. Both
balls began a downward plummet toward the floor.

"Got it," Drew said, catching one in each hand as if it
were the easiest thing in the world.

Each massive, strong, beautifully made hand.

"You with me, Violet?"

She tore her eyes off his hands. "Yes."

"Here, let's try this."

He positioned one ball in each of her palms before

moving behind her. Every nerve in Violet's body snapped to attention as Drew pressed close. He fitted his arms around her so the points of her elbows rested in the hollows of his. His forearms were long and solid and warm, and his fingers folded around hers, cupping each of her hands in one of his.

Violet sucked in a breath and resisted the urge to lean back against his chest.

This is crazy, this is crazy, this is crazy! her brain chanted. *More, more, more!* her body chanted.

Violet cleared her throat. "Now what?"

"Just follow my motion, and release the balls when I tell you to."

Violet's head was spinning, and she wondered if she'd be able to work her limbs at all if he weren't maneuvering her arms for her. His hands were warm and strong around hers, and his body was hard and solid behind her. She felt his breath rustle her hair again and shivered.

"This is the motion you're aiming for," he murmured close to her ear. "Feel that? That's what you want."

No kidding, Violet thought.

"Like this?" Her voice sounded high and strained.

"Perfect."

"Should I let go of the balls yet?"

"Not yet. I want you to get used to the rhythm first."

"Okay."

"Is it starting to feel natural to you yet?"

"Uh-huh…"

Her knees quivered and Violet could feel pinpricks of sweat dotting her skin. His arms were hot against hers, and she glanced down to admire the sinew of muscle and the dusting of dark hair. Her breath was coming fast now, and she knew it had nothing to do with the exertion of juggling. Drew was humming now, something whimsical and carnival-like. An '80s tune, of course… something by Kiss?

"'Psycho Circus'?" Violet asked.

"Good ear," he murmured, and kept humming.

The rumble of his voice in his chest vibrated through Violet's spine, and she pressed back against him just to feel more. She half expected him to pull back, to put a bit more distance between them.

Instead, he responded by pulling her closer. Violet felt her knees start to buckle. His mouth moved closer to her ear.

"Release," he murmured.

"Oh, God," Violet said, and dropped both balls.

He didn't catch them this time. Violet closed her eyes and fought the urge to whimper. Drew stopped moving and let go of her hands. Then he took a step back.

Violet turned and they both looked down at the balls on the floor. Then they looked up at each other.

His eyes were wild and a little unfocused. He blinked and took another step away. "That didn't go quite like I planned."

Violet licked her lips and stepped back, too. "I think I'll stick with accounting. That's safer."

"And psychic readings," Drew said. "Don't forget your new second career."

Violet winced. "I couldn't possibly."

Behind her, she heard footsteps.

"Ms. McGinn? I'm so sorry to keep you waiting. You're here for the paperwork, right?"

She turned around, straightening her shirt with one

hand as she wiped the other palm on her skirt. She extended her hand to shake, darting a quick glance at Drew as she did so.

Drew winked, and Violet felt her heart clench.

"Later, with the balls," he said.

Then, he was gone.

—⁓—

By the time Violet got back to her mother's shop, she had only ten minutes before her first appointment. She settled into Moonbeam's red velvet chair with a cup of chamomile tea and scanned the appointment book.

Gary Smeade. Violet sighed and set her tea down. *Detective* Gary Smeade.

It wasn't unusual for police personnel around the country to occasionally, albeit quietly, seek the services of clairvoyant professionals to assist in investigations.

There was a bit more history in her mother's relationship with Detective Smeade. The two had met fifteen years ago, when Moonbeam had contacted Detective Smeade, offering to use her psychic powers to find his runaway seventeen-year-old son. Violet knew her mother had relied less on psychic powers than on the knowledge that her yoga teacher had lured the smitten teen to her love den with the promise of sex and a hookah pipe, but no one had bothered splitting hairs. Moonbeam had done a good deed one way or another, and Detective Smeade was convinced Moonbeam was the real deal.

Violet had called Moonbeam at the hospital while driving to the shop and had been less than thrilled to hear her mother had already talked with Detective Smeade about the morning's psychic substitution.

"I let him know you're a highly skilled clairvoyant, dear," Moonbeam had said. "He was happy to hear you'll be able to help the police department get to the bottom of the robbery."

"But Moonbeam—" she'd started to protest.

"It will be fine," Moonbeam assured her. "Dear, I've always said you have the gift. Moss… haven't I always said Violet had the gift?"

In the background, someone made an affirmative noise.

"See, Violet?" Moonbeam said. "You'll be fine. Look, honey, can you call back later? Moss just arrived, and she's going to be doing some therapeutic harp playing."

"Mom—"

But Moonbeam had already disconnected the phone, leaving Violet woefully unprepared for her session with Detective Smeade. Then again, what could she possibly do to prepare? Spontaneously develop psychic powers?

The door chimed and Violet set the appointment book aside as she stood up to greet her visitor.

"Detective Smeade," she said, extending her hand. "So good to see you again. How's your son doing?"

Detective Smeade grimaced a little, but returned her handshake. "Still living with Clover. They just opened their own Bikram Yoga studio, so I guess they're doing well. How about you, Violet?"

"Great. Excellent, thank you."

He smiled. "Last time I saw you, you were posting Moonbeam's bail after she chained herself to that Dumpster at the courthouse and refused to leave until they improved their recycling program."

"Well, yes—"

"And then there was that indecent-exposure charge—"

"Well, technically, Moonbeam was wearing body paint."

He smiled at her. "So here you are again, bailing Moonbeam out. Always such a good girl."

Violet tried not to be annoyed at that. "Can I get you some tea, Detective?"

"No, I'm fine, thanks." He lowered himself into the red velvet chair opposite Violet and splayed his knees out to the sides, his hands resting awkwardly on his lap. Violet sat too, keeping an eye on the detective. He was clearly making an effort not to look out of place, surrounded by gauzy curtains and stacks of tarot cards.

Violet tried to do the same.

"So," she began. "I talked to my mother on the phone this morning, but why don't you tell me a little bit about the robbery."

"Well, it's pretty much like I told Moonbeam. Our perp visited the downtown branch of Pinewood Bank on Third and Washington about ten a.m. Thursday morning, wearing a black T-shirt and a pair of nude panty hose covering his head and face."

"Anything else?"

"Well, an orange tutu, but that's not really important. Anyway, he brandished a pistol and left with a rather significant amount of money. Three hours later, we received a tip that he was standing naked in the middle of Pioneer Courthouse Square, holding a Twix candy bar."

"Twix," Violet repeated, wondering if she should be taking notes.

"We apprehended him there, but by that time, the perp had already disposed of the money. What we're trying to determine is what he did with it."

"Right," Violet said. "That's a logical thing to wonder."

"Sure," Detective Smeade said, nodding at her as he placed his hands on his knees. "We've had investigators tracking down all kinds of leads, but, well, the trail's going a little cold, so I thought Moonbeam might be able to help."

"Good old Moonbeam," Violet said grimly.

"Or you. I'm sure you're every bit as good."

"I'm sure."

Detective Smeade gave her an encouraging smile and then looked around the shop. "So what do you use?"

"Use?"

"The glass ball thingy? Or that deck of cards? Trance?"

"Oh, right," Violet said, fighting panic. "Trance. Sure."

The detective smiled again, looking appeased. Violet gritted her teeth. Detective Smeade shifted in his seat and looked at her expectantly.

Violet sighed. She closed her eyes, more from exasperation than an intent to enter a cosmic state. She ground her molars together, wishing the earth would swallow her. She tried to remember what the hell Moonbeam would do in this situation. Then again, did it matter? It's not as if there was a rule book.

Violet took a deep breath and began to hum.

"Ommmmmmmmmmmmmmmmmmmmmmmm…"

She let her head fall forward slightly, opening her palms to the ceiling, hoping to God there were no hidden cameras in the shop.

"Ommmmmmmmmmmmmmmmmmmmmmmm…"

Violet opened one eye a fraction of an inch, peering at the detective from under her lashes. He was reclined against the red velvet, looking content and a little curious. That was good.

"Ommmmmmmmmmmmmmmmmmmmmmmm…"

How long could she keep this up? Sooner or later, she'd have to come up with something to tell him. Maybe she could say the guy had thrown the money in the river. Or burned it in his backyard. The thief was crazy, right? Maybe the cops would just give up and leave her alone if they thought the money was destroyed.

"Ommmmmmmmmmmmmmmmmmmmmmmm…"

There was a metallic thump on the other side of the wall, the sound of something powering up in the strip club next door. Was that static? Electric guitar?

"Smooth up in ya…"

Violet opened her eyes. Detective Smeade blinked at her. Violet dug her nails into her palms.

"Sorry," she said. "There's a, um, bar next door. They must be testing the sound or picking songs or something—"

"Not a problem," Detective Smeade assured her. "I can't even really hear it. Moonbeam usually just keeps going. Unless that sort of thing breaks your concentration?"

Violet frowned. "Moonbeam keeps going?"

Detective Smeade nodded.

Violet sighed. She closed her eyes again.

"Ommmmmmmmmmmmmmmmmmmmmmmm…"

On the other side of the wall, the BulletBoys howled for several more choruses. Then, the music stopped. Violet wasn't sure whether to be relieved or disappointed at the loss of the distraction.

She stole a peek under her lashes again. Detective Smeade looked calm, relaxed. A whole lot calmer than Violet felt.

Next door, the sound system screeched again. Violet tried not to flinch. Tried harder not to grimace when she recognized the first few chords of another '80s classic. Was that Billy Idol? Billy Squier? Violet couldn't remember.

"Stroke me, stroke me—"

"Ommmmmmmmmmmmmmmmmmmmmmmmm…"

Violet sucked in her breath and stole another look at Detective Smeade. He looked oblivious. What the hell?

"Ommmmmmmmmmmmmmmmmmmmmmmmm…"

Next door, the sound system squawked again. The music cut off abruptly. Then the bass began to thump again. Violet's head began to pound in time to the music. Drums thudded, an electric guitar screeched, and Aerosmith's Steven Tyler let out a primal shriek.

Violet smacked her palms against the arms of her chair. "For the love of God, who strips to 'Love in an Elevator'?"

"What?"

Violet opened her eyes and blinked. "What?"

"What did you just say?"

Violet swallowed, suddenly very aware that the music had gone silent. "Nothing, I was just… it was the trance."

"Because it sounded like you said something about an elevator."

"Oh, well, I was just—"

"And there's an abandoned elevator shaft in the perp's apartment building. The super said the doors have been padlocked for years. No one can get in there. But maybe—"

"Well, I wouldn't jump to any conclusions."

But Detective Smeade wasn't listening. He was fumbling in his pocket and looking a little bit crazed. "My God, he must have a way in. That's it, isn't it? Jesus, wait 'til I tell Johnson."

By now, Detective Smeade was standing up, rapidly hitting buttons on his cell phone with one hand.

Violet sat up straight in her chair, gripping the arms so hard her knuckles were pale. "Detective Smeade, let's not get carried away—"

He held up his hand, silencing her. "Johnson? Call up that super again. We need to check the abandoned elevator. I don't care if he doesn't have the key to the padlock—we'll get a warrant if we have to."

Violet closed her eyes again and put her head in her hands, slouching in her chair as she tried to tune out the rest of the detective's phone call. What had she done?

"Okay, I'll see you over there." Detective Smeade clicked off his phone.

Violet sat up in her chair, trying to look like someone who hadn't just lied to a police officer. "Detective Smeade—"

"Thanks a bunch, Violet. I've gotta run. Just have your mom send me the bill like she always does."

"But—"

"We appreciate it. You've been a great help."

And with that, he dashed out the door.

Violet stared after him, willing him to come back and tell her he'd just been kidding. That he wouldn't really order the city's police force to follow the accidental directions of a fake psychic with a bad hangover.

Next door, the sound system screeched again. Def Leppard began to howl. *Thud, thud, thud—*

"Goddamit!" Violet yelped and leaped out of her chair. She stomped past the storage area and into the shared hallway, not even bothering to knock before grabbing the knob that led to Drew's bar. She flung the door open with such force, she half expected the handle to snap off in her palm.

"Dammit, Drew, what's with the noise?"

Drew looked up at her in surprise. He was crouched over a complicated-looking stereo system to the left of the bar. His hair was rumpled, his jeans were holey, and his expression was bemused.

He grinned at her. "Hello, Violet. Been practicing your juggling?"

"No, I haven't been practicing my juggling. I've been trying to *work* next door, but you're blasting glam rock loud enough to peel paint off my walls."

"You mean butt rock?"

"What?"

"I prefer the term *butt rock* over *glam rock*, but I suppose we shouldn't split hairs. Actually, *hair metal* is another common term—"

"Drew!"

"What?"

"I had a client this morning! Why are you playing music this loud at ten thirty on a Saturday morning?"

"Checking the speakers... and tonight's set list. It never seems to bother Moonbeam."

"Of course it doesn't," Violet muttered, channeling a string of mental curses at her mother. "She's probably in the midst of an astral flight."

"Maybe you should try that."

Violet took a deep breath, trying hard to get her temper under control. It wasn't his fault, really. He was just doing his job. Doing it *loudly*, of course, but if Moonbeam had never complained before...

"Look, I'm sorry I yelled," she said. "I'm just not used to practicing in this sort of environment. The music is a little… well, distracting."

Drew stood up, sending whatever was left of Violet's temper right out the window. "Apology accepted," he said. "And I'm sorry about the music. I'll try to keep it down from now on. And look, I got a present for you."

Startled, Violet reached out and accepted the small bag she recognized from the toy store down the street. She knew what it was before she'd even finished pulling it out of the bag.

"A Magic 8 Ball," she said flatly.

Drew grinned. "I figured you might need it. For the psychic readings."

"Psychic readings?" asked a booming voice from the other side of the stage.

Violet turned to see the tallest, blondest, most vacant-looking man she'd ever seen. And she was seeing a whole lot of him, since he was clad in nothing but a pair of boxer briefs and a tool belt. Beautifully chiseled, beautifully clueless, the man moved toward her with such an earnest expression that Violet wanted to warn him about playground bullies.

He smiled at her, looking a lot like a cocker spaniel on steroids. "Did you guys say psychic readings?" he asked. "I haven't seen the lady next door for awhile. Is she okay? You're pretty."

Violet smiled, charmed in spite of herself. She glanced at Drew, who kicked a stray cord out of Jamie's path.

"Careful, Jamie," Drew said. "Don't trip again."

"Thanks, boss."

"Violet," Drew said, "meet Jamie. The best thing I got to keep from my divorce."

"What?"

"Jamie used to be my brother-in-law, but he's now one of our top male entertainers on Friday and Saturday nights. He's actually the one who came up with the idea to expand the bar's offerings to include special performances."

"It was always a dream of mine," Jamie said, reaching out to pump Violet's hand. "Stripping, I mean. It's my art."

Drew cleared his throat. "And Violet is the daughter of Miss Moonbeam from next door."

Jamie beamed. "Wow, are you psychic, too?" he asked, his eyes wide. "I didn't know that sort of thing ran in families. That's really cool."

"Yes," Violet said, throwing Drew a pointed look. "It *is* cool," Violet said. "My mother is the best-known psychic in Portland, and I'm filling in for her while she recovers from an accident."

Violet shot another look at Drew, daring him to say something snarky about her lack of psychic skills. Drew just went back to fiddling with his sound system, his expression irritatingly smug. Violet gripped the handle of the bag containing her Magic 8 Ball.

"Wow," Jamie said, still beaming obliviously at Violet. "Think maybe you could give me a reading sometime?"

"Oh. Well, sure. I could check the appointment book, or maybe it would just be better if you waited until my mother comes back in a few weeks…"

"No, I want you," Jamie said. "Not in an inappropriate way, I mean. I hope you don't think—"

"Of course not."

"It's just that I noticed you here last night, and you just seemed like you had a very kind, generous soul."

"Generous soul?" Violet asked, doing a quick mental wade through the previous night's drunken sludge.

Drew looked up from the wire he was threading into the back of a speaker. "I think he's talking about the hundred you stuffed in the front of Barry's shorts," Drew offered helpfully.

Jamie gave her a serious nod. "You said it was for his mother's surgery."

"Nice of him to buy his mom new boobs for Mother's Day," Drew agreed.

Violet grimaced, but turned back to Jamie, feeling determined. "Yes, Jamie, I'd be happy to help you with... um, well, whatever it is you need. Why don't you stop by the shop later this afternoon to make an appointment?"

Drew grinned at her. "I could spare him for a few minutes right now, if you like. We were just wrapping up here anyway. You could even use your new tool."

Jamie gave her a hopeful look. "New tool?"

Violet shook her head. "It's nothing. Drew's just being funny. I actually can't fit you in today though. I'm heading over to the hospital to see my mother."

"Give her my regards," Drew said.

"Oh... give her my tips from last night," Jamie said, stuffing his hand into the front of his boxer briefs. "Medical bills are expensive."

"Um, that's okay," Violet said, stepping back a little as Jamie continued to dig. "But I appreciate the thought, Jamie. That's really very sweet."

Jamie kept his hand in his shorts and beamed at her,

probably because it was the first time anyone had ever appreciated him for his thoughts.

"You have a good visit with your mother," he said. "I'll come see you later."

"I'm looking forward to it," Violet said, not looking forward to it at all.

———

To Drew's surprise, Jamie actually had enough tact to refrain from commenting on Violet until she'd left the room.

"Wow. She's really pretty, boss."

"Hmmph," Drew replied, feigning intense interest in his subwoofer.

"Is she your girlfriend?"

"What?" Drew dropped his wire cutters. "Of course not. Why would you ask that?"

"I've been taking classes in social anthropology, and I just noticed that when you were talking to each other—"

"No," Drew said firmly. "Definitely not."

"But she's lots smarter than the women you always go out with. That's a good thing."

"That's not a good thing."

"And she's psychic. That's a good thing, too."

"Again… not a good thing."

"Okay. Well, I just wanted to make sure it wouldn't upset you if I went to see her for a reading. You know, like a fox paw."

"A fox paw?"

"When you break a rule of etiquette—"

"Oh, a faux pas."

"Exactly. Spending time with the boss's girlfriend—"

"She's not my girlfriend, so be my guest." Drew glanced up at Jamie and sighed. "You might want to consider putting some clothes on, though."

"Yeah?"

"At least a pair of pants."

"Good idea," Jamie said. "Maybe I'll get dressed now. You don't need me anymore?"

"You go ahead," Drew said, adjusting his midrange driver and firing up another '80s tune. "I need you here at seven tonight instead of eight. Dan twisted his knee again."

"Sure thing, boss," Jamie said, and lumbered away.

When Jamie was gone, Drew flicked the sound system off and sighed.

He'd rather remove his own leg hair with hot pliers than date a whip-smart vixen with a type-A personality. He'd been married to one of those before, thank you very much, and it was the last thing in the world he needed now.

He'd been stupid to grope her at the juggling store. *Really stupid.* He hadn't meant for things to get so heated. One minute, he was giving her an innocent lesson in the fine art of ball handling, and the next minute he'd been remembering every detail of what her breast had felt like pressed against his palm the night before.

No. Forget about it.

Violet was *not* what he needed. Violet with her sharp mind for data and numbers and statistics, and her high-powered career back in Maine.

Not his type.

Ditzy women were good. Ditzy women with uncomplicated careers who didn't nag him about *his* career choice were even better.

Drew's thoughts swayed back to the way Violet had felt in his arms at the juggling store. The precise moment she'd dropped that stuffy, accountant façade and melted back into his arms, her spine pressed against his chest, her ass tight and round and—

No. Don't go there.

Okay, fine. So he'd deliberately cranked up the sound system this morning, hoping she'd come stomping over, beautiful in her fury. And yeah, he'd been thinking about her when he grabbed that Magic 8 Ball at the toy store, enjoying the thought of making her laugh, watching her lips curve in a smile, her eyes dance with laughter. Was there really anything wrong with that? With ogling an attractive, intelligent, slightly insane female?

"There's a whole lot wrong with that," Drew said aloud, and went to pour himself another cherry Coke.

Chapter 4

WHEN VIOLET ARRIVED IN HER MOTHER'S HOSPITAL room, she was surprised to find Moonbeam alone. Her mom looked pale and rumpled and a little dazed as she leaned back against her pillow, reading a copy of *Super Psychic* magazine.

"What, no séances this afternoon?" Violet asked, slinging her purse into a chair as she strode into the room. She bent to give Moonbeam a kiss on the cheek, noticing how soft her mother's skin was, even after fifty-eight years. Score one for organic skin care.

"No, the nurses kicked everyone out after the incense lit the curtains on fire again," Moonbeam said, setting her magazine aside. "But I'm so happy you're here. I just heard from Detective Smeade about your reading with him this morning."

"Oh?" Violet said, feeling the panic rise like bile in her throat.

"Congratulations, honey. They found the money right where you said it would be."

"What?"

"In the elevator shaft. Isn't that the craziest thing? But of course, you knew it all along, so—"

Violet sat down hard in the chair, her head spinning again in spite of the fact that her hangover had long since passed. She gripped the arm of the chair as her mother kept chattering, the words washing over her without actually sinking in.

When Violet found her voice, it was hoarse and far away.

"They found the money in the elevator?" she asked, certain there'd been a mistake. "At the thief's apartment building?"

"Detective Smeade said you led them right to it. I'm so proud of you honey. Didn't I always say you had the gift?"

"Jesus," Violet said, glancing up at her mother's IV bag. Was there anything worth drinking in there?

"Anyway, honey, you have Sandra Cooley coming in at three p.m. for a reading, and she's a tough one. Don't forget what I told you yesterday about—"

"Did the doctor give you any sort of timeline for recovery?" Violet asked. "Any chance you'll be returning to work soon?"

"Well, dear, Dr. Abbott should be here any minute to check on me and hopefully give me a better idea when I might be released. But of course, there's the physical therapy and bed rest and I'm really not supposed to be up moving around for at least a few weeks."

"A few weeks?" Violet choked. "But what about the shop?"

"Well, you're doing such a great job, honey, and I do feel like I'm getting good care, and it's so nice to know the shop is safe in your hands."

"Well, I don't know about—"

"Just make sure you chase away that Drew Watson if he shows up with a tape measure and starts talking about expanding his bar. He's been eyeing my space for years. But really, I know I have nothing to worry about with you in charge. You're such a smart girl and a good psychic and I know you'll take care of everything."

Violet grimaced, not sure how much longer dumb luck would hold out for her. She couldn't keep faking her way through readings like this.

Then again, isn't that what Moonbeam had been doing for almost thirty years?

Feeling guilty for disparaging her mother—even silently—Violet stood up and bent down to fluff Moonbeam's pillow. "So really, Mom, how are you feeling?"

"Oh, well, I wasn't happy about the tainting of my karmic balance with the chemicals and medications, and the doctors refused to use a natural, herb-based form of anesthesia, but—"

"We did the best we could," announced a voice from the doorway. Violet turned to see Dr. Abbott grinning at them. He made his way to the edge of hospital bed, pausing to offer Violet a pleasant smile before turning to Moonbeam.

"How are you feeling today, Ms. McGinn?"

Moonbeam grinned, grasping his hand as he rolled a wheeled stool to her bedside. "I've told you to call me Moonbeam," she scolded without venom.

"I'll try to remember," he said seriously, glancing at Violet. "You can go ahead and keep chatting with your daughter if you like, Moonbeam. I'm just going to check your stats for a sec, and then we can talk about our plans for you."

"I can leave the room, if you like," Violet said, picking up her purse. "If you need privacy or—"

"No, please," Dr. Abbott said. "The distraction is helpful."

He didn't say for whom, but Violet sat back down and

grasped her mother's free hand. "So, Mom. Everything's going great at the shop. Just concentrate on getting better and don't worry too much about your clients or the shop or anything."

"Oh, I don't worry at all, honey. I know you're a wonderfully talented clairvoyant, so everyone's in great hands."

From the corner of her eye, Violet saw Dr. Abbott's eyebrow lift. She winced, bracing herself for the barrage of skeptical questions—none of which she'd blame him for.

"You're psychic?" he asked. He glanced up at her with interest as he jotted something on her mother's chart.

"Oh, well, I'm just filling in for Mom while—"

"Violet is one of the most talented young clairvoyants practicing right now," Moonbeam boasted. "Why just today, she solved a major crime for the Portland Police Department."

Dr. Abbott looked impressed, his warm brown eyes crinkling pleasantly at the corners. "You have your own practice?"

"Oh, well, actually, I'm an accountant."

"A psychic accountant? I could use one of those."

Moonbeam looked up at Dr. Abbott and smiled. "She's an accountant in Portland, Maine, but I've always said that her true calling is in the psychic arts. Now that she's out here filling in for me, she's getting a chance to really showcase her skills."

Dr. Abbott nodded as he reached up and turned Moonbeam's IV bag. "Actually, I wasn't kidding. I really could use a good accountant. Temporarily, if you're interested. The accountant I normally use at my private practice just had a baby last week, and—"

"Oh," Moonbeam gasped, clutching his arm so tightly he dropped his pen. "A baby. How wonderful. She had a boy?"

Dr. Abbott's eyebrows went up. "Yes, as a matter of fact, she did have a boy."

Violet resisted the urge to roll her eyes. Fifty-fifty odds even on a wild guess, or if she knew Moonbeam, she probably studied the local birth announcements for just such an occasion.

"Anyway," Violet said. "I'm just filling in for Mom at the psychic studio for a few weeks until she's back on her feet and ready to take on her practice again. My employer back in Maine is letting me work remotely on a few projects, and I've been picking up some local jobs as well."

"She'd be happy to help you out," Moonbeam added.

Violet glanced at her mother. Since when was Moonbeam interested in her accounting career? Moonbeam didn't meet her eyes but kept up some lively chatter with Dr. Abbott about babies and careers and onion sprouts.

Moonbeam is up to something.

Violet did a mental shrug. Whatever it was, it couldn't be too dangerous.

"I'd be delighted to help with the accounting work," Violet said. "Just a few hours a week?"

Dr. Abbott smiled. "That's all Stacy spent on it, so I can't imagine it would take you any longer."

"Great," Violet said, licking her lips. "When would you like to meet?"

"Your schedule is open this evening, dear," Moonbeam volunteered.

"Mom—"

"Actually," Dr. Abbott said, "That would work just fine for me. We could get together, maybe go over the files?"

"Oh… well, yes. The sooner the better."

"Your last reading ends at four, right dear?" Moonbeam asked. "You could go out for drinks, maybe even dinner."

"Dinner?" Violet asked.

Dr. Abbott laughed. "I'm game if you are."

Violet returned the smile, feeling a pleasant tingle under her sternum.

"Portland City Grill has a nice happy hour," Moonbeam suggested. "Not that I'd actually eat there, since their vegan options are rather paltry, but both of you eat animal flesh, right?"

Violet grimaced at her mother's meddling, but Dr. Abbott didn't seem to notice.

"That sounds great," he said. "Would you like to meet there, or shall I pick you up?"

—◦◦◦—

Drew was focusing very hard on trying to remember his date's name. Did it rhyme with a fruit? No, that was the girl he'd gone out with last week.

It started with a *G*, he was pretty sure about that. Gilligan?

It didn't matter at the moment, since she hadn't paused for breath in over an hour.

"…and so then we broke up, but we had like five more months on our lease, and he couldn't find another place to live and I was like, 'Dude, I'm not leaving, this place is like four blocks from where I work,' so I told him he could crash on the couch as long as he stopped borrowing my underwear, and so…"

Drew frowned. Maybe her name didn't start with a *G*. It definitely sounded Middle Eastern. Or maybe it rhymed with a spice. Or was it something that sounded like a cleaning product?

"...so, you know, I like totally threw him out when he climbed into my bed when he was drunk, but he was all, 'Babe, it's totally not my fault,' and I was like..."

Drew swirled the cherry Coke in his glass and tried hard to remember her name. He could almost picture it on the slip of paper at the bar with her name and number scrawled in bubbly writing. How many of those scraps had he collected since his divorce? Too many to count. Too many to remember names.

God, you're a jerk, his brain told him.

Rhonda? No, that wasn't it. Persimmon? Bambi? *Dammit*. It was much too late to ask, since they'd been on this abysmal date for more than an hour now, and he'd been the one to invite her out anyway.

What a dumb idea.

But it had been his habit in the years since his divorce. Call up one of the dozens of girls who'd slipped him their number at the bar—a disturbingly frequent occurrence, in Drew's opinion. They'd meet for drinks at the Portland City Grill, and if the conversation sucked, at least the food was fabulous and there was always the beautiful view of the city.

He looked out the window and wondered if Violet had ever been here. Would she enjoy the view of the river or seize the opportunity to recite statistics about water pollution and Portland's freakishly high number of bridges? He wasn't sure he'd mind either way.

Stop thinking about Violet.

Bad idea on so many levels. He sure as hell didn't need another high-strung woman in his life. Not even if she had amazing eyes and beautiful hair and breasts that—

"Are you listening to me?"

Drew snapped back to attention. "What? Yes. Definitely."

"Because it seems like you're just looking out the window."

"I was listening," Drew insisted. "I was just enjoying the view."

The girl gave him a skeptical look. Mindy? Sarah? Was there any way he could bluff his way through the rest of this date without knowing her name? He felt like peeling the sole off the bottom of his shoe and beating himself on the forehead until he passed out.

"Hey!" his date squealed. Drew looked up to see she was waving at someone over his shoulder.

"That guy over there," she said. "He did my knee surgery last year, after I injured it in pole-dancing class."

Drew picked up his drink and scanned the crowd, noticing how packed the place was for a Monday.

He froze with his glass halfway to his lips. *Violet?*

She saw him at the same moment, and the shock registered plainly on her face. Drew watched in horror as Violet's companion followed the direction of her gaze right to their table.

"Hey!" called Drew's date again, waving madly as she sloshed her drink across the table. "Hello, Dr. Abbott! You want to come and sit with us?"

Drew frowned. "I'm sure he doesn't want to sit with us. He's on a date."

Something in his heart twisted at the word *date*, and

he looked at Violet again. She was smiling at the doctor, her beautiful eyes fixed on his face. Drew's heart twisted again, so he looked back at his own date.

She slugged him in the shoulder. "I think I hurt my wrist bowling the other night. I want Dr. Abbott to take a look at it."

Drew shook his head, not sure whether to be annoyed with her or with himself for asking her out in the first place. Normally he wasn't so easily annoyed, especially by a beautiful woman, but there was something different lately. Something he couldn't put his finger on.

It didn't matter, since Violet and Dr. Abbott were making their way toward the table. Drew tried not to stare, not to notice the luscious sway of her hips, the way her hand fluttered up to smooth her hair behind her ear.

God, she's beautiful.

"Wow, it's really packed in here," Violet said, clutching her little purse against her stomach. "You guys got lucky nabbing a window seat with these sofas."

"I come here every Monday night," Drew said. "Arriving early is the trick to getting good seats."

He saw something flash across Violet's face. Surprise? Irritation? He wasn't sure. She recovered quickly though, and placed her hand on the annoyingly broad shoulder of the man beside her. "Drew, this is Chris Abbott, my mother's orthopedic surgeon. Chris, this is Drew Watson. He owns the business next to Moonbeam's shop."

"Great to meet you," said the surgeon, giving Drew's hand a firm but friendly shake.

"It's so great to see you again, Dr. Abbott," piped up

Drew's date, scooting over to make room on the sofa beside her.

"You, too," said Dr. Abbott, no help at all with the name.

Violet looked at Drew, then at the girl, clearly awaiting an introduction. Drew opened his mouth to speak, but closed it again. He was completely, utterly blank.

Violet's eyes held his for a moment, intense and gorgeous and utterly spellbinding. He was pretty sure if he *had* known his date's name, he would have forgotten it right then.

God, those eyes.

"Drew, come sit over here by me so these two can have the other sofa to themselves," his date chirped.

He tore his eyes from Violet's and offered a weak smile. "Sure, good idea."

He grabbed his drink and stood up, relieved to realize he'd somehow gotten away with failing to introduce her. He gestured to the vacant sofa in an invitation to Violet. She moved past him, her hair brushing against his shoulder as she slid by. Drew breathed deeply, inhaling the scent of lavender and vanilla. He felt his hand start to rise, intent on stroking her hair.

Are you out of your fucking mind?

He dropped his hand. "Tight quarters."

She looked up quizzically, her big, violet eyes studying him with an unasked question. Drew lost his breath.

Then she cut her glance back at the other sofa and raised one eyebrow.

Shit. She'd noticed the skipped introduction. Drew raised one shoulder in a helpless shrug and moved around the table to sit beside his date.

Now she thinks you're a cad.

Okay, maybe he was. Since his divorce, anyway. Funny how it had never bothered him before.

He watched Violet settle onto the sofa and cross her legs primly. She folded her hands over her knees and Drew tried not to stare at her long, perfect fingers and rounded nails, bright with clear polish. He wondered what those nails would feel like dragging down his back and then gave himself another mental kick.

"So how long have you two known each other?" Violet asked as she signaled a passing waitress.

"Oh, this is our third date," chirped Drew's seatmate.

Really?

Drew took another sip of his drink and wondered if it might be wise pretend to go to the restroom and slip out the back door. He could just avoid this whole uncomfortable scene—the nameless date, the awkward conversation, the sight of Violet with another guy.

Then Violet recrossed her legs, her skirt riding up a little above her knee. Drew sat back in his seat, suddenly interested in sticking around awhile longer.

To his right, Drew's date had begun to chatter to Dr. Abbott about the pain in her wrist. Drew had to give Violet credit, she'd picked a nice guy. Most doctors he knew would have told the girl to book an appointment by now.

Something hit Drew in the foot. He looked down to see a fork lying beside his shoe. He glanced across the table at Violet, who shot him a quizzical look. They bent down to retrieve the fork at the same time.

Apparently, that was Violet's plan.

"You don't know your date's name?" she hissed in his ear.

Her hair tickled his nose, and Drew fought the urge to drag her down on the carpet and grope her under the table.

Classy, dude. Really classy.

"Help me out," he whispered back.

"Me?"

"I just need a clue."

"No kidding."

"Her name's been on the tip of my tongue all night, but I can't remember."

"Maybe you should be more selective in how you use the tip of your tongue."

He grinned. "Are you talking dirty to me under the table?"

"Merely pointing out that if you dated with your brain instead of your—" She bit her lip. "You wouldn't be in this mess."

"Please help?"

"What am I supposed to do?"

"I don't know… aren't you the psychic here?"

She smacked him on the arm and sat back on the sofa. Drew sighed and sat back, too. Okay, so the "psychic" jab probably wasn't smart. He was feeling desperate.

Drew looked over to see their dining companions were still chatting away like old friends. The waitress showed up at their table with glasses of water, and Violet ordered a complicated-sounding Chardonnay. The doctor ordered a gin martini, and Drew's date requested something fruity and neon colored.

"Cherry Coke," Drew said, lifting his empty glass.

Dr. Abbott raised an eyebrow. "Not a drinker, Drew?"

"On occasion. I just tend to prefer cherry Coke."

"Hmmm," said the doctor in a tone that suggested either disinterest or a belief that Drew had the maturity of a third grader.

Probably right, there.

As soon as the waitress had gone, Violet cleared her throat. "So what is it you do?" she asked Drew's date.

Excellent, Drew thought, shooting her a grateful look. *They can exchange business cards.*

Violet took a sip of her water and folded her hands again.

"Oh, I'm a cocktail waitress."

Drew sighed. No business cards.

"Actually," the girl chirped, patting her left boob, "I came straight here from work and almost forgot to take off my name tag. Can you believe it?"

A name tag, Drew lamented quietly. *So close.*

"So Drew," said Dr. Abbott. "What sort of business is it you own?

He looked at the guy and tried not to be pissed that the good doctor had scooted so close to Violet, he was practically in her lap. "A bar," Drew said. "Voted 'Best in Portland' two years running."

"They have the most amazing male strippers on Friday and Saturday nights," his date added. "Super hot."

"Thank you," Drew replied, feeling oddly proud.

"Male strippers," Dr. Abbot repeated, looking bemused. "That's... interesting."

Violet cleared her throat and jumped in. "Chris and I were just talking on the way over here and he mentioned that he was named after Christopher Latham Sholes—the guy who invented the typewriter in 1867. Isn't that interesting?"

Drew reached for the lifeline she'd thrown him—lame

as it was—reminding himself to show his gratitude in some way that didn't involve getting her naked.

"That *is* interesting," Drew said. "And you're named for the color of your eyes, right?"

Violet blinked at him. Drew lost his breath again.

"Should we order?" asked Drew's date, frowning at the menu. "Happy hour is almost over."

Drew slumped in his chair, defeated. He'd probably never know his date's name. The only thing mildly cheering was the knowledge that Violet and her date had nothing better to talk about than who invented the typewriter.

Then again, it's not as if he was wowing her with scintillating conversation. Toilet paper? Juggling? The superiority of the term *butt rock* over *glam rock*?

Drew slumped deeper in his chair and took another sip of his drink. Maybe he could make it through the rest of the night calling his date "pumpkin" or "love chicken."

The waitress appeared again, and Drew waited until the others had made their selections before placing his order, not bothering to consult the menu. Violet quirked an eyebrow at him.

"I always order the same thing," Drew said as he handed his menu back to the waitress. "I come here a lot."

"You mentioned that," Violet said dryly. "My mother, on the other hand, did not."

"What?"

"Nothing."

Violet reached for her wineglass and took a sip, apparently drinking more cautiously than she had the previous night. He studied the way she held the glass, her exquisite fingers curved around the stem. He wondered if she'd learned the precise way to hold a piece of stemware or if it just came naturally.

As if sensing his eyes on her, Violet turned back to Drew. "So, do you have some sort of low-grade hearing loss?"

"What?"

"You were blasting the music so loud, the mice woke up and started running in their wheel to the beat of 'Eye of the Tiger.'"

"Sorry about that. Moonbeam never seems to notice, but I'll try to keep it down."

"You weren't kidding about the eighties music."

Drew grinned. "We're actually doing this whole eighties theme next week. We were trying to find the right song for Jamie's routine."

"Sounded like you found the right one. Either that, or you just wanted to play that stupid '867-5309' song over and over and over—"

"'Jenny,'" he said, lifting a glass to the most famous—albeit the *only*—hit Tommy Tutone had ever recorded.

"Hey!" squeaked Drew's date. "That's how I got my name. My mom totally loved that song, and my dad was like, 'Whatever,' so that's what they named me, even though the song had been out for like five years by the time I was born."

Drew stared for a few beats, certain he couldn't possibly have gotten so lucky. "Jenny?" he asked. "That's your name? Jenny?"

She scowled at him. "What the hell did you think it was?"

"Jenny, of course," he backpedaled. "I knew it was Jenny. I just…" Drew picked up his drink and downed it in one gulp.

Jenny was glaring at him in earnest, and Drew wondered if she planned to throw her neon-pink drink in his face. He probably deserved it. Maybe he should save her the trouble and just pour it over his head and call it a night.

Across the table, Violet cleared her throat. "Didn't that song come out in 1982?" She shot Drew a look that said exactly what she thought of him dating a woman barely over the legal drinking age.

Jenny turned toward Violet, her drink-tossing plans momentarily forgotten. "Something like that, why?"

"No reason," Violet said. "Actually, 1982 was the year a brutal cold snap swept in from Canada and plunged temperatures in the Midwest to all-time record lows. Even Portland recorded a record low temperature for September, which was forty-one degrees Fahrenheit. Statistically speaking, a meteorological event like that—"

Drew sat back in his seat and let Violet carry the conversation away to safer, albeit weirder, territory. He was grateful. He was relieved.

He was also ridiculously, stupidly certain he was falling for her.

Idiot.

Chapter 5

AFTER ENDURING TWO HOURS OF DRINKS AND conversation with Drew and his ditzy date, Violet almost forgot there was a business reason behind her outing with Chris Abbott.

As the elevator doors closed behind them and they began their descent from the thirtieth floor, Chris turned and touched her elbow. Violet looked up at him, wondering if he was going to kiss her. Had she eaten too much garlic in the bruschetta?

He smiled. "Would you like to go get coffee someplace quiet so we can go over the books?"

"The books," Violet repeated, feeling her cheeks flush. The elevator doors opened and Violet stepped out onto the lower level, grateful she'd refrained from puckering up. "Of course. I think there's a little place just a couple blocks this way."

Chris fell into step beside her. "I wonder if they have matcha green tea? Moonbeam insists it's quite high in antioxidants."

"My mother, the fountain of health information." She hoped she sounded affectionate rather than snarky. She couldn't tell from the curious look Chris gave her.

"Are you and your mom very close?"

Violet shrugged. "As close as two people who live on opposite coasts can be."

"But it must be such an amazing thing, sharing the sort of bond you do. I mean, the psychic thing—"

"Right, the psychic thing," Violet said, trying not to sigh. "Isn't it a little unusual, you being a doctor and all, believing in the supernatural? I mean, most science-minded people are sort of skeptical."

Chris laughed, a warm, rich sound that made Violet crave a tall mocha. Good thing, since they'd just reached the coffee shop. Chris held the door open for her and followed her to the counter. Once they'd ordered and seated themselves in a quiet booth, Chris handed her a steaming mug and smiled across the table at her.

"To answer your question," he said, "I'm not all that skeptical of the supernatural. I've witnessed it plenty of times."

"You have?"

"Sure. The vegetative patient who opens her eyes when she hears her grandmother's voice. The heart-attack victim two hundred miles from a hospital who survives because a mysterious stranger appears and performs CPR. The guy everyone said would never walk again who suddenly stands up and takes a step when his wife calls his name."

"Wow. I never thought of it that way."

Chris shrugged. "Every doctor has a few stories to tell like that. We all choose to interpret them differently. Some attribute it to a higher power, or the supernatural, or even just dumb luck. Bottom line though, there's something more than science at play."

"Huh," Violet said, leaning more toward the dumb-luck theory.

"And there's you, of course."

"Me?"

"And Moonbeam. Clairvoyance is something that's always fascinated me."

"So you believe in psychics," Violet said, blowing on her mug.

He smiled at her, his eyes warm and pleasant. "I believe in you. I believe in your mom. She's doing great, by the way. What a fighting spirit."

Violet felt a funny swell of pride in her chest as she took a sip of her mocha. "Moonbeam certainly has her good qualities."

Chris laughed and touched the back of her hand. "Let's not talk about your mom. I can tell it makes you uncomfortable. Shall we go through some of the paperwork I brought?"

His fingers were warm against the back of her knuckles. Violet took a sip of mocha, thinking about how nice it felt to have his hand on hers. How safe and solid and *normal*.

She set her mug down and looked up at him. "Actually, let's talk some more," she said softly. "Get to know each other a bit. Do you mind?"

Chris squeezed her hand and smiled back. "I was hoping you'd say that."

On the other side of town, Drew was trying to figure out how to extricate his date from his passenger seat.

"So it was great to see you again, Jenny," he said brightly.

At least he knew her name now. He resisted the urge to tap out the song's drumbeat on the steering wheel just to remind himself.

Jenny smiled up at him, the glow from her front porch

light giving her face a weird orange hue. She looked at him from under her lashes. "Would you like to come in? I can open a bottle of wine, maybe show you what I learned in pole-dancing class last week."

"Wow. That sounds really"—Drew tried to think of an acceptable adjective—"interesting."

"Oh, it would be. Believe me."

"Well, actually—"

Something in the car buzzed. Jenny looked up at him with wide, startled eyes. Then she smiled, slow and seductive. She trailed a finger up his arm.

"Drew," she murmured. "That's a nice surprise."

"What?"

Something buzzed again and Jenny's smile widened.

"The vibrating seat. Do you have a remote control for that?"

Drew stared at her, baffled. Something buzzed again. Drew let go of the steering wheel and slid his hand under Jenny's butt.

"Wha... oh, my, *well*..." she squeaked.

Drew grabbed hold of the cell phone and pulled his hand back. He held up the phone for her to see. "It's set to vibrate."

She smiled. "Great idea. I do that with my phone all the time."

"No, it's not mine."

It was Jenny's turn to look confused. "You vibrated me with someone else's cell phone?"

"No, it's not... I didn't... Never mind. Violet must have left this in the car last night."

"Violet?" Jenny frowned. "The uptight woman at the restaurant? You're dating her?"

"No, no… of course not. I just gave her a ride home last night. She must have dropped this on the seat."

Jenny plucked the phone out of his hand and studied it. "Moons and stars? She doesn't look like a moons-and-stars kind of girl."

"She's a little unpredictable," Drew said, and tried to decide if that was a good or bad thing.

"Well, since we have this extra cell phone, and since it's already set to vibrate, what do you say we go inside and—"

"I'm not using someone else's cell phone as a sex toy," Drew said, not bothering to hide his exasperation. "Look, Jenny, let's just call it a night. I'm tired, and I have to get up early tomorrow."

She rolled her eyes and handed him the phone back. "Fine. Call me next week?"

"Sure."

Jenny leaned forward, her cleavage spilling out of the top of her blouse as she grabbed the back of his head and mashed her lips against his. Startled, Drew kissed her back, enjoying the pressure of her breasts against his chest. They weren't real—he could tell silicone even through two layers of fabric—but what the hell. He briefly considered taking Jenny up on her offer. It's not like he was a monk. It's not like she was a nun.

It's not like she's Violet, he thought.

Exactly. Violet's the last thing you need.

Jenny leaned back, her breath a little ragged as she looked into his eyes. "Come on, Drew. Let's go inside."

~~~

Violet had only been home for fifteen minutes, and she'd spent most of it fighting with Moonbeam's stereo.

It wasn't that the device was so technologically advanced. Quite the contrary, really. Moonbeam refused to purchase new electronics, so everything she owned was "rescued" from secondhand stores, complete with remote controls that may or may not correspond to any of the devices.

"Dammit," Violet muttered, slamming down another useless remote.

She only wanted to unwind with a little music, maybe a nice glass of wine. She had changed into cozy silk pajama pants and a threadbare cami top, and had opened a good bottle of Chianti. She'd even managed to find a wineglass among her mother's array of recycled glassware.

Starting up the stereo was another matter. She'd tried just pressing the power button right on the stereo, but no dice. She'd even checked to be sure it was plugged in. She was on the verge of filling the bathtub with water and tossing the damn thing in.

She took a sip of wine and picked up another remote control from the pile. She hit the power button and watched as the ceiling fan whirred to life. She clicked off the fan and grabbed another remote, muttering to herself as she clicked some more buttons.

"How many goddamn remotes does one person need?"

The hall lights flickered off and on, so Violet tossed the remote aside and picked up another. She took a sip of wine and hit the power button.

Ding-dong.

Violet frowned down at the remote. Why would Moonbeam have a remote control for her doorbell?

She started to hit the button again when a knock at the door startled her out of confusion. Setting down her wineglass, Violet trudged to the door with the remote still clutched in one hand. She peered through the peephole and felt something flutter in her belly.

"Drew?"

He waved at the peephole, clearly aware he was being watched. "Hey, Violet. Long time, no see."

"What are you doing here?"

He held up something purple and glittery. "I brought your cell phone."

Violet opened the door and felt her nipples contract from the cold and, admittedly, from having Drew in such close proximity. "I have my cell phone in my purse. I just used it a few minutes ago."

"Well, this definitely isn't mine," he said, and held it out to her.

Violet studied it, admiring the silver moons and stars on a bright purple background. "Oh, right. That's Butterfly's phone." Violet reached out and took it from him, ignoring the way her nerves jumped as his fingers brushed hers. "She asked me to hold it last night so she wouldn't be tempted to drunk-dial her ex. I guess I forgot to give it back."

"Makes sense. It didn't look like something you'd have."

"What does that mean?"

Drew shrugged and leaned against the doorframe, grinning at her. "Just that your phone is probably plain black with the factory ringtone."

"Are you calling me a cliché?"

"In the most affectionate way possible."

She stared him down, wanting to feel annoyed, but also wanting to feel his hands on her body.

She cleared her throat. "Speaking of clichés, did you

have a nice time on your date with the infant whose
name you can't recall?"

Drew's grin faded. "She's fine. Thanks for the help
with the name thing."

"No problem."

"I'm not usually such a jerk with women."

"No?"

"Not always. Since the divorce, I guess I just—"
He frowned down at the remote clutched in her hand.
"You're playing with a radio-controlled car?"

"What?"

"That's what that remote control goes to. Some sort
of radio-controlled vehicle."

"Oh." Violet looked down at it. "That's why it didn't
work on the stereo."

"That might explain it. Moonbeam has a remote-
controlled car?"

"No, it's a Humvee. Someone bought it for her last year
as a joke after she sold her Prius and vowed to go totally
green and eliminate automobiles from her life. She acted
annoyed, but I've caught her playing with it a few times."

Drew laughed. "That sounds like Moonbeam."

Violet looked down at the remote again and sighed.
"I suppose this is a sign I should just give up on the
stereo and go get ready for bed."

"Want help?"

Violet looked up at him, alarmed. Her pulse sped
up, and she felt a warmth flooding her arms and legs.
She wished it was indignation, but it felt a lot more like
intrigue. Was Drew propositioning her?

His eyes widened a fraction, almost as if he were
reading her thoughts. "Help with the stereo," he said,

swallowing hard. "Not getting ready for bed. I wasn't…
I mean, I didn't…"

"I knew what you meant," Violet lied.

"Right. So, the stereo? I'm happy to help. I play with
sound systems all day long."

Violet nodded and stepped aside. "Thank you. That
would be great."

Drew eyed the neat row of clogs and Birkenstocks at
the door. "Should I take my shoes off?"

"If you don't mind. Moonbeam is very particular
about maintaining proper feng shui in the home environment. There's a basket of slippers right there, if you
want something to put on."

Drew glanced down at an array of colorful raw silk
and tie-dyed cotton. "Thanks, I'm fine in my socks."

"Okay, so the stereo is this way."

Violet led him past Moonbeam's psychokinesis practice studio and through the kitchen. She stepped down
into the sunken living room, conscious of the thick carpet under her bare toes, of Drew's eyes on her back. She
stopped in front of the stereo cabinet and pointed. "If I
could just turn it on…"

"That's Moonbeam's stereo?" Drew asked, stepping up beside her. "Is she aware that technology has
advanced beyond the eight-track?"

"It's recycled."

"It's older than I am."

"Are you going to help or are you going to mock?"

"I was kind of enjoying the mocking," Drew admitted.
"Tell me you at least have more advanced technology in
your life."

"I have an iPod, but I can't exactly hook it up to this—"

"Sure you can."

"What?"

Drew knelt down in front of the stereo. He looked down at the floor, momentarily distracted from the technology. "Hey, this carpet's really nice."

Violet shrugged. "It's made from recycled pop bottles. What were you saying about my iPod?"

"Right. There's an AV jack right here. You can have your iPod running through these speakers in no time."

"Really?"

"Sure. Go get your iPod."

Violet looked down at him, trying not to stare at his hands, trying harder to resist the urge to pounce on him. What was it about men who fixed things that was such as turn-on?

"Okay," Violet said, taking a breath. "iPod."

She padded out of the room, chastising herself a little for allowing a strange man into her mother's house at this hour. At least she was perfectly sober, unlike last night. Less risk of blurting out "I'm a fake psychic" and forcing him to grope her.

As she began digging through her suitcase for her iPod, she thought of her visit with Chris Abbott. They'd had a nice time at the coffeehouse, talking about their lives and careers and childhoods. *Bonding*.

Of course, her childhood had been a lot less normal than his. Violet envied him that. The son of a neurologist and a third-grade teacher, Chris had grown up in New Hampshire with an older brother and a younger sister. He played rugby in high school, studied biology in college, got perfect grades in med school, and enjoyed skiing and mountain biking in his spare time.

He was a very nice man. Perfectly attractive, perfectly wealthy, perfectly smart, perfectly *normal*.

Violet found her iPod and returned to the living room. Drew was just coming back through the front door, looking disheveled and a little rain soaked. Violet watched as he kicked off his shoes and headed back toward the living room.

"Found a cable," he said, holding up a snakey black cord.

"You always carry stereo cables in your car?"

"I use them to tie up my dates."

Violet rolled her eyes, pretty sure he was kidding. She followed him into the living room and set the iPod on the floor beside a speaker. Drew knelt down again and began fiddling with the stereo.

"Actually," he said, "it comes with the job. You'd be surprised how much time I spend messing with sound equipment."

"No I wouldn't. I have to listen to it every day."

"You get used to it. Just ask Moonbeam."

"Hmmm," Violet said. She stood a few feet behind him, admiring the view. Okay, so the jeans were a little ratty, but they looked soft as cashmere. Violet thought about stroking the back of his thigh and felt herself flush. Really, he filled out the jeans very nicely. The perfect curve right there—

"When you're done staring at my ass, would it be possible to get a glass of water?"

Violet jumped. "What? I wasn't—"

"I can see your reflection in the glass," Drew said as he tapped the cabinet door with his knuckle. He turned around and grinned at her. "Call it even. For ogling your ass right after we met. And when you were standing on the desk. And again at the juggling store. And again over dinner tonight."

"At least you admit you're a pervert," Violet called as she trudged to the kitchen.

"Certainly. Proud to be. Repressed people miss out on all the fun."

Violet reached up and grabbed a glass out of the cabinet over her head. "I have plenty of fun."

"You're saying you're repressed?"

"Isn't that what you were suggesting?"

He didn't answer, so Violet dropped ice cubes in a glass and filled it with tap water. She realized she was biting her lip and forced herself to stop. "Does Moonbeam know you go to the Portland City Grill every Monday?"

She looked across the counter in time to see him shrug. "Probably. I've even invited her once or twice, but she said there weren't enough vegan selections on the menu. Why?"

Violet moved back into the living room and handed him the glass of water. "No reason. She just seemed to want me to go there tonight with Dr. Abbott, that's all."

"Huh," Drew said, swallowing the water in three quick gulps. "Maybe she wanted me to know you're already spoken for?"

"I'm not spoken for. It wasn't even really a date. We were going over the books for his practice. I'm going to be doing some temp accounting for him."

Drew snorted. "He touched your arm at least a dozen times during dinner. He shared his sushi with you. I saw him look down your blouse twice. He thinks it was a date."

"He doesn't—"

"Trust me."

Violet shut up for a minute. "Well, that's a good thing, then. If you're right, I mean. I could do worse than a man like Dr. Abbott."

"Sure you could."

"He's good marriage material, don't you think?"

Drew didn't look up at her, but she saw his hands go still on the wire he'd been fiddling with. "Shouldn't you be on a first-name basis with the guy before you start planning your wedding?"

Violet ignored him. "*Chris* is a normal guy. A safe guy. A wholesome, healthy guy."

"You make him sound like a salad."

Violet glared at his back. Drew looked up and grinned. "Can I have a little more water, please? I've almost got you hooked up."

Violet grabbed the glass and marched back to the kitchen. "So what about you?"

"What about me?"

"You said you've been married before. How long?"

"Two years. It was a while ago."

"What was she like?" Violet asked, turning the tap on and filling Drew's glass.

"You."

Violet shut off the tap, not sure she'd heard him right. "What?"

"Nothing."

"It sounded like you said 'you.'"

Drew shrugged. "She was very high-strung. Divorce attorney. She wanted me to have a career that didn't involve sweeping peanut shells off the floor and hiring men to dance in their underwear twice a week."

"Imagine that."

Drew turned around and frowned at her, the playfulness suddenly gone from his expression. "I like my job. I worked hard to build this business, and I'm damn good at it."

Violet walked back to the living room and set the water down beside him, feeling cautious all of a sudden. "Hey, I'm not knocking it. You've built a pretty great place, from what I could see."

Drew took a sip of water, his happy-go-lucky expression back in place. "What you could see was filtered through four Manhattans, but thanks. Come over sometime. Sober, and not screaming at me. I'll give you a tour of the place."

"I'd like that."

Drew finished fiddling with the wires and took a sip of water. He sat back on his heels and looked at her. "Okay, you want to choose your songs here?"

Violet sat down on the sofa and picked up the wineglass she'd abandoned earlier. She took a small sip. "You choose. Something mellow. Something nice to listen to before bed."

Something flickered in Drew's eyes on the word *bed*. Something warm and dark and predatory. Violet felt her pulse kick up and she gripped her wineglass tighter. Still, she didn't look away. She held his eyes with hers and she thought about tearing her shirt off and begging him to touch her.

Why was that a bad idea again?

You're a fake psychic.

He wants to steal your mom's shop space.

He's not *the normal guy you're looking for.*

"Get a grip." She didn't realize she'd said it aloud until Drew smiled.

"Right. Good plan." He looked down at the iPod. "Mellow bedtime music, coming right up."

Violet watched as he sat quietly scrolling and pressing buttons. His head was bent in concentration, the dark, tousled hair falling over his forehead. She stretched her legs out along the sofa as she stared at his fingers working the iPod controls. There was something oddly erotic about that, watching him push buttons and swirl his fingertip over the control wheel. Violet took another sip of wine and felt her skin tingle pleasantly as she flexed her bare feet.

At last, Drew set the iPod down and stood up. He strode over to the sofa in three quick steps, then hesitated.

"Need me to move my legs?" Violet asked.

"Unless you'd like me to sit on them."

She grinned and started to draw her legs back toward her. That's when the spasm gripped her calf.

"Ow!" She yelped. "Dammit! Charley horse."

She started to set down her wine to massage the leg cramp, but Drew grabbed both her feet and pulled her legs straight. His hands were solid and commanding, and Violet went still at his touch.

"Relax," he said. "I've got it. Which one?"

"Left," she whimpered as the cramp twisted the muscle again. "Yeowch!"

He dropped onto the sofa and pulled both her legs onto his lap. He slid up the hem of her silk pajama pants to reveal her calves, and Violet said a silent prayer of thanks she'd remembered to shave. She expected his touch, but still gasped as his fingers slid over her bare skin. He cupped her left calf in one oversized palm and began to knead the muscles with his thumbs.

His hands were warm and skilled, and Violet stifled the urge to whimper. She lay back against the sofa cushions, enjoying the firm pressure of his fingertips, the squeeze of his palms, the roughness of his hands against the twisted muscle of her calf. She closed her eyes and sighed in bliss.

"God, that feels good," she murmured.

"The four second-best words in the English language."

"What are the four best?"

"Fuck me again, please."

She laughed in spite of herself. "Pervert. Did you make that up just then?"

"Not bad, huh?"

Violet smiled as her calf muscle began to relax under his touch. He could probably tell the cramp was gone, but seemed in no hurry to bring the massage to an end. His touch had lightened now, and he was no longer kneading deeply into the muscle with his thumbs. Instead, he traced his fingertips over her flesh, fluttering across her shin bones, dipping into the delicate hollow of her ankle, moving across the arch of her foot. His fingers were so light, so gentle, that Violet had to open her eyes to see what he was doing.

Drew was watching her.

He smiled. "Better?"

"Mmmm."

"I haven't learned to decode your groans just yet, but I'll assume that's a yes."

She closed her eyes again. "Yes. Oh, God—yes."

He laughed and shifted her feet in his lap. She expected

him to stop massaging, but instead he moved on to the other calf.

"Wonder what causes that?" Drew mused. "Charley horses, I mean."

"The most common causes are hormonal imbalance, dehydration, a buildup of lactic acid after exercise, or low levels of potassium or calcium in the blood," Violet replied dreamily. "Studies have shown vitamin B complex can occasionally alleviate them, as well as quinine, which has obvious side effects, and—"

"How about I just keep massaging," Drew said. "Since I don't happen to have quinine or vitamin B complex."

"Okay."

Violet sighed as she basked in the feel of his hands on her skin, the smell of rain pattering the ferns outside the open window, the sound of the music from Moonbeam's ancient stereo.

"Interesting musical choice," she murmured.

"How so?"

"Peter Gabriel's 'Mercy Street,'" she replied. "You remind me of John Cusack."

"I'm not sure I follow."

She gave a blissful sigh, then hoped he didn't mistake it for impatience. "There's that scene in the movie *Say Anything* where he stands outside her window with a boom box playing a Peter Gabriel song."

"'In Your Eyes,' right," Drew said, squeezing her calf. "I can change the song and go get a boom box, if you want."

Violet laughed and took another sip of wine. "I appreciate the offer, but you're fine right where you are."

"So when will Moonbeam be able to get back to work?"

"They want to keep her at the hospital for a few more

days and then transfer her to rehab. There's a sort of rehab halfway house near the hospital where she may end up going. That way she's close by and we don't have to shuttle her back and forth or make the house wheelchair friendly right away."

"How long can you be away from your other job?"

"They've been good about letting me work remotely so far," she said. "I've been stockpiling vacation time for years though, so I can dip into that if I have to."

"You don't take vacations?"

"Not much. I visit Moonbeam a few times a year."

"No beachcombing in the Caribbean? Hiking in the Alps? Leisurely stays at your favorite nudist colony?"

Violet shrugged. "I work a lot."

"Because you like it or because you have to?"

"Both."

Drew was studying her with a funny expression, and Violet felt oddly self-conscious. She sipped at her wine again, grateful for the steady pressure of Drew's hands on her calves. He trailed his fingers along her left shin and Violet gasped. He smiled and did it again to the other calf.

Maybe she *should* plan a vacation. She'd never seen Greece. She'd always wanted to go—

"Isn't there an expression about not taking vacations?" Drew said, interrupting her fantasy. "Something like 'All work and no play makes Jack a dull boy.'"

"If I'm supposed to be Jack here, that's not such a bad thing."

"You want to be dull?"

"I want to be *normal*."

Drew laughed. "I don't know about normal, but you're the furthest thing from dull I've ever seen."

Violet looked down at her wine, pretty sure she'd just been complimented. He slid his fingertips into the hollow at the back of her knee and she gasped.

"Ticklish?"

"No."

"Want me to stop?"

"*No*. Please."

He laughed and kept stroking her calf. The Peter Gabriel song ended, and Violet waited to hear what would start playing next. She wasn't sure if Drew had made a playlist or if he just programmed the iPod to pick songs to match the first one selected. She still wasn't certain when Howard Jones began singing "The Prisoner."

Drew looked at her, his expression serious all of a sudden. "So you want a normal life with a normal guy in a normal house in a normal town."

"I could do with an abnormal house. All the rest, pretty much."

Drew laughed. "At least you're honest."

Violet felt a small stab of guilt somewhere in the vicinity of her spleen. *Honest*. She was impersonating a psychic to support a business she wasn't sure she believed in. How honest was that?

Drew shifted a little, moving her feet closer to his knees. She glanced at his lap and resisted the urge to smile. Was it her imagination, or was Drew getting turned on? She couldn't quite tell, with the fly of his jeans in the way, but it looked like—

"You can't ogle my ass when I'm sitting down, so now you're staring at my crotch?"

She looked up and blinked. "What?"

"You know what." He squeezed her calf, but didn't

stop massaging. "You have a filthy mind, but you won't admit it. You also have a master plan for your life with no room for spontaneity."

"No," Violet said, hoping that covered both statements.

Yes, screamed her body.

Violet ignored her body.

Drew, however, did not. He slid his fingers farther up her leg, lingering for a few seconds in the hollow behind her knee before traveling higher. Her pajama pants were hiked above her knees now, exposing the bottoms of her thighs. Drew's fingers drifted there, stroking, teasing. Violet felt her pulse kick up. She was breathing fast now, her head swimming in a cloud of lust and a desperate urge to be touched.

She didn't bother to stifle the moan as his fingers traced the sensitive curve of her thigh. She closed her eyes again and leaned back against the arm of the sofa.

"Violet…"

"Yes?"

"I should probably stop."

"Oh, please don't—"

"Violet," he repeated, his voice tense now.

Violet opened her eyes and looked at him. His jaw was rigid, his eyes dark and dangerous. She watched him swallow, his eyes never leaving her face. "If I don't stop now, I'm not going to—"

"Don't stop," she said. "Please?"

They stared at each other for a few beats, neither willing to be the first to move.

Somewhere in a far corner of the house, Tarzan began to yodel.

Violet groaned, not in the good way this time.

"What is that?" Drew asked, sounding a little dazed.

"That's the boring factory ringtone you were so certain I had," she replied as she reluctantly lifted her legs off his lap. "And I'd better answer. It might be the hospital."

She stumbled to the entryway, where she'd hung her purse, her brain still fuzzy with lust and heat. Grabbing the cell phone, she fumbled with the buttons, not recognizing the phone number on the readout.

"Hello, this is Violet McGinn speaking."

There was a short pause, followed by an angry-sounding grunt. *"What the hell do you think you're doing?"*

Chapter 6

WHEN VIOLET HUNG UP THE PHONE, SHE DIDN'T LOOK good. Her face was pale, and her bottom lip looked like she'd been biting it for the last five minutes. Actually, that's exactly what she'd been doing. Drew had watched from his perch on the sofa, trying hard to focus on whatever grave news she was getting instead of on his fascination with her mouth.

Violet set the phone down and walked wordlessly back to the living room. Her posture was stiff, like someone had fused a stripper pole to her spine.

Hardly the woman who'd been melting into his lap mere minutes before.

"That didn't sound good," Drew said, watching her step into the living room. "Are you okay?"

Violet didn't say anything. She just sat down beside him and picked up her wineglass. Without a word, she tipped it back and drained the rest of it in one gulp. Drew watched her throat as she swallowed, feeling edgy.

Violet set the wineglass down and looked at him. Her expression was perfectly calm, but her eyes flashed fire. Drew scooted back a little, moving all extremities out of her reach.

"That was Frank," she said at last.

"Frank?"

"Mrs. Rivers's professional squash partner. You

mentioned him the other day when Mrs. Rivers came in for a reading and I told her Frank was cheating?"

"Sure, Frank. How's he doing?

Violet stared at him, unblinking. He saw her fingers clench in a fist. When she spoke, her voice was icy.

"Do you think, perhaps, that when you mentioned that Mrs. Rivers's cheating man was her professional squash partner, maybe that would have been a good time for you to mention the fact that he's also the owner of our entire fucking building?"

The last three words came out in a snarl. Drew tried to edge back farther, but his spine was already pressed against the arm of the sofa.

"I figured you knew."

"How the hell would I know something like that?"

"Well," Drew said carefully, "I assumed Moonbeam would have told you. Or that if she hadn't, your psychic powers might have clued you in."

The last words were a cheap shot, so he should have expected the blow. Even so, he didn't duck fast enough when the throw pillow came hurtling toward him. It grazed the side of his head, smacking his left ear. Drew reached back and caught the pillow before it hit the ground.

"Ouch," he said dryly.

"What am I going to do?" she cried. "He's mad as hell. He wants to see me as soon as he gets back from Chicago. He said we're running a crooked operation and that he has every right to kick me out of the building."

"He said that?"

"He's pissed. He's a professional athlete, and I told his partner he was cheating. Wouldn't you be mad?"

Drew tucked the throw pillow under one arm and considered the question. "Did he deny cheating?"

"What?"

"At squash. Did he tell you he wasn't cheating?"

Violet rolled her eyes. "We didn't discuss the fine points of the game."

"Did it occur to you that if he's that angry, you were right? He *is* cheating."

Violet stared at him, her expression still panicked. "How do you know that?"

"Cheaters get angry. Don't you remember anything from schoolyard politics?"

"Even if that's true, how does it help? He still hates my guts now and wants to kick us out of the building."

"He won't do that. He needs the tenants."

"But that's what he threatened."

Drew shrugged. "So what's the worst-case scenario? Moonbeam can move."

"You don't understand. She's been there for thirty years. Her location is everything. It's not just the auras and the alignment of the space with the moons of Jupiter and the feng shui—it's the walk-in traffic she gets from being right on the edge of the Pearl District."

"Okay, I see what you mean. Still, it's a moot point. He's not going to kick you out. He's just mad now, but he'll cool off."

Violet looked at him uncertainly. Now that she'd stopped spitting fire, he almost wanted to hug her. Maybe pick up where they'd left off. The thought of taking her in his arms and stroking her back, then maybe sliding his hands down and cupping her—

He stopped, aware that his eyes were probably

starting to glaze over. "Look, Violet," he said. "Just talk to him. Explain that you got a bad deck of tarot cards or your crystal ball was cloudy or something. Call Mrs. Rivers and tell her the whole thing was a big misunderstanding. I doubt she's reported it to the Professional Squash Association. I'm sure it's not that big a deal."

"You want me to lie," she said flatly. He saw her grip the remaining throw pillow so hard that her knuckles turned white.

"Well what the hell was the first reading, the biblical truth?"

She frowned. "Just because you're a nonbeliever doesn't mean—"

"Come on, Violet."

She didn't say anything for a minute. He expected her to keep fighting, but she just sat there, looking glum.

"But you just said he's cheating," she said at last. "Why would I need to lie about the reading?"

"Can you prove he's cheating?"

"No."

"Did your psychic powers really tell you that without a doubt, he's cheating at squash?"

Violet blinked.

"Exactly."

She slumped down a little on the sofa, looking defeated. "This is so stupid. I don't even know what professional squash *is*, much less how you'd cheat at it."

"Well, squash is a little bit like tennis, only it's played on a four-walled court with a small, hollow rubber ball. You've got singles or doubles, just like tennis, and professional players like Frank and Mrs. Rivers can actually make some decent money at it. You can cheat in several ways, like bribing an umpire or failing to clear the line quickly after a drop shot or—"

He stopped, conscious of the fact that Violet was staring at him like he had a scorpion crawling out of his nostril. "What?"

"How the hell do you know that?"

He shrugged. "I'm a guy. We're born with a compass and a sports almanac in our heads. You have your data and random trivia, I've got that."

Violet shook her head, but she wasn't frowning anymore. That was a good sign. Drew thought about covering her hand with his, but decided against it. She'd probably bite a finger off.

On the stereo, Sarah McLachlan began singing "Train Wreck." Drew could relate.

After a long silence, Violet sighed. "I'm sorry I yelled at you. It wasn't your job to tell me about Frank."

"I know."

"I'm just scared."

"I know."

"Moonbeam trusts me to keep her business running. It's my job to protect it... to make sure everything goes okay."

"I know."

She looked at him. "Is there anything you *don't* know?"

Drew thought about it for a minute. "I don't know what that blue stuff is in the Magic 8 Ball. That's always perplexed me."

"It's alcohol with blue dye dissolved in it."

Drew grinned. "Now my life is complete."

Violet sighed again. "I'm going to bed."

"Okay. Need company?"

He meant it as a joke—just something to make her smile—and he succeeded there. But there was something else in her eyes. A flicker of surprise, maybe intrigue. She just looked at him for a few beats, making him dizzy.

The room felt too warm all of a sudden. How high was the damn heat turned up? He was pretty sure Violet wasn't wearing anything under that thin little tank top. If he could just move his hands up her legs again…

Drew stood up quickly, knowing he had to flee before he did something wildly stupid.

"Fine, I can take a hint," he said. "I'm going home now. Try not to annoy any professional squash players between now and tomorrow morning."

"I'll try," Violet said faintly.

"And no more Manhattans," he added, practically running toward the door. He had to get away from her before…

Before what?

He didn't care, he just had to escape. He yanked the door open and felt instant relief as the cold wall of wet air hit him in the face. He headed out into the rain, picking up speed when he thought of Violet sitting there, so warm and soft and inviting.

He was halfway to his car before he realized he'd forgotten his shoes.

The next morning, Violet was tidying up in the shop after two back-to-back appointments. Both had been basic tarot-card readings, which was a relief. She had learned to shuffle a tarot deck before her childhood pals were playing old maid. Laying out a Celtic Cross spread and waxing philosophic about the culmination card was something she could do in her sleep.

She was standing on tiptoe to tuck the cards back in the cabinet behind Moonbeam's chair when Drew came barreling through the door. He looked disheveled and a little frantic. His eyes lit up the second he saw her.

"Thank God you're here."

"Oh," she said, and dropped the deck of cards. All seventy-eight of them went fluttering to the floor, the Lovers card landing face up on her shoe, while the King of Cups hit her square in the boob.

Drew dropped to a crouch and began scooping up the cards. "Sorry about that. Look, do you have an appointment right now? I could really use your help with something."

"My help? With what?"

Drew finished piling the cards in a neat stack and handed them back to her. Violet tried not to notice the buzz she felt when his knuckle grazed hers.

"I'm auditioning a new entertainer to replace a guy who just busted his knee. The first applicant is going to be here any second and Sam just called in sick."

"You can't do it alone?"

"No way. Sam's a woman, so she takes the lead on all the auditions. Otherwise—"

"Ah, I see," Violet grinned. "You don't want to look like a creepy guy who likes gawking at naked men."

Drew frowned. Violet laughed and reached up to tuck the cards back in the cabinet. She turned back to him and shrugged. "Well, I don't have anyone coming in for a couple hours, but really, I don't know anything about judging strippers."

"*Entertainers*. And there's nothing to it, I swear."

"Well…"

"Come on, Violet, please? I'm really in a bind here."

She grinned. "You're begging me to come watch good-looking men take off their clothes? I've gotta think about this."

He grabbed her by the elbow and yanked her toward the door. "Thanks, Violet, really, I'll owe you one. I'll buy you a drink or hook up another stereo. Whatever. Just get in here, fast."

Violet allowed him to march her down the hall and through the door, hating to admit she loved the forcefulness of his fingers clamped around her arm.

She blinked a little as they stepped into the dimly lit bar. Though the place wasn't open for hours, she half expected a naked man to jump out from behind the crates of liquor piled in one corner.

"So how does this work, exactly?" Violet asked as he deposited her in a chair directly in front of a round stage in one corner. "Do I have to throw dollar bills at him or anything?"

"Please don't throw money. And no drinking, either. Or shouting obscenities."

Violet raised an eyebrow. "So what *do* I do?"

"Here are their applications. The first guy will be here any minute; his application is on top. We have them do two songs, and they can pick the music. We're judging technique, charisma, overall appearance—"

"Wow, I feel like a guy. Can I get a cigar?"

"No. No cigars. And no touching."

"Do I need to take notes or something?"

"Here's a notepad. Pens are right there."

He squeezed her shoulder, sending shockwaves of warmth down her arm. Violet hoped she wasn't having a stroke.

"Thanks, Violet. I really owe you one."

"No sweat."

A bell chimed at the front door, and Drew raced off to answer it. Violet studied the application, not entirely sure what she was supposed to be looking for. An advanced degree in stripper science?

Moments later, Drew came trudging back to the center of the room, followed by a man who looked like he probably bench-pressed Volkswagens. He had dark hair, a tattoo of Tweety Bird on his bicep, and a small scar on the edge of his chin.

"Violet, meet Jerry," Drew announced. "Jerry, meet Violet."

Violet stood, not that it did her much good. Her eyes fell somewhere in the middle of his sternum. She looked up at him, admiring the view. "Pleasure to meet you," she said, extending her hand.

He gripped it in one meaty paw and pumped it so hard Violet staggered. "It's so good to meet you, really. So good. This is a big goal of mine. I've been practicing hard ever since I got out of prison."

"Oh, wow," Violet said, taking a small step back and retracting her hand. "That's really… ambitious."

"Sure is," he agreed. "When Mr. Watson here called me, I got so excited I shit myself. No joke, I had to go home and change my undershorts, and then—"

"Okay, Jerry," Drew interrupted. "Let's just move on to the audition, shall we?"

"Sure thing, Mr. Watson," Jerry said with a nod.

"We've already cued up the music you requested, so whenever you're ready."

Jerry nodded again and bent down to untie his work boots. Violet studied his application again, finding it more intriguing than watching Jerry unroll his tube socks. *Jerry Jester, age 24, a graduate of Sandy High School. Relevant experience: three bachelorette parties and one ballet lesson at age five.*

Violet looked up, pretty sure she wasn't going to form any useful opinions about Jerry from reading his application.

With his socks and shoes removed, Jerry took a deep breath and paused before marching up the steps like a man on a mission. He stood there at the center of the stage for a moment, hands clasped in front of him as though in prayer. He was wearing a police uniform with several buttons missing and a smear of something pink on one sleeve.

"Whenever you're ready, Jerry, just give me a nod," Drew said.

"Fuckin' A," Jerry said. He stood there for a few more seconds, looking very spiritual. Or constipated. It was tough to tell. Finally, he gave a solemn nod.

Drew pressed a button on a remote control in his hand. Instantly, the pulse of Rod Stewart's "Da' Ya' Think I'm Sexy" filled the room. Jerry began to undulate, performing some sort of pelvic thrust Violet figured might be sexy under a black light, with a crowd of intoxicated observers clustered around the bar.

Jerry reached up and tipped his police cap at Violet. It slid down over one eye. Violet pressed her lips together, trying very hard not to giggle.

The dance continued from there, with Jerry unbuttoning and unvelcroing to the beat of the music. Twice, Violet stole a look at Drew. He had an expression of trained seriousness, and was jotting notes at a feverish pace in a spiral notebook. Violet craned her neck, trying to see what he was writing. He had the messiest handwriting she'd ever seen.

Violet looked back at her own notepad, where she'd written three words: *Buy breakfast sausage*.

By the time Rod was done singing, Jerry was shirtless and had started to fumble with the button on his pants. He turned his back to them, shaking his ass so hard Violet worried he might fall over. Slowly, Jerry began to lower his pants. Violet bit her lip and looked at Drew.

"I'm not sure I'm ready for this," she whispered.

"Throw him a wolf whistle or something," Drew whispered back. "It's good for his self-esteem."

Violet turned back to the stage and looked at Jerry. He shimmied his pants down over his thighs, gyrating furiously as Justin Timberlake began belting out the lyrics to "SexyBack."

"Oh, my," Violet said.

"He could use some new boxer briefs," Drew remarked. "The fabric is frayed on the edge there."

She looked at him. "I can't believe you're really this secure in your masculinity."

Drew shrugged. "It's just business."

Jerry tossed his pants on the table in front of Violet. She looked at them for a moment, not sure what etiquette called for. Should she fold them?

She glanced over at Drew again. *Whistle*, he mouthed

at her. Violet stuck her fingers between her lips and made her best attempt. Instead, she spit on the bar.

Drew rolled his eyes at her. "That's the best you can do?"

"Can I whoop instead?"

"By all means."

Jerry was thrusting and bobbing on stage, looking more like an ill chicken than a sex object. He was smiling though, having a good time. Violet let out a spirited whoop, causing Jerry to stumble as he whirled around the metal pole at the center of the stage.

Violet leaned back toward Drew. "Do you provide training for the guys you hire?" she whispered.

"Jamie does. You met him the other day."

"Right, Jamie. He'd be good at that."

"He is."

"He'd look good naked," she said, just trying to get a rise out of him.

"He's my ex-brother-in-law. You can ogle him, but don't get any ideas."

"I wouldn't dream of it."

Drew kept his focus on the stage, but she thought she saw something twitch at the corner of his eye. "No cartwheels, Jerry," he called. "Save that for another time."

"Okay, boss."

Violet looked down at her notepad. *Schedule bikini wax*, she scrawled.

"Jamie's coming in to see me the day after tomorrow for a reading," Violet whispered.

This time, she got an actual wince from Drew. He was quiet for a moment, but she could tell he was processing something. He didn't look at her, but she knew she had his attention.

"Go easy on him, Violet," Drew murmured. "Jamie's a good guy. Don't—"

"Hey, don't tell me how to do my job."

He raised an eyebrow. "Your job?"

"My mother's job. Whatever. I'm not telling you how to run *your* business."

"Fine. Just… just be careful. Jamie's not like a lot of guys."

"What does that mean?"

"He's not a jerk. He's pretty sensitive, actually. Gets his feelings hurt easily, falls prey to scams, that sort of thing."

"You're calling me a scam."

Drew didn't respond at first, and his eyes were still fixed on the stage. When he looked at her, his expression was serious. "Just be careful with him. That's what I'm saying."

Violet gritted her teeth, not sure how to respond to him. Did he really think she was that irresponsible? That unethical?

Hell, wasn't she?

She was on the verge of concocting a smart-ass retort when Jerry's boxer briefs hit her in the eye.

Later that afternoon, Violet closed out the spreadsheet on her laptop and stood up, bumping her head on a wild branch from Moonbeam's lucky bamboo plant. Struggling to regain her dignity, she extended her hand to the serious-looking blonde across the desk.

"Ms. Zimmerman, it's been a pleasure working with you," she said. "I'll have the rest of those figures for you by the end of business tomorrow."

The woman returned the handshake, smoothing her Armani jacket with her other hand. "Yes, of course. You came highly recommended to us as an accountant. Of course, once we heard you were also psychic, that sealed the deal for us. Tell me, Violet, do you have much experience with the stock market?"

Violet cringed inwardly. "Actually, Ms. Zimmerman, I'm very conscientious about not mixing my accounting business with the psychic one. Too much potential for ethical dilemmas, you understand?"

"Of course, of course. Still, you would alert a client if you had any premonitions about… oh, say, an embezzlement conviction on the horizon? Hypothetically speaking."

"Ms. Zimmerman—"

"Technically, investment fraud isn't such a huge deal. If there were just a way to find out what the FBI knows already, we could—"

"You know, my psychic skills really don't extend into the criminal realm."

Her client frowned. "But I know your mother contracts with the police department, and the readout on your iPhone there says Detective Smeade has called twice in the last thirty minutes. Surely, you could—"

"You have a lovely evening, Ms. Zimmerman," Violet interrupted. "Try not to embezzle money, okay?"

Violet's cell phone was ringing before the door had swung shut behind her client. Violet snatched up the phone with one hand as she powered down her computer with the other. "Hey, Mom, how are you feeling?"

"Oh, sweetie. You sound tired. Late night last night?"

"Something like that," Violet said, her mind veering toward the feel of Drew's hands on her calves.

"So your date with Dr. Abbott went well?"

Dr. Abbott. Right.

"It wasn't a date. And was there a particular reason you sent us to Portland City Grill?"

There was a long pause, and Violet wondered if she'd misjudged. Maybe it *was* just a coincidence.

"What are you talking about, honey?" Moonbeam asked sweetly.

"You know exactly what I'm talking about. Drew goes to Portland City Grill several times a week. With any variety of bimbos, from what I understand."

"Oh, my. Are you getting friendly with Drew?"

Violet rolled her eyes, feeling like a teenager. "You knew Drew would be there, so you sent me with Dr. Abbott. Why?"

"Violet, honey, I don't know what you're talking about."

"So it's just a coincidence that I show up with a wealthy, single surgeon on my arm at the restaurant where a guy you dislike is having dinner with a floozy?"

"Violet. You already know, dear—there are no coincidences in the life of a psychic."

Violet sighed, and changed the subject. "How are you feeling?"

"Much better since you brought me my Zen garden. So what's new at the shop, honey?"

"Detective Smeade called again. He wanted to give me a heads-up that they're running out of leads on a burglary case they've been working on."

"Really? Is he going to need you?"

"He doesn't know yet. He just wanted to give me some advance warning."

"It's nice when he does that. Gives you time to prepare."

Violet waited, wondering if her mother would offer more explanation. Was she admitting she was a fake? Admitting Violet was a fake? Or just giving her genuine guidance? Violet had no idea.

"Anyway, I did a little online research, just to familiarize myself with the case," Violet said. "Hopefully he won't need me, but—"

"If he does, you'll be ready."

"I'll be ready."

Violet was quiet for a moment, not sure how to broach the next subject without sending Moonbeam's pulse rate through the roof. "Moonbeam?"

"Yes, dear?"

"You know that reading I did with Mrs. Rivers a few days ago?"

"Of course, honey. Your first reading."

"Right. Well, I might have told her that Frank was cheating."

"Her squash partner, yes of course. I think they're getting ready to head to Japan for the world championships. He's cheating?"

Violet gritted her teeth, trying to figure out if her mother was being exceptionally dense or exceptionally clever. "I don't know, but—"

"Of course you know, honey," Moonbeam said. "You're clairvoyant."

"Right, but Frank owns the building and he said—"

"Violet, honey. You know you need to trust your instincts."

Violet sighed. "He threatened to kick us out of the building."

Chapter 7

Violet glanced at her watch and then pressed the gas pedal to the floor. She was later than she'd expected leaving the hospital, which meant she was running late to meet Chris at his private practice.

"Dammit," Violet muttered as she spotted a traffic jam up ahead. She saw a cluster of police cars and slowed down, keeping an eye on the standstill traffic.

She cursed under her breath again as she brought the car to a halt, watching her windshield wipers work double-time to fight the afternoon rainstorm. She gritted her teeth as she stared at the immobile cars. This was not what she needed. She was trying to make a good impression on Chris. To let him know she was professional and responsible and prompt.

You make it sound so hot.

Violet didn't notice the police officer until he knocked on her window.

"Sorry to startle you, ma'am," he said when Violet rolled down her window. "There's a train wreck up ahead—"

"The light rail?"

The officer nodded. "Some guy played chicken with the MAX and lost, so we're rerouting traffic back the other way. Do you need help with an alternate route to wherever you're going?"

Violet shook her head, already mapping it out in her head. "I think I've got it. I grew up here."

"Okay then. If you hang a right over there on Mercy Street, it'll take you right back out to the highway."

"Thanks."

"Have a good day, ma'am."

Violet rolled up her window and watched as the little blue Honda ahead of her executed a U-turn. She steered her rental car in an arc, falling in line behind the Honda. She glanced at her watch.

"Dammit," she muttered again. She had told Chris she'd stop by his office at five to pick up a few more files. It was already ten after, and the reroute would cost her at least five more. She would have called, but her cell-phone battery had gone dead earlier in the day. She resisted the urge to smack her fist on the steering wheel.

By the time she wheeled into the clinic parking lot, Violet was fifteen minutes late. She cast a look around the parking lot, relieved to see there were still five or six cars. Lurching into the closest spot, she flew out of the car and sprinted to the front door of the clinic.

A pleasant, sanitized, air-conditioned gust greeted her as she pulled open the door. So did an equally sanitized-looking blonde with a face that had clearly seen one too many Botox injections. Her name tag said "Beatrice."

"Hello, dear," greeted Beatrice and her immobile forehead. "Do you need an appointment?"

"No, actually, I'm here to see Dr. Abbott. Chris, I mean. Not for a checkup or anything. Sorry, I'm late to meet him to pick up some files and—"

"Oh, you must be Violet," Beatrice said, beaming widely at her. "He's expecting you. We've all heard so much about you."

"You have?"

"Let me just let Dr. Abbott know you've arrived. He's with a patient right now, but I know he'll be so excited to see you."

"I'll just wait here and read."

Violet picked up a women's magazine off the table and smiled. Beatrice smiled back, probably wondering whether Violet planned to read "Seven Bad-girl Bedroom Moves" or "The STD You May Already Have." Violet sat down and began to leaf through the magazine. She ran her fingers through her hair, hoping she didn't look too disheveled. She wasn't good at being late. It wasn't in her nature.

She turned the page, trying to find something to take her mind off her tardiness. Before she knew it, she was thoroughly engrossed in an article about gynecological exams gone bad.

A door opened off the lobby, and Violet looked up to see Chris beaming at her.

"Violet, I'm so glad to see you! How was your day?"

Violet closed the magazine and stood up, trying to pretend *vagina* wasn't the last word she'd read. "Hey, Chris. Sorry I'm late. There was a train wreck and… well, anyway, it's good to see you."

"No problem at all. I had a couple appointments run late anyway, so you're right on time."

"Must have been a busy day?"

"Pretty standard, actually. Moonbeam is doing well?"

"Very well, thank you. She's receiving excellent care."

There was a brief pause, and Violet worried for a moment that they'd run out of mundane topics to cover. She considered inviting him to take the *Cosmo* quiz with her when he spoke up again.

"So Violet, can I get you water or coffee or anything?"

"No, thank you. I'm good."

"Well then, let me give you a tour of the office."

He led her down a narrow hallway lined with taste-ful watercolors and a series of golden oak doorways. He pointed out offices and exam rooms, leading Violet through a short maze of hallways. Everything was very tasteful, very sterile. Precisely how a doctor's office should be. Violet made appropriate sounds of apprecia-tion, nodding when he showed her his X-ray machine and noting the expensive furniture in his office.

"So you probably want to get those files," he said when the tour was over.

"That would be great."

"I don't suppose you're free for dinner, are you?"

"Dinner?"

"If you don't already have plans, of course. I've been wanting to try that German restaurant up the road a bit, and I'd love the company."

"Oh. Well, yes. That would be lovely."

He smiled at her. "Let me grab those files for you, and I'll be ready to go."

"Okay," Violet said. "I'll wait here and read about…" She glanced back at her magazine. "I'll just wait here."

Chris was only gone a few minutes. When he emerged again, he had traded the lab coat for an expensive-looking wool jacket. He held an umbrella in one hand and a briefcase in the other. Violet admired the aesthetic. Very debonair.

"Do you want to go in one car, or follow me there?" he asked.

"Carpooling makes sense. Saves fossil fuels and all that."

He grinned. "You are your mother's daughter, aren't you?"

Violet smiled benignly and followed him out to the parking lot, where he beeped open the locks on a shiny black Mercedes. He reached past her to open the passenger-side door for her.

"Thank you," Violet said, and got in.

Chris moved around to the other side, depositing the briefcase and umbrella in the backseat before moving to the driver's side and taking his seat.

"Pardon the mess," he said, and picked up a single gum wrapper out of the console. It was the only thing Violet could see that was out of place.

They rode in companionable silence, listening to the patter of raindrops and the swish of puddles beneath the tires. Violet thought about how pleasant it was to be comfortable enough with someone that there was no need to make trivial conversation. That was nice. Better than nice, that was really great.

Violet looked out at the rain, trying to remember the last time she'd seen unclouded skies. That was one thing she didn't miss about living in Portland, Oregon. Not that there were many things she *did* miss. She liked her life in Portland, Maine. It was perfect. Just what she'd always wanted.

She turned to Chris, tired of listening to her own thoughts. "You like living in Portland? I mean, you didn't grow up here, so I just wondered."

He gave her an odd look. "How funny you should ask that right then."

"Why's that?"

"I was just thinking about living on the East Coast

and how much I enjoyed my childhood there." He looked at her and smiled. "I guess I pretty much give up the expectation of private thoughts when I'm spending time with a psychic."

"Right. Well, it doesn't always work quite that way."

"No? Do you have to really focus on it or something like that?"

"Something like that," Violet agreed, desperate to get off the subject of psychic powers. "So you enjoy the East Coast?"

"Very much. Like I mentioned the other night, I grew up in New Hampshire, and my parents are still back there."

"You see them often?"

"Not as often as I'd like. They're getting older, and... well, you probably know how it is. I suppose it's the same for you, isn't it? Moonbeam's over here, and you live on the East Coast. You must miss her."

"Sometimes," Violet agreed, surprised to realize she wasn't lying.

Chris smiled. "It must have been interesting growing up with a mother who was so... so..."

"Wacky?"

"Well..."

"Infuriating?"

Chris laughed. "I was going to say spirited, but I suppose you'd know better than I would."

Violet shrugged, a little taken aback by the hero worship Chris seemed to direct toward Moonbeam. "It was interesting," she agreed.

"Were all your boyfriends petrified that she knew their innermost thoughts?"

Violet laughed. "I never thought of that. Maybe that's why I didn't have boyfriends in high school."

Chris raised an eyebrow. "I find that hard to believe."

"Believe it. I guess you'd say I was a bit of an outcast, growing up." She tried to say it with a nonchalant air, but she could see from Chris's sympathetic expression that she hadn't succeeded.

"So how about now?" he asked. "Do you date much?"

Violet smiled and looked down at her hands folded neatly in her lap. "Some. Nothing serious at the moment. How about you?"

"Nothing serious. I haven't really found what I'm looking for, I suppose."

"And what are you looking for?"

He smiled, his warm, brown eyes a little faraway as he looked out at the road. "Marriage, family, the whole nine yards."

"The two-point-four children, the cocker spaniel, the house with the big front yard?" Violet added, grinning.

Chris smiled back a little sheepishly as he wheeled into the parking lot of the restaurant. "I suppose that sounds a little boring."

"Hey, nothing wrong with boring. I love boring. Boring gets me hot." She hadn't meant to add that last part, but the way Chris's eyes lit up told her she'd managed to intrigue, not offend. Well, that was good.

Chris switched off the car and unbuckled his seat belt. Then he turned and smiled right into her eyes. "In that case then, let's head inside and have a perfectly boring dinner."

—◦◦◦—

By the time Chris walked her to the door at the end of their evening, Violet was more frustrated than she'd been in years.

Not sexually frustrated—that would have been a good sign, really. And not frustrated with Chris, either. He was perfect. Exactly the sort of man she'd been looking for. He'd been an absolute gentleman all evening, kind and well-mannered and intelligent and exactly—*exactly*—what she wanted.

Which is why she was so damn frustrated with herself. Chris was smart, charming, career focused, and attentive to her every need. Above all, he was *normal*. Just what she wanted.

Only… well, she wasn't really *wanting* him. Not the way she expected to want a good-looking, smart, single—

"You must be tired," Chris murmured as they stopped on the front porch.

"What?" Violet asked, hoping she hadn't missed some important thread of conversation.

"That's the third time you've yawned since we left the restaurant. I hope I didn't keep you out too late."

"Oh… no, of course not. I mean, it's not your fault I'm yawning."

It's not, Violet reminded herself. She was just tired. That was all.

"So Violet, I had a really nice time this evening."

"Me too."

"Is there any chance I could see you again? Maybe without the pretense of reviewing paperwork or looking at files?"

Violet smiled. A joke, he'd made a joke. Obviously he wasn't a boring man. She really *was* tired.

"I'd like that," she said with enough gusto to make Chris beam at her.

"I'm so glad. Shall I give you a call tomorrow night to set something up?"

"I might not answer my phone tomorrow night. I have a couple of outdoor readings scheduled after dark... full moon and all. Moonbeam books those appointments months in advance, so I'll be tied up with that."

"Sure, of course," he said as though it was the most natural thing in the world for her to go traipsing into the dark of night with total strangers to give psychic readings. "How about if I just call you sometime in the next couple days when we've both got our calendars in front of us?"

"That sounds wonderful."

"Okay, then." Chris leaned toward her. Violet knew what came next. She took a breath, steeling herself for the kiss. Her hands felt clammy, and her heart skittered a little in her chest. Violet closed her eyes.

She felt Chris's lips brush her cheek, so soft she might have missed it. She felt him draw back. She opened her eyes.

Is that it?

Of course it was. Chris was a gentleman. What did she expect? It wasn't as if he would throw her up against the side of the house and push his body against hers, his breath hot on her throat, his hand fumbling at the opening of her blouse the way Drew's had as she'd pressed her breast into his palm and...

Violet felt her cheeks go hot. She took a small step back and offered Chris a weak smile.

He smiled back, looking kind and pleasant and absolutely perfect.

What the hell is wrong with you, Violet?

"Good night, Violet," he said softly.

"Good night," she said, and went inside to beat her head against a wall.

Violet opened her eyes the next morning and felt the dread pooling in her gut. It was the day she'd feared most when she'd agreed to this ridiculous psychic scheme. The day she'd known would probably blow her whole cover. The day she was almost certain to humiliate herself.

Not coincidentally, it was also Moonbeam's favorite day each month.

"Fucking full moon," Violet muttered, and got up to take a shower.

For at least a dozen years, Moonbeam had expounded on the special boost in psychic energy she felt with the gravitational pull of the full moon. Violet had always assumed it was menstrual cramps, but whatever. The appointments booked up months in advance, with many clients happy to take early-morning appointments with no moon in sight. Many of them requested special out-door locales for their full-moon readings.

Moonbeam was happy to oblige.

"A clairvoyant's power is always at its peak when the lunar cycle correlates with the earth's geomagnetic field, and the solar geomagnetic flux is in a state of calm," Moonbeam had said so many times that Violet could recite the bizarre string of words backward and forward.

She had no idea what it meant. She only knew that Moonbeam was nuttier than normal when the full moon arrived, and so she dreaded it.

Now she dreaded it for another reason. People were going to expect her to *know* things. The people who booked these appointments were serious connoisseurs of psychic services. They wouldn't be fooled by fake trances or half-assed tarot-card readings or words of wisdom from her Magic 8 Ball.

Everyone would know she was a fraud.

That alone wasn't so bad—certainly Violet didn't believe in psychics herself—but at least Moonbeam knew how to pull it off. She'd had years of practice.

Violet didn't have a clue.

So her mother's reputation would be sullied, and it would all be her fault.

Damn full moon.

Violet toweled off and dressed in an amethyst cashmere sweater with slim black slacks. She topped it off with tall black boots and a spritz of her favorite perfume. Maybe if she smelled nice, no one would notice she didn't know what the hell she was doing.

In the kitchen, she ate some organic steel-cut oatmeal drizzled with wild-forest honey and nibbled a handful of locally grown raspberries. Collecting her keys from the basket by the front door, Violet marched out the door with the enthusiasm of a woman facing an executioner with exceptionally bad halitosis.

Once she was settled in with a mug of mint tea in Moonbeam's red velvet chair, she studied the appointment book.

Ann Marie Winston, age twenty-seven, Scorpio, residing just outside Tigard. These were the only facts available to her. Ann Marie was a new client who'd booked her appointment three months earlier. She'd given no indication what she wanted to talk about, probably because the appointment had been made so far in advance.

Moonbeam's only note, written in tiny, flowery script, read, *Moved from San Fran, had regular psychic there*.

"Maybe she'll have low expectations," Violet muttered to herself as the door chimed.

Violet stood as a fresh-faced blonde stepped through the door and surveyed her surroundings. Violet surveyed Ann Marie, scanning for designer labels, telltale facial expressions, something significant in her poise—anything that would give her a clue who Ann Marie was and what she expected.

Her pants were khaki, her expression was neutral, and her posture was unreadable. Violet sighed.

Ann Marie gave her a perfectly bland, perfectly useless smile. "You must be the psychic?"

"Hello," Violet said, extending her hand as she approached. "You're Ann Marie Winston?"

"Yes, I am. Are you Miss Moonbeam?"

"That's my mother, actually, but I'm filling in for her while she recovers from an accident."

"Oh, dear… I hope it's not serious?"

Sympathetic, Violet noted, hoping that might prove helpful. "She's recovering well, thanks for asking. I hope you're okay with the substitution?"

"Of course. I mean, I assume you're qualified?"

Ends all her sentences with a question, Violet noted, not sure what she could discern about Ann Marie from that. And how the hell did one define a "qualified" psychic?

"Of course," Violet said. "Can I get you some mint tea? I just brewed some."

"That would be lovely."

"Have a seat right over there and I'll be with you in just a moment."

Violet moved to the corner and began preparing the tea, not bothering to play guessing games with Ann Marie's sweetener preferences. She grabbed Moonbeam's small sugar bowl, poured a steaming mug of tea, loaded the whole thing on a rustic bamboo tray, and returned to the seating area.

She set the tray on the small table between them and watched as Ann Marie added a perfect teaspoon of sugar to her mug. She stirred twice, then rested her spoon in its saucer.

Tidy, simple, well-mannered, Violet observed, trying to come up with any way this could help her. She was stumped.

I'm doomed.

"So, Ann Marie, what can I help you with today?"

Ann Marie took a slow sip of tea, her expression unreadable through the faint steam from the mug. She set her mug down and reached into her purse. Pulling out a little blue notebook, Ann Marie flipped it open and looked at Violet.

"Well," Ann Marie said slowly, "I have some career questions."

"Career?"

"Yes. Things have been a little rocky, and I'm wondering about the direction my career is headed."

"I see," Violet said, not seeing at all. She tried to remember the rules of thumb she'd heard her mother drill into other aspiring psychics over the years. *Let the client ask you questions, not the other way around. Spend 95*

*percent of the reading sharing information with your
client, not requesting information from her.*

Of course, that made it markedly tougher to fake her
way through a reading. Violet took a breath. She had to
start somewhere.

"My mother's notes indicate that you've used psychic services a bit in the past," she began. "How do you
usually prefer to have your reading flow?"

Ann Marie gave her a pleasant smile. "Thank you
for asking, that's very kind of you. I'm sure you have
your own way of working, so I don't want to interfere
with that, but I really just like to hear what you have to
say. Can you... that is, um... are you reading my energy
right now?"

Violet nodded. "Loud and clear," she said, and took
a sip of tea. "Okay, then, you want to know about the
direction of your career."

"Correct."

"I sense that you're feeling uncertain."

"Well, yes..."

Violet did a mental eye roll at her own overstatement
of the obvious. *Isn't everyone who visits a psychic feeling uncertain?*

She gripped her tea mug harder and tried again.
"You're clearly at a crossroads here, with some very
significant decisions to be made quite soon, and—"

"Why, yes," Ann Marie said, looking a little surprised. "I just interviewed for a job yesterday and they
told me they'll make their decision later this week. Are
you... can you tell whether I'll get the job?"

Fuck, Violet thought.

"Well," she began. "I'm not able to read the energy

from the members of the interview panel, but I do have a very strong sense that you did your very best and that the interviewers were really impressed with… with your professionalism and your experience."

Jesus. Could she get any more vague? Violet wished like hell she'd done a background check. Something to tell her more about this woman, what she did for a living, what sort of person she was.

Kill me now.

Ann Marie looked at her, waiting. She didn't appear angry or skeptical. Not yet, anyway. She *wanted* to believe.

Violet wished she'd had the foresight to pay someone to pull the fire alarm.

A door creaked in the hallway, and both women turned to look. Drew emerged from his shop and crept discreetly toward the storage closet. He was moving quietly, evidently remembering Violet's scolding about making noise during her readings. As a matter of fact, she hadn't heard him playing music all morning. She hadn't even known he was around.

Now that she knew, she felt every nerve in her body snap to attention. She tried to look away, but her eyes were fixed on Drew as he unlocked the storage closet and reached onto the top shelf for a pack of lightbulbs.

From the corner of her eye, Violet saw Ann Marie frown. She leaned toward Violet, her voice a conspiratorial whisper. "That man should know it can be harmful to his auditory health to listen to music that loud."

Violet tore her eyes from Drew and looked at Ann Marie. "What?"

"Those iPod earbuds he's wearing—they've been

known to damage hearing when someone listens to music at that volume."

Violet looked back at Drew. She hadn't noticed it, but there were the telltale wires, the little earbuds tucked in place. Maybe that's why things had seemed so quiet.

"Honestly," Ann Marie whispered, "how can people stand to listen to music at that volume?"

Violet listened, trying to hear the dangerous decibels that had caught Ann Marie's attention. Her eyes were fixed on Drew, on the rumpled hair, the faded jeans, the way his head nodded in time to the beat.

"Nothing but noise, anyway," Ann Marie was saying. "All those electric guitars and that horrible hammering."

Violet barely heard her. She was focused on the music, picking out the familiar drumbeat, the recognizable pulse of the chorus. The hair on her arms began to prickle. Something niggled at the back of her brain. Something completely crazy. Something so ridiculous that Violet couldn't even form the thought.

She focused on the distant buzz of the music, Ann Marie all but forgotten. What was that song, anyway? It was on the tip of her tongue.

Van Halen, Violet thought. She listened harder, trying to remember the name of the song. Her pulse was starting to gallop as the tickling at the back of her brain became an irritating scratch.

The song. It was from the *1984* album. If she could just remember what it was called...

Violet turned to Ann Marie. Her heart was pounding hard against her ribs, and her hands had started to shake. Surely there was no way—

"'Hot for Teacher,'" Violet blurted.

"I beg your pardon?" Ann Marie looked alarmed.

Violet took a breath and looked down at her hands. They were shaking, making her mint tea slosh onto her knee. She could hear Drew relocking the storage closet, moving quietly down the hall and back into his shop, completely oblivious to the havoc he'd just unleashed behind him.

"Ann Marie," Violet said slowly, looking back at her.

Ann Marie nodded, her expression wary but curious. "Yes?"

"This job you interviewed for… Are you… that is, were you interviewing for a position as a… well, are you a…"

Violet set her tea down and took another breath. "Ann Marie, are you a teacher?"

Ann Marie looked startled for a moment. Then a slow smile spread over her face.

"Why, yes. Yes, I am."

Chapter 8

SOMEHOW, VIOLET MANAGED TO MUDDLE HER WAY through the rest of the reading. It helped that Ann Marie seemed sufficiently awestruck by Violet's ability to name her profession and pinpoint the fact that Ann Marie had left her last job after an obsessed male student began stalking her.

It probably didn't help that Violet was even more awestruck than her client.

Even so, Ann Marie tipped generously at the end and promised to book another full-moon reading the next month.

"Psychics are just so powerful at that time, don't you think?" Ann Marie asked.

Violet only nodded, still too stunned to even stand up and see Ann Marie to the door.

When the woman was gone, Violet reached into the drawer and picked up a spiral notebook and pen. Her hands were still shaking, and she glanced over at the door to make sure she was alone.

Okay, this was ridiculous. Really, there was no way—

"*Love in an Elevator*," Violet wrote. She frowned down at the paper. Okay, fine, so that's the song that had prompted her to accidentally direct Detective Smeade to find the missing money. The song Drew had played right then, at the precise moment she was giving Detective Smeade his fake reading.

That was weird. Weird, but not completely out there. Not proof of anything, really.

What else? She tried to remember the first song she'd noticed, maybe something the day she'd moved her desk in.

"*Photograph*," she jotted.

Okay, fine. Drew had come in right after that to help her hang that picture of Mount Hood, but that was just a coincidence.

She thought back to the rest of the day she'd met Detective Smeade. Dinner at Portland City Grill with Chris and Drew and—

"Jenny," Violet said aloud. "*867-5309.*" The song Drew was playing that afternoon, even though he didn't seem to know that was his date's name.

Eerie, definitely very eerie. Still, not proof of anything.

What had Drew played on her iPod that night when he'd dropped by and fixed the stereo?

Peter Gabriel, "Mercy Street," Violet wrote on her pad. *Howard Jones, "The Prisoner." Sarah McLachlan, "Train Wreck."*

She stopped writing and tapped her pen against her teeth. What the hell did those songs mean?

Nothing, obviously nothing.

But Drew had auditioned Jerry the very next day, and Jerry had mentioned spending time in prison.

And then there was the light-rail train wreck that had delayed her meeting with Chris later that evening, and the detour she'd had to take was on Mercy Street, and—

Stupid, you're being completely ridiculous, Violet told herself. *You're worse than Moonbeam.*

And then there was the Van Halen song, right when

she would have given anything to know her client's profession. "Hot for Teacher." Who the hell played that song anymore?

Okay, so even assuming there was something to it, it wasn't as if she was the only person who could hear the music, so clearly it didn't mean *she* was psychic. So maybe it was something with Drew? Maybe Moonbeam had noticed it before?

Coincidence, Violet told herself. *Nothing more than that*.

She heard her mother's voice in her ear. *"There are no coincidences in the life of a psychic, Violet."*

"Shut up, Mom!" Violet said aloud.

Someone chuckled in the hallway. Violet's head snapped up as Drew walked into the room, smiling at her with that same cocksure expression he'd worn from the moment she met him.

"Are you communicating with your mom telepathically?" Drew asked. "Or do you always tell her off when she's ten miles away and highly medicated?"

Violet stared at him for a few heartbeats.

Then she burst into tears.

The instant Violet started crying, Drew felt like a jerk. He hadn't meant anything with his comment. Hell, he was just trying to make her laugh.

Tears were not the reaction he'd expected.

"Violet, hey, I was just kidding. I talk to myself all the time. It's not a big deal. Sometimes I carry on full conversations."

Violet just shook her head, sobbing harder as she dropped her pen on the floor. Drew knelt down and picked it up. He remained there at her feet, kneeling in front of her as she struggled to stop crying. He touched her knee.

"What's the matter?" he murmured. "Was it something I said?"

Violet shook her head and sniffled loudly.

"Your mom? You're worried about your mom?"

She shook her head again and wiped her nose on the back of her hand. Very unhygienic, and her face was all blotchy, and…

Then she looked at him.

All the air went out of Drew's lungs.

Her eyes were striking under normal circumstances, that hazy shade of violet with sparks of silver. But now, shimmering with candlelight and tears and all that raw emotion…

"Jesus."

Drew winced. He hadn't meant to say it aloud. Violet seemed unfazed, focused as she was on collecting herself. Drew handed her the pen and tried a smile.

"You okay now?"

Violet nodded, but still didn't speak. Drew's hand was still on her knee, and it took every ounce of strength he had to keep himself from gathering her in his arms and kissing her senseless to make her forget her troubles.

"Look, I'm sorry I startled you," he said. "I just came in to apologize about walking through in the middle of a reading. I was trying to be quiet, and I would have waited until you were done, but I had an inspector coming and—"

"What were you listening to on your iPod?"

Drew frowned. "When?"

Violet took a shaky breath and looked straight at him. "When you came through to get the lightbulbs. You had your iPod on then. What song were you listening to?"

Drew stared at her, trying to figure out what the hell she was driving at. Had she found Moonbeam's stash of magic mushrooms in the back of the cupboard?

"Are you feeling okay?" he tried.

"What song?" Violet demanded. She winced, seemingly startled by the forcefulness of her own voice. "Please," she added.

Drew stared at her for a moment before he began to rack his brain for an answer. "I have no idea. Mötley Crüe, or maybe Van Halen. I was listening to the *1984* album earlier, so that's probably it. You couldn't hear it all the way over here, could you?"

Violet nodded and clutched the pen in her fist.

"Sorry about that," Drew said. "I didn't realize I had it up so loud."

"'Hot for Teacher'?" Violet said in a husky, tear-soaked voice that made him a little dizzy.

"What?"

"Is that the song you were listening to?"

Drew shrugged. "Probably. That's on that album. Why?"

Violet just shook her head, looking numb.

"Okay. Right, well then." He was suddenly at a loss for words. What the hell was Violet up to?

He glanced down at the notepad in her lap. *"Love in an Elevator?"* What was that about?

Violet covered the page with her hand before he could see anything else she'd written there. He looked back up at her and gave her knee a friendly squeeze.

"Hey, if you're jonesing for eighties music, you should come on by tomorrow evening. We're doing a theme night."

"Theme night."

"All eighties, all night. It'll be fun. Bring your mom's friend... was it Butterfly?"

Violet nodded again. "Sure. Eighties night. I'll think about it."

Drew eyed her for a moment, not sure it was safe to leave her alone. "You sure you're okay? You want me to call someone for you or—"

"No. I'm fine. Really. Just tired, that's all."

"You should go home early, maybe eat pancakes in bed and go to sleep at seven p.m. watching sitcoms. That always makes me feel better." He tried smiling again, hoping she might follow suit.

Violet just shook her head and looked down at her hands. "I can't. Moonbeam booked all these full-moon appointments. I've got two of them back-to-back at Council Crest Park just after sundown. I'll be too busy for pancakes and sitcoms."

"Some other time, then."

"Sure."

Drew looked down at his hand that still rested on Violet's knee. He should probably move it. Any minute now. Just as soon as he stopped enjoying the solid warmth of her thigh through the thin fabric and—

Drew pulled his hand back and stood up. "Okay then, I'm going to get back to work. You sure you're going to be all right?"

"Positive."

"Promise?"

Violet laughed, a dry, humorless sound that made Drew want to pull her into his arms.

Then again, was there anything about Violet that didn't make him want to do that? Even the snot hadn't deterred him.

"Promise," Violet repeated, shaking her head and giving him a sad little smile. "Sure. I promise. You can believe me, I'm a professional."

That evening, Drew was even more distracted than normal. That was saying something. He'd been wiping the same spot on the bar for fifteen minutes, just rubbing and rubbing and rubbing and—

"You got a hot date or something?"

Drew looked up to see his business partner, Sam, peering at him over a tray of empty cocktail glasses.

Drew frowned at her and tucked his rag beneath the bar. "No. Why?"

"You keep looking at your watch."

"Right. Just wondering about the time."

"It's about two minutes later than it was the last time you looked." She grinned at him and set the glasses down.

Drew looked away, not wanting to get drawn into this conversation. On the corner stage, Jerry was performing his first show of the night. Drew watched as a cluster of women celebrating a coworker's birthday began shrieking with delight as Jerry tore open his shirt.

"Jerry's doing pretty well for a first-timer," Drew said. "Thanks for getting that background check done so fast."

"No sweat. Nice of you to give him a shot, with the prison record and all."

Drew shrugged. "He's done his time. Everyone deserves another chance. Besides, once he explained the circumstances, how could I not give him a shot?"

"I hear you. He sure seems to love doing this."

Drew nodded and began restocking Sam's tray with fresh cocktails for the bachelorette party at the corner table. "Jerry and Jamie were practicing all afternoon."

"Jamie's a great teacher, isn't he?"

Teacher, Drew thought, dropping olives into martini glasses. Why had Violet been so hung up on that song? Maybe it wasn't the song at all. Maybe she was just nuts. It would make sense. That sort of thing ran in families, didn't it?

"Hello there, earth to Drew…"

He snapped back to attention at Sam's chiding. She was smiling at him, but there was a hint of concern in her expression, too.

"You okay, buddy? You seem sort of out of it tonight."

Drew sighed. "Look, Sam… it's kind of slow tonight. Maybe I'll just—"

"I *knew* you had a date. Blonde or brunette?"

"Sam—"

"No wait, let me guess. That little redhead who tried to slip you her number the other night but couldn't figure out how to spell *phone*."

Drew sighed. "Marcie. Or Macy. Or something like that. I went out with her last night."

He didn't bother adding that it had been one of the most boring dates of his life. Since when had a buxom redhead failed to hold his interest?

Okay, fine. He could pinpoint the exact date. It was the day Violet McGinn marched in with her tall boots and those crazy eyes and started sassing him about psychics and spouting random data and putting his hand in her shirt and—

"Go home, Drew," Sam said. "I've got things handled here. You've obviously got something going on."

Drew thought about arguing, but he just nodded. "Thanks, Sam. You're the best."

She grinned. "Does that mean you'll cover for me next weekend so I can take the kids to the beach?"

"Anything you want."

"You're a good man, Drew Watson."

"Don't tell anyone."

By the time he'd grabbed his jacket and rattled off a few last-minute instructions to some of the entertainers, it was just after ten p.m. Early for a bar, but pretty damn late for Violet to be hanging out in a park with clients who could be crazy or…

Okay, the crazy part was a given. They were seeing a psychic, after all. Still, there was bad crazy and there was good crazy. Good crazy could be sexy. Bad crazy could be dangerous.

He really should check on her. That would be the gentlemanly thing to do.

Then he thought about how soft and touchable she'd looked in that purple sweater, and suddenly his thoughts weren't so gentlemanly.

Before he'd even made up his mind where he was driving, he was following the road up to Council Crest Park. The gates closed at midnight, so in all likelihood, Violet would still be up there. He'd just drive past, make sure she looked safe and unharmed. Then he'd drive away. She'd never even know he was there.

He reached over to turn down his stereo, but decided against it. Axl Rose was just starting to wail on the chorus of "Sweet Child o' Mine." No reason to miss that.

As Drew cruised slowly through the parking lot, he caught site of her rental car. Just a few feet away stood Violet, her feet planted shoulder width apart as she stood there in the grass, looking up at the sky.

She was still wearing the purple sweater, but she'd changed into a slim black skirt and tall, pointy boots. Her hair was loose and wild, floating over her shoulders in the light breeze. The night was almost cloudless for a change, and the moonlight pooled around her, illuminating her like a spotlight. She had a disheveled, untamed look that made Drew's gut clench.

God, she's beautiful.

Beside her was a thin woman in a tight top and a billowy skirt, wearing Birkenstocks and a dreamy expression. Drew hardly noticed her at all. He didn't even blink. He was barely aware that his car was still moving, inching forward through the dark, mostly empty parking lot. All he could see was Violet.

Suddenly, both women turned to look at him. He saw the recognition register on Violet's face. Was she angry?

Just surprised, he decided. He stepped on the brake and gave her a small wave. Violet nodded and turned back to the woman in the skirt. The two of them spoke for a minute, laughing and relaxed in the moonlight. The chirp of crickets nearly drowned out the sound of Portland traffic in the distance. He cracked his window just a tiny bit and inhaled the scent of damp moss in the trees.

Violet glanced at him again, talking quickly now,

gesturing at the woman. Drew could hear her voice, barely a murmur over the sound of the crickets and the stereo—

Whoops. The stereo.

He reached over and turned off Axl. The song was almost over anyway.

He looked back at Violet, who was watching him oddly. She turned back to the woman and talked some more, stopping to point up at the moon. She was so lovely, silhouetted against a backdrop of dark trees, the city lights fanned out behind her like glitter.

Drew winced. He sounded like a stalker. He was sure as hell acting like one, just sitting there in his car, staring at her in the darkness.

He was just about to lift his foot off the brake and keep moving when Violet leaned forward and gave the woman a hug. Then the two of them headed off in opposite directions—the woman toward a tan Audi, Violet striding purposefully toward Drew.

Even though he saw her coming, he still jumped when she tapped on the window. She didn't wait for a response, just opened the passenger door and got in.

"I thought that was you," she said, smiling at him. "Showing up for your full-moon reading?"

"Thanks, I already consulted my Magic 8 Ball about my impending lottery win. Apparently, 'all signs point to yes.'"

Violet laughed. "Better buy a ticket."

Drew smiled back at her, feeling warm in spite of the cool night air trickling through the open window. "I see you're in better spirits than you were earlier."

"Sorry about the crying jag. I'm not sure what came over me. Hormones or something." She gave a stiff little laugh. "That would explain a lot, actually. Why I was practically crawling in your lap last night, and five minutes later, yelling at you about Frank."

Drew studied her for a moment, a little surprised she'd broached the subject at all. "Hormones, huh? What's my excuse?"

"You're a guy. You don't need an excuse. You're naturally more driven by lust."

"You think so?"

She bit her lip and looked away. "Generally speaking."

"Want to know what I think?" Drew didn't wait for an answer. He leaned closer and stroked her cheek with one finger. "I think you have untapped reserves of lust," he whispered. "Barrels of lust. Lust you don't even know exists, but it's always right there under the surface, just waiting to boil over."

Violet met his eyes, looking startled. Shaken.

And maybe, just maybe, a little lust-driven.

She licked her lips. "I don't—"

"Yes you do."

"I'm not—"

"Yes you are."

She laughed. "How do you know what I'm going to say?"

"The psychic thing is rubbing off."

She was quiet for a moment, studying the stars through his sunroof. When she turned back to him, her eyes were glittery in the moonlight.

"Was that Guns N' Roses you were listening to as you pulled up?"

Whatever he'd been expecting her to say next, it wasn't that. "Good ear."

She nodded, and Drew watched her hair, dark and

silvery, moving against the leather seat. He wanted to reach out and slide his fingers through it…

"I just told that woman she was pregnant."

Drew stared at her. "What?"

"My client. My *mother's* client, whatever. I told her she's pregnant."

Drew frowned, not sure if he was more confused by the turn in conversation or by what she was actually saying. "I thought the object with this psychic crap was to be deliberately vague—not to tell the clients something that can be easily disproven."

She shrugged and looked out the window. "Why are you so sure I'm wrong?"

"Statistically speaking—"

"I wasn't wrong. At least I don't think so. She looked really surprised at first, but then said she'd been feeling a little funny and her breasts were tender and her period is five weeks late and—"

"You can stop there."

Violet smiled. "Anyway, I think I'm right."

"You think?"

"I know."

"Well in that case, let's call the paper with the birth announcement. Or maybe we can still catch up to her and we can all go shopping for onesies and those things to mop up baby puke and—"

He stopped when he realized Violet was scowling at him. "What?"

"Why are you such a skeptic?"

"Aren't you the same woman who sat in that very seat less than a week ago and said, and I quote, 'Psychics don't exist'?"

Violet looked out the window again. "I was drunk. You were taking advantage of my inebriated state."

Drew laughed. "Honey, I still have claw marks on my wrist from where you held on so I couldn't pry my hand off your breast. Not that I'm complaining, but you really want to play the victim here?"

Violet bit her lip and looked at the trees outside. She said nothing for a minute. Then she looked back at him, eyes flashing. "How did you know I'd be here tonight?"

"Because you told me."

She frowned. "I did?"

"When you were sobbing over the Van Halen song. What was that about, anyway?"

She ignored the question. "So you came up here to make fun of psychics?"

"Since when are you the great defender of psychics?"

"There's a lot you don't know about me."

"I can only imagine."

He saw Violet's cheeks pinken, but she didn't take the bait. She did hold his gaze, those violet eyes unblinking, which was enough to make Drew forget his train of thought.

"You didn't answer me," she said slowly. "Why did you come up here?"

"I came up here to make sure you didn't get dragged into the woods by some depraved lunatic."

"Oh."

"I'm thinking I should have let the lunatic have you. Maybe he'd know why you're acting like such a nut job all of a sudden."

Violet's expression softened and she reached out and touched his hand. Drew tried not to notice the way his skin hummed under the warmth of her fingertips.

"Thank you, Drew," she said quietly. "Not for the nut-job comment. I mean, it was nice of you to check on me. Really, I'm sorry I'm being such a bitch. It's been a long day."

"For both of us."

"Why was it long for you?"

Drew sighed. "I had a surprise OSHA inspection this morning. That wasn't so weird, but the guy was asking a lot of questions about my square footage and which walls were weight bearing and which fixtures belonged to me and which ones came with the building."

"I don't understand."

"I'm not sure he was really an OSHA inspector."

"Who else would he be?"

"Someone scoping out the property. I heard through the grapevine that Frank put out some feelers about selling the building. Nothing too serious yet, but—"

"Oh, no."

Drew shrugged. "It's probably nothing, but Frank probably could make a good profit off the property. It's in a good location."

Violet grimaced. "It's probably my fault."

Drew said nothing. He hated to admit it, but the thought had occurred to him. Ten years he'd been in the building and the owner had never once hinted at selling. Now, just a few days after Violet had completely pissed him off, he was suddenly sniffing around the real-estate market?

Drew shook his head.

"What?" Violet asked.

"Nothing. So are you done for the night?"

"Yes. Celia was my last reading."

"You really told her she was pregnant?"

Violet sighed. "It wasn't a complete shot in the dark. Moonbeam had it in her notes that Celia and her husband have been trying to conceive for at least six months, and she did have a certain glow about her, and I noticed some dark pigmentation on her face, and—"

"What?"

"Melasma—also known as the mask of pregnancy. It's pretty common."

"Your wealth of bizarre trivia astounds me."

She smiled. "I should get home. Thanks for coming by. It really helped me out."

"Helped you out?"

"Made my night. Whatever."

Drew laughed. "If seeing me made your night, you need to get out more."

"I probably do." She was quiet for a moment. "Let's go somewhere."

"Now?"

"Sure. Maybe Bannings for chocolate cake or back to the Portland City Grill for a drink. Unless you have a date or something?"

Drew looked at his watch. "It's eleven p.m. on Wednesday night. Any woman I'd pick up for a date at this hour would charge by the minute."

"Ah, that's right," she said, grinning at him. "You're normally much more selective in your dating habits. Sam stopped by to thank me for filling in for her yesterday. We talked about you. She said you have a habit of dating bimbos."

"Is this conversation almost over?"

Violet grinned. "She said that ever since you and

your wife divorced, you've made it your mission to only date women who are the precise opposite of your ex."

"You can get out of the car anytime."

"She also told me you have commitment issues."

"The door handle is right there," he said without venom. "Unlocked and everything."

She laughed. Apparently, she wasn't buying his mock indignation.

"Well anyway," she said, "it explains a lot about you."

Drew frowned. "How much is this psychoanalysis going to cost me? Because if I'm paying for a full hour, I've got some dreams I'd like you to interpret."

"Oh, tell me about them," she said, leaning closer and smiling up at him.

"Well, there's one where you're naked and…"

He stopped, a little startled at his own words. He hadn't meant to say that out loud. He braced himself, waiting for the slap he probably deserved.

But instead, Violet grinned at him.

"Funny. I think I had that same dream."

And then she kissed him.

Chapter 9

VIOLET HADN'T MEANT TO KISS DREW.

Hell, she was annoyed with him for being a skeptic about psychics.

Then she was annoyed with herself for forgetting she was a skeptic.

Somehow her confusion got mixed up with the moonlight and the heady smell of damp earth and the buzz of pleasure that had been humming through her veins from the moment she'd spotted Drew in the parking lot, looking dark and smug and so damn hot.

Before she had a chance to stop herself, she was grabbing the front of his shirt and yanking him hard against her. She lost all conscious thought, except the one that was screaming at her to find a way to kiss him *right fucking now*.

It was more graceful when it happened in the movies. She yanked, he came flying forward, and their lips met with a lot more force than Violet intended. There was an audible click as their teeth collided.

Violet started to pull away, embarrassed, but Drew grabbed the back of her head and held her there. His mouth was soft and hot, and she suddenly forgot the awkwardness and just lost herself in the sensation.

He felt so damn good.

They were both breathing hard now, Drew's fingers sliding into her hair as he pulled her tighter against him.

He wasn't gentle about it, which only made Violet dizzier as she lost herself in the crush of his lips against hers, the firm planes of his chest pushed against her breasts.

His mouth left hers, and Violet started to whimper in protest. She stopped when he began to nibble his way down her throat, alternating the softness of his lips with the roughness of his teeth against her pulse.

"Oh," Violet said, closing her eyes and tipping her head back. Her mind swirled with color and sensation and so damn much pleasure that she opened her eyes again to keep from passing out.

Drew's mouth was on her throat and his hand was inching its way up her rib cage as Violet opened her eyes and peered up through the sunroof at the stars. Pinpricks of light flickered against the darkness while the moon shimmered at the edge of the sky like a giant amber disk. She sucked in a breath as he caught her earlobe with his teeth and nibbled softly.

"More," she gasped, and pulled him closer.

Drew didn't argue. Instead, he moved his hand up under her sweater, his large palm cupping her breast and making her whimper. His thumb stroked her nipple through the thin satin, and Violet felt her whole world tilt.

She grabbed at the hem of his shirt and yanked before remembering it wasn't tucked in to start with. She slid her palms beneath it, gasping as the heels of her hands connected with solid muscle and skin and so much heat. She stroked his chest like that, delighting in the noise he made deep in his throat as her fingernails grazed his nipples. He responded by sliding his hand up her thigh, under her skirt, his huge palm cupping her ass.

Violet moaned and slid one hand down his chest and

over his button fly, her fingers stroking his erection through the soft denim of his jeans. She fumbled for his belt buckle, wanting to feel him everywhere—under her, on top of her, inside her. She gripped him again through the denim.

"How does this move?" she gasped.

Drew looked down at her hand on his crotch.

"Not *that*," she said. "The seat. I want it back farther."

"Yes, ma'am," he said, and flipped a switch with his left hand. The seat began a slow crawl backward and Violet began a hasty crawl onto his lap. Her back scraped the steering wheel and her knee bumped something in the console, but she barely noticed. All she could think of was her desperate, urgent hunger to feel him moving inside her. She kissed him hard, pushing him back against the seat as she ground herself on him.

Drew laughed and broke the kiss. "Men are more driven by lust, huh?"

"Smugness is not becoming on you."

"This is where I make the joke about how if I were on you, I'd be coming."

"Pervert."

"Absolutely."

Any retort she might have made was cut off by her own gasp of pleasure as he moved his hand under her skirt and one finger traced the dampness between her legs.

"No panties?" he murmured against her throat.

"I couldn't find the ones that matched the bra."

"So you went without. Very sensible. Practical."

"Fuck me."

He laughed and began to kiss her throat. "I was getting to that."

She tilted her head back to give him better access, moaning as his tongue grazed the sensitive spot right above her collarbone. She stared up through the sunroof, amazed at how many stars were out. She'd never seen the moon so big, so round, so glowing, so—

"Moonbeam," Violet said suddenly, sitting up straight.

Drew froze with his mouth against her throat. He stopped kissing, but didn't pull back.

"Fond as I am of your mother, it's not a big turn-on to hear you say her name when I'm two minutes from sliding inside you," he murmured.

"Two minutes?" Violet said wistfully, sitting back farther. "No. Dammit, *no*. I'm so sorry, Drew, but I promised Moonbeam I'd meet her at the hospital. I totally forgot."

Drew gave her an incredulous look. His eyes were wild and unfocused, and his hand was still beneath her skirt. "Visiting hours ended ages ago," he said slowly. "Moonbeam is almost certainly asleep, hanging upside down from the ceiling in a cocoon of her own wings."

Violet shook her head and wriggled away, trying to pry herself off his lap. "No, really… it's a long story, but I have to meet her before midnight. I promised."

"Are you nuts?" Drew asked as Violet sat back in the passenger seat and tried to straighten her skirt. "Never mind, don't answer that. The hospital staff will never let you in at his hour."

"Moonbeam requested a special exemption on religious grounds. I'm sorry, Drew, I have to go."

Drew continued to stare at her with a dumbstruck expression. "In the last twenty minutes you've accused me of stalking you, invited me out for chocolate cake, bitched at me for mocking psychics, and then begged me to fuck you in my front seat."

Violet felt her cheeks heat up. "You didn't seem to mind."

"God, no. Believe me, I'm grateful. I'm just feeling a little dizzy from the roller coaster. Do you have a fetish for Toyotas?"

"What?"

"Not that there's anything wrong with that. It's just that you forced me to grope you here in the front seat the day after we met, and now here we are again—"

"Never mind," Violet said, reaching for the door handle. "You're right, this is a dumb idea. I have to go."

"I didn't say it was a dumb idea—"

"No, it is. You're the total opposite of what I'm looking for, and God knows I'm not a bimbo, and I know that's the sort of woman you're looking for."

"Are you always such a romantic, or is it just the full moon?"

"Good night, Drew. Thanks again for coming up here and checking on me."

"Sure," he said, looking at her like he expected her to leap onto the hood of the car and start baying at the sky.

Violet opened the door and got out, pushing it shut with more force than it required. She was determined not to look back as she ran across the grass toward her car. This was crazy, totally stupid, and she had to get out of here fast.

Lust makes you stupid, Violet.

Drew was not what she was looking for. And he was the last thing she needed. Jesus, a bar owner who employed strippers and knew she was a fake psychic. Pretty much the opposite of *normal*.

Not only that, he'd been feuding with her mother for the better part of a decade. Moonbeam had said Drew wanted her space to expand his bar. How far would he go to get it?

Violet shook her head as she fumbled for her car keys. What the hell had she been thinking?

When she got the car door open, she lost her resolve and finally stole a quick glance over her shoulder at Drew.

He was sitting in the driver's seat, lightly smacking his forehead against the steering wheel.

By the time Violet reached the hospital, it was ten minutes before midnight.

She had to check in at the nursing station where Moonbeam had already secured permission for their scheduled evening visit. After getting the go-ahead from the nurse, Violet made her way down the hall as silently as possible in stiletto boots.

She reached the threshold of Moonbeam's room and noticed the door was ajar. Should she knock or just walk in? Maybe Moonbeam was sleeping.

"Violet?" her mother called from inside the room. "I know it's you, I sense your presence, dear. Come in."

Violet rolled her eyes and stepped through the door, biting back the urge to ask her mother who else would be dropping by for a visit at midnight on a Wednesday.

She looked at Moonbeam, taking in the paleness of her face and the thin bones in her cheeks. Had her mother lost weight, or was it just the dim light?

"Hello, Mom," she murmured, trying to keep her voice low. "How are you feeling?"

"Very well, honey. I love the full moon, don't you?"

"You look tired. We could do this another time if you want."

"Don't be silly, dear. It's the full moon. We have to do it tonight."

"But—"

Moonbeam waved her hand, signaling the end of that conversation. "It's just this lousy hospital light."

"How soon until they transfer you to the rehab place?"

"Maybe as early as tomorrow. Let's get on with this now. Did you bring everything?"

Violet sighed and reached over to move the tambourine off the guest chair. She sat down beside her mother's bed and patted her purse. "I have it all right here."

"Even the snails?"

"They've been sitting in my car in a cooler since lunchtime."

Moonbeam smiled with obvious delight. "You think of everything, dear."

"That's me. A model of efficiency with mollusks and gastropods."

"You brought the string, too?"

"Red, just like you asked for. Are you sure this is really—"

"Violet, honey, as a skilled clairvoyant, you should know the importance of timing when it comes to placing curses. The full moon only happens once a month."

"But Mom—"

"No buts, dear. I need you on this."

Violet shut her mouth and ignored the pang of guilt radiating up from her gut. Her mother was counting on her. Not just for this, but to protect her business. Violet had already put things at risk when she'd drunkenly told Drew she didn't believe in psychics, and clearly he didn't intend to let her forget it.

She at least owed Moonbeam this much. She sighed. "Before we start, can I ask you something?"

"Anything, dear."

"It's about the music next door. From Drew's place?"

"Music?"

"There's this thing I've noticed," Violet began, feeling a little silly just saying it out loud. "The songs he plays sometimes correspond to what's going to happen, or to the client I'm meeting with, or…"

She stopped, noticing the look of genuine bewilderment on Moonbeam's face. "That's not ringing any bells?" she asked her mother faintly.

Moonbeam shook her head. "I really don't notice the music from next door. Of course, things are different for every psychic, and it could be that something in your aura is causing him to select music that corresponds to—"

"Never mind. Forget I said anything. Dumb idea."

She patted Violet's hand. "No ideas are dumb, Violet."

"Right." She glanced out the window at the full moon. "Shall we get started with this curse? I'm supposed to meet with Frank when he gets back from Chicago the day after tomorrow."

Moonbeam smiled and leaned back against her pillows. "Okay, take the photo of Frank that you downloaded off the Professional Squash Association website."

"Got it," Violet said, and pulled the printout from her bag.

"Move into the center of the room."

Violet stood up and trudged to a spot near the foot of the bed. "Fine. Now what?"

"Sit down cross-legged on the floor, facing the window. Isn't it wonderful they gave me a room with a window?"

"I'm sure this is exactly what they had in mind when they did it."

Moonbeam ignored her and reached over to the bedside drawer. "Now before we start, you'll need to get out the snails and this vial of urine I got from my catheter bag…"

Violet stared at her mother. Moonbeam smiled and held out the vial.

Violet closed her eyes and slowly shook her head.

"No dumb ideas, Mom. Right."

The next day, Drew was working on the weekly liquor order while Jamie coached Jerry on his dance routine.

Drew was trying very hard not to look.

"Like this, Jerry," Jamie said with obvious patience. "You have to really thrust your pelvis during the chorus."

"But it's a long chorus."

"Do you want to make lots of tips?"

"Well, sure."

"Then trust me on this. And don't forget to smile."

Drew shook his head and hit a few buttons on his calculator. He may not have had any interest in watching, but he was pleased to hear Jerry doing well, and even more pleased Jamie was part of it.

Earlier that morning, the three of them had driven out to I-5 to check out the new billboard for the bar. They'd parked on the shoulder with the hazard lights on, staring up at the full-color wonder that Drew had paid a hefty sum for.

It was worth it.

The billboard featured an enormous photo of Jamie in a cowboy costume with his shirt unbuttoned. He was smiling for the camera, and for every Portland commuter traveling this stretch of freeway. The bar's logo was prominently displayed over Jamie's crotch.

"Wow, that's really me," Jamie had said, staring up with awe.

"It's really you," Drew said. "Well, you with some Photoshop touch-ups."

"It's amazing," Jerry whispered, his tone reverent. "Someday, maybe I'll get to be on a billboard."

"It's good to have goals," Drew agreed.

"Fuckin' A," Jerry said.

"I still can't believe it," Jamie murmured, shaking his head. "I'm famous."

"You certainly are," Drew said, patting him on the shoulder before putting the car back in gear and pulling out onto the freeway. "I've already had calls from six bachelorette groups wanting to book private parties next month. This is the best marketing campaign we've come up with in years. Expensive as hell, but I think it's going to pay off."

Jamie beamed with pride as Drew drove the three of them back to the bar. He hadn't stopped beaming all morning as he'd coached Jerry through the newest routine. It was only ten a.m., still hours before the bar opened for the day, but Jamie was taking his training job very seriously.

Drew wished he had a million Jamies.

"Don't spread your legs like that," Jamie called to Jerry. "That's for female entertainers."

"Really?"

"Yeah. No one wants to see that. You can shake your butt, though. Girls like that."

"They do?"

"Trust me."

Drew shook his head and flipped a page on his order. He needed the distraction this morning. Lord knows he hadn't gotten much sleep the night before. The full moon had made it seem like daylight in his bedroom. He probably could have pulled the shades, but for some ridiculous reason, he wanted to look at the stars.

Damn Violet and her woo-woo astrology crap and her soft sweater, and her softer lips, so warm and inviting—

Drew shook his head again and scowled at the paper. *Dumb idea, Watson*, he told himself. *You heard her last night. You're not her type. God knows she's not your type. After everything you went through with Catherine—*

"Hey, boss?"

Drew looked up to see Jamie walking toward him, toweling off his broad shoulders as Jerry continued to gyrate on the corner stage to a cheesy George Michael song.

"What's up, Jamie?"

"I have my reading now."

"What are you reading?"

"No, I'm not reading… I mean I can read, but I'm kind of slow at it."

"Oh, your psychic reading." Drew nodded. "Right. That's today?"

Of course it was today. Drew had developed a knack for knowing everything he could about Violet's routine. He knew when she took lunch, what time she fed the mice, how she sometimes talked to herself when she thought no one could hear her.

Great, he was becoming a stalker.

"Right," Jamie said. "So I was thinking I could take a break and go over there now."

"Sure, Jamie. No problem. You've already put in plenty of overtime this week, so you can take as long as you need."

"Thanks, boss. You're the best. Anything you'd like me to tell Miss Violet for you?"

Drew thought about it. There were plenty of things he'd like to say to Violet, but Jamie wasn't the messenger he'd choose to send.

"No message. But remember what we were saying about pants?"

"Pants?"

"Put some on. It's the polite thing to do."

"Right, boss. Thanks."

~~~

Violet was feeding a french fry to one of the mice when Jamie came striding in, looking beautifully obtuse and characteristically cheerful.

"Hello, Miss Violet," he said, gripping her hand jovially. "I hope I'm not late?"

"Hey, Jamie. You're right on time. Have a seat right over there."

"Thanks!"

Violet smiled at him as she closed the mouse cage

and took a seat in the opposite chair. "I've never seen you wearing pants before. You look very nice."

"The boss told me that would be a good idea. I wasn't sure about a shirt, so I left that off."

"No problem. We're not too strict about the dress code around here."

Jamie smiled a little sadly. "I wish more restaurants were like that."

Violet clasped her hands together and cleared her throat. "Can I get you anything to drink? Water or tea or anything?"

"No thanks. I'm just excited to get started."

"Right. So, Jamie... is there anything in particular you'd like to ask about?"

"Are your breasts really real? Because one of the guys said something backstage the other night and I had to punch him because it was disrespectful, but—"

"I meant about you," Violet clarified, shifting a little in her seat. "Do you have any questions you want to ask... um, for psychic purposes?"

Jamie looked confused. Violet sighed.

"Yes, my breasts are real," she offered. "So is there anything in your life you want me to tell you about?"

Jamie beamed. "Well, I'm just wondering what my future holds."

"Oh. Right. Okay, well, let me close my eyes and concentrate on reading your energy."

"Do I need to close my eyes, too?"

"Sure. That helps."

"Right. Okay. You'll tell me when I can open them again?"

"Absolutely. All right, Jamie, before we begin, I just

have a couple quick questions for you. Does Drew choose your music for your dance routines?"

"Sure, most of the time. Sometimes I pick, but he always has such good ideas and he knows so much about music."

"That he does," Violet agreed, feeling a little guilty. "Has he chosen anything new for you lately?"

"Oh, sure, lots of stuff. I have this cool new routine I do to that theme song from *Top Gun*."

"You mean the one by Kenny Loggins? 'Danger Zone'?"

"That's it. I get to use these flashlight things like the guys at the airport use to guide the planes in, you know? And a pilot uniform, but that comes off pretty fast."

"Right. Any other songs?"

"Well, there's this Aerosmith one we've been working on lately—'Dream On'? We do this really cool thing with the black light and I wear this white costume with sequins on it and I have this thing I do on the pole where I go around and around and around and—"

"That sounds really cool. I'd like to see that sometime."

"Oh, I'm sure Mr. Watson would invite you."

Violet felt a warm heat creep up her neck at the mention of Drew, but she tried to concentrate. This was Jamie's reading, after all, and she owed it to him to focus.

You're a fraud, you're a fraud, you're a fraud, chanted Violet's inner voice.

Violet cleared her throat. "So Jamie, I sense that you have some very big goals in life."

"Uh-huh," Jamie replied in a reverent tone.

"You have a lot of dreams, but something's always holding you back from achieving those. Um, fear?"

"I'm not chicken."

"No, of course not. Definitely not. But sometimes dreams come with certain risks. Danger, if you will."

"Yeah," Jamie agreed. "Danger."

"But risks can be good. If it means achieving your goals, that is."

Violet gritted her teeth, not sure what the hell she was driving at. Maybe she should have asked for more songs. Or maybe this was a ridiculous theory, this stupid thing with the music. Just a few silly coincidences.

There are no coincidences in the life of a psychic, Violet.

Shut up, Mom.

"So anyway, Jamie, I get the sense that you have big dreams that you need to pursue in life, and that achieving those dreams won't necessarily be an easy thing."

"You got that right," Jamie said with a sigh.

"I did?"

"Sure. I mean, duh… You're a psychic."

"Oh. Of course. Anything else you'd like to know?"

"How soon should I do this? Chase my dreams and all?"

"Oh, as soon as possible. Really, life's too short."

God, you sound like a fucking fortune cookie, she chided herself.

Mmmm, Chinese food sounds good.

Focus, Violet.

"Anyway, Jamie, you're a good guy who's capable of achieving a lot of great things in life."

"Yeah?"

"Yeah. So dive in headfirst, do what you want to do, and you'll reach your dreams before you know it."

She opened her eyes to peer at him. He managed to look simultaneously amazed and befuddled, all with his eyes pinched tightly shut.

"Wow, Miss Violet. You're really good."

Violet tried to ignore her guilty conscience. All she'd really done was give him a pep talk. Nothing a motivational speaker wouldn't have done.

You're not a motivational speaker.

"Right, so Jamie… what other questions do you have?"

He opened his eyes and peered at her. "None. You did a really great job, Miss Violet. I know exactly what I need to do now."

"You do?"

"Sure. I've got a plan and everything."

"Great. That's really great."

"And I owe it all to you."

Violet tried not to feel uneasy about that. "So Jamie, are you performing tonight?"

He broke into a wide grin. "Nah, tonight's not a stripper night. I'm tending bar, though. You should stop by."

"Maybe I will. I know Drew is really happy with all the work you do."

"Yeah?" he said, beaming proudly.

"Definitely. He says you're a really good teacher, too, with that new guy he hired, Jerry?"

"I could teach you."

"Teach me what?"

"You know. Dancing. How to be a professional entertainer."

"Oh." Violet felt her face heat up. "No, that's okay. Thanks, but I already have a job and everything."

"This would give you something to fall back on."

Violet felt herself start to smile. "Sure, in case the psychic accountant thing doesn't work out."

"What?"

"Never mind. I just… it's not really me, you know?"

"Oh," Jamie said, looking disappointed. "Because you're smart and serious and stuff?"

"Well, I don't know about that—"

"It's okay. Sorry, I didn't mean to offend you. That was really dumb. I always do dumb stuff like that."

"No, it wasn't dumb at all. Really, Jamie, I'm flattered you'd offer."

He gave her a hopeful smile. "So you want to try?"

"Oh… well…"

"Just a few moves," Jamie said, standing up and extending a hand. "It's the least I can do for all the help you've given me."

Violet looked up into his earnest face, so trusting, so sweet, so very hopeful.

You owe me big for this, Moonbeam, she thought, and took Jamie's hand.

Chapter 10

VIOLET WAS JUST TIDYING UP AFTER HER LAST READING of the evening when she heard the front door chime. She looked up to see Chris Abbott standing in the doorway with a self-conscious smile and a small bouquet of tulips.

"So this is where the magic happens," he said, stepping toward her. "Literally, I suppose."

"Hey, Chris! What brings you out here?"

"I was just heading home from the hospital and I realized I'd never actually seen Moonbeam's place of business."

"You always travel with tulips?" she asked, offering what she hoped was a flirtatious smile. "Or did you steal those from one of your patients?"

Chris laughed, flashing a single dimple in his left cheek. "She was out cold, so she'll never miss them."

"I hope you stole her Jell-O, too."

"Absolutely." Still smiling, he handed the tulips to Violet. "Actually, I saw them in the window of the flower shop across the street and thought you might like them. The color reminds me of your eyes."

"In that case, I'm glad they aren't red roses." Violet sniffed them and then felt dumb. *Tulips don't have a smell, do they?*

"Let me find a vase for these," she said. "I'll be right back."

She headed toward the small kitchenette in the corner behind a gauzy curtain and found a little vase she filled with water. As she snipped off the ends of the stems, she glanced back at Chris through the opening in the curtain. He looked very sophisticated, leaning against the counter. Educated and kind and very successful. Exactly the sort of man she'd always pictured herself with. She snipped another tulip stem and silently resolved to do a better job of falling for him. Whatever the hell that entailed.

"So you've never been here before?" Violet called over her shoulder.

"Never visited a psychic at all, if you can believe it. Well, unless you count the palm reader at my sixth-grade school carnival."

"Hey, everyone's gotta start somewhere."

Violet finished arranging the flowers and turned around, parting the curtain as she moved toward the front counter to set the vase down. "I'd offer you a tour, but this is pretty much it. We do readings right here in these chairs, and you can see all the merchandise for sale. Over there is where I do my accounting work."

She looked at Chris, taking in the soft, sandy hair, the warm brown eyes. She felt something stir inside her. Was it lust? Not exactly. Hunger, maybe? She hadn't eaten since breakfast. She smiled up at him.

"Any chance you'd want to go grab Chinese food?"

Chris laughed. "And here I was trying to come up with a creative way to ask you out without seeming like I was assuming you didn't have anything better to do than accept last-minute dinner invitations."

Violet shrugged. "Moonbeam's busy doing a past-life-regression class for a couple of her nurses, and I already painted my toenails last night. I don't have much else going on."

"In that case, I'd love to accompany you. Any place in particular?"

"Fong Chong. You know where it is?"

"No, but I'll drive if you give directions."

"Deal."

Violet took a few moments to lock up before following Chris out to his car. He beeped the locks and opened the passenger door for her.

"Thanks," Violet said, and settled herself into the buttery leather seat. She quickly flipped down the visor and checked her makeup, grateful she'd touched up her lipstick earlier.

Chris got behind the wheel and turned over the engine. Violet gave him a few quick directions and he pointed the car northwest toward Chinatown. Violet watched the old brick buildings slip past, remembering the heady rush of skipping school on a rainy afternoon, biting into a steaming dumpling at her favorite corner table.

"How long did you say you've been in Portland?" Violet asked.

"Almost four years. I guess I haven't been adventurous enough to explore this area. I didn't even know there *was* a Chinatown in Portland."

"You'll love this place. It gets written up in all the travel magazines. It's just a couple blocks from the Portland Classical Chinese Gardens. We could visit there after dinner if you like."

"That sounds nice."

Violet smiled. *Nice*. Exactly. *Nice* was a good thing. "Turn right here on Fourth and just park along the curb.

There's a spot up there, if you don't mind walking a couple blocks."

"I don't mind a bit."

Violet watched as Chris executed the perfect parallel park before getting out and walking around to open her door. They fell into step together, and Violet felt his fingers brush hers. She held her breath, waiting for the tingle to start as he took her hand in his. Her hand was definitely getting warmer. Did that count as tingle?

He held the restaurant door for her and a waitress led them to a small table in the middle of the room before bustling away. Violet watched another server move through the room with a large cart laden with steaming food.

Chris touched her hand. "Tell you what. You're in charge. Just order whatever you think is good."

Violet laughed. "A man who's not afraid to hand over the reins."

She hadn't meant it to sound as suggestive as it did, but Chris just smiled at her and unfolded his napkin in his lap. Violet felt herself relax as the waitress approached with a cart piled with dim sum and a mountain of other delicacies for them to choose from.

Violet began to point out items on the cart. She picked out dumplings filled with shrimp and cabbage, a plate of sautéed broccoli greens, sliced barbecue pork, *shumai*, *dai jee gow*, and several more plates heaped with rice and noodles.

"Wow," Chris said once the waitress had unloaded their chosen plates and wheeled away the half-empty cart. "I have no idea what most of this is, but it looks delicious."

Violet pointed her chopsticks at a pinkish looking dim sum. "That's *har go*—the bay shrimp make it pink.

The ones on the carrots are filled with scallops. I'm not sure what's in that one—"

"I'm sure it's all great," Chris said, and picked up a fork.

Violet reached for her chopsticks and picked up a piece of shrimp, wondering if she should have brought cue cards to keep the conversation flowing. Okay, so things were a little slow. Did that really matter? And did it matter that she didn't want to crawl into his lap and lick soy sauce off his neck? Lust was the last thing she needed clouding her judgment right now.

"So it looks like Moonbeam will get to go home soon," Chris said as he forked up a piece of barbecue pork.

"She'll probably spend a little while in that outpatient-rehab place first. Butterfly—that's Mom's best friend—and I are meeting with the occupational therapist tomorrow to go through the house and decide what furniture needs to be moved around, whether we need any adaptive devices, that sort of thing."

"Your mom is really lucky to have you. Not just the shopping and the hospital visits, but the way you stepped in to keep her business afloat."

"Well, she's my mom. She's nuts, but I love her."

Chris nodded and looked at her thoughtfully. "It can't be easy stepping into someone else's psychic practice and just taking over like that."

If you only knew, Violet thought, and forked up a piece of broccoli. "I'm doing okay."

"Really, it's very admirable. I know Moonbeam appreciates it. And she's so proud of you. She talks about your psychic skills all the time."

Violet set down her chopsticks and picked up her tea,

downing it in two quick gulps. She tried to swallow her unease the same way, but it wasn't working. What was her problem, anyway? First she was annoyed with Drew for his constant teasing, for being such a skeptic about her mom. About *her*.

But now she was feeling irritated at Chris for his fascination with it, for finding all this psychic stuff so damn intriguing.

Honestly, there was no pleasing her.

Violet picked up her chopsticks again, trying to re-focus on the conversation. She was on a date with an eligible doctor. She should be ecstatic.

"So, Chris," Violet said, giving him a pleasant smile. "You said something the other night about wanting to move back East eventually?"

"Absolutely," Chris said, taking a sip of tea. "I like it out here, and the medical community is great, but you know how it is. My parents are getting older, and so I want to be closer to them."

"Sure," Violet said, and felt a sharp pain somewhere around her spleen. She didn't like to think of Moonbeam getting older. In her mind, Moonbeam was still a free-spirited thirtysomething, swathed in tie-dye and holding a picket sign outside a shop selling fur coats.

"So you'd be returning to New Hampshire?" Violet asked.

"Not necessarily. Everything's so close together back East that it doesn't really matter whether I'm in New Hampshire or Rhode Island or Vermont or even upstate New York. I'll still be close enough to visit my parents regularly."

Violet nodded and poked a dumpling with her

chopsticks. "That's one of the things that seemed so funny when I first moved to Maine. It takes eight or nine hours to drive east to west across Oregon, but you can cross most East Coast states in half that time."

"Traffic permitting," Chris added, taking a sip of water.

"True. Actually, the best thing about coming home is that I can see the mountains, the desert, the rain forest, and the beach all in the same state."

Chris gave her a quizzical look. "You still think of Oregon as home?"

Violet stared for a moment, retracing her steps in the conversation. She hadn't realized she'd used that term until just that moment. She took a sip of tea and considered the question. She hadn't lived here for almost twenty years. She'd been so eager to get away after high school, so determined to start her own life as far away from Moonbeam as she could.

Since when had she considered this home?

"Sometimes," Violet said cautiously.

Chris nodded and finished polishing off the barbecue pork. "It's a nice place," he said. "Your mom sure has a great location. I didn't realize until I saw it today that she's in such a nice part of town."

"She's been there for thirty years."

"It's funny, in most places that wouldn't be the case. Psychic studios and strip clubs and adult stores would be out on skid row or something."

Violet laughed. "Welcome to Portland. Or should I say *Porn*land."

"Pornland?"

"It's the running joke here. Oregon has the second-highest concentration of strip clubs in the nation."

"No kidding? What about San Francisco, Reno, Vegas..."

"Nope. We've got 'em beat."

Chris laughed. "You sound so proud."

Violet frowned down at her plate. Did she? That was new. Hadn't she spent most of her adulthood fleeing the odd?

Fortunately, she was saved from having to contemplate that further when a young woman arrived toting a little silver tray topped with two cellophane-wrapped cookies and the check. Chris picked up the latter without comment and held the tray out to Violet.

"You choose," he offered.

Violet shrugged and grabbed the cookie closest to her. She unwrapped it carefully, trying not to break the dainty edges. She split the cookie in half, careful not to get cookie pieces all over her black silk blouse. She unfolded the tiny piece of paper and looked at it.

"'You will get what your heart desires,'" Violet read.

Chris gave her a meaningful look. Violet felt herself flush.

"Interesting," Chris said.

"Oh, please," she said, setting the paper aside. "Who doesn't get what they want at least occasionally?"

"Certainly, but it says what your *heart* desires."

"Whoever writes these things knows exactly how to do it so anyone off the street could think it applies to them."

"The cynical psychic," Chris said with a laugh. "You should put that on business cards."

Violet laughed. "What does yours say?"

Chris cracked open his cookie and brushed the

crumbs into his palm. He deposited them onto his plate before unfolding the little scrap of paper.

"'You will receive a letter from far away,'" he read.

"Going out on a limb with that one," Violet said with a snort. "It's the electronic age. How often do people receive letters from someone in the same town?"

Chris grinned. "I get it. The psychic is threatened by the fortune cookie. Worried it makes the whole fortune-telling business look bad?"

Violet folded her hands together and looked at him. "Of course," she said, forcing a smile. "That's exactly what I'm worried about."

<hr>

It was nearly ten p.m. by the time Chris pulled up to the curb in front of Moonbeam's shop. Violet turned and smiled at him, oddly grateful she'd left her rental car here so she wouldn't have to play out this scene on the front porch of her mother's house.

"I had a really great time, Chris."

"Me too. Thanks for the suggestion."

"Anytime."

"Yeah?"

"Sure. Give me a call."

Violet bent forward and picked up her purse at her feet. When she sat back up, Chris was leaning close with a look that told her to expect more than a kiss on the cheek this time.

"Violet?"

"Hmm?"

"May I kiss you?"

Violet stifled a flicker of annoyance. He was asking

permission? Hardly a sign of great passion. He was so overwhelmed by his desire for her that he paused to make a polite request?

He's a gentleman, Violet scolded herself, and offered an encouraging smile. "Of course."

Chris reached out to cup her chin in his hand. He leaned in and pressed his lips to hers. Violet tried to think of what to do with her hands. Should she run her fingers through his hair? Touch his shoulder?

She tried to relax as his lips moved against hers, soft and obviously skilled. Violet tried to focus on the warm pressure of his fingertips against her shoulder, the pleasant scent of his aftershave. She kissed him back, ignoring the fact that her pulse wasn't pounding. It wasn't as if she needed to have a stroke every time she brushed lips with a man.

When Chris broke the kiss, he smiled down at her. He caressed her arm softly before drawing his hand back. "Good night, Violet."

"Thank you," she said. "I mean… for dinner. Well, for the kiss, too, of course."

Chris laughed. "I had a great time."

"Me too."

"Okay, then. Good night."

Violet stepped out of the car and gave him a little wave before fumbling for her keys. She unlocked the front door to Moonbeam's shop and stepped inside, inhaling the familiar scent of patchouli and candle wax. She turned back to Chris and waved again, letting him know she was safely inside. Then she closed the door behind her.

She didn't turn the lights on right away. She stood

there in the entryway for a moment, absorbing the glow from the lava lamp, listening to the muted throb of music next door. She wondered if Drew was over there. She hadn't been able to figure out his schedule yet, and there were some nights he left Sam in charge and went out on dates.

Was this one of those nights? If it was, who was he with?

"Why should you care?" Violet asked herself aloud, and then felt dumb for talking to herself. It was getting to be a habit. Blame it on Moonbeam.

Against her better judgment, Violet felt herself drifting toward the shared hallway, toward Drew's bar. *Jamie invited me*, she told herself. *He asked me to come tonight. I'm just being friendly with a client.*

But she knew it wasn't Jamie drawing her next door. And the way her pulse was pounding in time to the music didn't feel quite friendly.

She moved quietly through the side door, ready to retreat if one of the bouncers caught her. After all, she hadn't paid the cover charge.

But no one seemed to notice her as she slipped through the hall door and into the noisy bar. She stood there for a moment getting her bearings, absorbing the pulse of loud conversation and louder music. Just a few feet away, a group of women clinked glasses and laughed.

She surveyed the room, noticing the number of women heavily outweighed the men. Even on the evenings there were no performances, it was obvious the place still attracted the female demographic.

No wonder Drew loves it here.

"Hey, Violet!" boomed a voice behind her. Violet

turned to see Jamie striding toward her with a broad smile on his face. "Can I get you a drink?"

"Maybe in a minute or so. The place is packed."

"Yeah, it's been busy a lot lately. Even on nights no one's taking their clothes off."

"That's good."

"I'll go get Mr. Watson for you, okay?"

"You don't need to…"

But Jamie was already gone, disappearing into the sea of bodies and clinking glasses. Violet's hands were sweating a little at the thought of seeing Drew, which was silly. She'd already seen him today. He was the owner of the neighboring business, a friend, an occasional sparring partner, that was all.

A friend who could kiss like a god and had hands like a—

"Violet."

She turned around at the sound of Drew's voice, trying hard to radiate friendliness instead of lust.

But Drew's face wasn't radiating any of those things. In fact, he was practically vibrating with fury. Violet took a step back, her intrigue turning to confusion.

Drew folded his arms over his chest and stared at her coldly. "We need to talk."

"Oh, well I was just going to go home and—"

"Now," he barked, and grabbed her arm.

Chapter 11

DREW MARCHED VIOLET INTO MOONBEAM'S SHOP AND shut the door, making a conscious effort not to slam it behind him. Truth be told, he was angry enough to put his fist through it, but that wasn't going to do him any good.

Because mad as he was, he wanted to kiss Violet a whole lot more than he wanted to hit something. He wanted to tangle his fingers in her hair and feel her moan in his arms as she pressed her body against his. He wanted to bury his face against her neck and inhale the lavender-vanilla scent of her.

He also wanted to scream.

Maybe that's why you're so pissed off. You don't know what the hell you want.

"What is your problem, Drew?" Violet demanded, shaking her arm out of his grip and turning to face him.

He stared at her, wanting to hate her but just… well, wanting her.

That was enough to piss him off.

"Did you have a nice date?" He tried to sound cool and aloof, but just sounded like a jealous jerk.

God, you're bad at this.

Violet folded her arms over her chest and stared at him. "Is that what this is about?"

"No."

Yes, muttered a voice in the back of his head.

Great, now he was hearing voices. He was as bad as Moonbeam and Violet.

Okay, fine, he'd come a little unglued when he glanced outside to check the line at the front door and spotted Violet sucking face with the damn doctor in his damn Mercedes. Sure, it had irked him a little more than it should have. Was there something about her and the front seat of a sedan?

Why do you care?

He didn't. He *didn't* care.

And besides, that wasn't why he was angry.

"Jamie quit," Drew said.

Violet's eyes flew wide. "He what?"

"He quit. Just waltzed into my office after your little psychic reading and gave his notice. Said he needed to chase his dreams, to take risks."

Violet stared at him, unblinking. "I thought his dream was to be a better stripper."

"His dream is to build schools in Afghanistan. Or at least it is now, thanks to you."

"*What?* I never told him to go to a dangerous war zone and—" Violet stopped, struck midsentence by some thought she wasn't about to give voice to.

"Thought of something, did you?" Drew asked.

Violet narrowed her eyes. "I told him to take risks and follow his dreams. There's nothing wrong with that. It's nothing you wouldn't hear in any motivational speech or inspirational eighties glam-rock tune or in a goddamn fortune cookie."

"Well at least we agree on how to rank the validity of your psychic readings."

"What do you want from me, Drew?" she demanded, eyes flashing.

Drew lost his train of thought for a second. Damn Violet and her ridiculous eye color.

Actually, it wasn't so much the color as the—

Focus, man, focus.

Drew cleared his throat, wishing like hell he could snap his fingers to clear the anger before backing her up against her desk and...

"Jamie is a kind, compassionate, fragile guy," he said, fighting to keep his voice steady. "He's afraid of violence. The last place in the world he belongs is a fucking war zone."

"Maybe that's exactly where a kind, compassionate guy belongs, did you think of that?"

Drew gritted his teeth. Yes, he had thought of that. He'd been thinking of that nonstop in between imagining Jamie getting his sappy, happy smile blown off his face by a wayward grenade.

"You can't mess with people's lives like this, Violet."

"Whose life are we talking about now, Drew?"

Drew glared at her. He hadn't told her about Catherine. About what prompted his ex-wife to leave him. Had Moonbeam said something to Violet?

This has nothing to do with that, he told himself.

Drew folded his arms over his chest. "Jamie could be killed. He could get hurt or contract malaria or—"

"Are you this concerned about all your employees? Or just the ones on billboards, the ones who make you the most money?"

Drew felt his temper flare again. *This* was why he was mad, dammit.

"Oh, that's rich," he snapped. "A fake psychic talking to me about the ethics of running a business."

"I'm not—"

"Spare me, Violet."

She shut her mouth, and Drew instantly regretted his tone. Maybe he was being too harsh. Maybe he was just pissed that another fake psychic was screwing with his life.

Or maybe he really *was* pissed about the fact that less than twenty-four hours after locking lips with him in the front seat of the car, she'd been out there sucking face with that damn surgeon.

You're an idiot, Drew's inner voice told him.

He had to agree.

"Look, Violet… I don't want to see Jamie get hurt."

"You think I do?"

"I think you don't have the same compassion—"

"Fuck you, buddy. I have plenty of compassion."

He stared at her. "Let me know when the irony of that statement sinks in."

Violet scowled at him. "What I tell a client in a private reading is none of your business. And what Jamie decides to do in his personal life is also none of your business."

Drew took a deep breath, forcing himself not to yell. "You can sit here playing psychic all you want. You can make up your fake fortunes and pretend we don't both know what you're up to over here. But when you cross the line and start doing harm to my work or to people I care about, then it damn well *is* my business."

Violet opened her mouth to retort, but then shut it again. She seemed to be considering her words carefully. When she finally spoke, her voice was icy.

"I will tell my clients what they need to hear. And I

will do what I need to do to keep my mother's stupid business afloat."

Drew stared at her, his blood pressure rising. "I know you will. And that terrifies the hell out of me."

Violet was still steaming when she returned to her mother's house that night. She spent an hour tidying, preparing for Moonbeam's return home from the hospital. She made sure the sheets were clean and the hallways clutter free so Moonbeam could maneuver in her wheelchair. She poured all her furious energy into mopping floors and washing windows.

She decided it was time to stop when she scrubbed the toilet seat hard enough to leave scratches.

Damn Drew.

"Who the hell does he think he is?" Violet said out loud as she glared at the toilet. She stood up and grabbed a sponge and went to work on the sink with equal vigor.

What had gone wrong? She had been enjoying a perfectly pleasant, warm glow after her date with Chris.

Then Drew had shown up, and suddenly "pleasant" and "warm" just seemed dull. Even in his anger, even when he was being a complete butthead, Drew Watson was the most infuriatingly sexy man she'd ever met.

And even when Violet wanted to pick him up by the ears and shake him, she also wanted to tear his clothes off with her teeth and pin him up against the wall and—

Violet shook off the thought and stood up to rinse her sponge out in the sink. It wasn't quite as easy to shake the tingly, irritatingly captivating lust buzz that had seized hold of her.

How the hell had he gotten under her skin like that?

Violet set the sponge on the edge of the sink and looked at herself in the mirror. She was wild-eyed and flushed and looked a little crazed. She had to get a grip.

This was dangerous terrain, she knew. Why the hell had she confessed to being a fake psychic that night? And why the hell had Drew remembered? Couldn't he have just written it off as drunken rambling?

Drew had the power to single-handedly dismantle the quiet, normal life she'd built for herself. To ruin Moonbeam's business by shouting from the rooftops about this damn fake psychic ploy.

She had to stay away from him. It was that simple.

Violet was still muttering to herself when the phone rang. She thought of Chris as she ran for the phone, and she told herself to make her voice pleasant, happy.

Then she thought of Drew and just felt like snarling.

But then she remembered the feel of his hand on her thigh, his tongue on her throat, and she wanted to whimper.

By the time she answered on the third ring, Violet was feeling vocally bipolar.

"Hello?" she said in a tone she hoped was neutral but probably just sounded deranged.

"Honey, is that you? You sound like your extrasensory energy is all out of whack."

"Hi, Mom. My extrasensory energy is just fine. Why are you still awake?"

"Oh, I just finished up with my past-life-regression class and I realized that I forgot to tell you that the occupational therapist stopped by earlier today. She wanted me to tell you she's going to be about an hour late for your appointment with her tomorrow."

Violet frowned as she peeled off her cleaning gloves and flopped onto the sofa. "Why didn't she just call and tell me herself?"

"She offered to, but I told her I was going to talk to you anyway and she didn't want to interrupt you in the middle of a reading or your date with Dr. Abbott or—"

"How did you know I had a date with Dr. Abbott?"

"Violet, honey, I'm clairvoyant."

Violet rolled her eyes. "He must have stopped by the hospital to do rounds after we ate."

Moonbeam made a little snort of annoyance, but didn't argue. "Did your date go well, dear?"

"Very well, thank you."

"Did you sleep with him?"

"Mom!"

"Well, honey, sexual energy is a very beautiful and natural thing, so—"

"I'm going to hang up if you start in on your tantric sex lecture again."

Moonbeam gave an impatient sigh. "I just think the sexual act is a sacred ritual, don't you?"

Violet gritted her teeth. "Whatever, Mom. I haven't been engaging in any sacred rituals lately, not that it's any of your business."

"Really? Are the physical alpha body and the spiritual energies not achieving harmonic convergence in this union?"

"I don't even know what that means."

"Just that when you allow a man to enter your sacred circle, then your inner radiance should—"

"Mom, *please*."

They were both quiet for a moment. Violet was the first to speak. "Why are you so hung up on my sex life, anyway?"

"Just a feeling I have, dear."

"Did Chris say something?"

"Violet, honey, your aura just seems a little—"

"Does he think I'm not physically attracted to him?"

"Well I was reading your energy, and I have the distinct sense that—"

"Is this because the kissing wasn't crazy passionate? I mean, it's often awkward the first time or two, that's not a big deal. Nothing to be worried about. Is he worried? Did he say he was worried?"

"Darling—"

"Because I don't want him to think I'm not hot for him. I'm totally hot for him. I *am*."

"Violet—"

"Just because I'm not panting with lust every time I see him doesn't mean anything at all. I think he's very attractive. He's a doctor, for chrissakes, and he's nice and smart and I'd jump him right now, as a matter of fact."

"Of course you would, honey."

Violet fell silent, suddenly aware of the trap she'd walked into. "That's how you do it, isn't it?"

"What's that, dear?"

"How you get people to volunteer too much information so they think you're being psychic, but really it's just them doing the work for you."

Moonbeam was quiet for a moment. "Are you feeling all right? You sound a little strange."

Violet closed her eyes and sighed. "There's no such

thing as a psychic. I thought there was something going on with the music, but that's stupid. There's no way. It's a ridiculous idea, isn't it?"

"You know there's no such thing as a ridiculous idea. If you sense there's some sort of cosmic connection between you and Drew and these musical selections, then I think you should—"

"Forget it, Mom. Really, I'm sure it's nothing."

Moonbeam was quiet for a moment. "Are you sure you're okay, Violet?"

"Fine. I'm fine, Mom. Just tired." *And really, really confused.*

"How is Drew, anyway?" Moonbeam asked. "Has he gotten smarter about the women he's dating and realized he needs someone who stimulates him intellectually as well as physically?"

The thought of stimulating Drew sent Violet's brain reeling in a dangerous direction, but she cleared her throat and ignored the throb of hormones in her veins. "I have no idea. I'm really not interested in who Drew dates."

"Of course you're not, dear. That's probably for the best. He still hasn't forgiven me for that thing with his ex-wife. I hope he's not taking that out on you."

Violet frowned. "What thing with Drew's ex-wife?"

There was a long pause on the other end of the line. "He hasn't mentioned it?"

"Mentioned what?"

"Nothing, dear. It doesn't matter."

"Mom!"

Moonbeam sighed. "It was just a silly little situation a few years ago. Drew's wife was a lawyer. Very career driven. Of course I had never met her, since she never came around his bar... not that I blame her, such an atrocious exploitation of—"

"Mom."

"Right. Well, anyway, Catherine came to see me for a reading on the future of her marriage. I could tell she was unhappy and really questioning, so I suggested that—"

"Oh, shit," Violet said, realization dawning. "You told Drew's wife to leave him?"

"Violet, you know a psychic never tells a client what actions to take, and anyway, I didn't *know* she was his wife at the time."

Violet shook her head and clenched the phone tighter. "No wonder he's so upset about the thing with Jamie. It's not about Jamie at all."

"What's that, honey?"

"Nothing." Violet picked up a couch cushion and hugged it to her chest, trying to stop her head from swimming. She looked down at the pillow and remembered throwing it at his head the other night.

I have to stop getting so pissed at him.

"Violet, honey, are you okay?"

"I'm fine, Mom. Look, tomorrow is the day Frank shows up to have a word with me. Any advice?"

"There's nothing to worry about, dear. I'm certain our curse worked."

Violet gritted her teeth. "I'm sure it did, but maybe we should have a backup plan?"

"Like what?"

"I don't know. What if he tries to kick you out of the building or ruin your reputation or—"

"Oh, Violet. You worry too much."

"Mom," Violet said, struggling to hold her temper. "The man who owns the building in which you've built your entire business is royally pissed at me. This doesn't concern you?"

"Of course it concerns me, dear. I just know that everything is in good hands."

Violet closed her eyes and sighed, wishing like hell it were true.

Across town at the bar, Drew was having a slightly less restful evening.

The music was throbbing more loudly than usual, or maybe it was just his head. He normally enjoyed the pulse of the music, the hum of conversation, but tonight it just reminded him of a migraine.

A dreadlocked woman dressed in a bright orange caftan shouted for another round of drinks. Drew watched, recognizing a few of Moonbeam's buddies. Sam shoved an empty tray at him.

"Your turn with the hippie chicks," she said. "Are they part of that place next door?"

"Friends of hers, I think."

"Thought so. They had a couple of gift cards for a free cover charge. They said it was a present from Moonbeam."

Drew frowned at her. "Moonbeam gave them free passes?"

Sam frowned back. "You gave Moonbeam free passes?"

"I do it every week as a joke," Drew said with a shrug. "She gets mad and tears them up and lectures me about dishonoring the spiritual and physical body. It's our fun little ritual."

"If that's your idea of fun, you need to get out more. Speaking of which, you've been slowing down on the bimbos lately. What gives?"

"I'm pacing myself."

"Right," Sam said, shaking her head. "And Violet's just a friend."

Before Drew could snap off a clever comeback, she began piling drinks on the tray. "Here. Take this over to them. Greyhounds all around. If they ask, the juice is organic. And watch out for the blonde, she's a grabber."

Drew scowled at the table. Why the hell would Moonbeam send her friends in here? She hated him, hated his business.

Didn't she?

He sighed and carried the tray over to the table. "Good evening, ladies," he called as he began passing the drinks around. "How are you all doing?"

"Hey, I know you!" squealed the older woman at the end of the table, pointing a finger at Drew. "You're the owner!"

Drew squinted down the table at her, recognizing her as the woman who'd come in with Violet first night. Was that only a week ago?

"Butterfly, right?" Drew asked tentatively.

"That's right!" she said, beaming happily up at him. "These are my friends Sage, Petal, Harmony, Quinn, and Oat. This is Drew. He's the gay owner."

Drew gritted his teeth. "Actually, I'm not—"

"The manager, then. Whatever."

"No," Drew said with exaggerated patience. "I own the place, and I'm not gay. Seriously, I'm going to get a tattoo that says that."

"I can do it!" piped a perky blonde in a crocheted halter top, wearing a big crystal around her neck. "I work at a tattoo parlor part-time. Want me to schedule you an appointment?"

Drew paused for a moment to appreciate the pleasant bouncing going on under the halter top. "Um, thanks. Some other time, maybe."

"Are you really straight?" she pressed. "Moonbeam said you were straight, but Butterfly said you weren't."

"I'm straight. Really and truly 100 percent..." Drew frowned. "Why was Moonbeam talking about me?"

The girl shrugged. "Maybe you'd like to go out sometime."

"Aren't you already out?"

"Out with me, silly. On a date. With sex and stuff."

Butterfly smiled at the exchange. "Petal is very open with her natural sexual energies," she said proudly. "She's also a nude model."

"For sculptors," Petal declared. "*Artists*."

"Okay," Drew said, backing away a little. "Are you ladies having a good evening?"

Butterfly offered a broad smile. "Oh, we're having so much fun. That man over there gave me a very nice lap dance."

Drew peered in the direction she was pointing and sighed. "He doesn't work here. That's a customer. And this isn't one of the nights we feature male entertainers, so you really shouldn't be getting lap dances from anyone."

Butterfly waved a dismissive hand. "It's all part of the experience."

"Right," Drew said. "Well, looks like you're all set

with the drinks. I'm heading out, so if you need anything else, just wave at Sam or Jamie."

"Where are you going?" Petal chirped, jostling pleasantly under that flimsy top.

"Home to watch ESPN in my underwear."

"Boxers or briefs?"

"Yes."

"Can I come with you?"

Petal smiled, her eyes wide in her pixie face. She had a dainty floral tattoo around her bicep, and her arms were toned and attractive. Her blonde hair curled wildly around her ears, and she was definitely braless under that top.

Drew waited for his blood to heat up. There was a little percolation, but no boiling...

"What the hell, why not," Drew muttered.

"That's the spirit!" Petal said, and hopped up out of her seat. "Let's go!"

------※------

There was no way Drew was taking Petal to his house. That much he knew. He was willing to take her out for a drink, maybe go back to her place if things went well.

But if they didn't go well, he had the sense Petal was the sort of girl to cut his boxers into tiny scraps while he was still wearing them.

He drove in silence while Petal sat in the passenger seat, sending text messages on a cell phone dotted with daisies.

What are you doing, idiot? Drew asked himself.

Same thing I've done for years, he answered silently. *Going out with an attractive woman who throws herself at me at the bar.*

Drew frowned, annoyed to discover that his new-found inner voice was now having conversations with itself. That was almost as irritating as the realization that he really had very little interest in sleeping with Petal. Not even her hand sliding up his thigh was causing him to have thoughts more lecherous than wondering if he should stop for fuel at the next Chevron.

He shook his head and gripped the steering wheel tighter. This is what he needed to do. He had to get his mind off Violet. He had to get back to his routine, to his habit of meaningless sex with women who wanted nothing from him except a good time. Women who were *not* high-strung, who wouldn't try to control his life or—

"Where are we going?" Petal asked from the passenger seat.

"Doug Fir Lounge. It's a nice little bar just down the road a bit. Good music."

"You own a bar, but we're going to another one?"

"Sometimes it's nice to visit a bar I'm not paying for."

Petal seemed to mull that over as Drew pulled his car into the parking lot at Doug Fir. He killed the engine and got out, ready to walk around and open her door for her.

Petal scowled and flung her door open, narrowly missing his gonads. Drew jumped back.

"I am a liberated, independent woman and I can open my own door."

"By all means," Drew said, stepping aside.

"I can open the door to the bar, too."

"Hey, knock yourself out."

She flounced ahead of him and grabbed the handle of the bar's front door. Then she turned and threw him a coy smile over her bare shoulder. "I do give great blow jobs, though. I'm not too liberated for that."

"Can I maybe get a drink first?"

Petal laughed and heaved the door open. Drew followed, wondering why the hell he continued to do this.

You're trying to forget about Violet, he reminded himself. *And your ex-wife, too, while you're at it*.

Petal hopped onto a barstool and patted the one beside her as a stoic-looking bartender ambled over, wearing a black shirt.

"I'd like a screwdriver, but only if the orange juice is organic," Petal informed him.

"Cherry Coke," Drew said.

Petal frowned at him. "No alcohol?"

"Not often."

"Recovering alcoholic?"

"Nope. Just someone who believes in keeping his wits about him at all times."

"Control freak?"

"No."

Petal smiled and grabbed his crotch under the bar. "Nice," she declared.

Drew slid back on his stool and reached down to relocate her hand to his knee. "How about we talk a little first. So you're a tattoo artist?"

Petal shrugged. "Sometimes. And a nude model. And I do some weaving, too."

"That's very… interesting."

Petal grinned again and slid her hand back up his thigh.

As the bartender set their drinks in front of them, Drew took a big sip and considered the situation. He had a beautiful girl who was practically inviting him to fornicate with her on the bar, with no strings attached. A month ago, he would have jumped at the chance.

Well, maybe not the sex on the bar, but the rest of it would have been appealing. Lord knew there had been plenty of women like Petal, women with no interest in long-term commitment or running his life or obsessing over her career path or his.

What the hell is my problem?

"What the hell is your problem?" Petal asked beside him.

He looked up at her, startled. "What?"

"I asked you three times what kind of music you like."

"Oh. All kinds. Eighties butt rock mostly, but I listen to just about everything."

"You want to dance?"

"I prefer to leave that to the professionals."

"Party pooper."

"Pretty much," Drew agreed, taking another sip of his drink.

She looked at him. "You have nice eyes."

"Thank you."

"Did anyone ever tell you look like that one movie star? What's his name… wait, don't tell me."

"John Cusack?" Drew said and took another sip of his drink.

Petal frowned. "No. Brad Pitt. Or maybe Tom Cruise."

Drew stared at her. "No. I've never heard that one before."

Petal shrugged and quietly sipped her screwdriver. When the bartender returned to ask if they wanted a re-fill, Petal pulled out her wallet and began counting bills.

"I'm getting this round," she insisted as she peeled money out of an array of tiny pockets covering the wallet.

"I believe in paying my way. There's no reason a man should always be in charge financially, right? Hold on a second, I know I've got a twenty in here somewhere."

She tucked a couple bills between her teeth as she bent down to grab her purse, pawing through another series of pockets. Drew sipped the last of his drink as he watched her.

"You know, you really shouldn't put cash in your mouth," he said. "One of those bills might have been in someone's butt crack."

She stared at him. Slowly, she removed the cash from between her teeth. "I beg your pardon?"

Drew shrugged. "I'm just saying. You think of these things when you're in the business I'm in."

She frowned. "Are you always this charming?"

"I try."

Petal finally found the cash she was looking for and handed it over to the bartender. The bartender retreated and returned with their drinks a moment later. Drew thanked him and held up the glass in a mock toast to Petal.

"Thanks for this," he said.

"No problem," she said, surveying the bar, probably looking for someone more fun than he was. The way he was feeling at the moment, that wouldn't be tough.

She had a good point about the charm thing, he mused. He was hardly in top form tonight. It was all Violet's fault. She'd gotten under his skin, pissed him off, ruined his whole evening, really.

Maybe he should just blame everything on Violet. The fact that Jamie was quitting, that his landlord was taking a peculiar interest in the market value of his building, the fact that he was suddenly too distracted to take home a perfectly willing, perfectly lovely young woman.

It was all Violet's fault. Of course.

Stop thinking about Violet, he told himself.

"Ohmygod, I love this song!" Petal shrieked, grabbing his arm and making him slosh his drink down his sleeve. "Dance with me. Please? Just this once."

Drew frowned down at his spilled soda. "I don't dance."

"But you own a stripper dance club."

"It's a bar. It just happens to feature male entertainers two nights a week."

"Come on, just once? I'll teach you."

He looked up at the speakers and frowned some more. "Is something wrong with that speaker over there?"

"Just one dance… it's my favorite song."

"I've never heard it," Drew said, mopping the spilled soda with a napkin. "Who is this, anyway?"

"Coldplay. The lead singer is married to Gwyneth Paltrow."

"Who?"

Petal sighed in exasperation. "The song is called 'Violet Hill,' and if you don't get out there and dance with me right now—"

Drew felt all the blood drain from his face. "What did you say?"

"I said if you don't dance with me right now—"

"No, the song. The name of the song."

"'Violet Hill.'"

Drew stared at her. Slowly he thunked his glass down on the bar.

"Any chance I could get some bourbon in this?"

Chapter 12

VIOLET WAS SITTING ON THE SOFA WATCHING A NATURE special on TV when the doorbell rang. She glanced at her watch, frowning. It was almost midnight. Who the hell rang a doorbell at midnight?

Probably not a burglar, but she wasn't taking any chances. She looked around the room for something to serve as a weapon. Spotting an umbrella in the corner, she picked it up and carried it like a sword to the front door.

"Who is it?" she called, gripping her umbrella in one hand as she flipped on the porch light with the other.

"Drew Watson," replied a voice that sounded familiar enough, but strangely sluggish. "Drew. Watson, I mean. In case you know a lot of other Drews. I'm the one you were straddling in the front seat of a Toyota a couple nights ago. I'm not sure if that narrows it down, but you don't have to call me by my first and last name. Just Drew is fine…"

Violet swung the door open and stared at him. He was leaning lopsided against the deck rail, his eyes half-closed, a funny smile on his face.

"Drew?"

"Hey, Violet. It's raining."

"It's Portland. It's always raining."

"Inside?"

"What?"

He nodded at her umbrella. "If you can make it rain

indoors, I take back every skeptical thing I ever said about your magical powers."

She studied him cautiously, noticing he looked even more disheveled than normal. His hair was damp and spiky, and his shirt was buttoned crookedly. One shoe was untied, and he was rubbing a hand over the thick beard stubble on his left cheek.

He'd never looked hotter.

Violet swallowed hard, trying to tamp down the lust she felt bubbling in her belly. "Have you been drinking?"

He grinned. "Perhaps."

The word came out sounding more like *prahapsh*, so Violet had her answer right there. "You didn't drive here, did you?"

"Course not. My date dropped me off."

"You had a date?" Violet said slowly. "And you asked her to drop you off *here*?"

"She lives two blocks that way," he said, pointing. He frowned and pointed the other direction. "That way. She left my car over there and I walked her home. Then I came back here to say hello to you." He grinned drunkenly. "Hello."

Violet shook her head, trying not to feel flattered. A drunk guy turning up on her doorstep after a date with another woman was hardly a turn-on. Why the hell was her heart slamming against her ribs like some sort of defective power tool?

Drew cleared his throat. "May I come in?"

"That sounds like an epically bad idea, under the circumstances."

"Right. So can I come in?"

Violet bit her lip, considering. She really didn't want

him to drive. And she was pretty sure she could keep from touching him or crawling into his lap or—

"I'm going to start kissing you every time you do that," he said.

"What?"

"Biting your lip. It's the least I can do to keep you from damaging the most perfect mouth on the face of the planet. Not that I've carefully inspected all mouths to reach this conclusion, but I wouldn't mind spending a bit more time becoming more acquainted with—"

"No kissing," Violet said, stepping back from the door. "But you can come in for a minute. Only because I want you to sober up and tell me what you're doing on my doorstep at midnight, smelling like bourbon and cherry Coke."

"Fair enough," he said, and brushed past her on his way inside. He paused to kick off his shoes in the entryway, and Violet considered that he probably wasn't completely hammered if he was clearheaded enough to remember to remove his shoes.

She watched as he wove a crooked path en route to the living room. He flopped onto the sofa and turned to smile at her. Violet felt her heart clench as he patted the seat beside him.

"You planning to stand there all night, holding the door open?"

She shook her head, still stunned to see him here in Moonbeam's house. *Again*. She shut the door and padded toward the kitchen, where she pulled a glass out of the cupboard and filled it with water.

"Good memories on this sofa," Drew called as Violet retrieved two aspirins from the cabinet over the sink. "Need another calf massage?"

Violet trudged toward the living room, where she handed him the water and aspirin before sitting down beside him. He took both without comment, draining the water in two big gulps. Then he set the glass down and looked at her.

"Thank you."

"You're welcome. Why are you here, Drew? Your date—"

"Wasn't really a date. Not a serious one, anyway. I didn't sleep with her, if that's what you're asking."

"I wasn't asking," Violet replied, ignoring the flutter of relief in her chest.

"Are you sleeping with the doctor?"

"Are we really having this conversation?"

"Should we?" Drew looked at her a moment, then shook his head. "Never mind. None of my business, right?"

He glanced away, then frowned at the television. "What the hell are you watching?"

She followed his gaze to the TV screen, where two porcupines were engaged in an enthusiastic act of copulation.

"It's a special on unusual mating rituals in the animal kingdom."

"Is that your idea of porn?"

She smiled in spite of herself. "It's fascinating."

"I'm certain it is. Is this how you acquire so much random trivia?"

"I've been learning a lot. Did you know that female hyenas have a pseudopenis?"

"A what?"

"A fake penis. It's basically an enlarged clitoris the hyena can erect at will. In order to mate, the smaller, meeker male has to insert his real penis into it and—"

"This may be the hottest thing a woman has ever said to me."

She laughed. "If you came here to seduce me, you're not off to a very good start."

"That's actually not why I came here," he said, sounding surprisingly sober as he sat up straighter. "I came to apologize. For yelling at you earlier today. And for grabbing you. Well, I'm actually not that sorry about grabbing you, but the yelling... that was bad."

Violet swallowed and resisted the urge to reach out and touch his arm. "It's okay."

"No it's not. I can be kind of a hothead sometimes, but I shouldn't have gotten so angry. I'm sorry."

"I'm sorry, too," Violet said slowly. "My mom told me about your ex-wife, so I understand now why you reacted the way you did about Jamie."

Drew frowned. "What are you talking about?"

"I just thought... well, I thought maybe that's part of the reason you're so upset about Jamie. About any psychic conferring with someone close to you. Telling them something you don't want them to hear."

Drew closed his eyes and leaned back against the sofa. Violet watched warily, wondering if she'd said the wrong thing. Wondering if he was going to fall asleep or pass out. Maybe she should just cover him with a blanket. Maybe she should call him a cab. Or maybe she should give him a quick kiss on the forehead and—

"My wife didn't leave me because of a psychic reading," Drew said, opening his eyes. "My wife left me because it was a lousy marriage and we were lousy for each other. She just happened to beat me to the door."

"Oh," Violet said.

"I knew when I caught myself thinking Jamie was the best part of the whole union that the marriage was probably doomed. Catherine just figured it out faster than I did."

Drew held her eyes for a moment and Violet felt her breath catch in her throat. From the corner of her eye, she saw him start to lift his hand. Then he stopped, dropping it back in his lap, and Violet couldn't help but wonder if he'd intended to touch her. His eyes still held hers, the electric blue of them reminding her of the sapphire ring Moonbeam used to wear.

She broke the gaze first. "You need more water."

She grabbed his glass and stood shakily, feeling his eyes on her as she stumbled toward the kitchen again. In the background, the television droned on.

"The bonobo is a species of great ape, also known as Pan paniscus. *Sexual relations play a significant role in bonobo society, with sexual acts used as a form of greeting, a means of conflict resolution, and in exchange for food."*

Violet glanced at the refrigerator. "Can I get you anything to eat?"

"Will I have to exchange sex for it?"

"What?"

"Like a bonobo. Not that I'm protesting. It actually seems like a pretty good arrangement."

"I didn't mean—"

"I know, Violet. I was kidding. I'm fine. Come back and sit down."

Violet glanced at the bottle of Pinot Noir on the counter and thought about grabbing a glass for herself.

"Bonobos have been observed tongue kissing,

engaging in face-to-face copulation, participating in mutual masturbation, and performing oral sex on members of…"

"You can change the channel if you want," Violet called.

"Why would I want to change the channel? This is the best thing I've seen all month."

Definitely no wine, Violet thought. She flushed and gripped Drew's water glass in one hand before trudging slowly to the living room and handing it to him.

"Thank you."

"You're welcome."

He took a small sip and set the glass aside. Then he looked at her again. "Violet, we should talk."

She looked down at her hands and swallowed. "If it's something serious, do you think it should wait until you're sober?"

"I'm not drunk. I am very lightly buzzed, and that's only because you're everywhere—at the bar, on my dates, on my stereo. I can't get you out of my head."

Violet started to bite her lip again, then stopped. She flicked her eyes to the TV, where a pair of snails were circling each other in a flirtatious fashion.

"Though snails have both male and female sexual organs, they do not self-fertilize. Snails' genitalia are located on their necks, behind their eye stalks."

She glanced back at Drew, who was grinning broadly.

He reached up and skimmed a finger behind her ear. "Does that mean we've had sex?"

"What?"

"I was kissing your neck the other night," he said. "In a snail's world—"

"We should stop."

"We aren't doing anything."

Violet closed her eyes and concentrated very hard on her breathing. Slow and steady, not wild and lust fueled or frantic and passionate. *Nice and easy.*

"You're not my type," she said. "And I'm not your type. This is a bad idea."

She opened her eyes to see Drew still grinning at her.

"Is that why you're touching me?" he asked.

She looked down to see that she was, in fact, gripping his thigh through his jeans. She wasn't sure how it had happened, but seeing her fingers fixed around that denim-clad muscle didn't do much to make her want to draw her hand away.

"The argonaut, or paper nautilus, is a species of octopus with a highly divergent sexual dimorphism. While females can reach four inches, with shells spanning eighteen inches, the male of the species is only three-quarters of an inch long."

"Poor guy," Drew murmured, not looking at the TV. "Size matters. Or so I'm told."

Violet felt her stomach clench, remembering the feel of his erection pressed into her palm through his jeans when she'd touched him in his car the other night.

Based on her cursory examination, Drew Watson had nothing to worry about in that department. It also said something about the old wives' tale about the correlation between the size of a man's hands and the size of—

"The male argonaut has a special tentacle known as a hectocotylus. He uses his hectocotylus to produce a ball of spermatozoa, and when he encounters a female of the species, he detaches the hectocotylus to swim toward the female and…"

"So he removes his dick and sends it to her," Drew mused, sliding his hand over Violet's and holding it in place on his thigh. "Convenient."

Violet licked her lips. "Seems like that would defeat the purpose."

"Depends on the purpose you have in mind."

"Did you know that most snakes have two penises, also known as hemipenes?"

"Is this supposed to be turning me on? Because it kind of is."

"You'd be turned on by an armchair."

"If you were sitting in it, yes."

Violet flushed. "Drew, I don't think we should—"

Her protest was silenced by Drew's mouth moving over hers. She kissed him back, not remembering anymore why she wanted to protest in the first place.

Somehow, she found herself crawling on top of him, straddling him the way she had the other night in his car. She was wearing thin cotton shorts this time and panties under that, but she could still feel every inch of him straining against the fly of his jeans.

His hands slid around her back and he pulled her hard against him. Violet whimpered at the feel of her breasts pressed into his chest. She moved her hips, grinding against him, reveling in the feel of all that hardness between her legs.

"The Lake Duck can be found in Argentina and has the longest penis of any bird species. When a female attempts to escape from a drake's amorous efforts, the drake can use his corkscrew-shaped penis to lasso the female…"

"Oh, God," Violet murmured as she ground harder

against Drew. He laughed and began to kiss his way down her throat.

"It's only fair to warn you that I'm pretty sure the lasso thing is outside the realm of my capability—"

"Shut up, Drew."

"Right."

He kissed her again and slid his hands under her shirt. She wasn't wearing a bra—just the ridiculously useless shelf bra in the cami top—and his hands found their way under the elastic in no time at all. Violet gasped as the tips of his fingers grazed her nipples. She kissed him harder, tasting bourbon and cherry Coke and something she thought was desire.

She twisted her fingers in his hair, loving the soft disarray of it, the idea of rumpling him more than he already was. She slid her palms around to savor the roughness of stubble on his cheeks. Her neck already felt raw from beard burn, but the rawness of it just excited her more.

So did Drew's tongue, making a slow descent down her throat, her collarbones, the tops of her breasts. He used his chin to nudge one strap down on her top, freeing her left breast.

"Oh, God," she cried as his mouth found her nipple. She ground herself harder against him and felt Drew lift his hips in response, pressing against her.

He drew back slightly. "Isn't this where we were the other night? You on my lap, grinding against me? I believe your exact words were—"

"Fuck me."

"Yes."

"Now."

Drew looked in her eyes and smiled. He opened his mouth to say something.

"Screeeeeeeeeeeeeeeeeeeeeeeech!"

Violet blinked and sat back.

Drew winced. "Is that some sort of animal mating call?"

They both craned their necks to see the television.

"Screeeeeeeeeeeeeeeeeeeeeeeech!"

"What the—?"

"This is a test of the Emergency Broadcast System. This is only a test. If this had been an actual emergency…"

Violet fumbled for the remote control and flipped the mute button. Then she looked at Drew. He was wild-eyed and disheveled and so damn hot, her body ached.

He was also the last thing in the world she needed right now. What the hell was she thinking?

She sat back a little farther and swallowed. "We should stop."

He blinked at her. "Are you crazy?"

"No, but you're drunk."

"I'm definitely not—"

"And I'm seeing someone."

"I don't—"

"So are you, right? You said it yourself, you were just on a date."

"I hardly think… Where are you going?"

"To bed," she said as she slid off his lap and stood up. "*Alone*. You're welcome to sleep on the sofa so you don't have to drive. There are blankets in that chest over there, and you can use the bathroom around the corner to wash up."

She was talking too fast, like a crazy person, and

that's certainly how he was looking at her. But she had to get out. She needed to escape, to get herself back on solid ground. *Normal* ground.

He stared at her with an incredulous expression. "You're not really going to—"

"Good night, Drew."

She took two steps back, every inch of her body aching with the need to touch him again.

But this was for the best. She knew it was. She turned away.

"Violet, wait."

But she was already up the stairs, closing her bedroom door behind her, twisting the lock into place. She stared at the knob a moment, struck by the irony.

She wasn't worried about locking Drew out.

She needed to lock herself in.

Drew sat in stunned silence for at least three minutes.

Then he waited another ten to see if Violet would come skipping back down the stairs with her clothes off and her head back in the game.

No sign of Violet. He'd heard the sound of running water for a few minutes, and wondered if she might have taken a cold shower.

He could damn sure use one.

Drew rubbed his hands over his face and tried to regain his balance. What the hell had happened?

You drank too much at the bar and showed up on the doorstep of a woman who doesn't want to date you. Way to go, Einstein.

Drew shook his head, noticing the dizziness had

almost completely worn off. He'd only had two drinks at the bar, really not that much. True, it probably hit him a bit harder than most guys, since he didn't drink a lot, but that didn't mean he wasn't fully in control of his words and actions.

He glanced at the television, where one giraffe was gallantly bumping the other's backside with its head. Then the pair began a mating ritual that couldn't possibly be romantic, even in the giraffe world. He stared, fascinated, until the amorous twosome finished.

Then he looked down at the coffee table. It was covered with neatly aligned printouts of spreadsheets and three pencils in a tidy row. A glass of water sat perfectly centered on a coaster. A leather briefcase was propped on a nearby shelf, shiny and polished and exactly like the one Catherine used to carry.

Get out! screamed a voice in his head.

Dammit. Violet was right.

He stood up, aware of the blood making the slow return trip to his brain after spending some time in more pleasant places. He wasn't the least bit drunk now, not anymore. He was sober and clearheaded and perfectly aware of his need to get the hell out of this house before there was no turning back.

For either of them.

Chapter 13

THE NEXT DAY AT THREE O'CLOCK, VIOLET WAS READY to jump out of her skin. She had been pacing the same spot in the psychic studio so fiercely that she had to check to see if she'd worn a groove in the carpet.

When the door opened, Violet wasn't sure whether to scream or cry at the sight of Drew.

"You're not Frank," she said.

Drew looked down at himself, considering. "Nope," he said, looking back up at her. "'Fraid not."

"Frank's coming in to talk to me, and he's already five minutes late and I'm completely freaking out because—"

"Frank's always late, unless he's coming to pick up the rent check. Then he's early. Sit down a minute. I want to talk to you."

Violet folded her arms over her chest and tried not to notice her hands were shaking. "If this is about last night, I don't want to argue."

"I don't want to argue, either. You were right. We shouldn't be sleeping together. It's a bad idea."

"Oh," Violet said, annoyed to feel the sting of disappointment. "Of course I'm right."

"I mean, hell, we've known each other a week?"

"Right."

"And we've been at each other's throats for most of that time."

"True," she said, hating how much she wanted to

disagree, despite the fact that he was making the exact point she'd tried to make the night before.

"I'm the opposite of what you want, you're the opposite of what I want, and the whole thing is a really bad idea."

"Is this supposed to be making me feel better?"

Drew grinned. "Hey, if you want to feel better—"

"Stop," she said, not really wanting him to. "By the way, I'm sorry about Jamie quitting. That really wasn't my intent."

Drew nodded once and cleared his throat. "Jamie needs to do what makes Jamie happy."

"So you're okay with him leaving?"

"Of course not. Hey, I'm still pissed that what you told Jamie might potentially put him in danger. And I'm also pissed that I'm losing my top entertainer, plus he's sort of family—"

"But if this is what he wants to do with his life—"

Drew held up his hand. "I know. Look, I don't agree with the whole fake psychic hocus-pocus, but Jamie is a grown-up who can make his own decisions. And this seems like something he wants to do."

Violet nodded. "Thank you. I'm glad you see it that way."

"Oh, don't get me wrong. I still think you're full of crap and I don't like you messing with people's lives. That's a lousy way to make a buck, if you want my honest opinion. But I do think that in this particular situation, Jamie probably needed a nudge to do something new."

Violet sighed "You couldn't have just stopped with the apology?"

"Nope. Sorry. We can agree to disagree on this." He

grinned at her, giving Violet the urge to agree to just about anything he might suggest. Bending her over the desk, for instance, or sliding his hands up her torso to unhook her bra and—

"Fine. Fine, whatever." Violet glanced at her watch, distracted again. "Where is Frank? Why is he late? Do you think he's bringing a lawyer?"

"Driving. Because he's an inconsiderate prick. No."

"What?"

"Just answering your questions. In the order you asked them."

Violet frowned, trying to remember what she'd asked. "So no lawyer?"

"I doubt it. But just in case, I'm retreating back to my cave now."

"Afraid of lawyers?"

"Hell, yes. Terrified. I was married to one, remember?"

"Right. Good to see you're moving past that."

"Maybe with some quality counseling from a fake psychic healer—"

"Go!" Violet ordered without venom as she pointed at the door. "I don't mock you in your place of business."

"No, but your mother does. And then she sends her crazy friends in to hit on me."

She frowned at him. "What are you talking about?"

"Your mom. She gave free passes to Butterfly and a whole bunch of her new-agey friends last night. They all came by last night and spent the evening in there, drinking entirely too many greyhounds. I take it you weren't privy to that plan?"

Violet frowned, trying to figure out what the hell Moonbeam was up to now. "That's weird."

"So is your mother, but I choose not to judge. Look, I've gotta get back to the... to my... Hell, I don't have anything going on. I'm just hoping to avoid Frank. Good luck with that, okay?"

"Okay," Violet said, puzzling over his words as she watched him retreat.

She was still staring at the door after he'd vanished. Why would Moonbeam send her friends to Drew's bar, especially when she was so opposed to it? That made no sense at all.

She didn't have long to ponder it, as the front door chimed to announce a visitor. Violet snapped to attention and watched as a middle-aged bald man came marching through the front door. He was tanned, muscular, and so obviously full of himself that Violet half expected him to throw his shoe up on the counter and ask her to shine it.

Instead, he reached up and scratched his neck. Hard. And with all the tact of a highland gorilla. She tried to look away, but couldn't help but notice the weird growth just below his ear. What the hell?

When he finally stopped scratching, he looked at her without a smile. "You must be Violet," he grunted.

Violet breathed a sigh of relief that he didn't seem to want to greet her with a handshake. She took several steps forward to meet him at the center of the room, her hands clasped firmly behind her back.

"I am," Violet said, hoping her voice wasn't quivering. "And you must be—"

"Cut the crap, and let's get down to business. I'm Frank. You know why I'm here."

"Oh," Violet said, and resisted the urge to hit him over

the head with Moonbeam's lucky bamboo plant. Instead, she smiled warmly. "In that case, would it be considered *crap* to ask if you'd like tea?"

He laughed, a completely humorless sound that reminded Violet of the time she got a fork stuck in her garbage disposal.

"A smart-ass," Frank said, stepping into the seating area and looking around as if he owned the place. Come to think of it, he did. "I like that. Feisty and bitchy, just what I need. Sit down and let's talk."

Violet gritted her teeth, resisting the urge to say something snarky. This was the landlord. *The very angry landlord.* Even if he wasn't going to be polite, *she* should at least try to be.

She mustered as much dignity as she could and led the way to Moonbeam's seating area. Arranging herself regally on the edge of the red velvet chair, she waited for Frank to seat himself opposite her.

Instead, he devoted another two minutes to scratching his neck. This time, Violet had to look away. She developed a sudden, intense interest in the cactus garden arranged in a little clay pot on the edge of the coffee table.

Finally, Frank lowered himself into the chair and sat with his knees wide apart. He stared at her.

"Look," she began, "Can I just say something first, sir?"

"No."

"But—"

"I'm a very busy man so—"

"Tough," Violet said, a little surprised to hear her "corporate bitch" voice emerging in this setting. "I'm busy, too, and I just want to say that while I'm sorry if

I caused you any distress with what I told your squash partner, I don't believe in cheating, and I do think—"

"Oh, cut the bullshit. You're a liar, and I'm a cheater. The Professional Squash Association canned me two days ago after my so-called partner ratted me out and they caught me on video. Whatever, I was planning to retire next month anyway, and I have better things to do with my time now. That's where you come in."

Violet sat back in her chair and tried to mask her shock. This was not how she expected the conversation to go.

"So you... you... You admit you were cheating?"

Frank laughed and Violet thought of the fork in the garbage disposal again. "Of course I was cheating. And the fact that you seem surprised pretty much proves my theory that you know as well as I do that this psychic thing is total bullshit. That's actually perfect. Just what I need."

Violet stared at him, trying to follow the conversation. "I don't understand. And I'm not a liar, so—"

"Can it, babe. Here's the deal. I own a shit pile of properties around Portland, and this is just one of many. I've got an investor lined up to buy one of my places to open some sort of vegan café."

Violet started to reply, but lost her words as Frank reached up and gave his neck another violent scratch. This one only lasted less than a minute, but seemed to require a bit more digging than the last one had. She tried not to look, but there definitely was some sort of growth there...

"Do you need some ointment or something?"

"Not whatever you've got around here. Some new-agey bullshit? No thank you. It's a fucking allergic reaction or something. Probably the goddamn escargot I ate for lunch."

"You ate snails?" She remembered the TV special about snail genitals on their necks, and suddenly her brain was veering toward Drew, to the feeling of his mouth on her throat and his hands…

"I'm not here to talk about what I had for lunch, okay?"

Violet frowned and decided to ignore the scratching. "So this investor is looking for property somewhere in the city—"

"Not just any property. *My* property. He's narrowed his choices down to two places, both of which I happen to own, and one of which is worth a fuckwad of money."

"How convenient for you," she said, looking up at him with a scowl.

"Convenient," he scoffed. "I'm nailing the guy's wife on the side. She made sure he only checked out properties I owned."

"I don't understand—"

"Of course you don't," he interrupted as he rubbed his neck some more. "And you don't need to know all the details. Here's what you *do* need to know. This investor is a total nut job, which explains why he went gaga over this crappy little psychic studio when I showed it to him the other day. Wants to knock out the wall and combine it with that shitty bar next door and turn it into the biggest vegan restaurant in the city."

Violet felt her temper flare. "You showed him our space without giving us the legally required notice twenty-four hours in advance?"

Frank just snorted. "I gave proper notice. I called your mom at the hospital. What, she doesn't remember?

Must've been all those painkillers." He snorted again. "Sue me."

"Maybe I will," Violet snapped.

"You don't have a leg to stand on and you know it. Shut up and listen a minute. I don't want to kick you out of this shit hole."

Violet stared at him. "You don't?"

"Hell no. I want you to stay here as long as possible."

"Wow. Thank you. I mean—"

"I'm not being benevolent. I just want this asshole investor to buy another space I've got for sale. One right on the waterfront, three times the price."

Violet frowned. "What does this have to do with me?"

"It's real simple. You're going to give him a psychic reading."

"What?" Violet squeaked.

"He's going to call you sometime tomorrow to schedule an appointment. The name's Jed Buckles, and you're going to book him an appointment within the next week, and you will tell him that bad things will happen if he doesn't buy that other property. Or good things will happen if he does buy it. Whatever, I'll leave the details up to you. The important thing is that he buys the other fucking property."

Violet stared at him. "I'm not going to make up some ridiculous story to tell this guy, just so you can take advantage of him."

Frank snorted again. "Why? Because you're so goddamn ethical? Spare me. Look, lady, you do this or else."

"Or else what?"

"Or you and your mom and all those crazy-ass strippers next door will find yourselves out on the street."

"Are you threatening me?"

"Hell yes."

Violet took a breath, then a second one for good measure. "You can't evict us without cause."

"I don't have to have cause. Hell, I don't even have to evict you. It wouldn't take much to ruin your reputation, maybe send one of those professional myth-buster guys in here to prove you guys are full of shit. You want that to happen? Huh?"

Violet just glared at him, too angry to speak.

Or maybe it was fear, not anger. He was right, after all. She was a fake.

"Do you fucking want that to happen?" he asked again, this time with obvious fury. "You really want someone in here sniffing around, trying to prove this is a crackpot excuse for a business? That you just make this shit up and take the money of unsuspecting community members?"

"Why would anyone believe you, huh? You just lost your professional athletic career for cheating."

"It wouldn't have to be *me* going public with your misdeeds," Frank snapped. "It would be the newspaper I own, the friends I have with television connections, the word of mouth I could kick off. You wouldn't believe how many connections I have in this town."

Violet pressed her lips together, trying to hold in the curse that threatened to emerge. Next door, she heard the music start up. She tried to distract herself with the thrum of the rhythm, the faint urge to name the tune. She could just barely pick out a smattering of lyrics. It seemed like a smarter thing to do than reaching across the coffee table and grabbing that horrible excuse for a human by his scrawny little throat and—

Frank laughed. Then he scratched his neck.

Suddenly, Violet had had enough. She jumped to her feet and pointed a finger at him.

A trembling finger, but still.

"Get out!" she shrieked. She stepped to the other side of her chair, desperate to get away from him. "Now, out. *And stop scratching yourself like that!* It's disgusting. Didn't your mother ever teach you it's rude to do that in public?"

Frank shrugged and kept scratching. "I got this weird growth that just showed up the other day. It's sort of long and skinny and—"

"It's a goddamn snail penis!"

He stopped scratching and stared at her. "What?"

"Nothing. Never mind. Get out."

"No problem," Frank said, giving his neck one last scratch before standing up. "This place gives me the creeps anyway. Besides, I already said what I had to say."

"Out!" Violet repeated, pointing the door.

Frank snorted and began moving that direction. "Just don't forget… tomorrow afternoon. Jed Buckles. Give him an appointment, tell him what he needs to hear, and everything will be fine."

On the other side of the wall in Drew's bar, the song was still playing. The title clicked into place in Violet's brain just as Frank reached the door.

"'I Hate Everything About You.'"

"What?" Frank said from the doorway.

"Lyrics from the song they're playing next door. It's by Ugly Kid Joe. Came out in the early nineties, I think."

Frank looked over his shoulder at her and laughed. "You're a real fuckin' nut job, lady."

Then he walked out the door, scratching his neck as he went.

Chapter 14

VIOLET WAS JUST FINISHING UP WITH ONE OF HER accounting clients when Drew walked in the next morning under the pretense of getting toilet paper from the storage closet.

Okay, so he didn't really need the toilet paper. He needed to see Violet. Naked, preferably, but fully clothed would do.

"Thank you so much for pointing out we could deduct that trip to Europe," Violet's client was saying as he shook her hand. "I can't believe you even thought to ask if we'd traveled there."

"Yes, well, Europe was on my mind this morning and I knew you had business interests over there, so it seemed wise to check. I'm glad it all worked out."

"Me too, Violet." He laughed. "Heck, maybe me and the missus will start planning another trip."

He waved and headed out the door, a thick packet of papers tucked under one arm. Violet was still smiling as Drew approached.

"Europe, huh?" he said. "I've been playing their *Final Countdown* album all morning."

"Oh?"

"Maybe that's why it was in your head."

"Hmm," Violet said, glancing away. "Right. Well, it's a nice album. Did you need something?"

"Just wondering how things went with Frank."

Violet sighed. "Not great, but I don't really want to talk about it. Frank's the least of my concerns right now."

"And what are the most of your concerns?"

"I had a meeting earlier with the occupational therapist. She came through to check out the house and make sure it's safe for Moonbeam to come home the day after tomorrow."

"And did it pass muster?"

Violet shook her head. "It looks like there's a lot more to do than I realized."

"Like what?"

She shrugged. "Moving furniture. Building a wheelchair ramp. Stuff like that."

"You planning to do all that by yourself in the next twenty-four hours?"

"I can manage."

"Of course you can. Moving sofas alone is always a good idea."

"Well—"

"And I'm sure you flew out here with a Skilsaw and lumber in your suitcase. That should come in handy for building the ramp."

"I'll figure it out," Violet said, her jaw set with determination.

"I'll help you. Tonight at seven, how's that?"

"You don't have to—"

"Of course I don't, but I want to. It's what neighbors do. I'm sure your mom would do it for me."

Violet raised an eyebrow. "You think my mother would build you a wheelchair ramp?"

"Well, maybe not that, exactly. But she'd probably turn my coffee table into a toad so it'd be easier to move."

Violet laughed, a warm, musical sound that made
Drew glad he owned a Skilsaw and a hammer. Not in a
euphemistic way, but…

"Okay then, I accept your offer. Thank you. How
about if I make dinner?"

"Dinner," Drew repeated, with visions of tofu dancing unpleasantly in his head.

"What do you eat?"

"Well, there are the four basic food groups, and I
pretty much eat all of them."

"You're not vegan or vegetarian or on a free-trade
organic diet or anything?"

"How about if we just order in?"

A look of relief crossed Violet's face. "You like pizza?"

"Perfect. The more grease, the better."

She grinned at him. "I'll see you at seven."

—◇◇—

Violet kept her mom's business cell tucked in her back
pocket while she hustled around the house, moving the
smaller furniture and digging for tools in the garage. The
phone hadn't rung all afternoon, and Violet wasn't sure
if that was a good thing or a bad thing. Frank had said
Jed Buckles would call for his appointment today. What
was she going to say?

She had stopped by the hospital on her way home
from the shop. When she'd told Moonbeam the whole
sordid tale of Frank's threats, Moonbeam hadn't
even flinched.

"Well naturally, dear, a psychic can't be bought.
I'm sure Frank knows that in his soul. Maybe he's just
testing you."

Violet had gritted her teeth and stared at her mother. "He's not testing me. And he doesn't have a soul."

"No, but he does have a snail penis on his neck," Moonbeam had said with a gleam in her eye. "Tell me that part of the story again, dear. I enjoyed that."

The conversation had pretty much petered out after that, with Moonbeam remaining steadfastly convinced that Violet would "do the right thing," whatever the hell that meant.

Now, as she shoved an end table across the room, Violet glanced down at the phone for the hundredth time. Maybe Jed Buckles wouldn't call. Maybe he didn't really want a psychic reading.

Or hell, so what if he did? What was the harm in doing what Frank asked, really?

It's not like you haven't spent the last couple weeks making stuff up for everyone who comes to see you, Violet told herself.

But that wasn't the same thing. What she'd been doing before was harmless, a carnival act. This was something bigger. Not just a client wondering if she should talk to the cute guy at work, but someone with a lot of money at stake. Maybe his whole livelihood.

And then there was the possibility that she *wasn't* just making stuff up. A small possibility, but it was there, in every song Drew played over the sound system, his car radio, even hummed in the hallway. What the hell was that about? Obviously, other people could hear the music, so it wasn't like some magical cosmic thing that only she could sense. But Moonbeam seemed to genuinely have no idea what Violet was talking about when she'd mentioned it. So maybe it *was* just her. Or just her and Drew, to be precise. Maybe some sort of bizarre psychic connection between the two of them.

Or maybe it was just a ridiculous coincidence. That seemed a hell of a lot more likely.

The doorbell chimed and Violet jumped. She had been so braced for a phone call that she wasn't expecting anyone at the door. She glanced at her watch as she headed toward the front of the house, wondering whether it was Drew or the pizza arriving early.

But it wasn't Drew on her doorstep.

And if the unwashed, dreadlocked man standing there had a pizza anywhere on his person, Violet was certain she didn't want to eat it.

She opened the door cautiously and peered out at the man.

"Dude," he said in greeting, and flipped his butt-length dreadlocks over one shoulder.

Violet caught a whiff of sweat and patchouli and took a step back. "Um, hello?"

He looked up her up and down and nodded approvingly. "Duuuude. Nice."

Violet resisted the urge to close the door in his face. The man was wearing pants made of paisley patches of fabric, and a shirt that might have been a Hefty bag at one time. His feet were bare.

"Um, can I help you?" she asked.

That's when she noticed the hammer in his hand.

With a yelp, she grabbed the door and started to fling it shut.

"Dude," the man said in a reassuring tone as he extended his hammer-free hand. "Chill. Moonbeam sent me."

Violet stopped closing the door and stared at him. "Moonbeam?"

"I was visiting her at rehab and she said you, like, needed help."

Violet sighed. "Of course she did."

"She said you, like, had *needs*... both spiritual and physical." He grinned at her, showing a piece of spinach on one tooth. "I'm, like, here to meet your needs."

"Oh, well, that's very nice of you, but—"

"I thought we could, like, tend to the spiritual first. Tell me, what are you looking for in a life partner?" Violet closed her eyes and silently cursed her mother.

A familiar voice burst through Violet's thoughts before she could get very far with her curse.

"Am I interrupting a meditation here?" Violet opened her eyes to see Drew ambling up the walkway, casting a curious look at Dreadlock Dude as he climbed the steps onto the porch. Violet was so happy to see him, she almost shoved Dreadlock Dude aside and rushed out to hug Drew.

She thought better of it when she spied the arsenal of sharp-looking tools he was toting.

Drew raised an eyebrow at as he glanced at Dreadlock Dude. Then he met her eyes again. "I can come back later if this isn't a good time—"

"No!" Violet yelled, and threw the door open. "This is the perfect time."

"Dude," said the dreadlocked man, and stepped aside so they could stand shoulder to shoulder in front of the door.

Violet sighed. "Drew. This is... I'm sorry, what was your name again?"

"I don't believe in names," said Dreadlock Dude as he extended a hand to Drew. "They're, like, too confining."

"Sure they are," Drew agreed as he gave the man's hand an agreeable shake. "I wish some of the girls I've dated felt the same way. It would make things much easier."

"Right, because *Jenny* is so tough to remember," Violet muttered as she stepped aside to usher them both through the door. "I've got pizza coming in a few minutes, if you boys want to come in. I ordered extra, so I'm sure there's plenty for all of us."

"Excellent," said Drew, and set his tools down on the porch. Dreadlock Dude frowned and set his hammer beside Drew's Skilsaw. "I don't eat animal flesh or dairy products or nightshade vegetables or anything grown in a country that, like, violates the human rights of its citizens."

Violet sighed. "You can look through the fridge and help yourself. I'm sure everything's free-trade certified and organic. Moonbeam wouldn't have it any other way."

Dreadlock Dude nodded happily at her and ambled toward the kitchen. "Maybe after you and I have been dating for a while, we can, like, move in together with Moonbeam and form a communal cooking collective."

Drew grinned at Violet as he headed toward the kitchen to join Dreadlock Dude. "That sounds like fun," he murmured in her ear as he passed. "Let me know when the wedding is so I have time to shop for a gift that isn't a nightshade vegetable or something made with animal flesh or—"

"Shut up," Violet hissed as she stole a glance at Dreadlock Dude. He was rummaging through the fridge, searching for something ethical to eat. She leaned back toward Drew. "Moonbeam sent him. Apparently, she thought I needed help with the wheelchair ramp."

"Apparently that's not all she thought you needed help with. Maybe I should leave the two of you alone?"

Violet grabbed his arm so tightly she could feel the curve of his bicep. She ignored the flutter in her belly and looked up at him in panic. "Please don't leave me alone with him."

Drew grinned down at her, his mouth close to her ear as he kept his tone low enough that Dreadlock Dude couldn't hear. "I kind of like it when you beg."

Violet released his arm as the heat crept into her cheeks. She stepped away from Drew and wiped her palms on the front of her jeans. She cleared her throat and addressed both of them in a voice that sounded noticeably shakier than it had a few minutes ago.

"There's beer in the fridge, iced tea, and I bought a few different kinds of soda. The tea is herbal and free-trade certified, of course. Drew, you like cherry Coke, right?"

Drew shot her a grin as he joined Dreadlock Dude in front of the refrigerator. "Wow, you must be psychic."

Dreadlock Dude turned and beamed at Drew. "She *is* psychic. Like, a very gifted one, from what Moonbeam and Butterfly say."

Violet rolled her eyes and took three glasses out of the cupboard. She began filling them with ice as Drew slurped his cherry Coke right out of the can and Dreadlock Dude began unscrewing the cap off a jar of organic stone-ground mustard. He stuck his nose in and sniffed it, and Violet made a mental note to throw it away later.

"So how long have you two kids known each other?" Drew asked as he leaned against the counter.

"Dude, we just met, but clearly there's, like, an intense spiritual connection between us," said Dreadlock Dude as he smiled at Violet with mustard on his nose. "I've always believed marriage is a draconian and discriminatory institution, but, like, I'm open to considering a sacred union if you want to talk about that."

"Right," Violet said. "How about if we just eat pizza? It should be here any minute."

Dreadlock Dude shrugged and peeled the top off a container of tofu that had been in the fridge since before Moonbeam's accident. He gave it a sniff before pulling out a rubbery cube and dipping it into the mustard jar. Violet grimaced.

"So you're a friend of Moonbeam's?" Drew asked Dreadlock Dude as he took another sip of his soda.

"We're all part of the same psychic massage group where we use touch to harmonize the astral vehicles," Dreadlock Dude said. "I've only just met Violet, but of course I've been hearing about her for, like, ages. She's, like, way remarkable."

"Agreed," Drew said, taking another sip of his soda.

"And her ethical conviction is, like, totally admirable," Dreadlock Dude continued. "Moonbeam was saying that just yesterday, someone tried to blackmail Violet into compromising her integrity by, like, giving a fake psychic reading to someone."

Violet felt all the blood drain from her face. She opened her mouth to say something, but Dreadlock Dude was on a roll now.

"I mean, here's this big shot, like, making all these

threats, but here's Violet sticking it to the man, you know? It's, like, dude… her ethics totally aren't for sale. Moonbeam even said—"

"Dude," Violet interrupted. "Enough, okay? The story's complicated, and my mom wasn't there, so—"

"Sticking it to the man, huh?" Drew said, raising an eyebrow at Violet. "How unfortunate for the man."

Violet blinked at him. "It's not a big deal. It's just… maybe we can talk about this later?"

Drew shrugged. "None of my business, is it?"

Violet hesitated. Was that a real question, or a rhetorical one?

The doorbell rang, and Violet almost cried with relief.

"I'll answer it," said Dreadlock Dude as he set down his tofu and headed for the door. "Since I'll probably be, like, moving in here soon anyway, right? I mean, we'll both want to live with Moonbeam, of course."

Violet gripped her empty glass, feeling the chill of ice cubes against her sweaty palm. She waited until Dreadlock Dude was well out of earshot before she met Drew's unreadable gaze.

"Something on your mind?" Drew asked.

"Nope, you?"

Drew just looked at her and took another sip of soda.

Violet swallowed. Should she say something? Frank was Drew's landlord, too. Whatever she decided to do— give the fake reading, or just tell Frank to go to hell— that impacted Drew.

Violet bit her lip. "Drew, I—"

"Hey, dude," came a voice from the other side of the wall. "You're, like, dressed totally too nice to be a pizza man."

There was a long pause, followed by another familiar voice. "Actually, I'm a doctor, though certainly I do appreciate a good pizza. Is Violet home, by any chance?"

Violet closed her eyes again, not sure whom to curse this time, but wishing like hell the floor would just swallow her up.

She opened her eyes as Drew clunked his soda can down on the counter beside her.

"Your night just keeps getting better," he said, and moved past her on his way out of the kitchen.

Chapter 15

"CHRIS," VIOLET SAID, PASTING A SMILE ON HER FACE AS she nudged Dreadlock Dude out of the way and greeted her new guest at the front door. "It's so good to see you."

Chris beamed at her and held up a bottle of expensive-looking Pinot Noir. "Your mom said you could use some help with a construction project. I made a few calls, but the earliest someone can get out here to build a ramp is next week."

"But—"

"Don't worry, I've already pulled some strings, so Moonbeam's extended stay at the rehab facility will be paid in full."

"That's very thoughtful of you, but actually, I have it covered."

"What?"

Violet smoothed her hair behind her ears. "Right. Um, a friend of Moonbeam's and then you remember Drew, my mom's neighbor? They offered to help build the ramp and move furniture."

She felt Drew behind her and stepped aside, letting the three men come face-to-face. She saw Chris's smile falter for a moment, but he recovered like a gentleman and extended his hand.

"Good to see you again, Drew."

Drew shook it warmly and nodded at Chris. "Welcome to the party."

Chris's expression was more pained than festive, and he turned back to Violet as though expecting an explanation. Violet grimaced and turned to Dreadlock Dude.

"Um, Chris, this is… well, he believes names are too confining. He's a friend of Moonbeam's, and he came to help, too. And Chris here is my mother's orthopedic surgeon, so… wow."

"Dude," said Dreadlock Dude again as he stepped up for a handshake.

"Well," Chris said, looking a bit taken aback as he studied the assembled male faces. "It looks like we all had the same idea this evening."

"Sure," Drew said. "Helping Moonbeam, right?"

"Right," Chris said uneasily. "Helping—exactly."

Dreadlock Dude shrugged and shoved a piece of mustard-covered tofu in his mouth. "Actually, I was hoping to, like, get with Violet. In a spiritual way, you know?"

"Okay!" Violet said brightly, clapping her hands together. "Chris, I ordered a bunch of pizza and you're welcome to stay for dinner. I see the delivery guy pulling up, so let me just run out and take him some money and I'll be back in… well, in just a minute."

She dashed out the door with her face flaming, relieved at the sensation of raindrops slapping her cheeks. She darted down the driveway and gave some serious thought to just continuing down the street, running as hard as she could until the house, the town, and most importantly, the men were all out of view.

Instead, she reached the door of the delivery car and rapped on the window.

The driver gave her a startled look and popped open his door. "Um, that'll be—"

"Keep the change," Violet said, and thrust a fistful of bills at him. "I don't suppose you're hiring, are you?"

"Uh—"

"Never mind. I'm just contemplating a career change."

"Right. Here's your pizza, ma'am."

"Thanks. Have a good night."

"Sure," said the kid, and yanked his door shut.

Violet clutched the two large pizza boxes to her chest and marched back up the driveway to face her suitors. When she walked through the door, the three men were deep in conversation about the positioning of the couch.

"Gentlemen," Violet called. "Shall we eat first?"

"Certainly," Chris said, stepping up beside her and placing a possessive arm around her shoulders. "That was really nice of you to think of feeding everyone like this."

"Oh, well…" Violet tightened her grip on the boxes, tipping a little under the weight of his arm and the pizzas.

Without a word, Drew ambled over and relieved her of the boxes. He set them down on the table and then set about rifling through the cupboard for plates.

Dreadlock Dude sat down at the head of the table and began performing some sort of complicated looking prayer ritual.

Chris released Violet and headed into the kitchen. "Where do you keep the corkscrew?"

"It's right there in that second drawer. Let me get some glasses. Who else wants wine?"

Chris grimaced a little and bent toward her. "I didn't realize we'd be splitting this four ways," he whispered. "It's actually a very expensive Pinot."

Violet stared at him. "Would you like to just keep it for yourself?" she whispered back. "I don't think anyone would mind."

"No, of course not. I just thought… well, I was hoping to share it with you. Sort of a romantic thing, I guess."

"Oh. Um, well—"

"Never mind, it's not a big deal. The more the merrier, right?"

"Right," Violet said uneasily as she glanced back out at the other two men. Drew was studying her with a curious expression.

"Wine?" Violet asked weakly.

"None for me, thanks," Drew said, lifting his cherry Coke.

Dreadlock Dude opened one eye and looked at her. "Does it have sulfites?"

"God, I hope so," Violet said, and reached up to grab two glasses.

Once they were all assembled around the table, Drew opened up the pizza boxes and released the heavenly scent of sausage and mushrooms. Violet inhaled deeply, feeling some of the tension ease out of her shoulders.

Beside her, Chris frowned. "I hope the wine pairs all right with sausage."

"It'll be fine," Violet said, and took a healthy gulp of it. "Perfect."

Chris gave her an awkward smile. "I'm sure you're right."

"Want some?" Drew offered, nudging the box out to Dreadlock Dude.

"Dude, no. I don't do animal flesh or dairy or—"

"Right. Enjoy your mustard."

"Thanks, man."

Chris shoveled a piece of pizza onto his plate and smiled at Dreadlock Dude. "So Drew here owns a bar. What is it you do… uh…"

Dreadlock Dude wiped some mustard off his mouth with the back of his hand. "I'm an artist."

"How fascinating. What medium?"

"Medium?"

"Acrylics, pottery, metals…"

"Nah, man, I do dirt art."

"Dirt art?"

"On car windows. Like, if I see a car that's, like, really dirty, I'll study the windshield until the form, like, comes to me, you know?"

"Oh. I see." Chris nodded thoughtfully. "So how do you… well, I mean, how do you make money at that?"

Dreadlock Dude stared at him, uncomprehending.

Chris flushed a little and picked up his wineglass. "I'm sorry, maybe I misunderstood. Is it a hobby or a career?"

"Dude?"

"Well surely you have to make money to survive, to have a stable income, a sense of purpose, a retirement plan…"

"I don't believe in capitalistic greed, dude. It's like… totally a drag."

"But why do you—?"

Drew looked up from his pizza and stared at Dreadlock Dude. "Do you like doing dirt art?"

Dreadlock Dude swung his gaze to Drew and nodded. "It's my calling. My passion. The reason I was, like, placed upon this earth."

"Do you eat regularly?"

Dreadlock Dude shoveled another piece of mustard-covered tofu in his mouth and smiled.

"Okay then," Drew said as he picked up the pizza box. "Sounds like you're doing just fine. Anyone want another slice?"

Violet hadn't realized she was holding her breath until she felt Drew's words dissolve the tension like sugar in a glass of warm water. She held out her plate and smiled at him with gratitude.

"Thank you," she said.

"Here, have the one with all the good toppings on it," Drew said as he shoveled it onto her plate. "Anyone else?"

Chris shook his head and swirled his wine around in his glass before taking his sip. "So Violet, how's the life of a psychic accountant treating you?"

"Fine, thanks. Busy, really busy. Don't worry, though, I finished up your accounting paperwork last night."

"I'm not worried about that. Take your time on that, really. I'm just glad you're enjoying your mom's business."

"It has its moments," Violet said, and took another gulp of wine.

"Maybe sometime I could come in and watch you work?"

"Oh… well, I really don't—"

"Or I could book an appointment. That would be even better. What's your schedule like next week?"

His expression was so eager Violet didn't have the heart to tell him she'd rather stick bamboo under her fingernails and soak her hands in grapefruit juice than give a psychic reading to a man she was dating.

"Well, I'd have to check my schedule," she said slowly. "I know things are really booked up, though."

"I'm sorry. I didn't even think about the fact that there

might be ethical issues with doing a psychic reading for someone you've been... well..."

"Right," Violet said. "Ethical issues. Well, there is that."

"Violet's all about, like, ethical stuff," said Dreadlock Dude somberly. "Like this thing with her landlord—"

"Let me get you some ketchup to go with that," Violet said, standing up so fast she knocked her chair over.

Drew reached over and caught it with one hand, setting it upright without a word. Violet retreated to the kitchen and stuck her head in the refrigerator, determined not to meet Drew's eyes.

—⁓—

An hour later, Drew looked down at the growing pile of sawdust at his feet and tried hard not to feel depressed.

Once Dr. Abbott had realized the other two males would be wielding power tools in Violet's presence, he couldn't resist the urge to demonstrate the size of his testicles by donning a tool belt.

Backward, as it turned out.

That was pretty much how the whole operation was unfolding. Building anything with Chris and the guy Violet quietly called Dreadlock Dude was like trying to pound nails with a meatball.

Actually, that might have been more effective. After Chris kept missing the nails with the hammer, Drew had casually offered to take over that task while Chris wielded the saw. But after about five minutes of that, Drew found himself hoping like hell that Chris demonstrated considerably more precision in the operating room.

"How's this, Drew?" Chris called as he deposited a couple of chewed up pieces of lumber at Drew's feet.

"Looking great," Drew said. "Nice work."

Jesus, they looked like he'd gnawed them apart with his incisors, but Drew wasn't about to say so. Guys staked a whole lot of ego on their ability to use power tools. Even guys like Chris and Dreadlock Dude were no exception, and Drew figured it wasn't his place to suggest they might be better off moving furniture than out here trying to impress Violet using their prowess with a cordless drill.

But it was a damn good thing he'd brought extra lumber. At the rate these guys were going, they'd be building this ramp with popsicle sticks before the night was through.

"Dude, is this, like, sanded enough?" Dreadlock Dude called to Drew as he held up a piece of wood.

Drew grimaced. "Maybe try using the scratchy side of the sandpaper."

"Good idea. Hey, you're sure this wood is rescued?"

"Yup. I got it from the foreman at a construction site just down the street from me. It's all their scrap wood."

"I don't know," Dreadlock Dude said as he frowned down at the wood. "I think Moonbeam would rather have that stuff made from recycled plastic."

"I'm sure she would, but this was free, and it was going to end up in the landfill anyway," Drew pointed out. "Besides, this ramp is temporary, right?"

"Right," Chris said as he set down another piece of mangled wood in the pile beside Drew. "Moonbeam should only need the wheelchair for a couple months. Then she'll be back on her feet."

And Violet will be back in Maine, Drew thought, and tried not to feel glum. Really, he'd only known her for a short time. As soon as she left, his life could go back to the way it was.

That was a good thing, right?

"Here you go, Drew," Violet said as she stepped out onto the porch. "I found those extra nails you wanted."

"Thanks. Can you toss them in the box right over there?"

She leaned down, and Drew looked up just in time to catch a glimpse of black lace down the front of her shirt. He looked away quickly, feeling like a jerk. Then he saw the other two men staring openmouthed at the black lace.

He didn't feel like such a jerk anymore.

Violet straightened up, taking her black lace with her. "Want me to keep sanding, or can I help you get those rails erected?" she asked him.

Drew's thoughts veered dangerously close to middle school humor at the word *erected*, but he cleared his throat and shook his head.

"I think we've got it covered here," he said. "Actually, we should probably wrap it up for tonight. I'm not sure the neighbors will appreciate it if we're running power tools past their bedtime."

"Good point. In that case, could I borrow you for a few minutes?"

"Borrow me?"

"Inside. There are still a couple more pieces of furniture to move, and I could use a quick hand if you don't mind taking a break from this."

Drew looked up at her again, his eyes catching on the black lace for a few moments before they found their way up to her face. She raised an eyebrow and leaned closer.

"Actually, I wanted to talk to you alone for a second," she whispered in his ear, making Drew feel light-headed. "About what Dreadlock Dude was saying earlier about ethical issues and—"

There was a sickening *whack* followed by a howl of pain. Drew whirled around and saw Dreadlock Dude doubled over, gripping his hand.

"Shit, are you okay?" Drew asked, scrambling over to where he was hunched on the other side of the porch. "What happened?"

Violet dropped to her knees beside them. "Ohmygod, are you okay? What did you do? Can I get you some ice or a Band-Aid or—"

"I hit it with the hammer," he moaned. "My thumb. I think I broke it."

"Let's see it," Drew coaxed, shooting a quick look at Chris. He was a damn doctor. Why the hell wasn't he the first one over here?

Chris must have seen something in Drew's expression, because he set down the board he'd been measuring and walked over to where they were clustered.

"Let me take a look," Chris said with authority. "Did anyone see the mechanism of injury?"

"What?" said Dreadlock Dude.

"He hit it with a fucking hammer," Drew supplied. "That's pretty much it."

Chris nodded sagely. "Let's see it."

Slowly, Dreadlock Dude held out his hand and un-curled his fingers. Drew resisted the urge to grimace. Even with zero medical training he could tell the joint in his thumb had been completely smashed.

"Ohmygod, that looks horrible," Violet gasped.

Drew frowned at her. "Way to be supportive."

"Sorry."

Chris was studying the thumb, turning it over, muttering about the color and the condition of the joint. Finally, he looked up at Dreadlock Dude.

"You definitely need to get to the hospital. It appears you've shattered the joint. You need X-rays right away, probably surgery. Do you have health insurance?"

"No."

"No matter. You have to get to the ER right away."

Drew waited for a moment, expecting the esteemed doctor to offer to drive him. When he didn't, Drew stood up.

"I'll take him. Should we get some ice or—"

"Yes, absolutely," Chris said, and looked up at Violet... or down Violet's blouse, Drew couldn't really tell. "Violet, let's run inside and prepare an ice pack."

"Oh," Violet said, looking a little stunned. "Okay, sure, we'll get ice and then we can all go to the hospital together."

Chris nodded, though Drew saw him frown a little. Clearly, this was not his plan. "Sure, Violet and I will follow in my car," Chris said. "You two stay here for just a second and Violet and I will get the ice so you have it for the drive. Just hold the hand up like this. Keep it up, okay? We'll be right back."

Violet cast another worried look at Dreadlock Dude before turning toward the house. "I'll get some Tylenol, too."

"And maybe some of that wine?" said Dreadlock Dude. "I'm okay with the sulfites now."

Drew watched Violet and Chris disappear inside. He

entertained a few unkind thoughts for a doctor who'd use someone else's injury as a chance to get closer to a hot girl, even for a few moments.

Beside him, Dreadlock Dude moaned. Drew looked back at him. "Hurts like hell, huh? Sorry about that. I didn't realize you'd gone back to hammering."

"I was tired of sanding, dude."

"Right. Well, we can finish building later. Come on, let's get you in the car. Think you can walk okay?"

Dreadlock Dude nodded and stood up, swaying a little as he took a step. Grimacing at the smell of unwashed hair and patchouli, Drew helped him up and began walking him cautiously toward the car.

"Keep your hand up like the doctor said," Drew instructed. "Watch your step here."

"Thanks, man."

"No sweat."

Drew opened the door of his car and handed Dreadlock Dude into the passenger seat. "Need help with the seat belt?"

"Dude," he replied, moaning a little.

Drew started to bend down, wondering what the hell was taking Chris and Violet so long with the ice.

Dreadlock Dude caught his eye. "Dude," he said, grimacing a little. "You're not seriously going to let that jackwad have her, are you?"

Drew stared at him for a few beats. "What are you talking about?"

"The doctor. Violet. Come on, man, you know what I mean."

Drew shook his head and clicked the seat belt shut. "Violet isn't my type. Not even close."

Dreadlock Dude gave him a weird little smile. "You haven't experienced your conscious revolution yet, but when the blindness is removed from your third eye—"

"Are you feeling dizzy?"

Dreadlock Dude shook his head. "Dude. She already knows I'm not her soul mate. Now it's, like, your job to make sure she knows *he* isn't, either."

Drew just stared at him for a few beats, trying to find his place in the conversation. Was this guy delirious?

Or was he actually more lucid than Drew had realized?

Behind him, Drew heard Violet and Chris hustling out onto the front porch and slamming the front door. Drew looked at Dreadlock Dude and nodded.

"So Moonbeam sent you here, huh?"

An hour later, Drew wove his way through the hallway of the outpatient-rehab facility where Moonbeam was staying. Violet had told him how to find her, though she'd seemed leery about why he might want to.

Violet was still over in the ER with Dreadlock Dude, while Chris alternately assumed the role of compassionate doctor and stole peeks down the front of Violet's shirt.

Not that it was any of Drew's business.

And it sure as hell wasn't Moonbeam's, either.

He reached her doorway and knocked quietly.

"Drew?" Moonbeam called from within. "Is that you, dear? I sensed your presence."

Drew rolled his eyes and ambled into the room, holding out the small vase of lilies he'd picked up in the hospital gift shop.

"I don't suppose sensing my presence has anything to do with Violet calling to let you know I was coming?"

"Of course not, dear," Moonbeam said as she accepted the flowers with a grateful smile. "You have a very distinct aura."

"That's what all the girls say."

"What else did you bring?"

"Cherry pie," he said as he held out the box from the hospital cafeteria. "Two slices. I know it's your favorite."

Moonbeam sighed with bliss and set the flowers aside to reach for the box. "And they used recycled cardboard instead of Styrofoam," she gushed. "Thank you."

Drew handed her a fork and sat down in the chair beside the bed. He couldn't help but notice how pale she looked, how much more frail she seemed than the last time he'd seen her at the shop. She dug into the pie with surprising vigor.

"So how is Violet?" Moonbeam asked between bites. "You've been spending a fair amount of time together, haven't you?"

"Right. That's actually what I came here to talk to you about."

"Oh?"

Drew folded his arms over his chest. He looked at Moonbeam, studying her for signs of the scheming, unpredictable lunatic he knew her to be.

Moonbeam was busy forking up cherries, not meeting his eyes at all.

Drew cleared his throat. "Let me see if I can sum this up. You've spent the last few years hating my business and chastising me for the way I choose to make my living. If memory serves me right, you've described me as unenlightened, boorish, unesoteric, disrespectful—"

"I also called you a poor planetary citizen," Moonbeam said helpfully between bites.

"Right. So explain to me why you've been trying to set me up with your daughter."

Moonbeam widened her eyes at him. She touched a hand to her chest, probably getting ready to feign heart failure. "I don't know what you're talking about, dear."

"Please. Her first date with Dr. Chris, you sent her to a restaurant where you knew I'd be."

"I don't keep track of where you take your bimbos."

"Bimbos?" Drew snorted. "You've been snarling at me for years over unenlightened word choices."

"Well really, dear, that ad campaign you did that talked about trouser snakes and—"

"Never mind the trouser snakes. Or the bimbos. That's not the issue here."

"No? Have you been dating more enlightened women, then?"

Drew raised an eyebrow at him. "You mean Petal?"

"I beg your pardon?"

"You sent her to the bar. You told her to pick me up. And you knew she'd annoy the hell out of me before we even got out of the parking lot."

Moonbeam gave him a look of innocence that was almost believable. "But dear, she's exactly the sort of girl you like."

"So you did try to set us up."

"Of course not."

Drew sighed. "You've been shoving inappropriate

women at me, and inappropriate men at Violet, and trying to convince us both that we're meant to be together."

Moonbeam's eyes opened wide. "That's the most ridiculous—"

"Exactly what *I* thought. What I want to know is why?"

Moonbeam stared at him for a moment. Her expression was perfectly bland. He couldn't tell if she was angry, offended, or just annoyed at being busted. Maybe he'd guessed wrong here. Maybe…

"Well, Drew," Moonbeam said sternly, "you certainly think very highly of yourself. Why on earth would I want you dating my daughter?"

"Exactly. God knows she's not my type, and I'm sure as hell not hers."

Moonbeam pressed her lips together and looked at him. "I'd have to be crazy to want Violet involved with someone in such a despicable profession."

"I'm with you on the 'crazy' part. Not so much the 'despicable,' but I've been called worse."

"I'm certain you have."

"By you, mostly."

Moonbeam frowned and took another bite of cherry pie. When she finished chewing, she looked at him. "Let me ask you something, dear."

"Fire away."

"You've known Violet for almost two weeks now. Do you think she belongs with Dr. Abbott?"

"Hell no."

"Why not? Why doesn't my daughter deserve to date a smart, wealthy, successful doctor?"

"The damn doctor doesn't deserve *her*," Drew snapped, a little louder than he'd intended. "Violet has way too much spirit for him. Too much passion. He's all wrong for her."

"You think so?"

Drew frowned. "So do you."

"Hmmm," Moonbeam said, and took another bite of pie. Not a yes, not a no.

Drew huffed an exasperated breath. "Look, I'm sure he's a nice guy, but he's boring. Violet thinks that's what she wants, but it's not. The last thing in the world she needs is normal. Normal would drive her nuts."

Moonbeam eyed him carefully, the same calculated expression he'd seen her use with countless unsuspecting clients over the years.

"Well, dear," Moonbeam said slowly, "that may be the first thing we've agreed on in ten years."

"Let's not hug over this, okay?"

Moonbeam rolled her eyes. "You're precisely right. Violet does *not* need normal."

"Fine. We agree on that. But it's not your place to make those decisions for her. For *me*."

"I'm not making decisions for any of you, dear. You're both allowed to make your own choices. It's called free will. I'm just helping things along."

"Just what the world needs. A fake psychic matchmaker."

Moonbeam pressed her lips together and studied him. "You could do a whole lot worse than Violet, dear. I've seen you do it over and over again, as a matter of fact."

"I've enjoyed doing it, thank you very much."

"Past tense?"

Drew frowned. "I don't understand. You don't like me, Moonbeam. You've never liked me."

"I don't like your business decisions, dear."

"I'm not wild about yours, either."

"See? Something else we have in common."

"Mutual abhorrence for each other's career choices is hardly the basis for friendship."

Moonbeam shrugged and nibbled a piece of pie crust. "You said it yourself. The last thing Violet needs is normal. You certainly aren't normal. At least, not in the way she thinks she wants."

Drew scowled at her. "I'm not sure whether to be flattered or to smother you with your pillow."

"You're normal in the ways that matter, dear," Moonbeam said patiently. "You're a stable energy in Violet's life. She needs that. But she also needs passion. Positive energy. A yang for her yin. Inner divinity."

"What drugs did they put in that pie?"

Moonbeam pressed her lips together, looking serene and all-knowing. Then she forked up a giant, gloopy cherry, ignoring the question.

Drew scowled at her. "What makes you think I even want to date Violet? Or that she wants to date me?"

Moonbeam smiled and patted the back of his hand. He knew what she was going to say before the words even left her lips.

"I'm psychic, dear."

Drew sighed. "Of course you are."

Chapter 16

Violet was sitting in the ER waiting room, completely engrossed in an article about toenail infections, but she knew the instant Drew walked into the room.

She looked up at him and smiled. "You smell like sawdust and pizza."

He dropped into the plastic seat beside her. "That sounds like a marketable cologne to me."

"How's Mom?"

"Tired. I told her you wanted to come and visit as soon as you're done here, but the nurse chased me out and said no more guests tonight."

"That's okay. I'm exhausted anyway. Think I could get a ride home with you?"

Drew frowned. "Where's Dr. Chris?"

"He got called into surgery. Not Dreadlock Dude's surgery—some emergency hip replacement or something. He wasn't sure how long he'd be."

"What about Dreadlock Dude?"

"His mom got here a few minutes ago. They're back there now, talking to the doctor."

"They going to operate?"

"Probably not tonight, but eventually. I feel terrible about what happened. He was just trying to help me, and now his thumb looks like a zucchini."

"He wasn't just trying to help you," Drew pointed out. "He was hoping to see you naked. We all were, frankly."

Violet felt her cheeks pinken a little, and she looked down at her lap. "Even so, he shouldn't get stuck with huge medical bills for that."

Drew reached over and gave her knee a quick squeeze. "Moonbeam's homeowner's insurance should cover it. And trust me, plenty of men would gladly hammer the body part of your choosing for the chance to gawk at you for the evening."

"Hey," Violet said, trying in vain to work up some feminist indignation.

"He'll be fine," Drew insisted.

"I guess you're right."

She looked up at him. He held her gaze for a moment and Violet forgot everything about blackmail and broken thumbs and psychic drama and just lost herself in those cool blue eyes.

"You look tired," Drew said.

"I am. Exhausted, actually. How did it get so late?"

"Come on," he said, standing up and offering her a hand. "Let's get you home."

She placed her hand in his and allowed him to hoist her up, enjoying the firmness of his grip. He touched her elbow to steady her, electrifying her skin as they both stood there beneath the glare of hospital lights with their fingers intertwined.

"Thanks again, Drew. For everything."

"Don't mention it," he said, and released her hand.

They walked in silence out to the car, Violet shivering a little in the light Portland drizzle. Drew moved closer to her—not touching her, not quite, but close enough that she could feel his warmth.

We can talk on the way home, Violet thought. *About*

Frank, about Chris, about his chat with Moonbeam...
whatever the hell that was about.

It seemed like a good plan until she was snugly buck-led into the seat with the car's heater turned up high and the raindrops thrumming rhythmically on the car roof. Violet burrowed into her jacket as Drew backed the car up and turned around. Maybe it was the soft swish of the windshield wipers or the hum of the motor or the soft murmur of Pat Benatar crooning "We Belong" on the stereo.

Before Violet knew it, her eyelids felt like lead. By the time they reached the edge of the parking lot, her neck forgot how to hold her head up.

She woke to the sound of Drew's voice warm against her ear.

"Violet?"

"Hmm?"

"Violet, wake up."

She kept her eyes scrunched tightly closed, fighting consciousness as she snuggled into the crook of Drew's arm. She inhaled the smell of soap and sawdust, press-ing her cheek against all that beautiful muscle and soft cotton. She could feel his breath in her hair, warm and comforting, and she burrowed against him. Before she knew it, she'd drifted back into oblivion.

"Violet?"

"Hmm?"

"Violet, I really..." His voice sounded strained, gravelly.

Violet felt his fingers touch her hair, gentle as a whisper.

"Christ," he murmured.

Violet opened her eyes and blinked in confusion. In the dim interior of the car, she took in the steering wheel, the seat belt, the flash of light in Drew's eyes. He looked breathless and rumpled and more than a little dangerous.

"Oh," she said.

"'Oh' is right," Drew said, pulling back a little.

Violet sat up and straightened her blouse. "Well… wow. I'm sorry about that. I must… I guess I fell asleep."

"That you did."

"I'm sorry, I'd better get inside."

Drew nodded slowly, one hand drifting up to skim the hair off her face, one hand gripping the steering wheel so tight his knuckles glowed white in the eerie yellow dashboard light.

Drew swallowed. "I'd offer to walk you inside, but—"

"No, that's okay, you're right. That would be—"

"Risky."

"Right."

For a few seconds, Violet struggled to remember why risky was a bad idea. Finally, she took a shaky breath. "All right. I'm going inside now. Thank you for the ride. And the ramp. And… well, everything."

"My pleasure."

Pleasure. The word hung there between them for a moment, suspended by a thin, silk thread. Neither of them blinked.

Violet took another breath, fighting the urge to just flip the locks and pounce on him. The windows were starting to steam up, and the rush of warmth from the heater made her want to take her clothes off.

She was pretty sure it was the heater.

"Okay," she said, and opened the car door. "Good night."

"Good night, Violet."

She stepped onto the driveway and was just about to close the door behind her when she spotted his Skilsaw on the porch. She turned back to him, hesitating.

"Your tools."

Drew shook his head. "I'll get them later. Tomorrow, maybe."

"Right. I just thought—"

"Violet," he said slowly, and took a ragged breath. "If I get out of the car and follow you to the door, the only tool I'll be thinking about..." He paused. "Okay, that was a little cruder than I intended. What I meant to say—"

Violet shook her head. "No, you're right. Of course, you're right. Okay, so I'll take care of your tools..."

Drew grimaced.

"I mean, I'll just go ahead and shove them inside..."

Drew shook his head. Violet flushed.

"I just mean that it's kind of wet, so maybe if I just put some sort of cover over..."

Drew closed his eyes and sighed. "Good night, Violet."

"Good night, Drew," she said, and shoved the door shut before she could just say *to hell with it* and lunge for him.

The next morning, Violet was at the shop bright and early. She hadn't slept well the night before, and she had no one to blame for that but herself.

Well, maybe she could blame Drew.

She couldn't stop thinking about pressing her body against his chest. Or the tease of his fingers under her skirt as they steamed up the windows in the lot at

Council Crest Park. Or the feeling of grinding against him on the sofa the other night. Or—

Stop.

Violet shook her head and picked up the phone, frowning down at the caller-ID window. Still no word from Jed. She felt a flutter of relief. Maybe he wouldn't call. Maybe she'd be off the hook. Surely Frank couldn't expect her to feed lies to the guy if he didn't call for an appointment.

The phone trilled in her hand and Violet dropped it, startled.

Behind her, she heard a chuckle. Violet whirled around.

"Wow," Drew said. "You psychics just have to touch the telephone and it rings."

"Shut up," she snapped, and bent down to pick up the cordless. "And stop sneaking up on me like that."

"Hey, I'm just looking for the plunger. Unless you'd like to tackle the women's toilet yourself?"

Violet frowned as the phone trilled again in her hand.

"I can call a plumber," she offered.

"No need, I'm a handy sort of guy."

The phone rang again, and Violet decided to let Drew's comment slide. She hit the switch and smiled into the receiver.

"Miss Moonbeam's Psychic Pservices, this is Violet."

"Violet, hey… Gary Smeade here."

"Detective Smeade," Violet replied without enthusiasm, trying to ignore Drew as he pulled the toilet plunger out of the closet and began twirling it like a baton. "What can I do for you?"

"Good question. We've got another situation here. Something I'm hoping you can help with."

"Oh?"

"Since you did such a great job with the last one and all."

Violet grimaced. "Right. Right, the bank robbery. What's happening this time?"

"B and E. Quite a serious rash of it."

Violet frowned. "Like whips and handcuffs and things? I didn't know that was illegal."

There was a pause on the other end of the line. To her left, Drew stopped twirling his toilet plunger and looked at her.

Detective Smeade cleared his throat. "No, you're thinking of B and D... uh, bondage and discipline."

"Oh, right." Violet flushed. "I mean, I wasn't really thinking about bondage and discipline, but—"

"No, I'm talking about B and E. Breaking and entering. We've had several robberies in the Pearl District. Pretty close to where you are, as a matter of fact. Surveillance cameras have caught a couple shots of the guy, but he's real tricky—keeps his face averted, wears ski masks, that sort of thing."

"Okay," Violet said, still regrouping after the bondage talk. "Burglary, right. So what do you need me to do?"

"Well, I have a few items we know the guy handled. Everything's been dusted for prints, but the guy is good—wears gloves, the whole nine yards. But Moonbeam has this ability to touch things and get this sense of who else touched them, you know?"

"Touch things," Violet repeated, still trying to avoid looking at Drew. "Sure."

"Great, so you can do that too?"

"What?"

"How's two thirty? Do you have any openings?"

"Oh... well, I... Let me check the appointment book."

She set the phone down and walked over to the cupboard, her brain going a million miles a second. This was so not what she needed today. She was already trying to escape the need to lie to a perfect stranger. Now she was going to have to do it with a cop.

Again.

She picked up the appointment book and flipped to the appropriate day. Wide open. Just her luck. She turned and looked at Drew.

"Are you going to be working next door all day?"

"Pretty much," Drew said, balancing the toilet plunger by its handle in the palm of his hand. "We've got a couple guys working on some new routines, so I told them I'd help out."

"So you'll be playing music?"

Drew gave her a look. "Without the music, it's just a bunch of half-naked men gyrating around the room. That would be creepy."

"Right."

Drew grinned. "I'll keep the volume turned down this time, promise."

Violet looked at him for a moment and felt a sharp prick of guilt somewhere in her gut.

"Don't worry about it," she said, and picked up the phone again. "Detective Smeade? Two thirty will work just fine. I'll see you then."

Jed Buckles still didn't call. All afternoon, Violet's phone stayed eerily silent.

The sound system next door didn't, which left Violet scrambling for a pen every time a new tune came blasting through the wall. Several times, she had to look up lyrics on the Internet, trying to remember obscure '80s one-hit wonders from her childhood.

By late afternoon, Violet had a list of glam-rock tunes comprehensive enough to impress attendees at a mullet convention.

"What the hell am I supposed to do with this?" Violet muttered to herself as she tried to puzzle out the hidden meaning behind Ozzy Osbourne's "You Can't Kill Rock and Roll" and Night Ranger's "Sister Christian."

"Something about murder? Church?" she muttered again, tapping the pen against her teeth.

Maybe there was no meaning. Hell, it's not like every song had to mean something. Maybe just the ones that played during key moments? She was pretty sure Drew had to be the one picking the songs. Did she have to be the one to hear them in order for this to work?

Violet set the pen down and frowned. Maybe this whole song theory was stupid. That seemed a whole lot more likely than the possibility there was some mysterious psychic message in Billy Idol's "Flesh for Fantasy."

The door chimed, and Violet looked up to see Detective Smeade striding toward her with a black leather briefcase in one hand. He smiled when he saw her.

"Violet, good to see you again."

"Good to see you, Detective Smeade."

"How's your mom doing?"

"Much better, thanks. She should be able to come home soon."

"That'll be good for her. How long are you going to stick around?"

Violet toed the carpet, surprised to realize she hadn't given much thought to the duration of her stay. To the fact that it would need to come to an end fairly soon.

"Probably another week, maybe two," she said. "At least until Mom can get around okay by herself and start taking appointments again."

"You've been able to pick up enough accounting work to keep yourself busy?"

"There's been a surprising demand for it."

"Good, that's good." He laughed. "Bet the accounting thing isn't nearly as fun and interesting as what you're doing here."

Violet started to point out that "fun" and "interesting" were hardly the soundest reasons for a career choice, but she couldn't make her mouth form the words.

"Right," she said. "So shall we get started?"

"Absolutely. I know you're probably busy."

"Actually, today's been pretty quiet. Just waiting for the phone to ring, really."

Violet led the way to the back of the shop as Detective Smeade chuckled again behind her.

"Probably helps to know beforehand when that's going to happen. The phone ringing, I mean. I'll bet that's the best thing about being psychic. You're never caught on the can when an important call comes."

"Uh… right. Please, have a seat. Can I get you anything to drink?"

"No thanks, I'm good."

They both eased into the red velvet chairs, Violet not feeling any more relaxed than she had a week ago when they'd assumed these same positions. She sat there for a moment, noticing the sound system next door had fallen silent.

Shit. No music. Now what?

She took a breath and glanced to her left, where she'd left the notepad filled with songs from earlier in the day. Not a problem. She could still do this.

She looked back at Detective Smeade, who was eyeing her curiously. For the briefest moment, she considered telling him about Frank. About the threats he'd made, about what he'd asked her to do. Maybe that would put an end to all of this. Blackmail was illegal, wasn't it? Especially from a landlord. Violet bit her lip, considering her options.

No. She couldn't do it. She had promised to protect her mom's business, to keep it afloat while Moonbeam was out. And Frank had threatened to ruin it if Violet didn't tell Jed what Frank wanted him to hear.

Telling Detective Smeade was a bad, bad idea. Besides, what good could come from admitting to the police that she could be bought?

"I almost forgot," Detective Smeade said, holding out an envelope. "Here's the check from last time. Sorry it took so long. You know how it is with government offices."

"No problem," Violet said as she accepted the check with a fresh pang of guilt. "Shall we get started?"

"Right, right. Well, here's what I've got."

Detective Smeade bent down and picked up the briefcase. He set it on the table between them and flipped open the locks. Violet watched as he opened the case and began extracting items one at a time.

"This here is a makeup pouch we think the perp handled."

Violet frowned. "He was trying on makeup?"

"No, it was in a car he broke into. The victim says she left it on the passenger seat in front, but when she came back to find her car had been broken into, the makeup pouch and a bunch of other stuff had been thrown in back. We think it was just in his way."

Violet nodded and looked at the case in his hand. "Were there any fingerprints?

"Nope, none at all. That's why I thought maybe you could touch it… you know, get a sense of who this guy is, what he's thinking. You can do that, right? I mean even if he's wearing gloves?"

He held it out to her. Violet hesitated, staring at the case in his hand. Maybe this was her out. *Sorry, Detective, can't help you. I can't get the proper vibe from an object if the suspect wore gloves.*

Next door, the sound system was still infuriatingly silent. Detective Smeade smiled at her. "Moonbeam's always able to do this, but if you're not able to—"

"No, I've got it," Violet said, and she reached out to take the little pouch from him. "Anything else?"

"Well, he hit the adult store about six blocks that way," he said. "He cleaned out the cash register, nabbed a few other items while he was at it. He was wearing a mask, so the surveillance cameras couldn't get a clear shot of his face, but he did knock over a rack of clothing on his way in."

"Clothing?"

"Lingerie, French-maid costumes, those little marble-sack underwear for guys, that sort of thing."

Violet nodded. "So he touched the clothing when he knocked it over?"

"And when he picked it up. Damndest thing, he tidied up after himself. We grabbed a couple things that were hanging on the section of the rack where he grabbed it to set it back up. Here, try this."

He held out a scrap of fabric and Violet set down the makeup case to take it from him.

"Oh," she said, frowning. "It's men's underwear."

"Yeah? Boy, that looks uncomfortable."

Violet frowned. "He didn't try it on or anything, did he?"

"Nope, he's not that kind of pervert. He was pretty much after the cash, we think."

Something stirred in the back of Violet's mind. She fingered the underwear, frowning. She should probably be humming or faking a trance or whatever the hell Moonbeam did in these situations.

But that wasn't what she needed to do to bring things into focus. There was an idea forming in the back of her mind…

"Do you know anything about what this guy looks like?" Violet asked.

"Tall, maybe six-three, six-four. He wears a ski mask when he hits businesses, but we have some footage from an outdoor security camera that shows the same guy breaking into a car. No mask there, but he keeps his face turned away. Like he knows where the camera is."

"Do you know hair color or anything?"

Detective Smeade shrugged. "Dark. That's all we know. The security camera only shoots black and white."

Violet nodded and fingered the G-string. "Very interesting," she said, still grappling with her thoughts.

"Are you getting any sort of… uh… vibe?"

Violet avoided his eyes, pretending to be engrossed in the underwear. "Maybe."

"Here's something that might help."

Detective Smeade reached into the briefcase and pulled out a piece of paper. He handed it to Violet and watched her as she took the paper and studied it.

"That's a still photo from one of the surveillance videos," he said. "It's pretty poor quality, but you see the tattoo?"

Violet squinted at the grainy picture, trying to make out details. She could barely make out a human shape, never mind a tattoo. "I don't see anything."

Detective Smeade extracted another printout from the briefcase and handed it over. "Here's a blowup of that shot in the bottom corner there. This is his arm."

Violet took the paper from him and stared at it. She felt a shiver chatter its way up her backbone. She said nothing as she looked at the inky image, but her brain was going a million miles a second.

She thought of the day last week when Drew had called her in to watch the new guy audition. *Jerry*. She remembered the tattoo on his arm, the mention of a prison record.

"It's still too fuzzy to make out the details, but we think it's a cartoon character of some sort," Detective Smeade offered.

Violet looked up at him and swallowed. "Is this his right bicep?"

Detective Smeade raised his eyebrows at her. "It is."

"Tweety Bird. The tattoo, I think that's what it is."

Detective Smeade took the printout back and stared at it. "I'll be damned. I think you're right. There's the feet right here, and that big head and—" He looked up at her. "Did you get that from reading the aura when you touched that other stuff?"

"Um… yes."

"Wow. Can you tell anything else?"

Violet bit the inside of her cheek, thinking. Drew had hired the guy, hadn't he? The one with the prison record?

Violet looked down into her lap at the makeup bag. She ran a finger over the edge of the underwear, considering what to say to Detective Smeade.

Next door, the sound system was still maddeningly silent. No guidance there.

Violet kept her eyes down, pretending to be engrossed in aura reading or whatever the hell she was supposed to be doing. Should she tell Detective Smeade about Jerry working next door? Did she really want to point a finger at Drew, at his business?

The last time she'd meddled with one of Drew's employees was her reading with Jamie. Look how that had turned out.

She looked up at Detective Smeade. "I'm still trying to get a sense of who this guy is."

"Maybe you can get a name? An address? Some idea how we could track him down?"

Violet hesitated. If she sent the cops next door, Drew would know it was her. She'd thought he was angry when she benignly encouraged Jamie to follow his dreams, but what would he say knowing she'd sicced the police on one of his dancers?

A dancer who admitted he just got out of prison, Violet told herself.

Violet fingered the makeup bag, feigning intense concentration. Maybe there was a way to do this quietly. A way to make sure Drew didn't blame her for meddling with his employees, but she could still do the right thing by reporting a suspicious character.

Or maybe that wasn't the right thing to do at all.

Violet cleared her throat and returned her gaze to Detective Smeade. "I need to… uh… meditate on this for a while."

"Really?"

"Yes. I… the vision isn't solidifying in my mind. Maybe if I had a little more time?"

Detective Smeade frowned. "Well, we're in a bit of a hurry to close this case. How much time do you need?"

"Can I get back to you tomorrow morning?"

"Sure, sure." Detective Smeade nodded at the items in her lap. "You need to keep those?"

Violet looked down at the makeup bag and the underwear. "Oh… well, yes. That would help."

"Okay then. How about if I stop by around nine tomorrow morning to pick those up and see if you've learned anything new?"

"Sure," Violet said as she picked up the makeup bag and underwear from her lap and set them on the coffee table. "I'll take good care of these, don't worry."

Detective Smeade shrugged. "We already searched them for all the evidence we're going to get. What's left—auras or vibes or energy or whatever you want to call it—that's all yours."

"Great," Violet said, feeling grim.

Detective Smeade stood up and smiled at her. "Thanks, Violet. You've already given us a lot to go on. Identifying the tattoo is huge. Who knows? Maybe we'll be able to nab the guy just on that."

Violet bit her lip as she stood up. "That would be wonderful."

Detective Smeade grinned at her. "You've been a big

help, Violet. Wait'll the guys at the station hear what you said about the Tweety Bird thing. They've been trying to figure out what it is for days. Even our forensics guy couldn't get it."

"Oh… Well, if it's all the same to you, maybe don't mention me to too many people?"

Detective Smeade gave her a sympathetic smile. "I got it. You don't want every cop in the precinct down here begging you for information. Or every criminal off the street, for that matter."

"Exactly," Violet said, thinking that criminals and cops were the least of her concerns.

Next door, the sound system finally cranked to life. Violet turned her head to the side, straining to hear the first few notes.

Her heart lodged itself in the bottom of her throat the instant she recognized the song.

Completely oblivious, Detective Smeade grinned. "Wow, haven't heard that tune for a while. They sure don't play it on the radio much anymore."

"No," Violet said slowly. "No they don't."

"Always loved this group. Kiss, right?"

"Right," Violet said, feeling the dagger sink into her heart. The wave of guilt for something she hadn't done yet, but knew she was likely to do.

"What's the name of this one? Don't tell me, I'll get it."

Violet waited, not wanting to say the word, not wanting to hear him say it, either.

Detective Smeade snapped his fingers. "Got it. 'Betrayed,' right?"

"Right," Violet said, and sank back into her chair.

Chapter 17

DREW WAS JUST POUNDING THE LAST NAIL INTO Moonbeam's wheelchair ramp when he heard Violet's rental car pull up the driveway. He resisted the urge to turn around and watch her walk toward him, her crazy-colored eyes missing nothing as she admired the progress he'd made, studied the completed project.

But Drew kept his head down and continued to pound the nail long after it no longer needed pounding. The hammering covered the sound of her footsteps, so he didn't realize she was right behind him until he heard her voice.

"Oh, my God. You finished this all by yourself?"

He turned and sat back on his heels, giving her what he hoped was a casual smile. "There wasn't that much left to do."

"You mean once the other guys got out of your way?"

Drew shrugged. "They did a lot of the hard work."

"Please. It's really nice of you to cover for them, and I know they tried hard, but don't think I didn't notice you were the only one who knew which end of the hammer to hit things with."

"Well, we all have our strengths," Drew said, feeling an inexplicable swell of pride that she appreciated at least one of his.

She smiled at him, lighting up her eyes in a way that made Drew consider what other construction projects he might undertake to prompt her to smile again.

"This must have taken you a long time," Violet said. "I thought you had to work all day?"

"One of my guys didn't show up to practice, so I cut the day short."

"Which guy?"

"Jerry... you know, the new guy. The one you helped me audition?"

"Right, Jerry." Violet looked away, studying the railing.

"He's sure turning out to be great. I was worried about losing Jamie like that, but Jerry might just be able to fill his shoes."

"Good. That's good."

"Anyway, Jerry had the flu today, so he didn't make it in. And since I have to work late tonight, I took off around one thirty so I could come here and finish this up before I have to go back."

"So you left before two?"

"Yeah, why?"

Violet shrugged and didn't meet his eyes. "That explains why I didn't hear any music later in the day."

Drew gripped the hammer in his palm and stood up, taking a step closer to her. "Sam was going to head in around three, so I hope the music started up again after that. Otherwise, something wasn't working right."

"No, I heard it then. Kiss, right?"

Drew stared at her mouth. "What?"

Violet flushed a little but didn't move away. "On the stereo. I think Sam was playing some old songs by Kiss."

"Oh. Right. Probably. That was on the set list I made up, so that makes sense. I told her to make sure to keep the sound down. I hope it didn't bother you."

Violet shook her head, still not meeting his eyes. "No, not too loud. Really, I've started to get used to the music."

"Yeah?"

She nodded. "I kind of miss it when I don't hear it."

"In that case, I'll keep the butt rock cranked."

"Glam rock."

"One of these days I'll get you to call it by its proper name."

"Since when is *butt* included in the proper name of anything?"

Drew laughed and watched her run a hand over the railing he'd just finished sanding. Her fingers trailed over the smooth surface, and Drew felt his mouth go dry at the sight of her caressing the wood.

Get your mind out of the gutter, he ordered himself.

Violet looked up at him and blinked, and Drew had a brief moment of panic.

No such thing as mind reading, he reminded himself. *Thank God*.

"Thanks, Drew," she said slowly. "There's no way I could have built this myself, and it would have cost a fortune to have someone else do it on short notice."

"No sweat."

"No, really. I feel like I owe you. Is there anything I can do for you?"

Drew gave some thought to making a crude comment, but decided against it. No sense going down that path again. He was still reeling a little from the double-entendre conversation about tools the night before.

"Just consider it a neighborly favor," Drew said. "Pay it forward or something."

"But you deserve something, too. I'm a terrible cook,

but I can take you out to dinner. Or what about accounting? Do you have any paperwork you need help with?
I'm good at that."

Drew entertained a quick fantasy of Violet bent low
over his ledgers, her blouse gaping open a little in front
as she studied the numbers with those wild eyes magni-
fied behind a pair of tortoiseshell glasses, and maybe
one of those plaid skirts with knee socks and—

"Drew?"

"Yes?"

"You had a funny look on your face."

"Oh. Just wondering if I should have used nine-penny
nails instead of sixteen."

Violet looked at him oddly. "I'm sure whatever you
used is perfect. Really, thanks so much."

"You're welcome. I was happy to do it. I might take
you up on your offer though."

"Which one?"

"The paperwork. It's the end of the month, and I still
have some organizing to do before I can hand everything
off to my bookkeeper."

"Oh… Well, I'm happy to do some bookkeeping
for you."

"No, I've got that covered. But I could really use a
hand getting my receipts organized, tallying up some of
the preliminary numbers. It's kind of grunt work, but—"

"Deal," Violet said, giving him another smile. "When
do you want me?"

Now, thought Drew. *Immediately. If I have to wait a
second longer, my brain might explode.*

"How about if I bring it by the studio in the morning?"

Violet frowned a little. "What time?"

"Nineish?"

"Can we make it ten?"

"Sure. Not a problem. You have an appointment?"

"Yes."

Violet was quiet for a moment, her fingers still trailing over the new rail. "How's Jamie doing?"

Drew felt a tiny flicker of irritation. He tried to ignore it, but it was still there, still reminding him that if it weren't for Violet, Jamie wouldn't be leaving. Wouldn't be putting himself in harm's way.

"Fine," Drew said, trying to keep the tightness from his voice. "Still talking about Afghanistan."

"So he's really planning to go?"

"Apparently. He's been talking to some not-for-profit organization that builds schools over there."

"So he'll be with someone? I mean… he's not just going to go wandering off by himself?"

"That's the plan, but it's hard to say what he'll do."

"But he'll definitely be safer if he's with a group."

Drew gripped the hammer a little tighter. He looked at it for a second, then bent down and set it carefully back in his toolbox. Avoiding Violet's eyes.

"Can we not talk about this right now?" he said finally. "I know we agreed that Jamie should do whatever he wants to do with his life, but I guess I'm still not used to this war-zone idea. He's a good kid, and if anything happens to him—"

"It's okay," Violet said quickly. "Sorry to bring it up."

"Look, I'm not still mad. It's just the whole thing about meddling with people's lives, with my business—"

"No, really. I understand. I know you worry about Jamie. I'm sorry if what I said prompted him to do this."

Drew nodded, but didn't say anything else. Violet just stood there looking miserable, and Drew wanted to kick himself for being a jerk. It wasn't her fault Jamie had quit. Not exactly. It probably would have happened eventually. So what if Violet had been the one to nudge him from the nest?

Drew was just about to open his mouth to say so when a car wheeled into the driveway. A black Mercedes. Drew stared at it, feeling his mood darken.

"Looks like your boyfriend's here," he said.

Violet looked at him, her eyes wide. "We've been dating, but he's not my boyfriend."

"Does he know that?"

Violet didn't say anything, but he saw her go stiff as Chris opened the car door. He watched as she made a conscious effort to paste a smile on her face.

"Chris, what a nice surprise," Violet called as he strode toward them, looking dapper and well dressed and so obviously smitten with Violet that Drew wanted to grab the hammer and knock the guy in the forehead.

He's a perfectly nice person, Drew told himself.

Still, the way he was looking at Violet…

"Hey, man," he called to Chris. "Good to see you again."

He caught a flicker of dismay in the good doc's expression, but Chris recovered quickly. Drew kicked the lid shut on his toolbox. No sense taking any chances with the hammer.

"Hey, Drew," Chris replied cheerfully as he took a couple more territorial steps toward Violet.

Jesus, he might as well lift his leg on her.

Chris surveyed the new wheelchair ramp, looking impressed. "Wow, did you finish all this today?"

"Ah, it was nothing," Drew replied. "We did most of the hard work yesterday."

Chris gave Violet a modest smile. "Well, hopefully this helps speed things along with getting Moonbeam home. I saw her today. She's looking great."

"She's feeling great, too," Violet agreed. "I know she's eager to get home."

"Rehab cleared her for release, so now it's just a matter of making sure everything's ready here."

"I think we're close. The occupational therapist is coming to check tomorrow."

"That's great. You must be so excited."

Chris shot a quick look at Drew, his expression friendly. But Drew could read the message in his eyes. *Leave.*

Drew folded his arms over his chest and smiled. "You kids have plans tonight?"

"Oh," Violet said, glancing at Chris. "I didn't sleep well last night, so I was hoping to go to bed early and—"

"Actually, Violet, I thought maybe I could take you out for dinner," Chris said.

Drew watched as Violet curled her fingers in toward her palms. She didn't answer him right away, and Drew saw the tension creep into Chris's smile.

"Dinner?" Violet repeated.

"Sure. There's this great little Italian place. Or if you'd rather stay in, we could order something casual."

Violet hesitated. Drew watched her eyes. Did she want to be rescued? Or did she want a quiet, romantic dinner with the doc?

None of his business. It was time to make his exit.

Drew cleared his throat. "I have to get back to work

before the evening crowd starts showing up. Violet? I'll see you tomorrow, okay?"

She turned and looked at him, her eyes wide, her smile tentative. What the hell was she thinking?

Drew had no idea.

"Thanks again, Drew," she said slowly. "I mean it, if you need anything besides the paperwork…"

Just you, thought Drew.

"See you tomorrow," he said instead, and stooped down to collect his toolbox.

When Drew was gone, Violet turned to Chris. She looked at his warm brown eyes, his perfectly attractive face, and felt nothing at all.

Dammit to hell.

He smiled at her. "I was hoping to spend the evening alone with you. Not that I wanted to scare your friend away, but I'm glad it's just the two of us now."

Violet stared at him. There was no part of her asking *What did I see in him?* It was pretty damn obvious what she'd seen in him. He was smart, wealthy, attractive, successful—everything she'd ever thought she wanted in a man.

"I think I was wrong," she said.

"What?"

Violet hadn't realized she'd spoken aloud, but now that she had, there was no turning back. She took a deep breath.

"Chris, look…"

She watched his features darken. He knew what was coming. It didn't take a psychic to figure that out.

Chris reached out and touched her hand. "Violet… what's going on?"

She looked down at her feet for a second, getting her bearings. When she looked back up, Chris was still studying her with an intensity she might have found endearing before.

Before what?

"I don't think this is going to work," she said slowly. "I mean, I know we've only been seeing each other a short time, but I think we both had the sense that it could turn into something serious, but now I think… well, I think it won't."

Chris looked at her, his expression grim but not heartbroken. "I see," he said.

"You're a really great guy, fabulous actually… an amazing catch, but—"

"It's Drew, isn't it?"

"What?"

"Drew. You're in love with Drew."

Violet opened her mouth to deny it, but no sound came out.

"It's okay," Chris said, still touching her hand. "Look, if it's any consolation, I knew the first time I saw you with him at the restaurant that night… well, I just knew."

"But I didn't—"

Chris laughed. Not a bitter sound, but not a joyful one, either. "Oh, I know. I could tell you were trying like hell to fight it. I don't really know what that's about, but I think it has something to do with your mom. Or maybe you just didn't picture yourself with a guy who owns a bar with naked men in it. Whatever. The point is, you were fighting it like hell. But it was obvious you were attracted to the guy."

It wasn't obvious to me, Violet thought.

But hadn't it been? Deep down?

"He's not my type," Violet said slowly. "He's all wrong for me."

"Maybe. Probably. But how often does it work out that people make their checklists of what they want in a partner and then go out and fall for precisely that person?"

Violet scuffed her toe on the pavement and tried to think of something deep to say. She was coming up blank. She wanted to argue, to tell him he was wrong about Drew, about her.

But she was so very tired of pretending.

Violet sighed and looked up at him. "But you're such a great guy."

Chris laughed. "Hey, I won't argue with you. You're a great girl. But we've known each other less than two weeks. It's not like we've made a lifelong commitment here."

"I know, but I hoped… I guess I thought…"

"I know," he said, giving her hand a squeeze. "I thought the same thing. But hey, if we'd given it a couple more weeks, I'm sure we'd have found a reason to hate each other."

"I could never hate you."

Chris shrugged. "Maybe not. But the opposite of hate isn't love."

Violet gave him half a smile. "You sound like Moonbeam."

He grasped her hand in his and pulled it to his lips. Softly, he planted a kiss along the bridge of her knuckles.

"Sounding like Moonbeam isn't such a bad thing, is it?"

Violet looked at him and shook her head. "No. No, I guess it's not."

After the requisite hugs and benign pledges to keep in touch, there was really nothing more for Violet and Chris to say to each other.

He didn't seem angry or even particularly hurt, but still. Violet felt like a jerk.

She spent the evening alone eating leftover pizza and organizing Moonbeam's CD collection. She kept her hands busy, but her brain was a million miles away.

Just before midnight, she walked into the kitchen and poured herself a glass of the terribly expensive Pinot they'd uncorked the night before. She carried her wine into the living room and dropped onto the couch, conscious of the fact that she was sitting in the spot where she'd practically torn off her clothes and begged Drew to make love to her just a couple nights earlier.

That would have been bad. He was drunk, for crying out loud. What kind of woman takes advantage of a drunk guy?

Violet took a sip of her wine and thought about Drew. About what it would be like to kiss him again, to go home to him every day, to be with him every night.

A terrible idea.

Isn't it?

They were all wrong for each other. He liked bimbos. He was crass and unfocused and goofy and nothing at all like the man Violet had pictured herself marrying someday.

But he was also funny and sexy and smart. He made her laugh. He made her stop taking herself so damn seriously.

That wasn't a trait she'd ever deliberately sought in a man, but now that she'd discovered the ability to laugh at herself, she couldn't imagine not doing it. Not having someone to make her do it.

She took another sip of wine and thought about Moonbeam. Once upon a time, Violet had built her life around doing precisely the opposite of what Moonbeam wanted. If her mother suggested Neapolitan ice cream, Violet chose vanilla. If Moonbeam offered to pay for massage-therapy courses after high school, Violet went looking for accounting programs on the opposite coast. If Moonbeam espoused her political views, Violet made it a point to take the other stance.

But somehow, Violet had lost her fondness for building her life around defying Moonbeam. Around not *becoming* Moonbeam.

So what did that mean for Drew and Violet?

Moonbeam abhorred Drew's business. That much was clear. She wasn't sure exactly what Moonbeam thought of Drew, but it couldn't be good.

Violet took a sip of wine and thought about that.

She'd spent the last two weeks thinking of a million reasons she didn't belong with Drew. He wasn't her type. He knew too many secrets about her, had a long-standing feud with her mother, had made no secret about wanting to get his hands on their studio space. He could bring the whole business toppling down around them.

He was a dangerous choice. A bad idea for a romantic entanglement.

Somehow, those reasons were starting to seem flimsy.

But on top of all the other reasons, there was this: she cared about what Moonbeam thought. After all these years of fleeing her mother's kooky shadow, she suddenly found herself craving Moonbeam's approval.

Even with her love life.

"How's that for fucking irony," Violet said aloud, and took another sip of wine.

Fine, forget about Moonbeam's approval. Forget about the business, the whole phony psychic thing, the fact that Drew would probably never be interested in a woman his own age with an IQ above eighty.

Aside from all that, Violet was leaving soon. She had a job back in Maine, a life.

True, it wasn't the most exciting job, or an exciting life. But since when had that mattered?

Since now, Violet thought.

She drained the rest of her wine and walked to the kitchen. She rinsed out the glass and set it out to dry. Then she walked upstairs to her bathroom and brushed her teeth with the organic toothpaste she remembered from childhood. It tasted like dirt and root beer, and Violet had hated it as a child. She remembered pleading with Moonbeam for Aquafresh, sneaking a smear of a friend's Crest at a sleepover in third grade.

Now, Violet looked at the tube in her hand and studied the lettering that touted all organic ingredients. Could she buy this stuff in Maine, or should she stock up here?

She sighed and rinsed out the sink before retreating to her bedroom. She changed into her favorite silk pajamas and tucked herself into bed. She lay there for a few minutes, blinking at the clock.

She hadn't slept well the night before, so she expected to fall right asleep. She waited for fatigue to overcome her, for her mind to drift into oblivion as her body became weightless and numb.

It wasn't happening.

Violet rolled over and curled into a ball, hoping another position might work. She counted sheep. She divided fractions in her mind. She tried to remember the lyrics to "You Shook Me All Night Long."

She rolled back over and looked at the clock.

It was after one a.m. Too late to go for a jog. Too early to get up and start her day. She didn't feel tired. She didn't feel like being in bed.

Okay, she *did* feel like being in bed.

Just not alone.

Violet flopped onto her back and stared at the ceiling.

After weeks of fighting it, pretending she wasn't interested, avoiding the obvious, Violet had to accept one simple fact.

She wanted Drew.

She wanted him very badly.

"To hell with this," she said out loud, and threw off the covers.

Chapter 18

"CAN I CALL YOU LADIES A CAB?" DREW ASKED A TRIO of intoxicated women hunkered down at the bar as he stole a quick glance at the clock.

It was 1:53 a.m.—just a few minutes before closing time at the bar—and Drew was more than ready to go home.

One of the women smiled up at him blearily. "Can't we get that guy to drive us home?" she slurred, pointing across the room.

Drew followed the direction of her finger to where Jerry was clumsily refastening the Velcro on his police uniform.

"He's not a cab driver," Drew said. "But how about if I call you a real one?"

"Can we put the tip in his pants?"

"I don't recommend it."

Drew headed to the other end of the bar and picked up the phone, hitting the speed-dial number for a cab company that frequently came to retrieve his more festive clients. He chatted with the guy for a few minutes, describing the clients and suggesting they send a car with an easy-to-clean interior.

As soon as he hung up the phone, he looked back at the women to be sure they were all still sitting upright.

He spotted a new face in the group. A familiar, disturbingly beautiful face.

"Violet?" Drew said.

He was at least fifteen feet away, but she looked up the instant he called her name and smiled at him.

"Hello, Drew."

He covered the distance to the end of the bar in just a few steps, his heart racing stupidly. "Is everything okay? Are you hurt? Drunk? Why are you here?"

She grinned at him and lifted a water glass she must have gotten from somewhere. "Yes. No. No. To seduce you."

He frowned. "What?"

"I was answering your questions. In the order that you—"

"Wait," he stammered as her words started to register. "Wh-what did you say?"

The drunk woman next to Violet smacked him on the shoulder so hard she teetered on her barstool. "She said she wants to seduce you, dumbass."

The woman laughed like this was the funniest thing she'd heard all night. She began to wobble on her barstool again, this time showing no signs of catching herself.

Drew reached across the bar and grabbed her by one shoulder while Violet propped the woman up from the other side. Sam swooped in and cleared away the women's empty glasses, leaving Violet's water in front of her. Drew stared dumbly at Violet, who was offering a kind smile to the drunk woman.

"Thanks for the translation," Violet told her. "He's a little slow sometimes."

"They all are, honey," the woman slurred. "They all are. Sometimes you gotta take the bull by the… by the… whatever. You know?"

"Sure," Violet agreed, taking a sip from her glass of water.

Drew was still two steps behind in the conversation. Had Violet really said what he thought she'd said? That she was here to seduce him?

"Hey, did you call for a cab?" Sam yelled from the doorway.

Drew waved a hand to catch her attention and pointed at the drunk women, one of whom was now sprawled out across the bar, fast asleep.

"Over here," he called. "Just these three. Violet's um… Violet's staying here for a bit."

Sam smiled at him and winked. "Gotcha," she said as she walked over and roused the sleeping woman. "Come on, ladies. Your chariot awaits."

The women grumbled and staggered, but began trudging reluctantly away from the bar. Sam strode over to the bar and held her hand out to Drew. "Can you grab my purse? It's under there, on the other side of the beer mugs."

Drew complied, still a little dazed, as Sam took the purse and began shepherding her intoxicated flock toward the exit.

"I'll lock up on my way out," Sam called as she headed for the door. "You kids have fun!"

"Thanks for the cherries," Violet yelled.

"My pleasure!"

"Cherries?" Drew asked, and Violet smiled at him.

"I was trying to practice tying the stem in a knot with my tongue as part of my seduction plan. It didn't work out so well, but they're good with the water."

She lifted her glass, trying to play it cool, but Drew saw her hand shake a little.

"Seduction plan," he said, still a little dumbfounded.

"What happened to 'We're all wrong for each other and this is the dumbest idea ever'?"

"I'm tired of fighting it. I want you. You want me. We both want each other."

"You sound pretty sure of that."

"Not really, but I fake it well."

Drew grinned. "For the record, that's not a great line to use on a guy you're trying to seduce."

Violet leaned forward on the bar, giving him a glimpse down the front of her blouse. "For the record, I never fake it. Any man worth seducing is willing to do the work required to get it right."

Drew opened his mouth to say something, but his tongue wouldn't cooperate.

Get it together, man. You'll probably be needing your tongue.

The bar was eerily silent now. He'd turned the music down to almost nothing, and he couldn't even make out the song that was playing. He could, however, make out the shape of Violet's breasts beneath her icy-blue silk blouse. She wore a slim black skirt and high-heeled boots that came up to her knees. Red lipstick. Smoky eyes.

She'd definitely dressed for seduction. Drew blinked, wondering if she was just a figment of his imagination. Could he really be this lucky?

"Where's Chris?" he asked. "Did you guys have a fight?"

"Chris?" She seemed genuinely perplexed.

"Right. The dashing doctor you've been knocking boots with. Stopped by your house this evening. Ringing any bells?"

Violet rolled her eyes. "We never knocked boots. We barely kissed, and even that wasn't great."

"I'm not disappointed to hear that. Any of it."

She drained her water glass and Drew reached over the bar and grabbed it. He refilled it slowly, not saying anything right away.

"Can I have another cherry?" she asked.

"Still planning to try the knot-tying thing with your tongue?"

"Would that turn you on?"

She was biting her lip again, equal parts bravado and nervous energy. He smiled to himself, intrigued by this new side of Violet, such a magnetic blend of confident seductress and quirky lunatic.

That's the turn-on.

"You don't need gimmicks to seduce me," Drew said as he set the water glass in front of her. "You just need to show up."

Violet nodded and gripped her glass with both hands. "I'm here. Now what?"

He grinned. "You're asking for seduction instruction?"

"Now there's a college course I never took."

"I'm pretty sure you've mastered it anyway."

She bit her lip. "Actually, I'm not so sure. I'm usually the one *being* seduced. The seductress role is new to me."

"You're doing great so far."

"Yeah?"

"Yeah."

Her eyes were flashing with the lights from the disco ball and with something like mischief. Drew felt an ache in his gut and wanted her so badly he could barely breathe.

Be cool, he told himself. *Don't blow this.*

They'd come so close so many times in the past few days. He was afraid to breathe, for fear of scaring her away. Maybe if he tried the slow, romantic approach. Maybe a glass of wine, a neck rub, some soft words whispered against her neck. He started to reach for her…

"Hey, I know!" Violet said, jumping off her barstool and grinning at him. "I could strip."

"What?"

"Jamie showed me how. He taught me some moves last week. That's seductive, right?"

"Are you serious?"

"Hey, I've seen *9½ Weeks.*"

She was heading for the center stage now, looking wild-eyed and so damn beautiful that Drew just stared after her. When she reached the steps, she cocked her head to the side.

"What's that song?"

Drew moved out from behind the bar and over to the sound system. He glanced at the readout as he picked up the remote.

"I'm surprised you could hear that," he said as he turned up the volume. "I had it almost all the way off."

Warrant's "Cherry Pie" came humming through the speakers, and the two of them locked eyes.

"Cherries," Violet said.

"Cherry pie, no less. Moonbeam."

Violet winced. "Maybe let's not talk about my mom when I'm trying to seduce you?"

"Right, right. Go ahead."

He watched as she mounted the stage with nervous

determination, her stride confident even as her hands twisted into shaky fists at her side.

Drew moved to the edge of the stage, his heart hammering hard in his chest. He took in the curve of her hips, the flash of thigh between the top of her boots and the hem of her skirt. Her hair was loose around her shoulders, dark and silky, and he ached to bury his face in the crook of her neck.

God, she's beautiful.

Violet reached the top of the steps and turned to look at him. She grinned and reached for the top button on her blouse. Her fingernails were short, but shimmery with some sort of pink polish. The blouse was silk, expensive. Drew longed to touch it, touch her. She swayed a little to the music, her hips moving just barely, just enough to tantalize.

She licked her lips and smiled at him, sliding her fingers into her hair. Then she reached down and flicked open the button just below her throat. Drew felt his heart clutch.

She grinned at him, her eyes locked on his, gauging his response.

Drew swallowed, completely speechless for the first time in his life. In all his years of dating, all the exotic dancers he'd seen in his club, he'd never had a woman strip for him. Not ever. Especially not one so beautiful, so classy, so unbelievably sexy.

Violet slid one hand up the side of her torso, her fingers moving delicately along the silk that covered her belly. Drew followed her hand with his eyes, mesmerized, watching as she caressed her rib cage and kept moving up.

"Oh, God," he said as she cupped her breast and gave him a wicked smile.

All the blood was draining from his brain, heading someplace else in a big hurry. Drew shoved his hands in his pockets and stared at her, trying not to let his mouth drop open as Violet circled her palm over cool blue silk, her fingers tracing the sharp peak of her nipple.

Her hips were still moving, and with the other hand, she reached up and flicked open a second button.

"Jesus," Drew murmured as he caught a flash of blue lace, the same color as her blouse.

Violet's nipples strained against the silk, and he ached to take one in his mouth. To touch her. To slide his hands up her thigh, up her skirt, and…

He took a step toward the edge of the stage and reached for her.

She took a step back, tantalizing him, keeping her body just out of his reach. She kept moving, her lips parted and smiling, her hips circling with aching slowness.

"You're making me crazy," he murmured.

"That's the idea," she said, pivoting a little to give him a glimpse of the most perfect ass he'd ever laid eyes on. She pivoted again and smiled at him, her fingers still stroking her breast.

Drew groaned. "You win. I want you so much I'm about to explode here."

She gave a pointed look at his crotch and grinned. "I can see that."

He stepped closer and reached for her again. She took another step back, still teasing, still drawing out the seduction. She wobbled a little on one heel, but seemed to catch herself. Then she took another step back.

"Oh!" she yelped, and toppled backward.

Drew leapt up and caught her around the waist, pulling her to him. Just in time.

Clang.

"Ouch!"

Okay, not just in time.

Violet rubbed the side of her head, looking jarred. She blinked up at him, a funny half smile on her lips.

"I brained myself on a stripper pole," she said, giggling a little. "Is this the most awkward seduction in history or what?"

Drew tightened his arm around her waist, determined not to release her now that he was holding her against him.

God, she felt good.

"Sorry about that," he murmured. "My fault. I should have warned you about the pole."

She grinned as he brushed her hair back from the side of her face. His fingers traced the rapidly swelling bump on the side of her head, making her wince a little.

"So much for seduction, huh?" she said, giggling again.

"Hey, it worked for me. You were amazing."

"Yeah?"

"Hot. Unbelievably hot."

She flushed a little. "My first time as a seductress. I didn't quite finish the job."

Drew grinned. "How about if you let me finish the job?"

"You're planning to strip?"

"Let's get some ice."

"Ice?"

"For your head."

"I don't need—"

But he scooped her into his arms, lifting her off the

ground and effectively cutting off her protest. She was surprisingly light as he carried her down the steps and away from the stage.

"Drew, I'm fine, I can walk."

"I know you can," he said as he moved around the bar and set her down on the edge of it. "This is just my excuse to get my hands on you. And to make sure you can't run away this time."

"How very caveman of you."

"Damn right."

Prying a reluctant hand off Violet's thigh, he shoved a handful of ice into a plastic baggie and zipped it shut. He set the baggie in her outstretched palm and reached for her again.

"Hold that on the swelling," he said, lifting her off the bar and into his arms again.

Violet grinned and slid the bag down his torso, going for his groin. He pulled her tighter against him, cutting off her path to his crotch.

"Not that swelling," he grunted, carrying her toward the back of the bar.

"Where are we going?" she asked, pressing the ice to her temple, her voice beautifully breathless.

"My office. You need medical attention."

She giggled again. "Oh, well, there's this doctor I know—"

Drew kicked his office door open, prompting a startled squeal from Violet.

"Forget about the doctor," he said.

"What doctor?" she gasped, and squirmed against him.

—⁓—

In all her years of dating, Violet had never had a guy sweep her off her feet and carry her around as if he were some sort of caveman.

Of course, she'd never brained herself on a stripper pole while trying to seduce a man, either.

This was definitely a night of firsts.

Drew kicked his office door shut behind him and set her on a leather sofa that was huge and surprisingly cozy.

"So this is your lair?" she asked, looking around the room as he released her just long enough to click the lock shut on his office door.

"One of several," he said. "I move whenever the space gets too full of mastodon carcasses."

"Hmm, yes, it's tough to drag women around by the hair with all those bones in the way."

Drew was back at the couch now, his hands huge and hot on her knees as he knelt down on the carpet in front of her. Violet gasped as his fingers slid along her bare thighs, pushing her skirt up roughly. His mouth found a spot on the outside of her left knee—hardly a familiar erotic zone—but Violet groaned with pleasure as his tongue made slow circles there and began teasing its way up.

"This time, you're not running away," he murmured.

"I promise not to try."

She tossed her ice pack aside and twisted her hands into his hair, leaning back against the sofa as Drew moved over the crest of her knee to nip the skin on her inner thigh. Then he slid back down to make lazy circles with his tongue on the back side of her knee.

"Oh, God," Violet whimpered, and felt herself slide lower on the couch. The hem of her skirt rode higher, giving Drew access to previously unclaimed territory.

She'd been eyeing his shoulders for weeks now, wondering how the broad expanse of muscle and bone would feel beneath her palms. Now she had a free pass to devour every curve of him, to trace each muscle with the tips of her fingers. She grazed him lightly with her nails, enjoying the tautness of flesh, the quiver of muscle.

More.

Drew slid one hand higher under her skirt, palming the curve of her butt while his tongue traced a nerve on the inside of her thigh.

Whimpering again, Violet sat up and clawed at the neck of his shirt, fumbling her way over his collar to reach the top button. She grabbed hold of it and yanked, feeling crazed, delirious, wanting him so much, her skin ached.

"Whoops." A button popped off and went skittering across the floor. "Sorry."

"Not a problem," Drew murmured against her thigh, somehow managing to shrug the shirt off the rest of the way without breaking contact between her flesh and his mouth. A few more buttons went bouncing under the sofa, but Violet barely noticed.

She drank him in with her eyes, marveling at all the muscle and flesh that was there for her use. It was like a buffet packed with amazing delicacies she never knew existed. She slid her hands around his back, clutching at his shoulder blades as Drew pushed her skirt up higher around her hips.

"Blue lace," he murmured appreciatively, sliding a finger along the waistband. "You found the matching set this time instead of skipping the panties."

She gasped as Drew slid a finger beneath the wispy

fabric. He barely made contact, but Violet felt stars explode behind her eyelids. His touch was delicate, slippery, slow, and Violet bit the back of her hand to keep from crying out.

Drew laughed. "No one's here. Feel free to make as much noise as you want."

Violet gasped as he stroked her again. She pressed against him, urging him to be rougher, to slide inside her. Drew pulled back, taking his time, teasing her.

"More," she whimpered.

"Not yet."

"Please?"

Drew just laughed and slid his finger away, moving along the edge of the lace, tracing her pelvic bone, the edge of her hip. His other hand still palmed the curve of her butt, his fingers digging roughly into muscle and flesh.

God, I want him.

Violet slid her fingernails down his ribs, the ripple of skin, the hardness of bone. She groaned and pulled him closer, his pecs tight against her bare knees.

She wanted to feel more of him. *All of him.*

She pressed a hand to his bare chest and pushed hard, toppling him backward onto the carpet. His expression barely registered surprise before Violet lunged for him, pinning him down between her thighs. Her skirt was still bunched around her waist as she clenched her legs around him and held him against her.

"I take it you wanted to change positions?" he said, fastening his hands around her hips.

"Yes," she moaned, partly to answer the question, partly because he felt so damn good pressed against her.

Violet felt the carpet grinding into her bare knees,

but she didn't care if it scraped them raw. She could feel the hardness of him straining against his jeans, the thin wisp of lace between her legs not offering any protection from the rough denim.

Good.

She ground against him, gasping at the sensation, writhing harder, craving more.

"God, you're so hot," Drew moaned, clutching her hips hard enough to leave marks in her flesh.

Violet reached up and fumbled with the buttons on her blouse, giving only a fleeting thought to the price of expensive silk as she tugged at the opening. Another button joined the growing pile on the floor.

She wriggled her arms free and tossed the blouse aside, giving Drew a full view of the lace bra. She was desperate to press her breasts against all that beautiful muscle and flesh. She bent forward, gasping as her nipples grazed the wall of muscle beneath her.

"Perfect breasts," he gasped, and reached around to cup them from the sides.

Violet sat up a little and moaned as his thumbs found her nipples and began making slow circles. His fingers dug into her ribs, not gentle, not that she wanted him to be. She gripped his shoulders hard.

"More," she gasped, and ground herself against him, feeling the seam of his jeans rough between her legs. He was so hard.

She slid down a little, reaching for his fly. The denim was damp—probably her fault, but she was way beyond caring. She wanted him so badly she was dizzy from it. She slid down farther, clawing at his belt buckle, yanking at the button fly on his jeans, ferocious in her desire.

Drew groaned as her fingernails raked the tender flesh of his belly, but he didn't pull away. He looked up at her, his eyes flashing with heat.

"We should have thought ahead and worn Velcro," he murmured, and reached down to help her yank his jeans the rest of the way off.

Violet smiled down at him, delighted to have him nearly naked beneath her. She reached for his waistband, ready to peel away the last layer.

"Wait," Drew gasped. "Condom. Top right drawer."

Violet grinned. "Wait," she repeated, her voice teasing. "Not just yet."

She reached behind her and found the ice pack where she'd dropped it at the edge of the sofa. Drew's eyes widened a little, but he didn't protest as Violet peeled the bag open and pulled out an ice cube. She held it between two fingers, touching it to his sternum and drawing it downward.

Drew gasped as she slid the melting cube along his chest, moving slowly, making wet circles around one nipple, then the other, the trail of chilly water sliding down his ribs.

He gasped as she leaned forward and slid her tongue up his rib cage, warming the chilled flesh. When the ice cube was completely melted, she sat up and grinned.

"Good thing there's more," she murmured, and started to reach behind her.

"Good thing," Drew agreed, and caught both of her wrists in one hand. He used his free hand to reach for the ice pack, grinning at her as he pinned her hands in place against his chest.

Slowly, he drew the ice cube along the thin flesh

on the inside of her arm. Violet shivered against him, wriggling as he licked his way toward the crook of her elbow. He held tight to her wrists, not letting her move.

"Very wet," he murmured.

"Don't stop."

Goose bumps pricked her forearms, but every other spot on her body was burning with heat. She writhed against him, wanting to feel more of him.

The ice melted and Drew released her hands. The second she was free, she grabbed for his waistband, tugging at the elastic of his boxer briefs. Her hands were greedy, searching, and she gasped as she wrapped her fingers around the length of him. Drew gasped too, as Violet gripped him hard, enjoying the solid heat in her palm.

She teased him like that for a few more seconds, sliding her fingers over him, stroking him, memorizing every beautiful inch of his hardness.

Drew moved against her, his hips rising to meet her, his hand gripping the edge of her thigh. He reached for her hand.

"You'd better stop," he murmured. "Unless you want this to be over before it starts."

She grinned and stroked him harder. "Make me."

"My pleasure."

Before she could say anything else, he flipped her neatly onto her back, pinning her beneath him. Violet's breath escaped in a whoosh as he used his weight to press her against the carpet, all that hot, heavy muscle against her. She was trapped. Possessed.

She'd never felt so desirable.

Drew grabbed her wrists again, his hands huge and

powerful as he pinned them over her head. She groaned as he pressed the tender flesh against the carpet, and Violet raised her hips to feel more of him.

She lifted her head and found his pulse with her tongue. She traced the curve of his neck, tasting salt, cedar, desire.

Drew groaned, his voice rumbling against her lips.

"I've wanted you from the first day I saw you," he murmured, drawing his teeth along the column of her neck. "Did you know that?"

"Yes," she gasped.

He laughed. "Modest."

"I wanted you, too."

"I know."

Violet opened her legs and clenched them around his hips, locking her ankles to pull him tighter against her. She groaned as she felt his hardness against the whisper of damp lace between her legs.

Drew was kissing her shoulder, moving his way down her sternum, his tongue hot and searching. He used his free hand to shove her bra strap to one side, releasing her left breast. His mouth covered her nipple, devouring her, and Violet moaned.

He circled slowly, using his tongue to tease, to make her mindless. He tugged her strap the rest of the way down and cupped her breast in his palm, kneading her roughly while his tongue made delicate circles. The contrast of soft and rough, gentle and firm, left her feeling dizzy, breathless.

She bucked against him, wanting more, wanting release.

"Please," she gasped.

"Not yet."

"Drew."

He laughed. "I love the way you say my name."

"So make me scream it."

She raised her hips again, harder this time, desperate to buck him off, to seize control again. He was stronger, but she had the element of surprise. Wrenching her wrists free, she raked her fingernails down his back. He rolled away, and Violet made her escape, her heart pounding hard with desire.

She grabbed for the ice again, grabbing a little more this time. She pushed against his chest with the heel of her hand, pressing him back down onto the carpet. He didn't resist, though it was obvious he could dominate her again anytime he wanted.

She smiled. "My turn."

With one hand still on his chest, she dragged the ice-filled palm down his torso and wrapped her fingers around him. He gasped—from shock or pleasure, Violet couldn't tell. Probably both.

She slid the ice down his hard length, taking care to let the heat of her fingers warm one spot of flesh while the ice slipped coolly along another. She glided her hand back up, then down again, then up, alternating pressure. He thrust against her palm, and Violet felt her pulse speed up. She twisted her grip, feeling the melted ice slide down her wrist. She bent to lick it off and paused to breathe warmly against Drew's abdomen.

"Violet," Drew gasped. "You'd better stop…"

"Hmm?" she said, letting her hair tickle his belly.

Drew sat up and caught her shoulders in his hands. His eyes were desperate, pupils dilated, his breath was ragged.

Violet sat back, triumphant, desperate, hungry.

"Now?" she gasped.

Drew grinned and flipped her over again, and Violet savored the weight of him once more. His chest was rough against her breasts, and she felt her hip bones pushing hard into him.

He sat up a little, his weight shifting as he reached across her to yank open his desk drawer.

"Good thinking," she gasped as he tore open the condom packet with his teeth.

"I've only got a few brain cells still functioning," he said, releasing her just long enough to sheathe himself.

He slid into her hard, so sudden it stole her breath. She arched against him and cried out, rising up to meet him as he thrust into her again.

She wrapped her legs around him, pulling him against her, wanting to hold all that sensation.

He moved slowly at first, gentle after all that roughness. She pressed her heels against his tailbone, urging him on, lifting her hips.

"So soft," he murmured against her throat. "You're so soft."

Violet gripped his shoulder blades and moaned, moving under him as he began to thrust harder, deeper. He was balancing his weight on his hands, trying not to crush her, but Violet wanted to be crushed. She pulled him down to her, kissing him deeply, pushing herself up against him.

"God, Violet."

He thrust into her again, hitting something that made her lose her breath. She gasped as he moved again, rocking into her harder.

Oh, Yes!

She began to lose her grasp on all the other sensations around her. She barely noticed the rug grating her elbows, the scent of leather, the hum of a long-forgotten '80s pop tune from the sound system on the other side of the locked door.

All she noticed was him. The movement of his hips, the slam of his heartbeat against hers, the sticky heat of his skin.

"Oh, God!" she shrieked as the first wave of sensation crashed into her, knocking her backward as she gripped him tighter.

"Christ!" he gasped in her ear, and drove deeper into her.

Violet screamed and raked her nails down his back, lifting her hips to take all of him, to contain the sensation.

He moved against her endlessly as her brain let go of reality, churning in a swirl of stars and cherry-hued light as she screamed his name again and again and again.

Chapter 19

DREW HAD ALWAYS PRIDED HIMSELF ON NOT BEING THE sort of guy to conk out immediately after sex. He was an old pro at postcoital pillow talk. He was even willing to spoon when the occasion called for it.

But the occasion of his first coupling with Violet called for IV fluids and a good long nap.

He awoke on the sofa in his office feeling parched and a little confused. Where was he? Where were his pants? Was it time to open the bar?

He looked down to see a waterfall of dark hair spilling across his chest, and his whole body relaxed in an instant.

Violet.

To hell with his pants and the bar.

Drew reached down and stroked her hair, enjoying the silky feel of it sliding between his fingers.

"Hmmm," Violet murmured in her sleep, and burrowed into the crook of his arm.

Drew looked at her for a moment, still a little awestruck. How had this happened?

Not that he wasn't glad. But after years of postdivorce determination never to get involved with another high-strung, type-A female, it was taking a few moments to adjust to the sight of one naked in his office.

He took in the perfect curve of her waist, the softness of her breasts on his chest, the flowery scent of her hair.

Okay, maybe it wasn't such an adjustment.

"Did you just smell my hair?" Violet murmured.

"No."

She sat up and gave him a sleepy smile. "Yes you did."

"Then why did you ask?"

"To see if you'd lie."

Drew grinned and kissed her forehead, aware that he probably had terrible morning breath, but willing to take the chance. "You caught me red-handed on that one," he said. "Probably better call the cops to arrest me."

He expected her to laugh, but instead, she sat bolt upright, her eyes frantic.

"What time is it?"

Unexpectedly dazzled by the sight of the world's most beautiful breasts, Drew took a moment to realize she'd asked a question.

He took another moment to realize his watch had been flung somewhere across the room. Maybe his pants were near his watch?

Violet jumped up, covering her perfect breasts with her perfect arm while she searched madly for a functional timepiece.

"Is the clock on your desk right?" she asked as she picked up the vintage Mickey Mouse alarm clock.

"Should be. What does it say?"

"Only six. Thank God. I have time to go home and shower before my first appointment."

Drew grinned and reached for her. "You told me earlier that your first appointment isn't until nine. You have time for more than a shower."

Violet flushed pink from her cheeks to her... well, other cheeks, but she didn't resist as he hooked his arm around her waist and pulled her back down on the sofa with him. He grabbed the quilt that normally rested on the back of the sofa—thank God for Sam's homey touches—and pulled it over them.

"You know," Violet said as Drew began to kiss his way down her throat. "This has to be the least romantic courtship in the history of the planet."

"How do you mean?" he asked, not really caring as his lips approached the slope of her breast.

She moaned a little and squirmed in his arms, but kept talking. "Well, you wooed me by juggling toilet paper, plunging the toilets, and building a wheelchair ramp for my mother—a woman you've been feuding with for the last decade."

"I wouldn't say *feuding*, exactly—"

"And of course, I seduced you by nearly knocking myself unconscious on a stripper pole."

"Always a fantasy of mine," he murmured as his tongue found her nipple. "Unconscious amateur strippers falling into my arms."

Violet gasped and arched her back, and Drew pulled her tighter against him, cupping his hand around the outside of her breast so he could savor the weight of it in his palm.

She moaned—part desire, part frustration, apparently—and pushed his hand aside. Sitting up on the couch, she gave a regretful sigh.

"I really have to go," she said, her breath a little ragged. "Sorry, but this appointment I have this morning at nine... well, it's complicated."

"Complicated how?"

She looked at him, not speaking for a moment. She seemed to be hesitating.

"Hey, don't worry about it," he told her. "We don't have to talk about work. In fact, we should probably make that a rule."

"Rule?"

"I don't know what's going to happen between us, but one thing I do know is that we need to stay the hell out of each other's business, right?"

Violet didn't say anything, but she nodded almost imperceptibly.

Drew planted a kiss on her hip as he rested his chin against her thigh. "Look, it's not a secret your mom isn't a fan of my business, and God knows I'm not wild about you two messing with people's lives over there with pseudopsychic stuff."

Violet's expression darkened, and Drew considered the possibility that it might not be wise to insult a woman's mother and profession with one's genitals exposed. He tucked the quilt tighter around his waist and looked up in time to see her open her mouth to protest.

"Drew, I—"

"Sorry. Look, I didn't mean that the way it sounded. I don't know what you do over there. It's not my business, and I'm sure you don't want to be involved in anything I'm doing over here, right? Let's just agree to leave work at work, okay?"

Violet looked at him for a moment, then stood up and began pulling on her clothes. "Okay. Fine. Your business is your business, and my business is… well, accounting. But for right now, my business is my mother's, so I'm going to keep doing that for at least a little while longer."

"Sure," he agreed, watching a little sadly as she began to dress, covering all the body parts he'd been hoping to fondle again. "So more importantly, when will we be getting naked together again?"

Violet looked up at him. Her smile wasn't as wide as it had been a few moments earlier, but it was still a smile.

"Soon," she said. "Tonight maybe?"

"How about now?"

She laughed and finished tucking her blouse into a skirt that looked a whole lot more wrinkled than it had when she arrived. The blouse was missing at least one button, and her hair was tousled into knots.

He'd never wanted her more.

"Oh, before I forget… you want me to take that paperwork now?" she asked.

"Here I am mentally undressing you, and you want to talk about paperwork?"

She smiled again. "You can bring it over later if you want. I just thought since I'm here…"

"Sure, might as well multitask," he said, rolling off the sofa with mock indignation. "A little striptease, a tryst on the office floor, and a bit of accounting."

Violet gave him a light swat on the butt as he leaned down to grab his boxer briefs off the floor. "It's okay, I can get it later," she said.

"No, I might forget later. Just give me a sec."

Drew pulled on his briefs and found an empty cardboard box in the corner. He reached for his inbox and began filling the cardboard carton with receipts and ledgers and a few other random bits of paperwork he'd been neglecting.

"You don't have to do this if you're busy," he told her. "Honestly, I'd rather remove my own armpit hair with my teeth than handle someone else's paperwork."

"A lovely image, but I actually enjoy it. I live to handle paperwork."

He stepped closer to her and set the box down on the edge of the desk. "If there's anything else of mine you'd like to handle, just let me know."

She grinned up at him before standing on tiptoe for a kiss. "Later. I'll handle whatever you ask me to."

"Promise?"

"It'll be my pleasure."

It was eight thirty by the time Violet got home and showered, changed, and returned to the shop to prepare for her visit with Detective Smeade.

She still had no earthly idea what she was going to tell him.

She looked at the underwear and makeup case he'd left on the coffee table, wishing there was such a thing as auras or vibes or whatever the hell Moonbeam claimed to be able to read from inanimate objects. Picking up the makeup case, she held it for a minute, just to see.

Nothing. No singing band of angels, no flashes of clarity, not even a funny feeling in her fingertips.

Violet sighed and set the case down. She eyed the underwear for a moment, but decided against picking it up.

To rat out Drew's employee, or to keep her mouth shut. That was the question. And Violet wasn't sure about the answer.

She spotted the Magic 8 Ball he'd given her and picked it up. Maybe this was the ticket. A simple question, a simple answer. Violet turned it over in her palm.

Ask again later.

"Go to hell," Violet said. She set the ball down and sighed.

Well, she might as well do a little tidying before Detective Smeade showed up. She noticed the half-wilted tulips Chris had brought a week ago and took them over to the sink to add some water. She took a rag and dusted off the Buddha statue. Returning to the seating area, she grabbed the box of Drew's paperwork and started to tuck it inside the cabinet.

That's when she noticed the piece of paper on top of the pile.

She reached inside, her fingers shaking a little.

"Jerry Jester," she read, pulling out the job application. *Desired position: entertainer. Desired salary: I'd do this for free. Most recent position: license-plate manufacturer, Oregon State Penitentiary.*

Violet winced and kept skimming, certain this had to be a mistake. What were the odds? Here was all of Jerry's contact information. His home phone, his address, his social security number, for crying out loud.

Okay, so she hadn't talked to Drew about it. She'd meant to, she really had. But after the fiasco with Jamie, after they'd woken up naked on the sofa together, after his speech about staying out of each other's business... well, it hadn't seemed wise.

How would she even broach the subject? "Thanks for the roll in the hay, and by the way, I'm thinking of telling the cops your favorite new employee is a criminal."

She looked down at the application again. Maybe it was a sign. Sort of like the music. Maybe she was just supposed to take this information and run with it.

If the guy was guilty, he'd go to prison and Drew

would be relieved of an untrustworthy employee. If he wasn't… well, if she didn't say anything to Drew beforehand, he wouldn't know to be pissed at her for making false accusations.

Violet bit her lip and took one last look at the application. Then she set it back in the box and shoved the whole thing into the corner beside the cabinet.

She was making herself a cup of lavender tea when the door chimed and Detective Smeade came strolling in. He was carrying the briefcase again, looking rumpled but eager.

"Hey, Violet. How's it going?"

"Good, thanks. Can I get you some tea?"

"None for me, thanks. Look, I'd love to stay and chat, but I've got something urgent I need to deal with this morning. Did you have any luck with the… with the auras and stuff?"

Violet bit her lip. She held the steaming mug between her palms, hesitating.

She saw him steal a glance at the clock over her shoulder. "Violet?"

"Yes."

"Yes what?"

"Yes, I had a… a vision."

Detective Smeade's eyes widened. "And?"

Violet swallowed and gripped the mug tighter. "My vision told me that the man you're looking for is named Jerry Jester. He lives at 3434 Borthwick in Northeast Portland."

Detective Smeade stared at her. "Oh, my God. Wow. Moonbeam's never able to give us such specific details. This is really… Hold on a minute, let me write this down."

He fumbled in his breast pocket for a small notepad and a piece of paper and Violet felt an instant stab of regret.

Shit. Why had she given him so much detail? Couldn't she have just given a first name and a street? Or hell, just a last name. There had to be several dozen Jesters in Portland.

"This is confidential, right?" Violet asked, taking a few steps closer to him. "I mean, I wouldn't want anyone to find out that I was the one who—"

"Don't worry, Violet," he said, clicking his pen closed and shoving it back into his pocket with the notebook. "We'll hold this in the strictest of confidence. You don't have to worry about any dangerous criminals coming after you."

"Dangerous criminals. Good."

"If I could just grab those items from you, I'll be on my way."

"Right," Violet said, turning to grab the makeup bag and the underwear on the table. "Here you go. They were very… um, helpful."

Detective Smeade stuffed the items into his briefcase and smiled at her. "Obviously. You have a great day now. And tell your mom hi for me, okay?"

"Sure."

"Thanks again, Violet."

She said nothing as she watched Detective Smeade hustle out the door and down the street. The door hadn't even swung shut all the way when Drew came waltzing in.

"That guy was in a hurry," he said with a glance back over his shoulder. "Did you bite him or something?"

"My client. He had another appointment. How'd you know I wasn't in the middle of a reading?"

"I'm psychic," he said, stepping close enough to brush her arm with his fingers. "Also, I walked by and saw you standing here by yourself, staring out the door."

Violet smiled, feeling some of the dread drain from her body. She looked at Drew, feeling her hands and feet begin to tingle at the thought of what they'd been up to on the other side of the wall just a few short hours ago.

The things that man can do with his hands—

"Hello? Earth to Violet?"

"What?"

Drew grinned at her, and Violet felt the tingle spread.

"I just wanted to drop off a few more receipts," he said. "I found them under the desk when I was tidying up. I also found a button that belongs to you, but you're not getting it back until you agree to have dinner with me tonight."

"So this is a hostage situation?"

"I like to think of it more like blackmail. You don't have any ethical problems with that, do you?"

Violet felt a sharp stab to her spleen, but she managed to smile. "None at all. How about seven?"

"I'll pick you up at your place. That way if you decide you just want to get naked and eat chili out of the can, we'll have the option."

"Are you always this romantic with women you've just slept with?"

"Nope. Just you."

"I'm touched."

"You will be," Drew said, and leaned down to kiss her.

The room whirled a little, and Violet gave up feeling guilty and just kissed him back. When Drew finally pulled away, he touched the side of her face and smiled into her eyes.

"We'll continue this later. Right now, I'm meeting Jerry to talk about taking over all the bachelorette parties he's covering after Jamie's gone. That's turned into a logistical nightmare."

Violet grimaced and took a small step back. "Good luck with that."

"Sure. Here, you want me to throw these in the box with the rest of them?"

Violet followed the direction of his gaze to the box tucked in the corner by the cabinet. Before she had a chance to say anything, he was striding over to it and peering inside.

Shit.

Did he even know he'd given her Jerry's application? Would he notice? Would he connect the dots back to her when the cops came looking for Jerry?

She breathed a sigh of relief as Drew dropped the paper into the box and turned back around. His expression was still cheerful as he moved back toward her. Clearly, Jerry's application wasn't as significant in his mind as it was in Violet's.

Why would it be? she asked herself. *He has no reason yet to think you're a traitor.*

"So I'll see you tonight?" Drew said.

"I'll be waiting."

He kissed her again, more softly this time, and then turned and walked away. Violet could hear him whistling as he disappeared down the hall. She caught herself trying to pick out the tune, wondering what message she could take from his song choice.

"No," she said out loud, and forced herself to start humming to drown out the sound of Drew's whistle. If his song choice was going to make her feel guiltier than she already did, she didn't want to hear it.

She was still humming two minutes later when the door banged open again and Frank stomped through the door and glared at her.

"'Bitch,' right?"

"I beg your pardon?"

"I hate that song you're humming, the one called 'Bitch.' My ex-wife used to play that all the time. It fucking figures."

Violet folded her arms over her chest and glared at him. "Good to see you again, too."

Frank stalked toward her and stopped three feet away, scratching his neck as he walked. "Why haven't you fucking talked to Jed yet?"

"Because fucking Jed hasn't fucking called yet," Violet shot back, trying to sound tough but instead sounding like a middle schooler.

"Listen, dammit. If you don't make this happen—"

"How exactly do you expect me to make this happen? What do you want me to do, call the guy and offer a free psychic reading?"

Frank snapped his fingers. "Exactly. That's a great idea."

"Don't be a moron. If I call to offer my services, don't you think it's going to make him just a little suspicious that I've got an agenda?"

"You *do* have an agenda. Your agenda is to make sure I don't ruin you and your crackpot mother."

Violet took a step forward and narrowed her eyes at him. "The only person who calls my mother a crackpot is me," she snapped. "And if you really think there's any way I can call this asshole without tipping him off to your ridiculous plan, you're dumber than I thought you were."

Frank's eyes flashed with fury, and for a second, Violet felt a zap of fear that she'd overstepped.

Then he laughed, a completely joyless sound that made Violet's skin crawl. "I like you. You're a lot like me, you know?"

"I'm nothing like you," she hissed.

"Yes you are. Totally without ethics, as long as you don't get caught. Tell you what. I'm supposed to bang Jed's wife again tonight while he's busy in some meeting. Let me see what I can do to hurry things along, okay?"

"I don't want anything to do with this."

"You should have thought of that before you went shooting your mouth off to my squash partner."

"Your *ex*–squash partner," Violet snarled. "I saw in the paper the other day that she just won some tournament with a new partner. Good for her."

"You really think I give a shit? If I close this deal, I'll make more in a single day than I would have made in a year of hitting that stupid little ball around."

As if the very mention of balls caused him to remember the snail penis on his neck, Frank reached up and scratched himself again. Then he pointed a finger at her, prompting Violet to take a step back.

"You're going to make sure this happens, you understand me? Unless you want Miss Moonbeam to end up out on the streets, you'll tell Jed Buckles what he needs to hear."

"Get out."

"I'm serious."

"Get out!" Violet screamed. "Get out, get out, *get out!*"

The hall door burst open and Drew stormed into the room, eyes blazing. He looked at Violet, then Frank, then back at Violet.

He moved closer to Violet, his arm snaking protectively closer to her. "Are you okay? I heard you scream. What's wrong?"

"Nothing's wrong," Frank snapped. "We were just having a friendly discussion, weren't we, Violet?"

Violet looked at Frank and blinked. "No we weren't."

Then she looked at Drew, taking in the concern etched on his face, the fact that he was here protecting her, looking out for her.

She owed him the same, didn't she?

She took a deep breath.

"Drew, I have to tell you something."

Chapter 20

In Drew's experience, no good news ever began with, "I have to tell you something."

That, coupled with the worried look on Violet's face, sent a shot of fear through his body.

"What's going on?" he asked, trying to keep his voice even. "Is there a problem?"

"Moonbeam's late with the rent," Frank blurted. "In fact, she's in great danger of losing her business. Isn't that right, Violet?"

Violet turned and looked at Frank, her eyes blazing with hot, purple rage. Drew hoped she never had a reason to look at him that way.

"No, Frank," Violet snapped. "Moonbeam is perfectly current on her rent. I just gave you the check last week."

"I'm warning you, Violet," Frank snarled, giving her a dangerous look.

Violet turned back to Drew, her hands shaking a little as she reached out and squeezed one of his. "Our landlord here has been trying to blackmail me."

Drew frowned. "What?"

"He told me that if I didn't give a fake psychic reading to an investor and convince the guy to buy some overpriced piece of property, he was going to try to ruin Moonbeam's business."

Drew looked at Frank, watching as the older man's

face went from pink to crimson in less than ten seconds. Drew stared, wondering what color might come next.

"It's not that hard to ruin this business with the truth," Frank snapped. "It's pretty fucking easy. I just have to tell everyone the sort of fake, crackpot bullshit you're doing here."

"Take it easy, Frank," Drew said. "You look like you're going to pass out."

"Go to hell," Frank snapped. "You think I can't do this? Moonbeam's been my tenant for years. The stories I can tell—"

"Shut up, Frank," Violet hissed. "No one cares what you have to say."

Frank sneered at her. "Plenty of people care what I have to say. Did I mention that in addition to owning a shit pile of real estate around here, I also own a newspaper? It's a little alternative weekly, but the circulation includes five hundred thousand of exactly the sort of hippie, new age, alternative loonies you people target. You didn't know that, did you?"

Violet just glared at him, her hands balled into fists at her side. She was breathing hard in a way that might have made Drew want to ogle her breasts if he weren't focused on making sure she didn't kill the landlord.

Frank was still talking, oblivious to the threat Violet posed to his life. "My reporters love this sort of investigative myth-buster crap. Besides the paper, I also know a guy on the production crew at that TV show that goes out and debunks all those phony things like ghosts and psychics and shit like that. One phone call from me and—"

"Listen, asshole," Violet said, taking a step closer to Frank.

Drew shouldered his way between them, holding Violet back. "Frank, I think it's time for you to leave," he said as calmly as he could manage. "This is enough. If Violet doesn't already have an attorney, I'm quite happy to recommend one to her who will be delighted to nail your ass."

Frank just laughed, his voice sinister and hoarse. "I get it now. You guys are fucking. This is great—Drew's gonna sic his ex-wife on me on behalf of his new bimbo. Let me clue you in here, buddy. Since your girlfriend seems intent on screwing up this real-estate deal, I'll have no choice but to sell this guy a different piece of property for his goddamn vegan restaurant. *This* piece of property, to be precise."

Drew stared at him, slowly processing the threat. Behind him, Violet was practically vibrating with fury.

Frank sneered again, pleased to have rattled them both. "You catch my drift, Drew? Moonbeam's not the only one who'll be out on her ass here. So will you. And it's all because your girlfriend, the fake psychic, wants to pretend to be all self-righteous. She's a crook, and if you don't know that, you're dumber than you look."

Drew glared at him, feeling a hatred he hadn't felt for another human since a customer made Jamie cry by saying he had fat thighs.

To hell with civil discourse. Drew reached out to grab the little fuck around the throat.

"Drew, no," Violet said, and stepped in front of him. "Let it go. Just let it go. Violence isn't the answer."

"It is to some questions."

"Please," Violet said, touching his shoulder.

Drew took a step back, willing to do pretty much anything for Violet, when she asked like that.

Frank sneered at him. "I'd wipe the floor with you, pansy."

"Nice action-hero line," Drew said with a sharp laugh. "It might have more punch if your fly weren't down."

Frank shot a startled look down at his crotch and began yanking at his zipper.

Violet raised her eyebrows. "Give my apologies to your wife. How disappointing that must be for her."

Frank's eyes snapped up at her. "You little bitch," he said, and grabbed her arm so hard her whole body jerked.

Violet cried out.

Drew didn't even think. He grabbed Frank's wrist and yanked up, rewarded by Frank's yelp of pain as he released Violet.

"You motherfucker!" Frank screamed. "That's it. I'm calling the cops. You'll be hearing from my lawyer."

"Phone's right over there," Drew said calmly as he dropped Frank's wrist. "Go ahead, I'd like to talk to them too, while you're at it."

Frank was still cursing and frothing, clutching his wrist as he backed toward the door with a little vein flickering on the side of his temple. "You will regret this," Frank hissed. "I can guarantee it."

"Have a great day, Frank," Drew called after him. "We'll have to do this again sometime."

When Frank was gone, Drew turned to Violet. "Are you okay?"

She nodded numbly, looking up at him with wide eyes. She didn't say anything at first. Drew reached for her.

"Let me take a look at your arm," he said. "Does it hurt?"

Violet allowed him to peel up her shirtsleeve to expose her forearm. Drew felt the anger well up again as he studied the angry red marks on her soft flesh.

"I should have done more than yank his arm," Drew muttered.

"It's okay. It really doesn't hurt."

"Maybe you should have it checked out. I can drive you to the hospital."

"I'm okay, really," she said, and drew her arm back. "I'm so sorry, Drew."

"For what?"

"For that. What happened with Frank."

"It's not your fault."

"It is my fault. Now we're both going to lose the building."

Drew tried not to look bothered by that, even though Frank's words hadn't stopped ricocheting through his brain for the last five minutes. "I'm sure it'll all work out," he told her. "I'll talk to my attorney—not my ex-wife, by the way. And you and I can both talk to the cops. Frank won't get away with this. Right now I think someone should look at your arm. He grabbed you pretty hard."

"The marks are already fading," she said with a sniffle as she looked up at him. "But if we lose the building—"

"We'll deal with it."

Violet shook her head sadly.

"If someone wants to buy this place and kick us out, there's nothing we can do about it. Even if Frank is a prick—"

"Quit it," Drew said, cupping her chin in his hand. "This isn't your fault, okay? I'm going to call the cops now, to let them know what happened. Can I use your phone, or you want me to go next door?"

"Here is fine. But really, I don't think—"

"Look, he threatened you, okay? He hurt you. We can't let him get away with that."

"But he'll ruin the business. Both the businesses—yours and Moonbeam's. You heard him."

Drew tried hard not to grimace. He couldn't consider that right now. Couldn't think about what would happen if he had to close down and relocate. Jesus, was that even possible? He had the best location in town. He'd already lost a lot of money on the billboard campaign he'd had to dismantle with Jamie leaving. Cash was tight. Having to move, to start over, to pay to remodel some new space—

Don't think about it.

Drew cleared his throat. "Whatever Frank's planning to do, he's going to do it whether we call the cops or not. At least this way we'll have our version of the story on record."

Violet nodded a little sadly as Drew picked up her phone and dialed. He spent ten minutes talking with a bored-sounding police dispatcher, explaining the situation and giving directions to the shop.

By the time he hung up, Violet was sitting in one of the big red velvet chairs in the corner, looking very tired. Drew walked over to join her, easing himself into the other chair.

"They'll be here in a minute," he told her. "You need anything before that? Ice for your arm? Voodoo doll?"

Violet shook her head. "It's okay, really. It's not even red anymore. I think you hurt him a lot worse than he hurt me."

"Good."

Violet looked at him. "So much for staying out of each other's business, huh?"

"Yeah, this wasn't really the plan."

"What are you going to do? If we lose the building, that is."

Drew shrugged. "I don't know. I'm not sure I could afford to relocate, and even if I did, I don't know that the customers would follow. Probably the same for you guys here."

He didn't add that it was probably a hell of a lot easier for a psychic studio to relocate than it would be for him. Jesus, the stages, the lighting, the sound system, the custom-designed bar… Sure, he could move some of it, but not everything belonged to him. There was no way he could afford to do it all again.

Violet sighed. "Well, if we're going down, I guess at least we're going down together."

Drew grinned, pleased with the opportunity for a subject change. "Speaking of going down…"

"You're not honestly thinking of sex right now?" She was smiling, relaxing a little. That was good.

"I'm thinking of sex anytime you're in the room," he said. "Most of the time you're *not* in the room, for that matter."

Violet flushed and looked down at her lap. When she looked back up at him, there was something else in her eyes. Something besides desire.

"Drew, I need to tell you—"

The front door banged open and a uniformed police officer came striding in.

Violet stood up, looking oddly relieved. Whatever she'd been about to say was forgotten for the moment. Drew watched as she moved toward the door in her tight black jeans, her hips curving in silhouette against the light from the front window. He glimpsed the outline of her right breast as she lifted her arm to extend a handshake to the young cop, who looked as dazzled by her as Drew did.

"Hello, officer," Violet said. "It's good to see you."

———✦———

Violet couldn't believe her luck. She'd been so sure she'd see Detective Smeade striding through that door, that *he* would be the one to respond to the call.

That was the way fate worked, wasn't it?

She had already begun to rehearse what she'd say to Drew when Detective Smeade began praising her psychic prowess, thanking her for leading them to Jerry.

But then that smiling young officer walked through the door, and Violet had to believe fate was cutting her a break.

Okay, so she should have told Drew about the thing with Jerry. She'd thought about it, she really had. Right after the blowout with Frank, after everything had gone so wrong, it seemed like she had nothing to lose.

After all, he'd handled the Frank thing okay, hadn't he? Violet stole a glance at Drew, watching his face as he answered the officer's questions. He seemed protective of her, not angry with her. At least on the surface. But maybe when he digested the information, realized she held some responsibility for the fact that they might all lose the building—

Okay, so she'd hold her tongue on the Jerry thing for now, hold onto her biggest secret.

Well, maybe not her biggest secret. There was the music thing, after all.

Violet sighed and watched as Drew and the officer began pacing off a spot in the reception area, discussing the sequence of events in the fight.

Hell, maybe she should just come clean about all of it. Tell Drew about Jerry, about the music, about how she'd been considering giving in to Frank's blackmail.

After what had happened between them, she owed him a little honesty, didn't she?

She tried to tune out her angst-fueled inner dialogue and concentrate on the fact that the officer was now turning his attention to her.

"So when did the landlord first threaten you?" he asked.

Violet thought about it. "I guess it would have been Friday."

She saw Drew's eyebrows rise. "Three days ago?"

Violet bit her lip. "Yes. Why?"

He shrugged. "Just surprised you didn't mention it earlier, that's all."

She nodded, trying to come up with something to say to that. "I was worried about the business."

Drew looked at her. "Just your mother's business?"

"What?"

"Because if I'm understanding Frank's threat, mine is in jeopardy, too. The whole building, right?"

"Right." She couldn't really think of anything else to say, and the officer was looking at her funny, so Violet turned her attention back to him.

As she continued answering questions, though, she could see something different in Drew's expression. Irritation, for sure. That she hadn't told him sooner? That she'd considered doing what Frank asked?

Or maybe that she hadn't done it... that she hadn't just lied to save them all.

Hell, maybe that would have been the easiest thing after all. What was one more fake psychic reading?

"Ma'am?"

Violet snapped her attention back to the young police officer. "I'm sorry, could you repeat the question?"

By the time she'd finished up with the police, Violet was running late to visit Moonbeam at the outpatient rehab facility. They had an appointment to meet with the occupational therapist to go over some of the last-minute details of Moonbeam's release, and Violet was already ten minutes behind.

She skidded into the room just as Moonbeam was hanging up the phone.

"Who was that?" Violet asked.

"No one, dear. You're here for the appointment with the occupational therapist?"

"Sorry I'm late. Did I miss her?"

"Actually, she had to cancel. Some sort of emergency with another patient. She dropped off a packet of information, though."

Violet took the thick blue folder and sank down into the chair beside the bed. She flipped listlessly through the paperwork for a moment, not really reading anything. The she closed it and looked at Moonbeam.

"I'm actually glad you're alone," Violet said. "I kind of need to talk to you."

"About having sex with Drew?"

"Not about..." Violet stared at her mother. "How did you—?"

"I'm psychic, dear."

Violet narrowed her eyes. "Is this like in high school, where you said your psychic powers told you I'd lost my virginity to Matt Martin in the backseat of your car and then I found out you'd read my diary?"

"I never read your diary, dear," Moonbeam said convincingly.

"Right. I always figured it was either that or you found the condom wrapper in the backseat."

Moonbeam said nothing, and Violet decided to just drop the subject. "So there's a problem."

"With Drew? Oh, dear. He didn't strike me as impotent, but—"

"No, not with Drew."

"So everything was in working order with Drew then?"

"Stop doing that."

Moonbeam smiled. "You're so transparent, dear."

Violet sighed. "Enough with the sex already. I have to talk to you about Frank and Jed Buckles and Detective Smeade and—"

"Oh, look. The Discovery Channel is rerunning that program about the lion cub."

Moonbeam grabbed for the remote and flicked off the mute button, looking delighted.

Violet closed her eyes and gritted her teeth. *"Mom."*

"Yes, dear?"

"We're going to lose the studio. And Frank's going to ruin us in the media. The space, your reputation... we're going to lose everything."

Moonbeam looked at her, an expression completely devoid of alarm or anger. "I don't think so, dear."

"You don't understand—"

"No dear, you don't understand." Moonbeam squeezed her hand. "Do you realize what you just said? *We're* going to lose everything. It's exactly what I've always known. You're as much a part of this as I am."

Violet looked at her mother. Part of her wanted to shake her hard, make her pay attention to the gravity of the situation.

Part of her wanted to crawl into Moonbeam's lap so her mother could stroke her head and tell her everything was going to be okay.

But that had never been Moonbeam's style, had it? Comforting reassurances, taking care of crises—that was Violet's style, not Moonbeam's. Her worries over Detective Smeade and Jerry and Frank, those were hers alone to deal with.

Violet looked at her mother, watching as her face lit up in the strange orange glow of the TV.

"I think I'm in love with Drew," Violet said.

Moonbeam didn't look away from the TV screen, and her face registered no surprise, but she patted Violet's hand. "I know you are, dear."

Violet stared at her. "I thought you hated him."

"I don't hate anyone, Violet. Like I told him the other night, the two of you are meant for each other."

"What?"

"When Drew stopped by to see me. That's what he wanted to talk about."

"Wait… Drew came here to talk about *me*?"

"Of course, dear. He's quite taken with you."

Violet sat quietly for a moment, trying to decide whether to be flattered or annoyed. Why the hell would Drew talk to her mom about his feelings before sharing them with her?

"Anyway," Moonbeam continued cheerfully, "I'm glad you two have found your happily-ever-after ending now."

Violet nodded, feeling a prickle of unease crawling over her skin. "We'll see."

―――⁓―――

It was a few minutes before Drew was due to arrive for their seven p.m. date, and Violet was feeling oddly flustered. She'd already applied her eye makeup twice, having necessitated a redo after poking herself in the eye with her mascara wand.

She'd spent a full hour putting her hair up, then letting it down, then putting it up again, compromising with a loose chignon she hoped was a good blend of sexy and sophisticated.

There was something oddly nerve-racking about having a date with a man she'd just slept with. There was a peculiar sense of "now what?"—a need to strike the balance between cool indifference and a desperate desire to do it again.

She was just straightening her cashmere pullover—no buttons this time—when the doorbell chimed. She hustled to the front of the house, stopping to check her lipstick in the hallway mirror.

The instant Violet threw the door open, she knew something was wrong. On the surface, Drew looked calm, composed, completely devoid of emotion.

But Violet had spent the last two weeks looking below Drew's surface.

He stood there motionless, his blue eyes boring into hers. When he finally spoke, his words were icy.

"So, Violet," he said, arms folded over his chest. "Would you like to talk about Jerry?"

Chapter 21

DREW WAS TRYING VERY HARD NOT TO LOSE HIS COOL.

Since his cool had pretty much evaporated the second Detective Smeade had arrived at the bar to question him about Jerry, Drew was already shit out of luck.

Violet gripped the edge of the door so hard her knuckles were white. So was her face, for that matter. She looked nauseous. Nauseous and a little scared.

Dammit.

His anger evaporated for an instant, and all he could think about was taking her in his arms and making her smile again.

Then he thought of Violet keeping secrets, jeopardizing his business, trying to control everything behind the scenes while he sat there like a schmuck and fell for her.

"We need to talk," he said, and pushed past her, ignoring the little whimper she made as he stalked through the entryway and headed straight for the living room.

He looked at the sofa and gave a passing thought to kissing her there, the feel of her hair sliding between his fingers, her breasts pressing into his palms as she writhed against him and—

He turned away from the sofa and chose a chair instead.

"Drew, I can explain," Violet said, hurrying into the room behind him. She hesitated a moment before dropping onto the edge of the sofa and folding her hands in her lap.

"You can? Good, because I'd really like to know how you thought it would be a good idea to rat out one of my employees without even talking to me about it."

"Look, I didn't know what to do. The detective showed me the pictures and I just knew it was Jerry. I couldn't cover it up, could I?"

"I wouldn't expect you to cover anything up, Violet," Drew snapped, fuming a little harder as his brain veered to the image of her covering her breasts with her arm just that morning. He fixed his eyes on the arm of the sofa, hoping the nailhead trim might dampen his libido. "What I'm saying is that you should have talked to me about it before you called the damn cops."

"Why, so you could yell at me again for meddling with your employees?"

"No, I—"

"So you could get pissed at me for getting involved in your business, for poking my nose where it didn't belong?"

"No, I—"

"So you could make fun of psychics again?"

"No!" he yelled, barking the word out as he smacked his hand on the edge of the chair. "So I could tell you that you're wrong. You were completely, one hundred percent wrong about Jerry."

"What?"

Drew took a breath, trying to keep his voice calm. "Your psychic reading? You were wrong. Jerry isn't the criminal they're after."

"How did you—?"

"How did I know Jerry didn't do it, or how did I know you used me to feed false information to the cops just to keep up your psychic charade?"

Violet opened her mouth as if to protest, then shut it, looking slapped.

Drew looked away, not wanting to see the stung expression in her eyes.

You're the victim here, he reminded himself. *And Jerry. And Jamie, dammit.*

"First of all," he said, "the name you gave the police is wrong. There is no Jerry Jester."

"What?"

"Jerry Jester is a stage name he invented for himself. One he put on his application before I told him it was a bad idea, and told him he'd only be using his first name anyway when he came to work for me."

"But how did the police—?"

"They showed up at his old address—another tip-off to where the information came from, by the way—and his ex-roommate told them where he worked."

Violet swallowed. "So that's how you knew."

"That you stole information off a confidential job application and fed it to the police? That you tried to use your relationship with me to further your mom's sham of a business?"

"Hey, I was trying to do the right thing: to get a criminal off the streets."

"Yeah, well the only thing Jerry is guilty of is exceptionally bad judgment when he tried to take the fall for a car-jacking last year to keep his brother out of prison. He was cleared by DNA evidence two months ago. Not that you bothered to come to me to find out any of that information before talking to the cops."

"I didn't realize—"

"He was getting a second chance here, getting his

life together, but you had to send the cops chasing after him."

"But the tattoo—"

"Is on Jerry's left arm, not the right one. Oh, and FYI, learn to distinguish between Tweety Bird and Marvin the Martian before you go accusing a man of crimes he didn't commit."

That last part sounded silly even to him, and Drew almost laughed.

But he was mad, dammit.

Stay mad. Don't notice how beautiful she is, how sad she looks. Whatever you do, don't reach out and touch her and—

Violet was blinking hard now, fighting back tears. She bit her lip and everything inside Drew twisted and ached.

"Drew, I'm so sorry," she said. "I feel terrible."

"Save your apologies for Jerry. I'm sure he'll be happy to hear them when he comes out of surgery."

Violet stared at him. "What?"

"When he saw the cops coming for him, he got scared and ran. Right out the door, and into the path of a bus."

"Oh, God."

Violet covered her face with her hands, and Drew tried not to feel sorry for her. She was messing with people's lives here, hurting people. It wasn't right.

Drew shook his head and looked down at his hands. "This has to stop. This fake psychic thing, these made-up predictions and visions and—"

"Drew, I think it's real." She uncovered her face and stared at him, those big violet eyes wild, imploring.

This time, the shock was his. "What?"

She swallowed, looking unsure. "I know I told you at first that I didn't believe in psychics. But that was before."

"Before what? A massive brain injury?"

"Before I started listening to the music you played. Before I realized what it was saying."

Drew stared at her. "Have you been drinking?"

Violet took a breath and started talking. Her words came out in jumble, a peculiar list of '80s tunes strung together in a chronology that made Drew's head throb. She talked about Jenny, about the client who turned out to be a teacher, the woman who turned out to be pregnant, the money in the elevator.

The story went on and on, and Drew grew numb to the endless string of song titles that previously been nothing more than a good beat for unclothed gyration: "Photograph." "867-5309 (Jenny)." "Love in an Elevator." "The Prisoner." "Train Wreck." "Hot for Teacher." "Sweet Child o' Mine."

"Enough," Drew said, shaking his head. "This is crazy. This is ridiculous."

"But it's true. You can't deny the coincidence. What else could it be?"

Drew's head was throbbing now as he thought about that night in the bar with Petal. The Coldplay song, "Violet Hill." Maybe there was really something to this. Some sort of bizarre connection between both of them—

"No," he said firmly.

"What?"

"This isn't possible. There's no way."

"But think about it, Drew. What are the odds?"

He did think about it. He thought about it hard. And

then he pushed all the other thoughts out of his mind and focused on a new one.

"So you used me."

"What?" Violet said, looking confused.

"You used me. For the songs, for the information about Jerry, for—"

"Wait, let me get this straight," Violet said, her expression going from baffled to annoyed. "You're pissed I'm using you for psychic skills that don't exist?"

"No!" Drew raked his fingers through his hair. "*Yes!* I don't—"

"You don't believe there could possibly be a way I could be channeling some sort of psychic information from the music you're playing, but you think I'm using you because I've been doing exactly that?"

Drew stood up, feeling dizzy from the anger and confusion and the fact that the thing he wanted most of all was to take Violet in his arms and make love to her on the sofa.

God, you're a mess.

She's trying to control you. Another woman thinking she knows best, going behind your back, taking charge instead of talking it out—

"I can't do this," he said, stalking past her and heading for the door. "You're nuts. Your mom is nuts. This whole thing with the music is—"

"Nuts? Really, Drew? Is that why you went to my mother to talk about your feelings for me without ever saying a word to me about it? Because we're all so nuts?"

Drew shook his head again and grabbed for the doorknob. "I have to get out of here."

He yanked the door open hard and stomped out into the chilly Portland air, slamming the door even harder.

But even the drum of his footsteps wasn't loud enough to drown out the sound of something being hurled against the door.

Or the sound of Violet crying as Drew trudged through the rain to his car.

—◦◦◦—

Violet didn't remember falling asleep on the sofa, but that's exactly where she woke up the next morning, feeling like she'd been run over by a bus.

"Shit," she said out loud, remembering that was exactly what had happened to Jerry.

All my fault.

As Violet stumbled to the bathroom, she glanced at the clock in the hallway. It was already ten thirty in the morning, though she couldn't remember truly sleeping all night.

She remembered crying into a throw pillow, sobbing at the knowledge that she had been right all along. She should have stuck with normal. She should have stayed on the East Coast with her safe job and her quiet life. She should be dating a banker or data analyst or an actuary. Not a bar owner, for chrissakes.

The thought of Drew sent a wave of nausea through her body. But there was also a tingle, familiar and joyful and delicate as bubbles.

Violet pushed aside thoughts of Drew as she slogged through showering, dressing, and eating big spoonfuls of organic cherry yogurt straight from the carton. She dragged her feet getting ready, not wanting to go to the shop, to risk seeing Drew again.

Finally, at noon, she was standing on the sidewalk

in the rain in front of Moonbeam's shop. The sight of a notice tacked to the front door wasn't even alarming. Violet pulled it off with the same sense of dread that had accompanied her all morning.

"Notice of sale," she read aloud as she held the piece of paper close to her body, trying to shield it from the rain.

The door to Drew's bar swung open and Violet turned to see Sam walking toward her, looking grim.

"You guys got one, too, huh?"

Violet nodded. "I've never seen one of these before."

"It's not really an official document," Sam said. "Just something Frank made to rub it in."

"So he really sold the building?"

"I guess the guy signed the paperwork last night. Frank's washing his hands of the whole thing."

Violet looked back down at the paper and tried not to cry. "So how does this sort of thing work? We have thirty days to get out or what?"

Sam shrugged. "I guess so. I'm not really sure. Drew left a couple messages for the new owner, but he hasn't heard back yet."

"So we're all moving," Violet said glumly.

"Maybe. You guys should be able to find a new place fast. Your space needs are pretty limited."

"But what about you guys?"

Sam shrugged again and wrapped her arms around herself, shivering in the light Portland drizzle. "It's not as simple for us. Building out a new space to operate this sort of business takes a lot of money. Stages, lighting, disco balls, a new bar—that's a whole lot of capital."

"But it's a successful business," Violet said. "Drew must have some savings or—"

"His ex-wife took all the cash," Sam interrupted. "That was the agreement when they divorced. Drew kept this place, and she pretty much wiped out the savings."

"A loan then?"

"Maybe. I guess he'd have to weigh whether it's worth it. Whether the clients would even follow us to a new location."

Violet clutched the note in her hand as a tear slid down her cheek.

"Hey, don't cry," Sam said. "It'll all work out. Don't you believe that?"

"I don't know what to believe anymore."

Sam gave her arm a squeeze and Violet took a breath, trying to steady herself. "How's Jerry doing?" she asked. "Drew told me what happened."

She didn't add "when he was yelling at me" or "it's all my fault," but that was in the back of her mind. She wondered how much Sam knew.

"Jerry's doing well," Sam said. "They actually think he'll be able to come back to work in a few weeks."

"You've seen him?"

Sam nodded. "Jamie and I went to visit him at the hospital this morning. Jamie had all these plans for incorporating Jerry's cast into a dance routine. He even had this idea where the two of them would pretend to get into a fight and—"

"Wait, I thought Jamie was leaving. Afghanistan, right? Isn't he going to build schools?"

Sam shook her head. "Now that Jerry's hurt, Jamie doesn't want to leave him. He said Jerry needs him here. He thinks that may be his mission, to help Jerry recover."

"But… what about Jamie's big plans?"

Sam shrugged. "This seems to be his new plan. I don't know if it's a good one, but we're glad to be able to keep Jamie safe here for a little while longer."

Violet sighed and stuffed the notice into her purse. "That's good news. I mean, not that Jerry got hurt, but—"

"I know," Sam said. "I know what you mean."

Violet turned away and stuck her key in the door. Behind her, Sam cleared her throat.

"Drew was asking about you this morning."

"Oh?"

Violet didn't look up, but she felt her heart starting to hammer in her chest.

"Look, I don't know what happened between you two—it's none of my business, really—but, well, just don't give up on him. He needs you. You're good for him."

Violet swallowed back the tears and turned to look at Sam. She gave a dry little laugh, figuring it was better than a sob. "I don't think I have any say in it. Drew's the one who made it pretty clear he wants nothing to do with me."

"He'll change his mind. He's stubborn and a little hotheaded sometimes, but he's smart. He knows you're the best thing that's ever happened to him. Just give it time."

"Time," Violet repeated. She shook her head and pushed open the front door. "You want to come in for a cup of tea?"

"Thanks, but I have to run. Think about what I said though, okay?"

"Okay. And Sam? I'm really sorry about everything."

"Don't be."

With a sigh, Violet yanked the key out of the door

and stepped inside, flipping on the lights. She spent the next few minutes robotically going about the business of watering the plants, feeding the mice, checking the messages. There were none from Jed Buckles, and Violet allowed herself to wonder briefly what the hell had happened there.

If only he'd called.

If only Violet had just gone through with the damn appointment, told Jed what Frank wanted her to say.

None of this would have happened.

Okay, some of it would have happened. The thing with Jerry, the fight with Drew, her stupid, idiotic confession about the songs.

Violet winced, remembering the way Drew had looked at her. Like she was crazy, and not in a good way.

Hell, maybe she was. Maybe it was a stupid theory. She'd been a moron to blurt it out like she had, when he was already poised to hate her. She might as well have lit his hair on fire and then peed on him to put it out.

The phone rang, and Violet picked it up, depressed at the thought of giving yet another psychic reading.

"Miss Moonbeam's Psychic Pservices. This is Violet."

"Violet, honey… this is Mom."

"Hi, Moonbeam," she said, tucking the phone against her shoulder. "I was just getting ready to come visit you."

Moonbeam gave a familiar squeak of delight. "Your gift just keeps getting more attuned, Violet. I was calling to ask you to come down here. It's like we're cosmically connected, dear."

"That's great, Mom," Violet said without enthusiasm.

"Just let me wrap up a couple things here and I'll be there in about an hour, okay?"

"Actually, honey, can you get here a little sooner than that? There's someone here I'd like you to meet."

"Mom, I had a really rough night last night and I've got some bad news to share. I really think it would be best if we could talk alone for—"

"Jed, dear, would you hand me that glass of water?"

Violet stopped talking. "What did you just say?"

"Sorry, honey, I wasn't talking to you. Thanks, Jed, you're an angel."

Violet swallowed. "Mom?"

"Yes, dear?"

"Who is your visitor?"

"Oh, he's a wonderful new client I just met last night and—"

"Is his name Jed Buckles?"

"Why yes, dear," Moonbeam breathed. "My goodness, your psychic skills are just uncanny. I was just telling Jed that—"

"I'll be right there, Mom. Don't let Jed leave."

Chapter 22

VIOLET COVERED THE DISTANCE TO THE REHAB CENTER in a fraction of the time it normally took. When she reached her mother's room, her blouse was clinging to her sweaty back, and she was panting so hard one of the nurses frowned at her.

Classy, Violet thought, and stopped in the doorway of her mother's room to straighten her blouse and catch her breath.

"Violet, dear, is that you? I sense your presence."

"Sure, Mom," Violet said, not bothering to make a snarky comment as she strode into the room trying to project competence and professionalism.

She stopped marching as she spotted the man lounging in the chair beside Moonbeam's bed. He wore an off-white caftan tunic over loose-fitting trousers. His goatee looked like a breeding ground for a family of hamsters, and what little hair remained on his head was gathered in a sloppy braid at the nape of his neck. He looked like any other happy hippie in her mother's circle of friends.

But this happy hippie held her mother's whole future in his happy-hippie hands. Did Moonbeam even know that?

"Violet, honey," Moonbeam said from her bed. "This is Mr. Jed Buckles. Jed, this is my daughter, Violet."

"It's a pleasure to meet you, Violet," he said, rising to take her hand. "I've heard so much about you."

"You have?"

"Oh, yes. Your mother has told me what a gifted clairvoyant you are. It actually made me feel shame for my actions, but everything has its purpose, don't you agree?"

"I—" Violet stopped, not sure she was following the conversation. She looked to Moonbeam for guidance, and quickly realized how bizarre that was. Things were really going downhill fast if she was seeking guidance from her mother.

"Jed called me yesterday evening, dear," Moonbeam said. "He wanted to consult with a psychic, and when he heard I was here—"

"It's nothing against you, Violet," Jed interrupted. "I'm sure you're every bit as talented as your mother says you are. But I've wanted a consultation with Miss Moonbeam for years, and when I heard she'd been injured… well, I just had to come here and see her. I was certain her powers would still be strong even in an environment like this."

"He'd heard about me all the way from Santa Fe," Moonbeam said, beaming. "Isn't that something?"

"That is something," Violet said, still trying to find her way through the conversation. "So Mr. Buckles, what brings you out to Portland? Besides my mother, that is."

"Oh, I've had a second home here for years. My wife is an artist, and she teaches classes at Reed College from time to time."

Violet winced a little at the mention of his wife, remembering Frank's repeated claims of intimacy with the woman. Still oblivious, Jed kept right on talking.

"Anyway," Jed said, "we've been looking to buy

some investment property here for years, and my wife has been talking with your landlord for quite some time."

"Talking," Violet repeated carefully.

"Well, fucking, too. We have an open marriage, you see."

Violet stared at him, completely speechless.

Jed carried on, looking like it was the most natural thing in the world to discuss his sexual practices with a woman he'd just met.

"So Meredith—that's my wife—she and I want to open a vegan café. Frank showed us a number of different properties that would be just perfect, including the one that currently houses Miss Moonbeam's shop."

"And Drew Watson's bar," Violet added, instinctively wanting to remind them all there was more at stake here than just one person's livelihood.

"Right," Jed said. "We were really torn about what to do. The other property is down on the waterfront, and just perfect for the restaurant, but we just loved the aura of your building."

"Well, the aura actually gets smelly from time to time," Violet pointed out, hoping there was still a chance to change things.

Moonbeam shot Violet a quick frown before smiling serenely back at Jed.

"Jed and Meredith consulted the stars and talked with their syncretistic guide and even used peyote to induce an altered state, but they still weren't certain what to do," she said. "So they came here last night for a private consultation."

"You… you gave them a psychic reading?" Violet asked. *"Here?"*

"Of course, dear. I know the doctors said I shouldn't, but this seemed like a special occasion I should make an exception for. The three of us joined hands and—"

"So you're not buying our building?" Violet asked Jed, feeling a flood of relief. "Moonbeam told you it was a bad idea?"

Jed gave her a perplexed look, stealing quick glance at Moonbeam. "No, Moonbeam said it was a wonderful idea."

Violet blinked at her mother. "I don't understand."

"Violet, honey, I just follow what the voices say."

"The voices," Violet repeated, her own voice tinged with disbelief. "The voices said to displace two businesses that have been thriving there for years? The voices said it wouldn't matter that Drew will have an impossible time trying to start over again? The voices said—"

"Violet, honey," Moonbeam said, looking baffled. "We're not going anywhere. Neither is Drew."

"What?"

"That's the best part, dear. I consulted with the higher powers, who suggested that Jed and Meredith should purchase our property and leave everything exactly the same."

"It's an excellent investment," Jed said proudly. "With such established tenants who pay the rent on time. And I just feel such a cosmic connection to that space, the idea of owning the building that houses Miss Moonbeam's Psychic Pservices."

Violet shook her head. "But what about your vegan café? Are you buying Frank's other property, too?"

"Heavens, no," Jed said. "As a matter of fact, Miss

Moonbeam offered us some invaluable guidance there, too."

"She did," Violet said flatly.

"Yes, it seems there's a viable market for legalized medical marijuana in this state, and Moonbeam has identified a tremendous opportunity for the three of us to enter into a mutually beneficial growing and distribution operation together."

Moonbeam smiled. "Dr. Abbott stopped by to check on me when we were hammering out the details, and he said he might consider partnering with us as well. Offering medical consultation and a bit of extra capital."

Violet stared at them. "You're starting a pot plantation together."

"Perfectly legal," Moonbeam piped up. "I applied for the permits two months ago. All I needed was a business partner."

A business partner with cash, Violet thought.

She looked at her mother, not sure whether to be aghast or proud. Or some combination of both.

The story of your life, Violet.

"Wow," Violet said, bending down to kiss her mother on the cheek. "Congratulations to all of you. I'm sure it will be a mutually beneficial partnership."

"Oh, certainly," Jed said, beaming. "Once Moonbeam is healed, we've invited her to take part in our swingers group."

Moonbeam nodded, but Violet caught just the faintest hint of a grimace. "Just as soon as my doctor clears it."

"You're totally welcome to participate, Violet," Jed offered. "I mean, if that wouldn't be too strange for you, with your mother and all."

"My mother," Violet repeated, shaking her head as she looked at Moonbeam. "Strange doesn't even begin to cover it."

———∙∙∙———

Down the hall, Drew was playing a ferocious game of old maid with Jamie and Jerry in Jerry's hospital room. He was pretty sure Jerry was cheating, but he didn't care enough to call him on it.

Hell, he didn't care about much of anything right now.

"Everything okay, boss?" Jamie asked.

"Yeah, why?"

"Well, that's the third time you've tried to play the two and the three of spades as a pair."

"Right," Drew said, looking down at his hand. "Sorry. My mind's not really on the game right now."

"His mind is on Violet," Jamie said knowingly to Jerry. "She's the one who almost got you arrested."

"Bitch," Jerry said without venom. "Hey, is it my turn?"

Jamie held up his cards for Jerry to take one. "You should probably think about forgiving her," Jamie pointed out. "Maybe once the cast comes off."

"Maybe," Jerry agreed. "Hey, don't let me forget there's a show about monster trucks that's on in fifteen minutes."

Drew waited for more deep thoughts from Jamie or Jerry, but apparently they'd said all they needed to say.

Clearly they hadn't grasped the severity of the situation. Clearly they didn't realize the trouble they were in with the business. Clearly they didn't know what a phony Violet was. Clearly they weren't in love with her…

In love?

Jesus, he wasn't in love with her. Not in a million

years. So they'd had phenomenal sex. So he found himself listening for her voice every day, watching for her
in the hall, thinking about her when she wasn't around.

That didn't mean anything. He was just horny. That
was all.

"So you think we can get one of those new black-
light things for the corner stage, boss?" Jamie asked,
shuffling the cards nonchalantly. "I saw one online and
it's really cool."

"Sure. Whatever."

Drew felt a stab of guilt not cluing the guys in about
the sale of the building. He hadn't decided yet what to
do. Whether he could cobble together the funds to start
over again someplace else, or if he should just throw in
the towel. He wished there were someone he could talk
to, someone with a good head for numbers.

"Violet," Jamie said.

Drew looked up, startled. "What?"

"In the doorway," he said, waving over Drew's
shoulder. "Hey, Violet. Want to play old maid?"

"Bitch," said Jerry without menace before turning
back to Jamie. "Dude, do you have a king?"

"Hello," Violet said from the doorway. "I just brought
these for Jerry, but I can come back—"

"Woah!" Jamie said. "*Stripper Dude* magazine.
Where did you find those?"

"There's a magazine shop downtown that has a
lot of unusual selections," she said, taking a cautious
step into the room. "I just thought maybe while Jerry's
recovering—"

"Bitch," said Jerry, but reached out eagerly to take
the magazines.

"I'm really sorry, Jerry," she said. "I didn't mean to cause you trouble. I jumped to a bad conclusion. Can you forgive me?"

Jerry looked up from the pile of magazines in his lap and frowned at her. "You think you could get me some extra Jell-O?"

"What color?"

"Red. They only have green and yellow here, but I want red."

"Sure. Whatever you want."

"A blowjob?"

"Um…"

"Don't be disrespectful," Jamie said, flipping through one of the magazines.

Jerry sighed. "You can play old maid with us if you want."

"Thanks, Jerry," Violet said. "That means a lot to me. Maybe a little bit later?"

Drew watched the whole exchange with his heart in his throat. When Violet's eyes swung toward him, he felt his heart twist.

"Drew, could I maybe talk to you alone for a minute?"

Drew blinked and tried to remember why he hated her.

"Please?" she asked, and touched his arm.

Drew stood up and set his cards down on Jerry's tray table. "I'll be right back, guys."

He followed her out into the hallway. He expected her to stop in the waiting area, but she kept going, trudging through the parking lot and into the parking garage. Drew tagged along, feeling like an idiot, but also intrigued. She pushed the button for the elevator.

"Where are we going?" he asked.

"My car."

"Am I being kidnapped?"

She looked at him. "You're free to go."

He shrugged. "I'm curious what I'm worth in ransom."

Violet sighed. "Drew, I'm sorry. I already said so. I should have talked to you about Jerry before I talked to the police."

Drew said nothing, but he nodded once. They stepped into the elevator and Violet pressed the button for the sixth floor. They rode in silence for a few seconds, Violet standing so close to him he could smell her shampoo. He felt himself getting light-headed and had to remind himself to be angry.

"The thing is," Violet said, "I wanted to protect my mother's business and her reputation. And I also thought I was doing the right thing by alerting the police to the presence of a dangerous criminal." She held up her hand as Drew opened his mouth to object. "I know… *I know* it turned out Jerry wasn't really a criminal. But I didn't know that before. And even though I screwed up, I was trying to do the right thing. Don't I at least get credit for that?"

The elevator jerked to a stop, sending Violet lurching against him. He caught her arm to steady her and felt his stomach ball up. God, she felt good.

No she doesn't.

Yes she does.

Drew was still holding her when the elevator doors swished open.

"Thank you," she said.

"No problem," Drew replied, still holding her against him.

If Violet noticed or cared, she didn't say anything. The elevator doors started to close, and Violet pulled away from him to hold them open. She stepped out into the parking garage, looking visibly shaken.

Drew followed, struggling to remind himself to be pissed. Why was he mad again? It had something to do with cops, he was pretty sure.

Violet aimed her key at the rental car and the locks clicked open. She went around to the driver's side, so Drew headed for the passenger side. He opened the door and wondered briefly if it was a bad idea to get into a car with a crazy woman.

Crazy is exactly why you fell for her, he told himself, and got into the car.

She sold you out, whispered the voice in his head. *She used you, she wants to control you—*

"Shut up."

Violet looked him. "I didn't say anything."

"What? Never mind. Where are we going?"

"Nowhere."

"Good way to improve gas mileage."

"Turn on the radio and pick a station."

"What?"

"You heard me. I want to prove my theory about the music. I don't understand it, but I know it has something to do with you making a selection, maybe something to do with both of us or—"

"Violet, this is nuts—"

"Do it!" she snapped, and Drew reached for the radio dial. He flicked it on to the buzz of static. He briefly considered the five preset buttons in front of him. It was a rental car, after all, so maybe they weren't set to anything, but then again, Violet had been driving it for two weeks, so maybe—

"You're thinking too much," Violet said. "It has to be random."

"Sorry, I forgot to read my psychic handbook."

"Just pick something."

Drew hit the button that said "seek." He listened.

Violet's face crumpled. "A vacuum-cleaner commercial?"

"I hear it's a very good brand," Drew offered.

"Wait, try again."

Drew reached up and flicked the stereo off. Then he turned in his seat and looked at her. "Violet, I don't care."

There was a flicker of something in her eyes... pain? A plan to maim him? Drew caught her hand before she could take a swing or turn the radio back on.

"I don't mean I don't care about *you*," he said. "I do. God knows I didn't mean to, but there it is."

"But—"

"Oh, I'm still mad about the thing with Jerry. But I'll get over it. And I'm bummed to be losing my business, but I know that isn't your fault. The thing is, though, I don't want to lose *you*. That's one thing I absolutely couldn't handle."

"But—"

"Let me finish."

Violet closed her mouth and looked at him, those beautiful eyes studying him with unnerving intensity.

"What was I saying?" he asked.

"You don't want to lose me."

"Right. See, the thing is, I'll get over being annoyed with you. But I know I'm not going to get over being in love with you. That's something I figured out... well, just now. On the way up in the elevator, actually."

Violet stared at him, stunned. She opened her mouth to say something, but no words came out. Belatedly, Drew realized he'd used the *L*-word, and maybe that wasn't a good idea when he'd only known her two weeks and she was probably leaving town anyway and—

The hell with it. It's the truth, isn't it?

Drew swallowed. "So the deal is, I don't care about the music thing. I mean, I don't care if it's hogwash or there's something to it or—"

"Wait, you're acknowledging there might be something to it?"

Drew sighed. "There was this thing in a bar and this Coldplay song came on and... never mind. That's not the point. The point is, I'm willing to consider the possibility that there might be things going on in the world or right next door that I don't understand. You know?"

"I know," Violet said, a little breathlessly. "Believe me, I know."

"Anyway, I'm sorry, too."

"For what?"

"For being a total fucking caveman and grabbing you right now and kissing you before you have a chance to fight me off."

He hesitated a second anyway, giving her a chance to shove him away—he could be a gentlemanly caveman, after all—but Violet grabbed him by the front of the shirt and jerked him to her, kissing him so hard Drew forgot to breathe. He leaned into her, pressing her back against the door of the car, grateful he hadn't bothered with his seat belt, just so damn glad to feel his hands on her again.

When he pulled back, he was breathing hard and his head was swimming a little. Violet smiled.

"What is it with us and cars?"

"I don't know, but I think I might have to buy one without a steering wheel. It gets in the way. Hell, maybe I'll throw in the towel on the bar and open an auto dealership filled with cars for people to make out in. I'm sure there's a market for it."

"It's a nice idea, but you'll have to keep the bar, too."

"What?"

"The new owner isn't closing us down. In fact, he's got a whole list of tenant improvements he'll be doing for both of us."

"What?"

"I met with the new owner. Apparently, he and my mother are growing pot together and maybe having an inappropriate sexual relationship. It's a long story."

"I can only imagine."

"But the short version is that we're not getting kicked out. None of us are."

Drew looked at her. "How plural is that?"

"What do you mean?"

"I mean, are you staying in Portland?"

Violet grinned at him. "That depends."

"On?"

"Well, first I'd have to get one of the accounting jobs I'm interviewing for next week."

"And second?"

"What do you think my chances are of getting my hands on one of those cars without the steering wheel?"

"About the same as the chances of me getting my hands on you."

She reached for the front of his shirt again, pulling him to her. "I'll have to consult my Magic 8 Ball, but right now, *signs point to yes*."

"Thank God," Drew said, and pulled her to him.

Acknowledgments

It isn't possible to thank everyone who helped shape this book unless I walk the streets of Portland and personally express my appreciation to every odd duck and strange soul in the city. I tried that, but I got spit on a lot.

I owe the deepest debt of gratitude to my amazing critique partners, Linda Brundage, Cynthia Reese, and Linda Grimes, as well as my terrific beta readers, Larie Borden, Bridget McGinn, and Minta Powelson. Thank you for not allowing me to sound like an idiot. Much.

A million thanks to my fabulous editor, Deb Werksman, publicity goddess Danielle Jackson, and the wonderful staff at Sourcebooks for making me look much cooler than I am.

Thank you to my terrific RWA chaptermates of the Rose City Romance Writers and Mid-Willamette Valley RWA. It's been lovely knowing I'm never in this alone and there are hundreds of you who hear the voices, too.

A huge round of applause for my incredible agent, Michelle Wolfson, for going so far beyond the call of duty that she probably can't even hear duty anymore. (And thanks also for always laughing at my *duty/doody* jokes.)

Thank you to the very best parents on the planet (a claim I will fight to the death to defend), Dixie and David Fenske. You guys made me who I am, and I'm pretty sure you could be prosecuted for that in a court of law. Thanks also to Aaron "Russ" Fenske, who may not recognize my name on the cover of this book, because to the best of my knowledge, he's never called me anything besides "butthead."

And thank you to Craig for holding my hand through the lousy stuff, and for proving over and over that the best is still to come.

I said *come*.

About the Author

Tawna Fenske is a third-generation Oregonian who revels in writing about the quirky little things that define her home state and its residents.

She's the author of the romantic comedy *Making Waves* and the popular daily blog *Don't Pet Me, I'm Writing*. A member of Romance Writers of America, Tawna holds a degree in English lit and makes a living pretending she knows something about marketing and corporate communications.

Tawna lives in central Oregon with a menagerie of well-loved (albeit ill-behaved) pets. *Believe It or Not* is her second novel.

Making Waves

"I'M SORRY, HE WANTS ME TO DO WHAT?"

Juli Flynn didn't think to hide the incredulity in her voice. She did, however, think of hiding beneath her mother's kitchen table. If it weren't for the memory of her brother wiping boogers there thirty years ago, she probably would have crawled right under.

Juli stared at her mother. Tina Flynn was chopping carrots for a Jell-O salad that would, in all likelihood, hold as much culinary appeal for the funeral guests as the actual corpse.

"You know you were always Uncle Frank's favorite," Tina said in the same voice she'd used to suggest her children not stick lima beans up their noses. "I think you should be flattered."

"Mom. I'd be flattered if he asked me to read a poem at the funeral or look after his cat or take his clothes to Goodwill. But this—this is just weird."

"Don't be so dramatic, Juli."

"Dramatic? Dramatic is making a deathbed request that your niece travel to the freakin' Virgin Islands to dump your ashes over the edge of a boat near St. John— that's dramatic. Why not spread them off the Oregon coast or on Mount Hood or something?"

Tina finished with the carrots and began chopping beets, her knife making neat little slivers of purple that scattered over the green countertop. Juli sighed and began hunting in the cupboard for sesame seeds to add to the Jell-O.

"Frank had fond memories of his years sailing over there," Juli's mother said.

"He had fond memories of the Polish hooker he traveled with while he was fleeing that federal indictment."

Tina smiled and set her knife down. "That's right—what was her name? Olga or Helga or something like that?"

"Oksana," said Juli, thinking this was *so* not the point.

Juli closed her eyes, hating the fact that at age thirty-seven, she felt like a petulant toddler. She had a sudden urge to stomp her feet and bang her fists on the counter in a full-blown tantrum.

It's not like she and Uncle Frank had been *that* close. She'd been living in Seattle for the past six years, coming home to Portland for the occasional holiday. Until last week, she hadn't even seen Uncle Frank since her birthday party a year ago when he'd gotten drunk on a quart of vanilla extract from Tina's baking cupboard and spent the evening pretending to be a stegosaurus. The rest of the family had been embarrassed. Juli had been delighted that, for once, she wasn't the oddest member of the family. That common bond was the reason she and Uncle Frank had always enjoyed a special relationship.

Well, that, and the fact that advanced dementia had led him to believe his niece was Celine Dion.

"You didn't happen to tell Uncle Frank that I'm—"

"Terrified of the ocean? No, I didn't have the heart to mention that."

Juli nodded and watched her mother consult her hand-written recipe before reaching for the Worcestershire sauce.

"Did Uncle Frank say when I need to complete this mission?" Juli asked, grabbing three packets of orange Jell-O and her mother's fish-shaped Jell-O mold. "Do cremated remains have—um—a shelf life or anything?"

"He didn't really say. He was choking on his tongue a lot there at the end, so it was hard to understand him. Could you hand me that feta cheese?"

Juli gave her the container and scooted a knife out of the way, aware of her mother's tendency to drop sharp objects on her bare feet.

"So maybe you didn't understand him right?" Juli asked hopefully. "Maybe instead of 'throw my ashes off a fishing boat,' he said, 'roll my ass over, you stupid whore'?"

"Those bedsores were sure something! Hand me those Junior Mints?"

Juli sighed, sensing the conversation was going nowhere. Maybe she was arguing the wrong point.

"I can't just pack up and go to St. John. I have a *life*."

Tina beamed at her daughter. "Are you dating someone new, sweetie?"

Juli scowled. "That's not what I meant. I haven't dated anyone since—well, for a long time."

"Oh. Well, you know it can be a little bit intimidating for some men to date a woman with your particular—"

"Mom, can we not talk about this now?"

"Sweetie, I don't know why you're always so embarrassed about your special—"

"Please, Mom," Juli said weakly, feeling her ears flame the way they always did when someone drew attention to the fact that she was—well, *different*. She touched her fingers to her lobes, trying to cool them. "Could we just stick with the subject of Uncle Frank?" she pleaded.

"Of course, dear. Can you hand me the dill?"

Juli spun the spice rack and located the appropriate jar. "I have a job, Mom. I have a bank account that can't exactly handle the strain of a Caribbean vacation."

"Well, Uncle Frank left a little bit of money in his will to cover some of the cost of your travels."

"Okay. That's half the equation. What about my job?"

"Didn't you say they asked for people in your department to volunteer to take a little time off? That sounds so nice."

That sounds like a layoff, Juli thought, biting into a carrot as she watched her mother mix the Jell-O.

Not that the idea didn't hold some appeal. She'd worked in the marketing department of a software company for less than a year and already she was so bored her skin itched. She'd hardly bothered to hide her delight the week before when the vice president had stood at the center of their cube-farm, running his fingers through his comb-over, asking if anyone was interested in a severance package of three weeks' salary and a scone-of-the-month club membership in exchange for "taking a little time off. *Indefinitely*."

Later that day, Juli had flung herself onto the sofa in her therapist's office and sighed. "I feel like my career is going nowhere," she told Dr. Gordon.

"What makes you say that?" he'd asked, looking wise and vaguely constipated on the edge of his orange armchair.

"The fact that my boss told me yesterday, 'Juli, your career is going nowhere.'"

"Right," Dr. Gordon said, nodding. "And how does that make you feel?"

Juli shot him a look. "Terrific."

Dr. Gordon was not amused. Dr. Gordon was seldom amused. Juli had fantasies about pinning him down on the carpet and tickling him until he peed.

"Juli, we've spoken before about the social oddities you've developed as a coping mechanism to deal with your self-consciousness and your lack of a sense of belonging, which is the direct result of the attention you've generated in the scientific community and the media for your—" He stopped and stared at her, then shook his head. "Are you covering your ears so you don't have to listen, or are you cooling them like you always do when you're embarrassed?"

"A little of both," she admitted, lowering her hands.

"I see," Dr. Gordon said, looking morose. "You're uncomfortable with this subject. Let's talk about your career. What did you want to be when you were a child?"

"The Bionic Woman."

Dr. Gordon didn't smile. "What was your first job after college?"

"I was a newspaper reporter for three months before an on-the-job injury forced me to change careers."

"Injury?"

"I fell asleep in a City Council meeting and stabbed myself between the ribs with a pencil." She lifted the hem of her shirt. "Check it out, five stitches right here—"

Dr. Gordon sighed and began to flip through his notes. "Let's go back over some of the other jobs you've held. After you were a reporter, you spent some time as a data analyst?"

Juli lowered her shirttail and sat up straighter. "Oh. Sure, there was that. And marketing, of course. And I got my helicopter pilot license about seven years ago, and there was that stint as a pet store manager, and four months as a scout for forest fires, six months working in that hat shop, and—"

"Juli, your employment history leaves something to be desired."

She nodded, pleased to be understood. "You're right. I've never been a brain surgeon."

"It's very typical for someone with your IQ level to—"

"Are those new drapes? I like the little tassels."

Dr. Gordon sighed again. "Juli, if you're ever going to have close, intimate relationships with people, you're going to need to work on grounding yourself a bit more."

"My mother never believed in grounding—always thought time-out was a much more effective method of punishment."

"Juli—"

"I know. *I know*. I was making a joke."

He didn't smile. "Why don't you start by taking a step back and reevaluating your career and life choices? Gain some new perspective."

Perspective. That's what she needed.

She'd raced home to Portland from Seattle the day she'd heard about Uncle Frank. Now here she was, chopping steak for her mother's Jell-O salad on the afternoon of her uncle's funeral, wondering if a spur-of-the-moment jaunt to St. John might not be the best thing for her. Or maybe the worst.

"Honey, could you hand me those garbanzos?"

No. Not the worst. Not quite the worst.

Available now from Sourcebooks Casablanca

Romeo, Romeo

by Robin Kaye

Rosalie Ronaldi doesn't have a domestic bone in her body...

All she cares about is her career, so she survives on take-out and dirty martinis, keeps her shoes under the dining room table, her bras on the shower curtain rod, and her clothes on the couch.

Nick Romeo is every woman's fantasy— tall, dark, handsome, rich, really good in bed, AND he loves to cook and clean...

He says he wants an independent woman, but when he meets Rosalie, all he wants to do is take care of her. Before long, he's cleaned up her apartment, stocked her refrigerator, and adopted her dog.

So what's the problem? Just a little matter of mistaken identity, corporate theft, a hidden past in juvenile detention, and one big nosy Italian family too close for comfort...

Praise for **Romeo, Romeo***:*

"Kaye's debut is a delightfully fun, witty romance, making her a writer to watch."—*Booklist*

For more Robin Kaye books, visit:

www.sourcebooks.com

Breakfast in Bed

by Robin Kaye

He'd be Mr. Perfect, if he wasn't a perfect mess...

Rich Ronaldi is *almost* the complete package—smart, sexy, great job—but his girlfriend dumps him for being such a slob, and Rich swears he'll learn to cook and clean to win her back. Becca Larson is more than willing to help him master the domestic arts, but she'll be damned if she'll do it so he can start cooking in another woman's kitchen—or bedroom...

Praise for Robin Kaye:

"Robin Kaye has proved herself a master of romantic comedy."—*Armchair Interviews*

"Ms. Kaye has style—it's easy, it's fun, and it has everything that you need to get caught up in a wonderful romance."—*Erotic Horizon*

"A fresh and fun voice in romantic comedy."—*All About Romance*

For more Robin Kaye books, visit:

www.sourcebooks.com

Too Hot to Handle

by Robin Kaye

———〰———

He sure would love to have a
woman to take care of…

To Dr. Mike Flynn, there's nothing like housework to help a guy relax, while artist Annabelle Ronaldi doesn't have a domestic bone in her body.

When they meet at her sister's wedding, Mike is sure this is the woman he wants to take care of forever. While Mike sets to work wooing Annabelle, she becomes determined to sniff out the truth of the convoluted family secret that's threatening to turn both their lives upside down.

———〰———

Praise for Too Hot to Handle:

"Entertaining, funny, and steaming hot."—*Book Loons*

"A sensational story that sizzles with sex appeal."—*The Long and Short of It*

"Witty and enchanting."—*Love Romance Passion*

"From the brilliant first chapter until the heartwarming finale, I was hooked!"—*Crave More Romance*

For more Robin Kaye books, visit:

www.sourcebooks.com

Line of Scrimmage

by Marie Force

—⁓—

She's given up on him and moved on...

Susannah finally has peace, calm, a sedate life, and a no-surprises man. Marriage to football superstar Ryan Sanderson was a whirlwind, but Susanna got sick of playing second fiddle to his team. With their divorce just a few weeks away, she's already planning her wedding with her new fiancé.

He's finally figured out what's really important to Him. If only it's no too late...

Ryan has just ten days to convince his soon-to-be-ex-wife to give him a second chance. His career is at its pinnacle, but in the year of their separation, Ryan's come to realize it doesn't mean anything without Susannah...

—⁓—

Praise for Line of Scrimmage:

"An awesome novel... their passion simply sizzles as they work through their problems."—*SingleTitles.com*

"I will definitely be reading more Marie Force."—*Revisiting the Moon's Library*

"Hands down, *Line of Scrimmage* is the best romance I've read this year."—*J. Kaye's Book Blog*

For more Marie Force books, visit:

www.sourcebooks.com

Love at First Flight

by Marie Force

***What if the guy in the airplane seat next to you
turned out to be the love of your life?***

Juliana, happy in her career as a hair stylist, is on her way
to Florida to visit her boyfriend. When he tells her he's
wondering what it might be like to make love to other women
she is devastated. Even though he tries to take it back, she
doesn't want him to be wondering all his life. So they agree
to take a break, and heartbroken, she goes back to Baltimore.

Michael is going to his fiancee's parents' home for an
engagement party he doesn't want. A state's prosecutor,
he's about to try the biggest case of his career, and he's
having doubts about the relationship. When Paige pulls a
manipulative stunt at the party, he becomes so enraged that
he breaks off the engagement.

Juliana and Michael sat together on the plane ride from
Baltimore to Florida, and discover they're on the same flight
coming back. With the weekend a disaster for each of them,
they bond in a "two-person pity party" on the plane ride home.
Their friendship begins to blossom and love, too, but life is full
of complications, and when Michael's trial turns dangerous,
the two must confront what they value most in life...

For more Marie Force books, visit:

www.sourcebooks.com